Penguin Books
The Appren

David Mackenzie
$7.99

P9-DGV-228

Mordecai Richler was born in 1931 in Montreal, of a
Jewish family which came to Canada from Russia and
Poland two generations ago. He was educated in Montreal
at Sir Williams University. He was awarded a
Canada Junior Arts Fellowship in 1959, had it renewed in
1960, and in 1963 he went to the United States on a
Guggenheim Fellowship for Creative Writing; in 1966
he was awarded a Canada Arts Council Senior
Fellowship. When he was twenty-two, after spending a
year in Europe, he finished his first novel, *The Acrobats*,
and has since become one of Canada's best-known
writers with his other novels, *A Choice of Enemies*, *Son of
a Smaller Hero*, *The Apprenticeship of Duddy Kravitz*,
The Incomparable Atuk, and *Cocksure*. His most recent
book is *Hunting Tigers under Glass* (1969). His articles
and stories have appeared in the *New Statesman*,
Encounter, the *New York Review of Books*, *Kenyon Review*,
Commentary, and other journals.

Mordecai Richler is married and has three children. He
has lived in England for the last twelve years.

Mordecai Richler

The Apprenticeship of Duddy Kravitz

Penguin Books

Penguin Books Ltd, Harmondsworth,
Middlesex, England

Penguin Books Australia Ltd, Ringwood,
Victoria, Australia

First published by André Deutsch 1959
Published in Penguin Books 1964
Reprinted 1967, 1968, 1969, 1970, 1971

Made and printed in Great Britain by
Cox & Wyman Ltd, London, Reading
and Fakenham
Set in Monotype Imprint

FOR FLORENCE

Author's Note

Because I was awarded a Canada Council Junior Arts Fellowship in April 1958, I was able to write this novel free from the usual financial pressures, and for that I am most grateful. I would also like to thank Albert Gomberg, who was kind enough to correct all the legal and real estate errors in the manuscript.

All the characters and incidents described in this novel are fictional and any similarities to characters living or dead are, as they say, purely coincidental.   M.R.

Part One

Chapter One

What with his wife so ill these past few weeks and the prospect of three more days of teaching before the weekend break, Mr MacPherson felt unusually glum. He trudged along St Dominique Street to within sight of the school. Because it was early and he wanted to avoid the Masters' Room, he paused for an instant in the snow. When he had first seen that building, some twenty years ago, he had shut his eyes and asked that his work as a school master be blessed with charity and achievement. He had day-dreamed about the potential heritage of his later years, former students – now lawyers or doctors or M.P.s – gathering in his parlour on Sunday evenings to lament the lost hockey games of twenty years ago. But for some time now Mr MacPherson had felt nothing about the building. He couldn't describe it or tell you how to get there any more than he could forget that Shelley's 'Ode to the West Wind' was on page eighty-nine of *Highroads to Reading*, the central idea being the poet's dedication to a free and natural spirit.

Since he had first come to the school in 1927 – a tight-lipped young Scot with a red fussy face – many of Mr MacPherson's earliest students had, indeed, gone on to make their reputations in medicine, politics and business, but there were no nostalgic gatherings at his home. The sons of his first students would not attend Fletcher's Field High School, either. For making their way in the world his first students had also graduated from the streets of cold-water flats that surrounded FFHS to buy their own duplexes in the tree-lined streets of Outremont. In fact, that morning as Mr MacPherson hesitated on a scalp of glittering white ice, there were already three gentiles in the school (that is to say, Anglo-Saxons; for Ukranians, Poles, and Yugoslavs, with funny names and customs of their own, did not count as true gentiles), and ten years hence FFHS would no longer be *the* Jewish high school. At the time, however, most Jewish boys in Montreal who had been to high school had gone to FFHS and, consequently, had studied history out of *The World's Progress* (revised) with John Alexander MacPherson; and every old graduate had an anecdote to tell about him.

Mr MacPherson's most celebrated former student – Jerry Dingleman, The Boy Wonder – liked to tell the one about the merit cards.

Once Mr MacPherson tried giving out merit cards to his students for such virtues as exceptionally high examination results, good behaviour, and neat writing. Each month he collected the cards and gave the boy who had earned the most of them the afternoon off from school. But at the end of the third month it was Jerry Dingleman who stood up to claim and, on demand, produce, a suspiciously high stack of soiled merit cards. Now Mr MacPherson knew that he had never awarded Dingleman, a most inattentive and badly-behaved boy, one single card. On the threat of a week's expulsion from school Dingleman confessed that he had won all the cards playing nearest-to-the-wall with the other boys in the toilet, and so the system ended.

Many of the other anecdotes, especially the more recent (and vastly exaggerated) ones had to do with Mr MacPherson's drinking habits. It was true that by 1947 he was a heavy drinker, though he was certainly not, as they say, a problem. He was still much slimmer than his first students, but his face seemed more bitingly angry and the curly black hair had greyed. Mr Mac-Pherson was more inclined to stoop, but, as on his first day at FFHS, he still wore the brim of his battered little grey fedora turned down, rain or shine, spoke with a thick Scots accent, and had yet to strap a boy.

If Mr MacPherson had altered somewhat with the years the school building had remained exactly the same.

Fletcher's Field High School was five storeys high, like the Style-Kraft building that flanked it on one side and the tenement on the other. Across the street at Stein's the bare-chested bakers worked with the door open even during the winter and, at school recess-time, were fond of winking at the boys outside and wiping the sweat from under their armpits with an unbaked kimel bread before tossing it into the oven. Except for the

8

cracked asphalt courtyard to the right of the school, separating it from the tenement, there was little to distinguish this building from the others.

There were, of course, the students.

At that moment several of the older boys leaned against Felder's frosted window. The biggest sign in Felder's tiny tenement store, DON'T BUY FROM THE GOYISHE CHIP MAN – FELDER IS YOUR FRIEND FOR LIFE, was no longer needed. The last time the chip man, an intrepid French-Canadian, had passed with his horse and wagon the boys, led by Duddy Kravitz, had run him off the street.

Duddy Kravitz was a small, narrow-chested boy of fifteen with a thin face. His black eyes were ringed with dark circles and his pale, bony cheeks were criss-crossed with scratches as he shaved twice daily in his attempt to encourage a beard. Duddy was president of room forty-one.

'Hey, guess what,' Samuels shouted, running up to the boys. 'Mr Horner's not coming back. He's got triple pneumonia or something. So we're getting a new class master. Mac, of all people.'

'Mac'll be a breeze,' Duddy said, lighting a cigarette. 'He never straps or nothing. Mac believes in *per*-suasion.'

Only Hersh failed to laugh. 'We're lucky to get Mac,' he said, 'so let's not take advantage like.'

Mr MacPherson didn't want to cross the street in order to chastise the smokers, but the boys had clearly seen him.

'Weasel! Can the cigs. Here comes Mac himself.'

'I should care,' Duddy said.

'Kravitz! Put out that cigarette immediately.'

'My father is aware that I smoke, Sir.'

'Then he's not fit to bring up a boy.'

'He's my father, Sir.'

'Would you like to stay on in this school, Kravitz?'

'Yes, Sir. But he's my father, Sir.'

'Then let's not have any more of your cheekiness. Put out that cigarette immediately.'

'Yes, Sir.'

No sooner had Mr MacPherson turned his back on them than Duddy began to hum *Coming Through the Rye*. But, turning sharply into the boys' side of the courtyard, Mr MacPherson guessed that he was far enough away to pretend that he hadn't heard.

'Boy, are you ever lucky,' Hersh said. 'Horner would've strapped you ten on each.'

Mr MacPherson began to climb the icy concrete steps that led into the school. When he was on the last step a high-pitched shriek rose among the students. He felt a plunk on the back of his neck as the snowball smashed to smithereens just above his coat collar. Particles of snow began to trace a chilling pattern down his back. Mr MacPherson whirled about and turned on the students, knitting his eyebrows in an attempt at ferocity. An innocent bustle filled the courtyard. Nobody looked at him. Mr MacPherson fled into the dark stuffy school building. His horn-rimmed glasses fogged immediately. Ripping them off, he prepared to be vile in class all day.

Duddy Kravitz bobbed up in the middle of a group of boys. 'How's that for pitching?' he asked.

'Oh, big hero. You didn't mean to hit him. You meant to hit me,' Hersh said.

'Mighty neat, anyway,' Samuels said.

The bell rang.

'Nobody gets away with insulting my old man,' Duddy said.

When Mr MacPherson entered room forty-one a few minutes later he was no stranger there. This was his first day as class master, but he already taught the boys history three times weekly and so knew them all by name and deed. Some, it should be said, stayed in room forty-one longer than others, par for the course being two years, grades ten and eleven.

The undisputed record-holding resident of room forty-one was, in 1947, still there. His name was Stanley Blatt, but everybody called him A.D. because, in flunking one among hundreds of oral exams, he had permanently endeared himself to the school inspector by insisting that A.D. stood for 'After the Depression'. A.D., already sporting a moustache, had first entered room forty-one and found it was good in 1942, and there he had rested, but not non-stop, for he had served three years in the merchant marine during the war.

Room forty-one had a reputation for being the toughest class in the school. There were those, Mr MacPherson knew, who thought he was too soft a replacement for Horner. Only yesterday Mr Jackson had said, 'You shouldn't have put John at the mercy of Kravitz & Co. He's in no shape to cope these days.'

'He's right, Leonard. Poor John hasn't stepped out of the house once since Jenny took ill.'

'I've got a feeling he's usually up half the night with her, too.'

'You should have given me room forty-one,' Mr Coldwell had said with appetite. 'I would have strapped plenty of respect into Kravitz.'

The boys had been unusually quiet when Mr MacPherson had entered room forty-one after the first bell. On the blackboard, drawn in a clumsy hand, was the chalk figure of a lean man being crushed by a snowball. Underneath was the inscription, OUR MAC. Mr MacPherson contrived to appear calm. 'Who did it? Whose filthy work is this?' Fully expecting the answering quiet, he smacked his copy of *The World's Progress* (revised) against the desk and sat down. 'We shall remain seated until the coward who has done this owns up.'

Ten minutes passed in silence before somebody giggled in the back row. Mr MacPherson whipped out his attendance book. 'Hersh, erase the boards.'

'But it wasn't me, Sir. I should drop down dead it wasn't me.'

Small, squinting Hersh was the butt of the class. His undoing had been a demonstration against the rise in the price of chocolate bars. A photograph on the back page of the *Telegram* had shown Hersh, his attempt to hide behind taller members of the Young Communist League unsuccessful, holding high a placard that read, DOWN WITH THE 7 CENT CHOCOLATE BAR.

'Erase the boards, Hersh.'

Mr MacPherson called out the names in his attendance book, asking each boy if he was responsible for the 'outrage' on the board, and eventually he bit into Kravitz's name with special distaste.

'Present, Sir.'

'Kravitz, are you responsible for this?'

'For what, Sir?'

'For the drawing on the board.'

'Partly, Sir.'

'What do you mean, partly? Either you are responsible or you are not responsible.'

'Sir, it's like – '

'Stand up when you talk to me. Impudent!'

'Yes, Sir. If you want to know the truth we're all responsible like. But we only meant it for a joke, Sir.'

'Do you mean to insinuate that I haven't got a sense of humour?'

'Well, Sir . . .'

'Answer my question.'

'No, Sir.'

'All right then, whose idea was this little prank?'

'I'm telling you we're all responsible.'

'Was it your idea?'

No answer.

'This class will not go to the basketball game this afternoon, but will stay in for an hour after school is out. And you, Kravitz, will do the same tomorrow and the next day.'

'That's not fair, Sir.'

'Are you telling me what's fair?'

'No, Sir. But why am I different from everybody else?'

'I don't know, Kravitz. You tell me.'

Mr MacPherson smiled thinly. Everybody laughed.

'Aw, Sir. Gee whiz.'

'This class may do anything it likes for the next period. I absolutely refuse to teach the likes of you.'

'Anything, Sir?'

'Look here, Kravitz, you're a brat and an exhibitionist. I'm – '

'You said my father wasn't fit to bring me up. I've got witnesses. That's an insult to my family, Sir.'

' – not going to strap you, though. I won't give you that satisfaction. But – '

'You think it's a pleasure or something to be strapped? Jeez.'

' – I know you're responsible for the drawing on the board and I think it cowardly of you not to have taken complete responsibility.'

'*I'm* a coward. Who's afraid to strap who around here?'

'I'm not afraid to strap you, Kravitz. I don't believe in corporal punishment.'

'Sure.'

'*Sir*.'

'Sure, Sir.'

Outside, Duddy slapped Abrams on the back. 'Mac is gonna wish he was never born,' he said. 'It's the treatment for him.'

The treatment took more than one form. With Mr Jackson, who wore a hearing aid, the boys spoke softer and softer in class until all they did was move their lips in a pretence of speech and Mr Jackson raised his hearing aid to its fullest capacity. Then all thirty-eight boys shouted out at once and Mr Jackson fled the physics lab holding his hands to his ears. The boys retaliated against Mr Coldwell by sending movers, taxis, and ambulances to his door. Mr Feeney was something else again. He would seize on each new boy and ask him, 'Do you know what the Jewish national anthem is?'

'No, Sir.'

So Mr Feeney would go to the board and write, 'To the Bank, To the Bank.'

'Do you know how the Jews make an "S"?'

'No, Sir.'

Mr Feeney would go to the board, make an 'S', and draw two strokes through it. Actually, he meant his jokes in a friendly spirit and the sour reactions he usually got puzzled him. Anyway, the boys got even with Mr Feeney by filling out coupons for books that came in plain brown wrappers with his daughter's name and, with cruel accuracy, by writing away for bust-developers for his wife.

Duddy pretended he was dialling a number on the telephone. 'Hey! Hullo, hullo. Is Mac in? Hey, Mac? Em, this is The Avenger speaking. Yep, none other. Your days are numbered, Mac.'

The boys split up. Those who had after-school jobs, like Hersh, went one way and the others, led by Duddy Kravitz, wandered up towards Park Avenue.

To a middle-class stranger, it's true, one street would have seemed as squalid as the next. On each corner a cigar store, a grocery, and a fruit man. Outside staircases everywhere. Winding ones, wooden ones, rusty and risky ones. Here a prized plot of grass splendidly barbered, there a spitefully weedy patch. An endless repetition of precious peeling balconies and waste lots making the occasional gap here and there. But, as the boys knew, each street between St Dominique and Park Avenue represented subtle differences in income. No two cold-water flats were alike. Here was the house where the fabulous Jerry Dingleman was born. A few doors away lived Duddy Ash, who ran for alderman each election on a one-plank platform: provincial speedcops were anti-semites. No two stores were the same, either. Best Fruit gypped on the scales, but Smiley's didn't give credit.

Duddy told the boys about his brother Bradley. 'I got a letter from him only yesterday aft,' he said. 'As soon as I'm finished up at Fletcher's Field he wants me to come down to Arizona to help out on the ranch like.'

Leaning into the wind, their nostrils sticking together each time they inhaled, Abrams and Samuels exchanged incredulous glances, but didn't dare smile. They were familiar with the exploits of Bradley. He had run away to the States at fifteen, lied about his age, joined the air force, and sunk three Jap battleships in the Pacific. They were going to make a movie about his life, maybe. After the war Bradley had rescued an Arizona millionaire's beautiful daughter from drowning, married her, and bought a ranch. Familiar with all of Bradley's exploits the boys also suspected that he was a fictional character, but nobody dared accuse Duddy of lying. Duddy was kind of funny, that's all.

'Hey,' Abrams shouted. 'Look!'

Right there, on St Joseph Boulevard, was a newly opened mission. The neon sign outside the little shop proclaimed JESUS SAVES in English and Yiddish. Another bilingual sign, this one in the window, announced THE MESSIAH HAS COME, over open copies of the Bible with the appropriate phrases underlined in red.

'Come on, guys.' Duddy said.

Somewhat hesitant, the boys nevertheless followed Duddy inside. Trailing snow over the gleaming hardwood floor, they ripped off their stiff frozen gloves and began to examine the pamphlets and blotters that were stacked in piles on the long table. A door rasped behind them. 'Good afternoon.' A small rosy-faced man stood before them, rubbing his hands together. 'Something I can do for you?'

'We were just passing by,' Duddy said. 'Hey, are you a Hebe?'

'Of the Jewish faith?'

'Yeah. Are you?'

'I was,' the man said, 'until I embraced Jesus.'

'No kidding! Hey, we guys would like to know all about Jesus. *Isn't that right, guys?*'

'Sure.'

'How we could become *goyim*, Christians like.'

'Aren't you a little young to – '

'Could we take some of these pamphlets? I mean we'd like to read up on it.'

'Certainly.'

'Blotters, too?' A.D. asked quickly.

'*For keeps?*'

'Of course.'

Duddy gave Samuels a nudge. 'Hey, Sir,' he asked, 'you ever heard of FFHS?'

'I'm afraid not.'

Duddy told him about it. 'I've got an idea for you, Sir. Lots of guys there are dying to know about Jesus and stuff. Our parents never tell us anything, you know. So what I'm thinking is why don't you come round at lunch time tomorrow and hand out some of these *free* pamphlets and stuff to the guys, eh?'

Racing down the street A.D. goosed Samuels and Duddy pushed Abrams into a snowbank. The boys stopped short outside the Lubovitcher Yeshiva and began to arm themselves with snowballs. 'They'll be coming out any minute.' Duddy said.

They had come to torment the rabbinical college students before. During another cold spell they had once given one of the smaller boys the alternative of having his face washed with snow or licking the grill of the school fence. Stupidly, the boy had chosen to lick the grill. And there he had remained, his tongue adhering to the iron, until medical help had come.

'Here they come, guys!'

'Jesus saves. Read all about it!'

The alarmed students drew back into their school just as the FFHS boys began to pelt them with pamphlets and snowballs. Two bearded teachers, armed with brooms, charged down the steps and started after the boys. Duddy led the retreat across the street. There, joining arms, the boys marched along, stopping

at the corner of Jeanne Mance Street to stuff a mailbox with
snow. They sang:

> '*Oh, Nellie put your belly close to mine.*
> *Wiggle your bum.*'

Chapter Two

After he left the school that afternoon Mr MacPherson decided that rather than getting right on a streetcar, instead of waiting in the cold and fighting for a place in the rush hour, he would go to the Laura Secord Shop to buy a box of chocolates for Jenny. Directly across the street from the shop was the Pines Tavern.

Once in the tavern Mr MacPherson was careful to seat himself two tables away from the nearest group of labourers. He decided that he had been morally right to call Kravitz a coward. But after he had delayed his trip to the Laura Secord Shop twice more he admitted to himself that there were more urgent reasons why it had been wrong to insult Kravitz. Tomorrow or the next day the bottle of ink on his desk would have been mysteriously overturned. Pencils and sheets of foolscap paper would disappear from his drawers. The boys would be given to fits of coughing or, at a secret signal, would begin to hum *Coming Through the Rye*. On his side Mr MacPherson would bombard the boys with unannounced exams and cancel all athletics, assign at least two hours of homework nightly and expel a few boys from school for a week, but he would not use the strap.

Long ago Mr MacPherson had vowed never to strap a boy. The principle itself, like the dream of taking Jenny on a trip to Europe, keeping up with the latest educational books, or saving to buy a house, was dead. But his refusal to strap was still of the greatest consequence to Mr MacPherson. 'There,' they'd say, 'goes the only teacher in FFHS who has never strapped a boy.' That he no longer believed in not-strapping was beside the point. As long as he refused to do it Mr MacPherson felt that he would always land safely. There would be no crack-up. He would survive.

Outside again, waiting for his streetcar, Mr MacPherson kept kicking his feet together to keep them from freezing. Flattened against the window by the crush of people in the rear of the streetcar, anxious because the man next to him was sneezing violently, he thought, another eight years. Eight years more, and he would retire.

Only when he hung his coat up on the hall rack did he realize that he had forgotten to buy that box of chocolates for Jenny. There were two strange coats on the rack. The woman's coat was grey Persian lamb. Briefly Mr MacPherson considered slipping outside again.

'Is that you, John?'

'Yes.'

'Surprise, John. We have visitors. Herbert and Clara Shields.'

Ostensibly her voice was cheerfully confident, but Mr Mac-Pherson was familiar with the cautionary quality in it, and the fear also. Calling out to him, even before he got out of the hall, was a warning. Automatically Mr MacPherson reached for the package of Sen-Sen he always carried with him. He also lit a cigarette before he entered the bedroom.

Jenny sat up in bed. Her mouth broke into a small, painful smile. Mr MacPherson smiled back at her reassuringly and averted his eyes quickly. 'Hello Herbert, Clara,' he said. 'How nice to see you again.'

Big, broad Herbert Shields charged out of his seat and grabbed Mr MacPherson's hand. 'You old son-of-a-gun,' he said.

'Herbert and Clara are in Montreal for the Pulp and Paper Convention. They're going abroad this summer. Herbert's been made an assistant to the vice-president. Isn't that lovely, John?'

'It is indeed. I'm very happy for you, Herbert. How nice of you to remember us. Really I – '

'Look at him, Herbert,' Clara said. 'He hasn't changed one bit. He's still our John. I'll bet he thinks we're dreadful. Materialists, or philistines. John, are you still a what-do-you-call-it? A pacifist?'

'You old son-of-a-gun,' Herbert said.

The Shieldses had kept in touch with most of the old McGill crowd. And Mr MacPherson knew that Clara would write letters to all of them, explaining why they never heard from John. 'He's a failure, my dear, absolutely, and the Colby girl, the minister's daughter if you remember, well, she's turned out an invalid.'

After the Shieldses had left, first making him promise that he would call them at the Mount Royal Hotel, Mr MacPherson gave Jenny her medicines. He had meant to work on his history test papers, long overdue, but he was too tired. So, remembering to unhook the phone, he got into bed. He told Jenny about Kravitz.

'But what a rude thing for you to have said about the boy's father. I'm surprised at you, John.'

'You ought to meet my boys one day.' Mr MacPherson laughed out loud. He reached over and touched Jenny's forehead. 'Good night,' he said.

Jenny awakened him around three in the morning, complaining of a nagging pain in her chest. He thought of calling Dr Hanson. But Dr Hanson would say that Jenny must get a month's rest in the mountains or he wouldn't be held responsible for the consequences, and then he would shake his head, mildly exasperated, and prescribe the usual sedatives, so MacPherson administered the sedatives himself.

'Would you like me to read to you for a while?' he asked.

'Thanks, anyway, John. But I think I'll be able to sleep.'

Mr MacPherson sat down in his armchair and passed the night overlooking her difficult sleep, squeezing his hands together whenever she coughed.

Chapter Three

Duddy didn't get home until after seven o'clock. His father was out, but he found his brother Lennie in the bedroom.

'Hi!'

'Duddy,' Lennie said, 'how many times have I asked you not to barge in here when I'm studying?'

Duddy's face flushed.

'Look, Duddy, half the guys who flunk out do it in their second year. Anatomy's the big killer. Your supper's on the kitchen table.'

Duddy ate his frankfurters and beans standing up, poured himself a glass of milk, and returned to the bedroom. 'We got a new class master today,' he said. 'Mac, of all people.'

No answer.

'Hey, guess what? I heard a rumour that a sort of mission's opened up on St Joseph Boulevard and the jerk who runs it is going to hand out pamphlets and stuff at FFHS. Isn't that an insult to our religion like? I think somebody oughta complain.'

'Look, Duddy, I really must get back to work.'

Duddy jumped up. 'You don't have to worry about your fees next year. I'm going to get a job as a waiter up North for the summer and you can have all my tips.' Embarrassed, he fled.

'Duddy!'

'I know,' Duddy said, half into his coat. 'Uncle Benjy is gonna take care of your fees.'

'I think I'm going to be free Saturday afternoon. You want to come to the movies with us?'

'Aw, Riva wouldn't like it. I'd be a fifth wheel like.'

It's true, Lennie thought, and come Saturday morning he'd regret that he had asked Duddy to join him. 'You're coming with us, that's definite.'

'Sure.'

'Hey, where are you going?'

'I'm invited to a musical evening at Mr Cox's house. All the guys are.'

Young Mr Cox, the newest teacher in the school, was, in Duddy's opinion, the World's No. 1 Crap-Artist. Once he had dropped into Irving's Poolroom after school to talk to the boys – a terrifying intrusion. Another crazy thing he had done had been to come to the Students' Council Tea Dance in the gym one day – not *so* crazy when you remember that he danced three slow numbers with Birdie Lyman. But, whackiest of all, he invited the boys round regularly for musicales. Mr Cox's music was a bore. But there were plenty of cokes, hot dogs sometimes, and lots of laughs. Best, of course, was Mrs Cox, who was always chasing after you with questions like are you jealous of your younger sister and how do you feel about restricted hotels, as if their parents could afford them.

After the second musicale Mrs Cox tried to do something about the boys' language. 'I know very well,' she said, 'that you only use those words for their shock value and that's silly, because you can't shock me. You know the *correct* words, anyway. We can begin by naming the parts of the body. Do you all know what a penis is?'

'Sure,' Duddy said. 'A penis is a guy that plays the piano.'

That ended the language lessons, but not the quarrels about Jane Cox. One night the boys detected the shadowy shape of an unmistakably black lace brassiere under Jane's white cotton blouse and this prompted Duddy to observe, 'A broad who wears a black brassiere means business.'

'Maybe it wasn't black, smart guy. Maybe it was just a dirty pink one.'

At this Duddy howled derisively.

'O.K.,' Tannenbaum said, 'it's black, let's say, but she could wear it only for her husband's sake.'

'She wouldn't need it for Cox, you jerk, because he can see her *completely* naked any time he feels like it.'

This silenced everybody but Hersh. 'You have to make everything dirty. Nothing's good for you, unless you can make it dirty.'

That night, while the others were pretending to listen to a symphony, Duddy slipped out into the hall to examine the bookcases. He did not notice Jane Cox hovering over his shoulder until she coughed. Blushing, he shut the book quickly and retreated. 'I was reading a book, that's all. I wasn't stealing anything.'

'But nobody accused you of stealing anything.' She picked up the book. *U.S.A.*, by Dos Passos. 'Do you usually read such heavy stuff?' she asked with a faint smile.

'Why not, eh? You think I have to be a moron just because my old man is a taxi driver? My brother's studying to be a doctor. I read lots of books.'

'Are you sure,' Jane asked, still smiling, 'that you didn't pick up this book simply because you were looking for . . . sexy passages?'

'Look, I'm not the kind of a shmo who has to get his sex second-hand.'

Jane brought her hand to her mouth, suppressing a giggle. 'Don't be alarmed. When I was your age I used to flip through modern novels for the same reason. It's normal. You're just at the age when a boy becomes aware of all the secret powers of his body.'

'Oh, will you leave me alone? Will you please leave me alone?'

Duddy rushed into the bedroom, grabbed his coat, and ran down the stairs. Outside, it was snowing and he had to wait a long time for a streetcar. He sat down on the seat over the heater and melting snow ran down his neck. Later, he thought, Jane would tell Shmo-face Cox about catching him with that dirty book. Tomorrow Cox would repeat the story in the Masters' Room and everybody would have a good laugh at his expense. The hell with them, Duddy thought. He walked up to Eddy's Cigar & Soda, across the street from the Triangle Taxi Stand, and there he found his father drinking coffee with some of the other men. Josette was there, too.

'Duddy,' Max said gruffly. 'I thought you'd be home in bed by this time.' Turning to the others with a wide smile, he added, 'You all know my kid.'

'*That's* Lennie?' Drapeau asked.

Max laughed expansively. 'Ixnay. He's not gonna be a saw-bones. Duddy's a dope like me. Aren't you, kid?' He rumpled the boy's snow-caked hair. 'Lennie's twenty-one. He's had scholarships all through school.'

A big man, burly and balding, with soft brown eyes and an adorable smile, Max Kravitz was inordinately proud of the fact that he had, several years ago, been dubbed Max The Hack in *Mel West's What's What*, Moey Weinstein's column in the *Telegram*, and that, as a consequence, he (along with West's most puerile Yiddish-isms) had gone by that name ever since. Max was said to be on first-name terms with The Boy Wonder and, as Mel West would have put it, a host of others.

Max, in fact, delighted in telling tales about the legendary Boy Wonder. His favourite, a story that Duddy had heard over and over again, was the one about the streetcar transfer. Max loved to tell this tale, one he believed to be beautiful, to new-comers; and earlier that evening he had repeated it to MacDonald. Not just like that, mind you, because before he could begin Max required the right atmosphere. His customary chair next to the coke freezer, a hot coffee with a supply of sugar cubes ready by his side, and a supporting body of old friends. Then, speaking slowly and evenly, he would begin, letting the story develop on its own, never allowing an interruption to nonplus him and not raising his voice until Baltimore.

'He was broke,' Max began, 'and he hadn't even made his name yet. He was just another bum at the time.'

'And what is he now? The gangster.'

'I'm warning you, MacDonald, if the Boy Wonder knocked off his mother Max here is the guy who would find an excuse for him.'

'I mean you could say that,' Max continued. 'We're like this, you know, and I'd say it to his face even. *The Boy Wonder was just another bum at the time.* Funny, isn't it? I mean his phone bill alone last year must have come to twenty G's (he's got lines open to all the tracks and ballparks all day long, you know), but only ten years ago he would have had to sweat blood before he coulda raised a lousy fin.'

'No wonder.'

'How that goniff manages to keep out of jail beats me.'

'It's simple,' Debrofsky said, 'the whole police force is on his pay roll.'

Max waited. He sucked a sugar cube. 'Anyway, he's broke, like I said. So he walks up to the corner of Park and St Joseph and hangs around the streetcar stop for a couple of hours, and do you know what?'

'He trips over a hundred dollar bill and breaks his leg.'

'He's pulled in for milking pay phones. Or stealing milk bottles, maybe.'

'All that time,' Max said, 'he's collecting streetcar transfers off the street and selling them, see. Nerve? *Nerve*. At three cents apiece he's up a quarter in two hours, and then what? He walks right in that door, MacDonald, right past where you're standing, and into the back room. There, with only a quarter in his pocket, he sits in on the rummy game. Win? He's worked his stake up to ten bucks in no time. And what does he do next?'

'Buy a gun and shoot himself.'

'I got it. He donates the ten spot to the Jewish National Fund.'

Max smiled indulgently. He blew on his coffee. 'Around the corner he goes to Moe's barbershop and plunk goes the whole ten spot on a filly named Miss Sparks running in the fifth at Belmont. On the nose, but. And you guessed it, MacDonald, Miss Sparks comes in and pays eleven to one. The Boy Wonder picks up his loot and goes to find himself a barbotte game. Now you or me, MacDonald, we'd take that hundred and ten fish and buy ourselves a hat, or a present for the wife maybe, and consider ourselves lucky. We mere mortals we'd right away put some of it in the bank. Right? *Right*. But not the Boy Wonder. No Sir.'

Max dropped a sugar cube on to his tongue and took some time sucking the goodness out of it.

'Picture him, MacDonald, a twenty-nine-year-old boy from St Urbain Street and he's not even made his name yet. All night he spends with those low-lifes, men who would slit their mother's throat for a lousy nickel. Gangsters. Graduates of Saint Vincent de Paul. Anti-semites, the lot. If he loses, O.K., but if he wins – *If he wins*, MacDonald? Will they let that little St Urbain Street punk, Jerry Dingleman, leave with all their money? He's up and he's down, and when he's up a lot the looks he gets around the table are not so nice.' Max cleared his throat. 'Another coffee, please, Eddy.'

But Eddy had already poured it. For, at this point in the transfer story, Max always ordered coffee.

'Imagine him, MacDonald. It's morning. Dawn, I mean, like

at the end of a film. The city is awakening. Little tots in their little beds are dreaming pretty little dreams. Men are getting out of bed and catching shit from their wives. The exercise boys are taking the horses out. Somewhere, in the Jewish General Hospital let's say, a baby is born, and in the Catholic hospital – no offence, MacDonald – some poor, misguided nun has just died of an abortion. Morning, MacDonald, another day. And the Boy Wonder, his eyes ringed with black circles, steps out into God's sunlight – that was before his personal troubles, you know – and in his pocket, MacDonald, is almost one thousand de-is-ollers – and I should drop down dead if a word of this isn't true.

'But wait. That's not all. This is only the beginning. Because the Boy Wonder does not go home to sleep. No, Sir. That morning he takes the train to Baltimore, see, and that's a tough horse town, you know, and they never heard of the Boy Wonder yet. He's only a St Urbain Street boy, you know. I mean he wasn't born very far from where *I* live. Anyway, for six weeks there is no word. *Rien.* Not a postcard even. Imagine, Mac-Donald, try to visualize it. Has some dirty nigger killed him for his roll, God forbid? (There are lots of them in Baltimore, you know, and at night with those dim street lamps, you think you can even see those black bastards coming?) Is he a broken man, penniless again, wasting away in a hospital maybe? *The public ward.* Six weeks and not a word. Nothing. Expect the worst, I said to myself. Goodbye, old friend. *Au revoir.* Good night, sweet prince, as they say, something something something. Then one day, MacDonald, one fine day, back into town he comes, only not by foot and not by train and not by plane. He's driving a car a block long and sitting beside him is the greatest little piece you ever saw. Knockers? You've never seen such a pair. I mean just to look at that girl – And do you know what, MacDonald? He parks that bus right outside here and steps inside to have a smoked meat with the boys. By this time he owns his own stable already. So help me, MacDonald, in Baltimore he has eight horses running. O.K.; today it would be peanuts for an operator his size, but at the time, MacDonald, at the time. And from what? Streetcar transfers at three cents a piece. Streetcar transfers, that's all. I mean can you beat that?'

Whenever he told that story Max's face was suffused with

such enthusiasm that the men, though they had heard it time and again, sure as they were that it would come out right in the end, unfailingly moved in closer, their fears and hopes riding with the Boy Wonder in Baltimore, who, as Max said, was only a St Urbain Street boy.

But they were extremely fond of Max, anyway. He didn't push, he was always good for a fin, and though he never complained it had been hard for him since his wife had died.

Minnie had died nine years ago and that, Max figured, was why Duddy was such a puzzle. A headache, even. All he ever wanted to do was play snooker. Max, of course, was anxious for Duddy to get started in life. About Lennie he had no worries: not one.

'Awright, Duddy, since you're here already, what'll you have?'

'A scotch and soda.'

Max shook with laughter. 'Some BTO my kid.'

'Getting much?' MacDonald asked, winking at Duddy.

Drapeau guffawed and Debrofsky gave Josette a meaningful poke. But Max frowned. 'You shouldn't talk like that, Mac-Donald. He's only a kid.'

Small, sallow MacDonald smiled thinly. 'Well, if he can drink Scotch . . .'

'Okey-doke, Eddy, give my boy a Grepsi and a lean on rye. I'll have the same.' Max sat down beside Duddy at the counter. 'Keep away from MacDonald,' he said in a low voice. 'He's new here and I don't like him.'

Duddy told his father about Mr MacPherson. 'He said you weren't fit to bring me up, the bastard.'

'If your teacher said that he had a good reason. What did you say first?'

'Do I always have to be in the wrong? Jeez. Why can't you stick up for me? Just once why can't you – '

'You're a real trouble-maker, Duddy, that's why. Lennie never once got the strap in four years at Fletchers.'

Duddy repeated to his father the rumour about the missionary who was going to distribute pamphlets outside FFHS. 'Something oughta be done,' he said. 'The PTA oughta complain.'

'That's true,' Max said. 'It's not like we were chinks or something.'

But Duddy sensed that his father wasn't listening to him. He seemed edgy, and from time to time he glanced anxiously at Josette.

Josette was a handsome whore with splendid black hair and enormous breasts. 'She wears a sign under her bra,' Duddy had once overheard Max say, 'and you know what it says? It says look out for the four foot drop.' She often came in to drink coffee with the drivers and occasionally when there was no game going on in the backroom she went there with one or the other of them. In exchange, the men tried to be helpful. Josette was obviously drunk and seemed to be in a black mood.

'You finish your sandwich,' Max said to Duddy, 'and I'll drive you home. It's time to pack in, anyway.'

'Hey, c'mere kid,' MacDonald said. 'Got something to show you.'

'You put those cards right back in your pocket, MacDonald.'

'You were glad enough to look through them, so why can't the kid . . .?'

'Because he's a kid.'

'Aw, come on, Daddy, lemme look at the cards.'

'Your old man figures you still think it's got no other use but to piss with.'

The phone rang and Debrofsky went to answer it.

'Don't needle me, MacDonald.'

MacDonald flipped his deck of cards.

'When I lose my temper,' Max said, 'I lose my temper.'

MacDonald looked closely at Max and retreated. Josette tittered. Max grabbed his boy firmly by the arm. 'Let's go,' he said. But Debrofsky blocked his way. 'It's for you, Max.'

Duddy, left alone, looked longingly at MacDonald. MacDonald smiled his thin, humourless smile, and walked towards the back of the store. Just as Duddy started after him Eddy called out, 'You sit right down here and finish your sandwich like your paw said. Come on, Duddy.'

'I'm not a kid any more.'

'You're a kid,' Eddy said.

MacDonald began to lay out his cards face up on the pinball machine and the other drivers moved away from him.

'How're you doing at school?' Debrofsky asked.

'Aw.'

Max stepped out of the phone booth and took Josette aside. They whispered together.

'I can't drive you home,' Max said to Duddy.

'Why?'

'I've got to take Josette somewhere.'

Josette began putting on more makeup.

'Where?'

'I can't take you home. You'll have to walk, that's all.'

'I'll drive him home,' MacDonald said.

'He'll walk.'

'Why can't Debrofsky take Josette?'

'It's gotta be me. No more questions. O.K.?'

Duddy kicked an empty cigarette box with his toe.

'I can't explain,' Max said. 'Now will you go home, please.'

Duddy hesitated.

'He gets it off the top,' MacDonald said.

Max flushed. He took a deep breath, and the only sound was the click of Josette's compact. MacDonald slipped behind a chair, ready to pick it up, and Max started for him. He was stopped by the expression on Duddy's face.

Duddy smiled; he laughed.

'Jeez,' he said proudly. 'That's something. Jeez.'

Max slapped his face so hard that Duddy lost his balance and fell against the counter.

'Get out of here. Go home.'

Finger-marks had been burnt red into the boy's cheeks. Max buried his hands in his pockets.

'You're a pimp.'

'Get out, Duddy.'

Duddy got up and ran.

'I didn't mean to hit him so hard,' Max said to the other drivers.

'He had it coming to him.'

'Easy, Max. It wasn't your fault.'

Max took Josette by the arm. 'Awright,' he said. 'I haven't got all night. Let's go.'

'You're hurting me,' Josette said.

Chapter Four

In the Masters' Room of FFHS the next morning Mr MacPherson was interrupted when Mr Coldwell burst angrily into the room. 'If I ever find out which one of them phoned me last night,' he said, 'I'll fix it so that he can't get into any school in the city.'

'So they've been calling you too,' Mr Jackson said.

'Are you sure it's the students?' Mr MacPherson asked sleepily.

'Did you call me at one a.m. John? Shout obscenities into my ear and hang up?'

'I believe,' Mr Jackson began, applying his years of intimacy with the scientific method to the present banality, 'I believe – now we must allow some margin for doubt – but I *do* believe I recognized Kravitz's voice last night.'

Mr MacPherson began to read his history test papers.

'Damn it, John,' Mr Coldwell said, 'strap the little bastard and put an end to this nonsense.'

'Strapping,' Mr MacPherson began in a small voice, 'has never been a solution to . . .'

'Sure, sure,' Mr Coldwell said, 'but until your socialist messiah comes along I'd like my sleep undisturbed by obscene phone calls. Strap him, John.'

'I refuse to strap Kravitz.'

Mr Cox lowered his newspaper. 'As a matter of fact,' he said, 'Kravitz and the rest of the Dead End Kids were at our place last night. I played some records for them.'

'Young man, you'll hear more about this. I think we've had quite enough of your musical evenings.'

'Why don't you try strapping me, Coldwell? You can make the same deal with me as you made with Kravitz. If I say nothing about my wrists bleeding you'll promise not to mark it in your book.'

Even Mr MacPherson joined in the ensuing laughter.

'Really, Cox,' Mr Feeney said, 'you don't believe that story, do you?'

Mr Cox's face turned white.

'What would you say,' Mr Coldwell said, his anger gone, 'if Kravitz told you I beat him with chains?'

Luckily for Mr Cox the first bell rang just then. He caught up with Mr MacPherson just outside Room forty-one. 'I want you to know,' he said, 'that I'm with you all the way in this. Strapping is the worst kind of reactionary measure. I'm a socialist too,' he added warmly.

Mr MacPherson saw Coldwell walking towards them. 'Socialism is strictly for young men,' he said loudly. 'I hope you too will grow out of it in time.'

A typed note was waiting for Mr MacPherson on his desk in room forty-one.

KRAVITZ MAY BE A BRAT AND AN EXHIBITIONIST
AND A COWARD, BUT THE GUY AFRAID TO STRAP
HIM MUST BE A REAL CHICKEN.

Mr MacPherson crumpled the note into a ball and tossed it into the wastepaper basket. 'I'm warning you I won't stand for any nonsense today. If anyone so much as talks without raising his hand he's as good as asking for an expulsion.'

When Mr MacPherson got home that afternoon there was yet another note waiting for him.

Dear John,
Dr Hanson wants you to call him as soon as
you get in. He gave me an injection and
something to make me sleep.

Jenny

Mr MacPherson phoned. Dr Hanson was out on a call, Miss Floyd said, but Mr MacPherson was to come to his office at nine a.m. tomorrow morning, without fail. Yes, he would have to miss school. This was urgent.

No sooner had he hung up than the telephone rang again. 'Yes,' he said tightly.

'Guess who?'

'Look here, Kravitz, I'm warning you –'

'Oh, dear, do I sound Jewish, John?'

'I shall have you expelled for this. That's a promise.'

'John, pet, it's *me*.'

'Who's speaking, please?

'Clara Shield-berg. Und vat's new vit you, Abie?'

'Oh, it's you Clara. I'm sorry. You see, sometimes my students – '

'Never mind your students, pet. You get right into a taxi this minute and come over here and have a drink with us. We're in Room 341.'

'Oh, I couldn't do that. Jenny isn't well and besides I – '

'If you don't come over here this minute Herbert says he'll report you to the police for having stolen his car.'

The party, centred in room 341, actually embraced the two adjoining rooms as well. Even the surrounding halls swarmed with merry-makers. A lot of the men wore badges with their names and addresses typed on them and, underneath, the one word, 'DELEGATE'. All the women were smartly dressed. Embarrassed, Mr MacPherson edged into a free corner and hastily lit a cigarette.

'It's great to see you again,' said Herbert. 'What brand of poison do you prefer, Mr Chips?'

Clara kissed Mr MacPherson on the cheek and it was a long time and lots of whiskies later when he next looked at his watch and discovered that it was three a.m. He had only meant to stay for an hour. Horrified, Mr MacPherson rushed for his coat, ran outside, and hailed a taxi.

Once in the taxi he recalled how Herbert had introduced him to a group of strangers. 'I want you to shake the hand of the most brilliant student of our class at McGill. He could have been a success at anything he wanted. Instead he's devoted his life to teaching.' It was clear that they still took him for the freshly scrubbed idealist who had left McGill twenty years ago. They had no idea that he was exhausted, bitter, and drained, and that given the chance to choose again he would never become a teacher.

Perhaps, he thought, there's still time. He hadn't strapped a boy yet, had he? Cox admired him. Next year, he remembered, two more young veterans would be joining the staff. Together, maybe, they could help the boys. A club could be formed, perhaps, as was usually done in movies about delinquents. *There might still be nostalgic reunions in his parlour.* Mr MacPherson began to feel much better. Cheerful, even. There's still hope, he thought.

Mr MacPherson tip-toed into the bedroom, but Jenny wasn't there. He found her crumpled up on the hall floor. The receiver dangled idiotically from the hook above her. Mr Mac-Pherson, who was still only vaguely conscious of what had happened, snatched it up immediately, but the party at the other end had hung up. So he stared accusingly at his wife on the floor, not knowing whether to rip his clothes into shreds or hold her dry hand in his or go out for another drink. After he had hovered over her dumbly for a time he knelt down and discovered that she was still alive. Quickly he telephoned for an ambulance.

Chapter Five

Weidman and Samuels were playing OXO on the board.

'Hey Duddy,' Abrams shouted, 'guess who's coming back today?'

'Not my favourite Scotchman?'

'It's not so funny,' Hersh said. 'His wife died.'

'Too bad it wasn't Mac,' Abrams said.

'You know what,' Cohen said. 'My brother met Mac in the Pines Wednesday aft. And man o man was he ever shot! So anyways my brother pats him on the shoulder. "How's about a beer on me," he says. So you know what? So Mac slaps him across the face.'

Weidman and Samuels stopped their game on the board.

'So what did your brother do, Jerkovitch?'

'What do you mean what did my brother do? He let him have it smack on the jaw, Bango!'

'Smack on the jaw. Yeah, I'll bet.'

'O.K., ask Mac when he comes in, smart guy.'

In the uproar that followed nobody noticed that Mr Mac-Pherson had, indeed, entered the room, until he smacked his briefcase down on the class master's desk.

'Well, well, welcome back, Sir.'

Mr MacPherson silenced Duddy with a scowl. The other boys scrambled for their seats.

'Glad to have you back, Sir,' Hersh offered timidly.

Clutching the class register tightly Mr MacPherson began to call out the boys' names in alphabetical order. 'Abrams,' he began.

'Present, Sir.'

He belched when he got to 'Waldman'.

'He's drunk,' Duddy howled. 'Drunk as a lord.'

The boys watched predatorily as Mr MacPherson fiddled with the straps of his briefcase.

'Hey, Sir. How's about a few pints after classes, eh?'

No reply.

'Is it true that Cohen's brother let you have it, Sir?'

Hersh squeezed his hands together. 'Cut it out,' he said. 'Leave him alone, please.'

Duddy Kravitz shook a fist at Hersh. 'We know how to deal with *tuchusleckers* here,' he said. Then, turning to Mr Mac-Pherson, he asked, 'How's about a free period, Sir?'

'All right.'

Two minutes later Duddy shot up in his seat. 'Sir, there's something I'd like to ask you. I've been looking at my hist'ry book and I see there's only one paragraph on the Spanish inquisition. You don't even mention it in class, so seeing we got lots of time now I thought you might like to tell us something about it,'

'The trouble with you Jews,' Mr MacPherson said, 'is that you're always walking around with a chip on your shoulder.'

'Hey! Hey, there!'

'What exactly do you mean *you Jews?*'

'This isn't Germany, you know.'

'He's a nazi fascist!'

Chapter Six

The man to avoid, as far as strappings went, was Mr Coldwell. Mr Coldwell strapped from an angle, so that the tongue curled around your hand and rebounded hard on the wrist. Usually he strapped a boy until he cried; then he'd say, 'I'd hoped you'd take it like a man.' Next came Mr Feeney. Mr Feeney took three steps backwards with the strap resting lightly on his shoulder, charged, and struck. Mr MacPherson, however, did not even know how to hold the strap properly. So when he led Duddy Kravitz into the Medical Room that afternoon, breaking with a practice of twenty years, the actual blows were feeble, and it was Duddy who emerged triumphant, racing outside to greet his classmates.

'Hey, look! Look, jerkos! Ten on each. Mac strapped me. Mac, of all people.'

Mr MacPherson strapped fifteen boys that week, and his method improved with practice. But the rowdiness in class, and his own drinking, increased in proportion to the strappings. He began to sit around the house alone. He seldom went out any more.

And then one night, a couple of weeks after he had returned to school, Mr MacPherson sat down before his dead fireplace and broke open a new bottle of whisky. He sat there for hours, cherishing old and unlikely memories and trying to feel something more than a sense of liberation because Jenny, whom he had once loved truly, was dead. Half the bottle was finished before all of Mr MacPherson's troubles crystallized into the hard, leering shape of Duddy Kravitz. Mr MacPherson chuckled. Staggering into the hall, pulling the light cord so hard that it broke off in his hand, he rocked to and fro over the telephone. It did not take him long, considering his state, to find Kravitz's number, and he dialled it with care. The telephone must have rung and rung about fifteen times before somebody answered it.

'Hullo,' a voice said gruffly.

Mr MacPherson didn't reply.

'*Hullo*. HULLO! Who is that anyway? Hullo.'

It wasn't Kravitz. He would have recognized Kravitz's voice. The room began to sway around Mr MacPherson.

'Who's speaking?' the voice commanded.

'Mr MacPhers—'

Mr MacPherson slammed the receiver back on the hook and stumbled into the living-room, knocking over a lamp on his way. The first thing he saw there were the history test papers. He ripped them apart, flung them into the fireplace, and lit them. Exhausted, he collapsed into his armchair to watch them burn.

Chapter Seven

Leonard Bush, the principal of FFHS, was a man with many troubles. Only this morning a letter had come from the general manager of the Blue-Top Milk Co. to protest that Joseph Dollard, one of their drivers, had been innocently collecting empty milk bottles outside FFHS when somebody standing in a fourth floor window had urinated on him, which – Mr Bush would certainly agree – could not have been accidental. Attached came a bill for cleaning charges. There was also a letter from the vice-president of the PTA to ask about the man who had been handing out free copies of the New Testament outside FFHS. For, with all due respect, Mr Bush would certainly agree that this was an insult to people of the Jewish faith.

Leonard Bush was a capable, soft-spoken man in his early fifties. His first visitor that morning, a Mrs Yagid, wanted to know why her Herby, a remarkable boy – and I don't say that because he's my own, we're not such common types – why her Herby was not an officer in the FFHS Cadets, not a sergeant even, when that stinker Mrs Cooperman's boy next door, the one with the running nose, was a captain? His second visitor, Glass the used-car dealer, told him it would be a shame, stupid even, to make his boy repeat grade ten again over a lousy two per cent, and besides he had a little hunch that if Mr Bush dropped in to his lot tomorrow there might be a bargain, a real steal, of a car there for him. Leonard Bush's third visitor was Max Kravitz.

'I mean saying such a thing as "you dirty Jews" to a bunch of boys. I mean a phone call at three o'clock in the morning, Mr Bush. You know what I ask myself? What kind of men are teaching my boy. How can they expect to make decent citizens of them when they themselves are like bad children? Tell me if I'm wrong, sir. You can be honest with me, and I'll be honest with you. That's what I'm like.'

'We like honesty here too, Mr Kravitz.'

'You call me Max. I'm a simple man, Mr Bush, a taxi driver. But a taxi driver, Mr Bush, is a little like being a doctor. Night and day, rain or shine, I am at the service of John Q. Public. You'd be surprised at the things that come up in my life. Pregnant women to be rushed to the hospital, accidents, fights, and older men with fine reputations, if you'll pardon me, trying to have sexual relations with young girls in the back of my taxi. No, thank you. But, like I said, it is nothing for me to be called to an emergency in the middle of the night so, as you can well understand, I can't afford to have my sleep disturbed for nothing.'

Mr Bush assured Max Kravitz that Mr MacPherson had never called the boys dirty Jews. He also said that it was certainly not Mr MacPherson who had telephoned in the middle of the night. It was, in his opinion, a student imitating Mr Mac-Pherson. But it was no use. Something, Mr Bush knew, would have to be done. At first the staff had been sympathetic about Mr MacPherson's loss, but his drinking had since become the school joke. So the next morning Mr Bush suggested to Mr MacPherson that he would like to have a quiet chat with him after school was out. That morning, three weeks after Mr Mac-Pherson had returned to school, he was confronted with the problem of the history test papers.

Duddy dashed out his cigarette. 'My dear Mac,' he said, 'the room forty-one gang doesn't care how many times a week you go out to tie a load on. But, if you don't mind, our parents work hard to keep us here. Our reports are supposed to come out next week. We want the results of our hist'ry test.'

The boys applauded and Duddy bowed ceremoniously and sat down.

And it all came tumbling down on Mr MacPherson; the drinking, the phone call, how Kravitz was master of the class-room and he was being ostracized in the Masters' Room. A quiet little chat after school was out, that's what Mr Bush had said. My pension, he thought. They'll take away my job.

'C'mon! What about our marks?'

Mr MacPherson pounced on the register. Abrams, he called. Abrams cupped his hand under his armpit and made a foul noise, Abromovitch, Bernstein. Nobody answered. He hadn't checked the attendance all week. But he kept on reading. 'Kravitz!'

'Yes, Your Highness.'

Something about him, the look in Mr MacPherson's eyes maybe, made Weidman scramble back to his seat sure that Mac had finally gone off his rocker. Cohen clutched a ruler in his hand, waiting. Mr MacPherson walked slowly down the room towards Kravitz.

'It was you who phoned, wasn't it?'

'I don't know what you're talking about.'

'It was you.'

'So help me, Sir, it wasn't.'

'You killed my wife, Kravitz.'

'Stay away from me. I'm warning you.'

'You killed my wife.'

Duddy put up his fists. 'Why don't you have another drink, eh? You should be locked up, that's what. You have no right to be with children.'

'You murdered her, you filthy street arab.'

'Leave him alone,' Abrams whined.

'Please let him go, Sir. We'll be good.'

Mr MacPherson mumbled something inarticulate and passed out. In falling, he banged his head against a desk.

'Duddy! Get the doctor. Hurry! I think Mac is dead!'

Hersh began to sob. 'We killed him,' he screamed.

Duddy stamped his foot on the floor. 'What does he mean I killed his goddam wife? I didn't mean nothing all the time. Nothing. We're all in this together, you understand?'

Once the doctor had assured him that Mr MacPherson had revived completely, though he was still in a shocked state, Mr Bush stepped into the Medical Room to speak to him. Mr Mac-Pherson, resting on the cot, immediately asked, 'Have you come to strap me, Leonard?'

'I'm glad to see you still haven't lost your sense of humour, John.' Mr Bush laughed uneasily. He told Mr MacPherson that he thought it would be best if he took a few days off. There would be plenty of time for their little chat another day. Outside, a taxi was waiting.

'I don't want a taxi,' Mr MacPherson said. 'I'd rather walk.'

Mr MacPherson stopped short when he noticed Kravitz and the others idling outside Felder's store. The boys seemed subdued and unsure of themselves. Duddy started to walk towards him, but then he apparently changed his mind, for he turned around to rejoin the boys.

'Kravitz.'

Duddy stopped.

'You'll go far, Kravitz. You're going to go very far.'

Mr MacPherson, smiling a little, walked away towards Pine Avenue.

*

THE MARCH OF THE FLETCHER'S CADETS

Lance-corporal Boxenbaum led with a bang bang bang on his big white drum and Litvak tripped Cohen, Pinsky blew on his bugle, and the Fletcher's Cadets wheeled left, reet, left, reet, out of Fletcher's Field, led by their Commander-in-chief, that snappy five-footer, W. E. James (that's 'Jew' spelt backwards, as he told each new gym class). Left, reet, left, reet, powdery snow crunching underfoot, Ginsburg out of step once more and Hornstein unable to beat his drum right because of the ten-on-each Mr Coldwell had applied before the parade. Turning smartly right down Esplanade Avenue they were at once joined and embarrassed on either side by a following of younger brothers on sleighs, little sisters with running noses, and grinning delivery boys stopping to make snowballs.

'Hey, look out there General Montgomery, here comes your mother to blow your nose.'

'Lefty! Hey, Lefty! Maw says you gotta come right home to sift the ashes after the parade. No playing pool she says. She's afraid the pipes will burst.'

Tara-boom, tara-*boom*, tara-BOOM-BOOM-BOOM, past the Jewish Old People's Home where on the balcony above, bedecked with shawls and rugs, a stain of yellowing expressionless faces, women with little beards and men with sucked-in mouths, fussy nurses with thick legs and grandfathers whose sons had little time, a shrunken little woman who had survived a pogrom and two husbands and three strokes, and two followers of Rabbi Brott the Miracle Maker, watched squinting against the fierce wintry sun.

'Jewish children in uniform?'

'Why not?'

'It's not nice. For a Jewish boy a uniform is not so nice.'

Skinny, lumpy-faced Boxenbaum took it out on the big white drum and Sergeant Grepsy Segal, who could burp or break wind at will, sang,

> BULLSHIT, that's all the band could play,
> BULLSHIT, it makes the grass grow green.

Mendelsohn hopped to get back into step and Archie Rosen, the FFHS Cadet Corps Quartermaster who sold dyed uniforms at $8.00 each, told Naturman the one about the rabbi and the priest and the bunch of grapes. 'Fun-*ny*,' Naturman said. Commander-in-chief W. E. James, straight as a ramrod, veteran of the Somme, a swagger stick held tight in his hand, his royal blue uniform pressed to a cutting edge and his brass buttons polished perfect, felt a lump in his throat as the corps bugles blowing approached the red brick armoury of the Canadian Grenadier Guards. 'Eyes . . . RIGHT,' he called, saluting stiffly.

Duddy Kravitz like the rest turned to salute the Union Jack and the pursuing gang of kid brothers and sisters took up the chant,

> *Here come the Fletcher's Cadets,*
> *smoking cigarettes,*
> *the cigarettes are lousy*
> *and so are the Fletcher's Cadets.*

Crunch, crunch, crunch-crunch-crunch, over the powdery snow ears near frozen stiff the FFHS Cadet Corps marched past the Jewish Library, where a poster announced,

Wednesday Night
ON BEING A JEWISH POET IN MONTREAL WEST
A Talk by H. I. Zimmerman, B.A.
Refreshments

and smack over the spot where in 1933 a car with a Michigan licence plate had machine-gunned to death the Boy Wonder's uncle. They stopped in front of the YMHA to mark time while the driver of a KIKKOLA truck that had slid in a No. 97 streetcar began to fight with the conductor.

'Hip, hip,' W. E. James called. 'HUP-HIP-HIP.'

A bunch of YMHA boys came out to watch.

'There's Arnie. Hey, Arnie! Where's your gun? Wha'?'

'Hey, Sir! Mr James! You know what you can do with that stick?'

'Boxenbaum. Hey! You'll get a rupture if you carry that drum any further.'

'Hip, Hip,' W. E. James called. 'HIP-HIP-HIP.'

Geiger blew on his bugle and Sivak goosed Kravitz. A snowball knocked off Sergeant Heller's cap, Pinsky caught a frozen horse-bun on the cheek, and Mel Brucker lowered his eyes when they passed his father's store. Monstrous icicles ran from the broken second floor windows of his home into the muck of stiff burnt dry goods and charred wood below. The fire had happened last night. Mel had expected it because that afternoon his father had said cheerfully, 'You're sleeping at grandmaw's tonight,' and each time Mel and his brother were asked to sleep at grandmaw's it meant another fire, another store.

'Hip. Hip. Hip, hip, hip.'

To the right Boxenbaum's father and another picketer walked up and down blowing on their hands before the Nu-Oxford Shoe Factory, and to the left there was Harry's War Assets Store with a sign outside that read, IF YOU HAVEN'T GOT TIME TO DROP IN – SMILE WHEN YOU WALK PAST. Tara-boom, tara-*boom*, tara-BOOM-BOOM-BOOM, past the Hollywood Barbershop where they removed blackheads for 50 cents around the corner of Clark where Charna Felder lived, the FFHS Cadet Corps came crunch-crunch-crunch. Tansky started on his drum, Rubin dropped an icicle down Mort Heimer's back, and the cadets wheeled left, reet, left, reet, into St Urbain Street. A gathering of old grads and slackers stepped out of the Laurier Billiard Hall, attracted by the martial music.

'Hey, Sir. Mr James! Is it true you were a pastry cook in the first war?'

'We hear you were wounded grating latkas.'

'There's Stanley. Hey, Stan! Jeez, he's an officer or something. STAN! It's O.K. about Friday night but Rita says Irv's too short for her. Can you bring Syd instead? Stan! STAN?'

Over the intersection where Gordie Wiser had burnt the Union Jack after many others had trampled and spat on it the day Ernest Bevin announced his Palestine policy, past the house where the Boy Wonder had been born, stopping to mark time at the corner where their fathers and elder brothers armed with baseball bats had fought the frogs during the conscription riots, the boys came marching. A little slower, though, Boxenhaum puffing as he pounded his drum and thirteen or thirty-five others feeling the frost in their toes. The sun went, darkness came quick as a traffic light change, and the snow began to gleam purple. Tansky felt an ache in his stomach as they slogged past his house and Captain Bercovitch remembered there'd be boiled beef and potatoes for supper but he'd have to pick up the laundry first.

'Hip. HIP. Hip, hip, hip.'

To the right the AZA Club House and to the left the poky Polish synagogue where old man Zabitsky searched the black windy street and saw the cadets coming towards him.

'Label. Label, come here.'

'I can't, zeyda, it's a parade.'

'A parade. *Narishkeit*. We're short one man for prayers.'

'But zeyda, please.'

'No buts, no please. Rosenberg has to say kaddish.'

Led by the arm, drum and all, Lionel Zabitsky was pulled from the parade.

'Hey, Sir. A casualty.'

'Chic-*ken*!'

Past Moe's warmly lit Cigar Store where you could get a lean on rye for 15 cents and three more cadets defected. Pinsky blew his bugle faint-heartedly and Boxenbaum gave the drum a little bang. Wheeling right and back again up Clark Street five more cadets disappeared into the darkness.

'Hip. Hip. HIP, HIP, HIP.'

One of the deserters ran into his father, who was on his way home from work.

'Would you like a hotdog and a coke before we go home?'

'Sure.'

'O.K., but you mustn't say anything to Maw.'

Together they watched the out-of-step FFHS Cadet Corps fade under the just starting fall of big lazy snowflakes.

'It's too cold for a parade. You kids could catch pneumonia out in this weather without scarves or rubbers.'

'Mr James says that in the first world war sometimes they'd march for thirty miles without stop through rain and mud that was knee-deep.'

'Is that what I pay school fees for?'

Chapter Eight

Where Duddy Kravitz sprung from the boys grew up dirty
and sad, spiky also, like grass beside the railroad tracks. He
might have been born in Lodz, but forty-eight years earlier his
grandfather had bought a steerage passage to Halifax. Duddy
might have been born in Toronto, that's where his grandfather
was bound for, but Simcha Kravitz's CPR ticket took him only
as far as the Bonaventure Station in Montreal, and he never did
get to Toronto. Simcha was a shoemaker, and two years after
his arrival he was able to send for his wife and two sons. A year
later he had his own shop on a corner of St Dominique Street.
His family lived upstairs, and outside in the gritty hostile soil of
his back yard, Simcha planted corn and radishes, peas, carrots,
and cucumbers. Each year the corn came up scrawnier and the
cucumbers yellowed before they ripened, but Simcha persisted
with his planting.

Simcha's hard thin dark figure was a familiar one in the
neighbourhood. Among the other immigrants he was trusted,
he was regarded as a man of singular honesty and some wisdom,
but he was not loved. He would lend a man money to help him
bring over his wife, grudgingly he would agree to settle a dispute
or advise a man in trouble, he never repeated a confidence, but
about the conditions of his own life he remained silent. His wife
was a shrew with warts on her face and she spoke to him sharply
when others were present, but Simcha did not complain.

'He's only a shoemaker,' Adler said, 'so why does he act so
superior?'

Once Moishe Katansky, a newcomer, dared to sympathize
with Simcha Kravitz about his marriage, and Simcha looked up
from the last and stared at him so severely that Katansky understood and did not return to the shop for many months. Simcha's
shop was a meeting place. Here the round-shouldered

immigrants gathered to sip lemon tea and to talk of their fear of failure in the new country. Some came to idolize Simcha. 'You could,' they said, 'trust Simcha Kravitz with your wife – your money – anything.' But others came to resent their need to go to his shop. They began to search him for a fault. 'Nobody's perfect,' Katansky said.

Simcha's stature increased immensely when it became known that he was respected even among the gentiles in the district. That came about after Blondin the blacksmith had been kicked by a horse. Simcha, not the first man on the scene, forced Blondin to drink some brandy and set the broken bone in his leg before the doctor came. After that whenever there was an accident as far as the lead foundry eight blocks away on one side and the saw mill nine blocks away on the other, Simcha was sent for.

The old grizzled man would not talk about his private life, but there was one thing that even he couldn't hide. His firstborn son, Benjy, was a delight to him. The others would often see Simcha Kravitz coming out of the synagogue and walking down St Dominique Street holding the boy's hand and that, if you knew the man, seemed such a proud and difficult display of intimacy that the others would turn away embarrassed. Those who liked him, the majority, and knew about his bad life with his wife, hoped that Benjy would justify his love. But some of the others, men who had broken down in the shop and still more those who owed him money they couldn't repay, sensed that here at last Simcha was vulnerable and they wished bad luck on Benjy.

'He's got his mother's dirty mouth.'

'He's fat and feminine. Poor Simcha. He doesn't see.'

But fat, caustic tongue, and other failures too, Benjy prospered. And more. He revered his father and did not once abuse the old man's love. He was a shrewd boy, intelligent and quick and without fear of the new country and he undoubtedly had, as Katansky put it, the golden touch. The fat teenage boy who ventured into the country to sell the farmers reams of cloth and boots and cutlery was, at twenty-six, the owner of a basement blouse factory. From the beginning he paid the highest wages and like his father lent money and, though he was loquacious, he never repeated a confidence.

On Saturday mornings father and son could be seen standing side by side in the synagogue, and when Benjy began to read Mencken and Dreiser and no longer came to pray his father said, 'Benjy does what he believes. That's his right.'

Nobody, not even Katansky, could have accused Benjy of marrying for money. The bride was a pants-presser's daughter. A beauty. Ida was a slender girl with curly red hair and a long delicate neck and white skin. She went everywhere with Benjy and everywhere she went with him she could not stop looking at him. The old man adored her too. He often brought her vegetables from his garden and on Sunday afternoons the three of them had a habit of going for a drive, leaving Mrs Kravitz and Max and Minnie and their children to wait at home. A year later when Simcha's wife died he refused to go and live with Benjy and Ida; he said it would not be wise, and he continued to live alone. Then the trouble started.

'I went to see Benjy in his office yesterday,' Adler said, 'and I'd swear he was drunk.'

Ida began to take trips alone and the round-shouldered men in the shoe repair shop began to ask questions.

'When are they going to have children?'

'These modern marriages. Oi.'

Simcha never replied and the questions stopped for a time. Then one day Adler came into the shop and patted Simcha tenderly on the back. 'I'm sorry,' he said.

Simcha was hurt because Benjy did not visit very often these days and when he did come to the house it was only after he had a lot to drink.

'I hear your daughter-in-law's off in Miami again,' Katansky said.

At the synagogue the other old men became sad and gentle with him. Simcha never asked why. He took his regular seat every Saturday morning and acknowledged the others' sympathetic looks with the stiffest of nods. But he began to look at the rest of his family with more curiosity and, without any pre-amble, he took Duddy into the back yard one Sunday morning to teach him how to plant and fertilize and pull out the killing weeds. Then, one day soon after Ida had left on another trip, he actually sent for Benjy. This was the first time he had ever actually asked his son to come to see him.

'If there's something the matter with her I'm your father and you can tell me.'

Benjy turned to go.

'Strangers know something I don't know.'

'It's Max. He talks too much.'

'Max is a fool.'

When Benjy came again about six months later Duddy was working with his grandfather in the back yard. He watched his uncle follow his grandfather into the kitchen. Duddy couldn't hear what was said, but only two minutes later Uncle Benjy came out of the house carrying what looked like a little jar of preserves. Seeing Duddy, he stopped and gave the boy a frightening look. 'If you hurt him . . .'

'Wha'?'

But he didn't finish or explain. He walked off, staggering a little, and Duddy went back to pulling weeds. Simcha joined him about a half hour later. 'Your grandfather was a failure in this country,' he said.

'Why?'

'Your Uncle Benjy with all his money is nothing too. Of your father I won't even speak.'

The old man squashed a mosquito against his cheek with a surprisingly quick hand.

'A man without land is nobody. Remember that, Duddel.'

Duddy was seven at the time and a year earlier his mother had enrolled him in the Talmud Torah parochial school. Uncle Benjy was going through his Zionist phase at the time, and he paid the tuition. Uncle Benjy also knew that his father, whom he hardly ever saw these days, walked hand in hand with Duddy on St Dominique Street. But the round-shouldered men did not wonder or turn away when they saw Simcha walking with his grandson. The old man had no more enemies – even Katansky pitied him .The round-shouldered old men looked at Duddy and decided he was mean, a crafty boy, and they hoped he would not hurt Simcha too hard.

Chapter Nine

At the parochial school until he was thirteen years old Duddy
met many boys who came from families that were much better
off than his own and on the least pretext he fought with them.
Those who were too big to beat up he tried to become friendly
with. He taught them how to steal at Kresge's and split streetcar
tickets so that one could be used twice, how to smoke with bubble
pipes, and the way babies were made. After he had been at the
school for three years mothers warned their children not to play
with that Kravitz boy. But boys and girls alike were drawn to
dark, skinny Duddy and those who were excluded from his
gang, the Warriors, felt the snub deeply.

Such a boy was blond, curly-haired Milty Halpirin, the real
estate agent's son. Milty's mother drove him to school every
day. He was an only child and he was not allowed to ride a
bicycle or eat crab-apples. Duddy delighted in tormenting him.
While Milty, on his side, yearned to join the Warriors. So one
day Duddy said it would be O.K. if only Milty agreed to drink
the secret initiation potion first. The potion, made up of water,
red ink, baking soda, pepper, ketchup, a glob of chicken fat and,
at the last minute, a squirt of Aqua Velva, went down with
surprising ease. Afterwards, however, Duddy feigned hysteria.

'Jeez. This is terrible. I made a terrible mistake.'

'What is it?'

'The wrong recipe. Jeez.'

'But I drank it. You said if I drank it I could become a Warrior. You swore to God, Duddy.'

'It's terrible,' Duddy said, 'but this means your beezer is a
cinch to fall off and you'll never grow a bush. And Milty if a
guy doesn't grow a bush . . .'

Milty ran off crying and that night he was violently ill.

'What is it, pussy-lamb?'

'I'm never going to grow a bush, Mummy.'

'*What?*'

'Duddy Kravitz says . . .'

Max Kravitz was called in once more by the principal and Duddy became the first boy ever to be expelled from the parochial school: he was sent home for a week. Milty was terrified. He lived in an enormous house alongside the mountain, and it was he who answered the door when Duddy showed up with three other Warriors the following Saturday afternoon. 'What do you want?' he asked in a small voice.

'Why Milty, boy, we've come to play with you.'

'Hiya, Milty old pal.'

Milty hesitated. The maid had gone out for a walk; he was all alone.

'You never came to play with me before.'

'Jeez. Aren't you going to let us in, Milty?'

'No.'

'Wouldn't you still like to become a Warrior like?'

'You mustn't touch anything,' Milty said, opening the door. 'You promise?'

Duddy crossed his heart. So did the others.

'Some dump, eh, guys? Where does your old man keep his cigs?'

'You can't stay. You have to go.'

'Gee whiz, Milty.'

'You want to play Monopoly?' Milty asked.

'Monopoly! Jeez. Where do your mother and father sleep? Have they got the same bed like?'

Milty bit his thumb.

'He's going to cry, guys.'

'I thought you wanted to play with me?'

'Sure. Sure we do.'

Milty watched, terrified, as Duddy wandered about the living-room examining china figurines here and there. A rubber plant stood before the glass doors that led into the garden. It reached almost to the ceiling. Duddy stopped to stare at it.

'Why don't we sit in the garden, Milty?'

'We mustn't.'

Mrs Halpirin, an amateur horticulturist, was strict about the garden.

'I thought we were pals, Milty.'

Milty led the boys into the garden. The five of them sat down on the swing and Duddy told them a story about his brother Bradley. 'The poor jerk. Jeez. I got a letter from him only yesterday aft and he's going to try and escape. Otherwise he'd have to stay in the Foreign Legion for another two years, you know.'

'No kidding?'

'If he makes it he's going to come back here for me. He's going to take me to South America. We're going to get a yacht. I mean all he has to do once he's out is dig up that buried money and – '

'How could he write you he's going to try and escape?' Milty asked. 'Don't they read his mail? My father told me that in the army letters – '

'You poor, stupid jerk-head. Haven't you ever heard of invisible ink? Hey,' Duddy said, jumping up, 'what's wrong with the tulips?'

'What do you mean what's wrong with the tulips?'

'Why they're closed.' Duddy looked horrified.

'So what?'

'Tulips should be opened,' Duddy said.

'Should they?'

'Hey, what kind of a stupid jerk are you anyway? Ask Bobby.'

'Sure they should be opened.'

Duddy bent down to pluck a tulip.

'Don't touch anything.'

'I just wanted to show you.'

Milty hesitated. 'All right,' he said. 'But only one. Promise?'

'On my word of honour.' Duddy picked up a tulip and opened it carefully. 'There,' he said, 'doesn't that look better?'

'Wow.'

'How beautiful.'

Even Milty had to admit that the tulip looked better opened and, as a nice surprise for his mother, he helped Duddy and the others open every tulip in the garden.

'My mommy will be home soon,' Milty said. 'She'll give us milk and apple pie.'

'Naw,' Duddy said. 'I think we'd better go. See you.'

51

Duddy Kravitz's Warriors operated in war-time and many of their activities were coloured by the conflagration in Europe. Take their tussle with the CPC, for instance.

What with so many of its able-bodied young men already stationed overseas, in 1943 Montreal, the world's largest inland sea port, seemed to invite enemy attack. The Nips and even the hated Huns, it's true, were some distance away, but remembering Pearl Harbour the city played it safe. Older citizens, those who couldn't fight in the regular army, joined the Canadian Provost Corps, a sort of civil defence organization. Members of the CPC were issued with steel helmets and dark blue zipper suits of the type that Churchill had made popular. The officer in charge of Duddy's neighbourhood – tubby, middle-aged Benny Feinberg – was seldom without his helmet, his suit, or an enormous flashlight that he wore strapped to his belt. Feinberg's zeal did not go down well on St Urbain Street and the first time he marched past Moe's Cigar Store, the dangling flashlight inspired some rather obvious jokes. To these Feinberg was too dignified to make a reply, but when Moe observed, 'No wonder we haven't opened a second front yet. With Montgomery tied down in Libya and Feinberg looking after things here who have they got left to take command?', Feinberg felt that he had been pushed too far.

'A bunch of slackers,' he said, 'the whole lousy lot of you.'

The Warriors, to begin with, were on the side of the CPC to the man. Feinberg had assured them that in the event of an air raid they would all be evacuated to the mountains. Some of them, he said, might even be orphaned before the war was done, and this they took to be a promise. Feinberg and a few other CPC enthusiasts aside, the Warriors probably longed for the devastation of Montreal more than anyone. A direct hit, Feinberg warned them, might kill and maim 'untold' hundreds of people. They were left with only one worry. The bombers might miss their chosen targets. Long into the night they once debated whether or not it would be sabotage – could a boy be hanged, for instance – if he painted a bullseye on the roof of the Talmud Torah.

Then the tide, so to speak, turned. The Warriors discovered that behind their backs Feinberg had given instructions and issued a real first aid kit to a YMHA club, and Duddy decided to fix him. His first chance came the night of the blackout. It was, to be sure, only a practice blackout, but real sirens were to sound the alert. The streets were to be cleared and all blinds were to be drawn. The CPC was to be out in force checking for offenders and, according to Feinberg, saboteurs and dirty spies.

Five minutes after the sirens wailed, leaving the city in darkness, the Warriors, faces smeared commando-style with mud, crept two by two down St Urbain Street, spilling kerosene on the street here and there; and then they dispersed to the balconies and rooftops. After Feinberg and his men had passed, searching windows for tell-tale strips of yellow, Duddy slipped two fingers into his mouth and whistled as loud as he could. All along the street clothespin guns came out and matches were slipped into place. Duddy counted to ten and whistled again. The guns were fired simultaneously. As the matches struck the pavement most of them ignited immediately and in an instant St Urbain Street was ablaze with light. As it so happened an airplane, probably New York bound, was flying overhead at the time. Feinberg, they said, was the first to take cover, but there were those who insisted that Lance-Corporal Lerner beat him to it. Others, like Shubin, did not dishonour the blue zipper suit. Shubin rushed quickly to the scene of the enemy action and, if it were not for the fact that he had put on his gas mask in some haste – an impediment to movement and vision – he would have caught Duddy Kravitz anyway. As it was, all the Warriors escaped.

When the all-clear sounded several theories were hotly disputed at Moe's Cigar Store. During the blackout OPEN UP A SECOND FRONT NOW stickers had been pasted on many windows and it was Debrofsky's theory that the communists were responsible for the street fires too. Lyman didn't agree. He believed that Adrien Arcand's boys, the local fascist group, were responsible for the fires. Moe muttered something about the newly-arrived refugee who had moved in around the corner and was rumoured to have a short wave radio set. But when the incident was mentioned in the *Gazette* the next morning it was clearly stated that a group of juvenile delinquents had been responsible for the outrage.

'Of course. What else do you want them to say?' Feinberg

demanded when cornered. 'You expect them to admit we got spies in Montreal?'

But a week later Feinberg stopped wearing his blue zipper suit and the St Urbain Street section of the CPC could no longer be considered an effective fighting force.

Chapter Ten

Duddy Kravitz's other parochial school activities were decidedly more commercial. He got his start in stamps, like so many other boys, by answering an advertisement for salesmen in *Tip Top Comics*. The company, one of many, sent you stamps on approval sheets to be sold. In payment, you got some free stamps, catalogues, and sometimes even a commission. Unlike the other boys, however, Duddy soon established two fascinating facts about the companies in question. Once you had sold successfully two or three times, making a prompt return of money to the company, you were sent a truly expensive kit of approvals to handle. The other fact was that a minor couldn't be sued – certainly not by an American company. So dealing with seven companies he eventually worked each one of them up to the truly expensive approval kit point under a variety of pseudonyms, and then he was never heard from again.

Some of his stamp business profits Duddy invested in the comic book market when, during the war, American ones were hard to come by due to dollar restrictions. (Canadian comics, not even printed in colour, were unreadable.) He bought, at 20 cents apiece, a considerable quantity of contraband American comics, and these he rented out for 3 cents a day until glue and scotch tape would no longer hold them together. This led him into another and more questionable channel of distribution. One of Duddy's comic book suppliers, a Park Avenue newsstand proprietor named Barney, showed him one day a sixteen page comic-book-like production titled *Dick Tracy's Night Out*. The drawings, crude black and white, were obviously the work of a local artist and printer. The books looked shoddy. In the very first frame, however, Dick Tracy, sporting an enormous erection with the words 'drip, drip, drip' and an arrow pointing to it from underneath, looked ravenously at Tess Trueheart.

Miss Trueheart was clad only in black panties. The adventure, begun there, continued for fifteen more action-packed pages, and the whole book sold for 75 cents retail. There were many other volumes available in the same series, i.e., *L'il Abner gets Daisy Mae*, *Terry and the Dragon Lady*, *Blondie plays strip poker*, *Gasoline Alley Gang Bang*, and more.

The Talmud Torah boys were getting older, American comic books were beginning to trickle into the city again, and so Duddy was attracted by this new line. After some haggling he agreed to order by the dozen if, in exchange, he was given exclusive rights to a territory that, after even more bargaining, included three Protestant schools, two parochials, the Bnai Brith Youth House, a yeshiva, and at least four poolrooms and a bowling alley. This venture was the first of Duddy's to end in disaster. Three weeks later when the going was really good Barney was picked up by the police and fined. Duddy, unfortunately, was caught with a large stock on hand. He took fright and threw them in the furnace.

Other projects, like the hockey stick sideline, were more profitable.

At the age of twelve Duddy discovered that smiling boys with autograph books could get in to hockey practises at the Forum. Getting in to see minor league teams like the Royals was a cinch; and, if you were quick or smart enough to hide in the toilet after the Royals had left the ice you could also get to see the Canadiens practise, and those were the years of Lach, Blake, and the great Maurice Richard. While they were on the ice the players' spare sticks, kept in a rack against the wall in a gangway leading into the passages out, were guarded by a thirteen-year-old stick boy. Duddy guessed that these sticks, each with a star player's name stencilled on it, would be treasured by many a fan. So he worked out a system. Getting another boy, usually A.D., to come along with him and talk to the stick boy, leading him gently away from the rack, Duddy would then emerge from under a seat, grab as many sticks as he could manage, and run like hell. The sticks netted him a tidy profit. But, even though the stick boy was changed from time to time, making further forays possible, the business was a risky one. It was only seasonal, too.

Duddy took his first regular job at the age of thirteen in the summer of 1945. He went to work in his Uncle Benjy's dress factory for sixteen dollars at week and here he sat at the end of a long table where twelve French-Canadian girls, wearing flowered housecoats over their dresses, sewed belts in the heat and dust. The belts were passed along to Duddy who turned them rightside out with a poker and dumped them in a cardboard carton. It was tedious work and Duddy took to reversing the black and red and orange belts in an altogether absent-minded manner. Supporting the poker against his crotch he'd roll the belts over it one by one. The girls began to make jokes about his technique, but Duddy did not understand at first what the fuss and giggles and slow burning looks were all about.

The girls, however, seemed agreeable enough. Funny-looking and thin mostly, that was true; one with a squint and three with crucifixes, five with black hair worn pompadour-style and two with wedding rings and another, without a ring, who was pregnant. Gabrielle had a bad rumbling cough and when the one with the squint lowered to thread a needle you could see something of her bosom. She had the biggest one of the twelve. Her name was Thérèse and there was always a Pepsi beside her machine. She usually consumed at least four by noon and as the day wore on big wet patches spread under her armpits and she began to smell bad. The girls punched in each morning at five to nine and by nine a.m. they had all assumed their places by the machines: a tense crouch. At one minute past nine there was a bell, a whirr, the machines began and the girls, taking a deep breath, bent their heads lower over their work. One of them, Jacqueline, was a chain-smoker and by ten-thirty her smock and everything around her was littered with ashes.

Around the time when Duddy began to understand the jokes about his method of rolling belts he also noticed that only two other men worked on the third floor. Malloy, who dusted coats on manikins at the far end of the floor, was an old man with a fierce tattoo on his chest. Herby, the sweeper, was a coloured boy, and Duddy always watched him for the pink flash of his tongue and the palms of his hands. Other men – even Uncle Benjy himself – occasionally passed through the third floor. Manny Kaplan, the (as he put it) personnel manager and a nephew on the other side of the family, came in once in the morning and again in the afternoon. He swept in with a big frenzied smile and shouted, 'Atta boy,' at the girls, 'Atta boy,' and leaning and looking he counted how many belts they still had to do, making a note of who was behind and who was absent. Much more popular was little Epstein the silverhaired cutter who came once a day with chocolate cookies, a pound of Bing cherries maybe, or two dozen plums for the girls, always stopping to pinch or kiss them, rolling his eyes and saying 'Mmmm' in a way that made the girls laugh and feel good.

Duddy noticed that there were only two other men on the floor and that when he supported the poker against his crotch Adèle, the youngest girl at the table, watched him out of the corner of her eye. She was a nervous girl, too, forever getting up to go to the toilet. One hot afternoon, after Duddy had got up to let her pass, Thérèse indicated with a jerk of her head that Duddy ought to follow her. He waited a moment, coughed, and excused himself. The other girls giggled when he went off.

Unfortunately for Duddy his Uncle Benjy passed by a half hour later and saw that Adèle and Duddy were gone and guessed where they were. Uncle Benjy had Duddy transferred to the cutting room.

Uncle Benjy was a wealthy man. A disappointed one too. His wife, Ida, went to Florida every winter. And when they were together for an important wedding or an old friend's funeral or the summer they both had a lot to drink before going to bed.

'They say there's a new doctor in Los Angeles who can work miracles.'

'Benjy, please.'

'What harm could it do to give him a try?'

'You ought to leave me, Benjy. I'd understand.'

'Got yourself lined up good in Miami, eh? Some ritzy bachelor who can make his ears wiggle.'

'Benjy.'

'Or maybe that physio-what's-it you told me about. You know, the blond exerciser with the Ph.D.'

'Gil?'

'That's the one. Come clean, Ida. I can take it.'

She would pass out at last and Benjy would get out of bed and gather up her dress and girdle and stockings where they had fallen on her way to bed. Afterwards he would usually sit up in the kitchen for hours. A short fat man in enormous blue shorts with a golf ball pattern, he might fry himself a couple of eggs and read the socialist magazines he subscribed to that came from England and the United States. These bored him even more than Miami. Foolishness, romance, about what the workers were, and advertisements for family planning and summer camps where solemn negroes sang progressive songs.

Always, before going to sleep, he kissed Ida on the forehead. Sometimes, more drunken times, he would hold her close, his head squeezed against her breasts, and she would waken dizzy and afraid. He never knew that. She made sure he never realized that her sleep had been disturbed. But come morning Ida would be gone again.

Finally Benjy's father called him to the house. 'Why are there no children?' he asked.

'I'm impotent.'

The old man gave Benjy a bottle. 'It's made from herbs. An old country recipe.'

At home Benjy flushed the bottle's contents down the toilet and he and his father never discussed the matter again. Meanwhile, Benjy made more money and enemies. He refused to contribute to the synagogue building fund. 'Praying went out with the spears, Sam. You can quote me.' A known supporter of communist causes he was always good for a touch when there was a strike or a defence fund or the *Tribune* was in trouble. He enjoyed bragging about these contributions in the company of other manufacturers.

'Comrade Peltier – he drops in from time to time, you know – told me the other day that when we get round to nationalizing the needle trade I'm likely to be in charge.'

'Another season like this and you can take charge tomorrow.'

'That means that in your sweatshop, Sam, you'd have to allow a union.'

'Over my dead body.'

'Alright. Over your dead body, then. And Harry here is going to have to put paper and soap in those filthy toilets of his.'

Uncle Benjy got along no better with the communists who came to him for money. He couldn't forgive them their abuse of Trotsky and they were unhappy about his little irreverences, like making an ostentatious sign of the cross when Peltier mentioned Stalin. Books, probably, gave him the most enjoyment, and Benjy was a prodigious reader. But here too there was more disappointment than pleasure. Tolstoi, yes, and Balzac. Gorki, too. But where among the modern belly-achers was there a writer to teach him about a fat factory owner, hopelessly in love with a woman who dyed her hair, wore too much rouge, and preferred contract bridge to Bach. A foolish woman. Ida. 'Even if we could have a son,' he often thought, 'Ida would be no fit companion for my old age, so why . . .' He didn't understand why and nobody could tell him. Meanwhile, he helped keep the family together and drank alone.

When Max had come to tell him he was getting married Benjy had said, 'Bring her around, sure. I can hardly wait. The girl who would marry the likes of you I have to see to believe.' His wedding gift was to set Max up with a taxi cab. 'I'd give you a job in the factory but I happen to be in business to make a profit.' And Max, familiar with his older brother's acid tongue, had smiled affably and made no reply. 'Imagine,' he told Debrofsky, 'not being able to get it up. Ever I mean.'

'No wonder he's such a lush,' Debrofsky had said.

'Once,' Max had said, dropping a sugar cube on his tongue, 'just after he began to make his name but before his personal trouble, the Boy Wonder won a bet by spending a night in the Ford Hotel banging three different broads. He's got a whang that could choke a horse. *I* know, we had a leak together once . . . But to get back to poor Benjy, he's got his good points, you know. For my Lennie he'd do anything.'

It was true.

Benjy was in the hospital the night Lennie was born and he held him and bloodied his knuckles the day he was circumcised. He had a specialist flown in from Toronto when Lennie developed an unusually severe case of rheumatic fever and he picked the boy's school, the books he ought to read, and took him to every circus that came to town.

'It's not right, Max,' Minnie said. 'You're the father.'

'I'm the father. Sure I'm the father. But Benjy can't – well, you know.'

Uncle Benjy took pride in all of Lennie's achievements. The medals, the scholarships, and ultimately his acceptance by the McGill University faculty of medicine. He paid the boy's fees, gave him a weekly allowance, and was certainly prepared to set him up in practice when the time came.

Uncle Benjy felt differently about Duddy, but it did not come out until the boy went to work for him. He did not like Duddy on sight, it's true. The thin crafty face, the quick black eyes and the restlessness, the blackheads and the oily skin, the perpetual fidgeting, the grin so shrewd and knowing, all made a bad impression on Uncle Benjy. He was prepared to give Duddy a chance, however, but Duddy went and loused it up. Two weeks after he had been transferred to the cutting room he charged into Uncle Benjy's office and told him, 'That old geezer in the cutting room, Laroche, is swiping lengths of cloth. I saw him.'

But Uncle Benjy had looked at him with displeasure.

'What's a matter?'

'I'm not interested.'

'He's stealing from you. Jeez, aren't you gonna fire him?'

'Next time you come in here with a story like that I'll fire you.'

Duddy leaped to his feet.

'Wait.' Uncle Benjy could see that the boy's eyes were full, but he could not stop himself. 'In all my years in the trade I've never hired anyone to spy on the workers here.'

'Why?'

'What?'

Duddy smiled thinly and his voice quietened. 'Are you afraid that there are even more of them stealing?'

'What?'

'That maybe with all your loans and favours to them they still think you're the boss like?'

'Some kid. Some kid you are.'

'Not like Lennie?'

'You're only here a week and already you may have got a girl in trouble. Two weeks in the cutting room and you come to me with this story about Laroche. Manny tells me you've been selling the girls underwear and stuff you get from some mail order house. Is that true?'

'How did you make all your money Uncle Benjy? Tell me that.'

'Some kid.'

'Sure. Why not?'

61

'I don't like squealers. Try to remember that.'

'Why don't you fire me, Uncle Benjy?'

'I'm not going to fire you because it would hurt your grand-father.'

'Is that so?'

'You're some kid, Duddy, some kid, but this much you ought to know. If you ever do anything to hurt your grandfather I'll break every bone in your body beginning with the little fingers.'

'How come you care so much? You never even go to visit him any more.'

Uncle Benjy pushed his chair back from his desk. 'I think you'd better get back to work,' he said.

Uncle Benjy, Duddy figured, had humiliated him, and he would remember that.

'When the Boy Wonder,' Max had once told him, 'loses his temper he could eat bread and it would come out toasted. That's the size of it.'

Duddy liked to think that his anger was made of the same hot stuff. He liked to think, in fact, that point for point he was a lot like the Boy Wonder before he had made his name. Duddy had seen him stepping outside the synagogue on Yom Kippur once, before his personal trouble, and left and right men had waved heartily or turned pale and the women had followed him with their eyes. The Boy Wonder was no atheist, like Uncle Benjy. Even, as Max had once explained to him, if Yom Kippur fell on the same day as the Kentucky Derby and a heavyweight cham-pionship fight together, the Boy Wonder would place no bets. Max knew because, even though he was a taxi driver, he was an intimate of the Boy Wonder and one day he would intro-duce Duddy to him.

'Not yet. Next year maybe. When you're ready.'

But it was a promise all the same.

Meanwhile Duddy worked on the weekends and each sum-mer (though never for Uncle Benjy again), and he continued to put money in the bank. For Duddy had never forgotten what his grandfather had said: 'A man without land is nobody.'

Duddy wanted to be a somebody. Another Boy Wonder maybe. Not a loser, certainly.

*

COMMENCEMENT

They arrived by fives and eights and threes. A surge of mothers and fathers and brothers and sisters and grandparents to a hot sticky gym. They came with smiles and jokes and embarrassment, the men pulling at their ties and the women choked by their girdles, walking through the halls of learning to see their sons and daughters, the class of '49, graduate classes one, two and three from Fletcher's Field High School to – as Leonard Bush, M.A. (McGill), said each year – the wide world. Here, Max Kravitz said, was the door to the sub-basement where the Boy Wonder had organized a lunch-time crap game. There with the red face goes Feeney, an enemy of our people. Here comes Mendelsohn's boy, the scholarship winner. There was the exact spot, Benny Rabinovitch pointed out, where Mickey 'The Mauler' Shub had KO'd the sometime principal of FFHS Dr Ross McEwen.

The men mopped their necks with handkerchiefs and the women wearing too much make-up fanned themselves with programmes that announced GREETINGS GRADS, from MORRIE THE TAILOR, and scholarships for $100 donated by Steinberg's Groceterias and for $50 in everlasting memory of Mrs Ida Berg.

'It goes off the income tax,' Sam Fine said.

They arrived too soon and thirsty and proud, and immediately shamed their sons and daughters by waving and whistling at them.

'Yoo-hoo.'

High over the platform loomed the mighty black and green crest with the inscription, WORK AND HONOUR.

'Well, well, if it isn't Tannenbaum in the flesh. You got a son here?'

'Why not?'

'Is yours going to a nightclub afterwards? I gave mine a ten spot. Aw, what the hell I said to myself. Next week he goes to work in the store.'

'Mine's going to McGill to be a lawyer.'

'The way you operate, Tannenbaum, you'll need him.'

Fanning themselves they watched as the staff filed in, silent and severe, and took their places on the platform at last.

'White men,' Panofsky said sourly.

'Whatsa matter with women teachers that they never have no watermelons?'

'Sam, please, people can hear you.'

One chair was empty. Mr MacPherson wasn't there.

'That's Coldwell, the torturer. Yeah, that one.'

Mr Feeney sat next to Mr Cox. Mr Gyle who had failed engineering and decided to become a teacher sat next to Miss Bradshaw. Mr Jackson adjusted his hearing aid.

'Becky! *Bec-cky!* No, over *here*. Why does she turn away, Louis?'

The choir of two hundred boys and girls came marching in according to height, the boys in white shirts and black bow ties and the girls in school tunics.

'Listen, with the speeches and everything we'll be lucky to get out of here by two o'clock.'

'Sh.'

> *Ten men went to mow,*
> *went to mow a meadow,*
> *ten men, nine men, eight men,*
> *seven men, six men, five men,*
> *four men, three men, two men,*
> *one man and his dog*
> *went to mow a meadow.*

'A Yiddish song they couldn't sing? It would be against the law?'

Martin Abromovitch, his adam's apple making his black bow tie bobble, strode across the platform to play a Chopin Polonaise.

'I know that. It was in *A Song to Remember*.'

'Sh.'

'Oh sh-sh yourself. Pain in the neck!'

There was some mistaken applause at the end of the first section, more at the end of the second and still more, decidedly resentful, at the end of the third. When Martin Abromovitch finally finished playing the wary ones among the audience waited until he stood up and bowed twice before joining in the ovation with warm charitable looks for the uncultured early applauders among their neighbours.

'So, Abromovitch, are you proud of your grandson?'

'He played without a hat.'

'Paw. For Christ's sake!'

'It would hurt him to wear a hat?'

'Have you ever heard of the wheel, Paw? Some damn fool invented this thing you attach to a wagon and it turns. We've got this business called electricity too now. You press a button, see, and . . . THIS IS MODERN TIMES.'

'He doesn't wear a hat and he can't speak Yiddish.'

'Neither could Chopin.'

'Who?'

'Skip it. Never mind. Look, there's the speaker.'

Captain John Edgar Tate, author (*Canada – Land of Contrasts*), famous broadcaster and lecturer, journalist, explorer (first white man to paddle and chart all the tributaries of the Peace River), world traveller and proud descendant of a family of United Empire Loyalists, clutched the speaker's rostrum like a ship's prow, cleared his throat fiercely and looked down from under greying beetle brows at his audience of small sceptical round-shouldered men, women with too much rouge, and children – some restless and yawning and others inclined to pick their noses – looked down and stroked a puffy red cheek and measured and realized too late that he had brought the wrong speech with him. But he did not falter. He spoke feelingly of the Red Indian and the first British and French-Canadian settlers who came to the country and he talked about Jacques Cartier, LaSalle, and General Wolfe.

'You see that red nose he's got? That comes from too much Johny Walker.'

'Louder. LOUDER, PLEASE.'

'Why couldn't they have invited one of our own to speak?'

'Who, for instance?'

'Dr Rosen, there's a speaker for you. To hear him talk about cancer . . .'

Captain John Edgar Tate shifted his attention to the present age, the wide world today's graduates would have to contend with, and after some dark warnings about the communist threat, he concluded: 'Don't drop the ball. Because if you drop the ball you're passing it to Uncle Joe.'

There was some mild applause.

'In Japan, when a man gets up to speak he has to hold

icecubes in his hands, and he can only speak for as long as he can hold them. That's for me.'

'I'll tell you, Sydney, this speaker – '

'Don't tell me. *I know*, Paw. He doesn't wear a hat.'

'Oh, am I ever dying for a cold drink.'

'How's about some watermelon instead, Harry? Ice-cold.'

'Hoo-haw. Don't speak.'

At last the graduates were called up to get their diplomas. First came small, squinting Hersh (he had come second in the province and won a scholarship to McGill), and behind him came Mendelsohn's boy, another scholarship winner, and Rita Bloom, who had come fifth in the province.

'My boy's in the minors,' Brown said. 'He probably doesn't get his diploma until three in the morning.'

Shmul Berger was presented with the Ida Berg Memorial Scholarship.

'It's a gyp. He should have been disqualified.'

Shmul's father, Rabbi Isaac Berger, was supposed to have a photographic memory. They said he could stick a pin through any volume of the Talmud and, given the number of the page it had come out on, tell you the exact word it had punctured.

'That's the last of the prize winners. Main event now.'

'About time.'

One by one to milder and milder applause the boys and girls stepped up to shake the hand of Leonard Bush, M.A., and take their diplomas.

'There he is!'

Duddy Kravitz was the four hundred and tenth boy to be handed his diploma. He had graduated third class with failures in History and Algebra II. He accepted his diploma with a thin smile, turned sharply away from Mr MacPherson's empty seat on the platform, and walked away on squeaky black shoes.

Max Kravitz clapped loudly. 'Atta boy, Duddy. Atta boy.'

'Sh,' Lennie said.

Uncle Benjy turned to his father and the old man looked at the floor.

'Atta boy,' Max said.

Chapter Eleven

Duddy found the land he wanted quite by accident.

That summer, the year he graduated from FFHS, he went to work as a waiter in an hotel in the Laurentian mountains. Rubin's Hotel Lac des Sables was in Ste Agathe des Monts and of all the waiters taken on for the summer only Duddy was not a college boy. The others were first and second year McGill boys, none had ever been to FFHS – they came from more prosperous families – and Duddy found it difficult. Some of the other employees, like Cuckoo Kaplan, the recreation director, and the boys in Artie Bloom's band, had their own rooms, but all the waiters slept in the same dormitory over the recreation hall that extended above the lake. After a long day's work they often shared a bottle of rye and sang songs like,

> *We are little black sheep who have gone astray,*
> *bah-bah-bah,*
> *Lost from here to eternity,*
> *bah-bah-bah.*

Duddy, leaping into a lapse in the harmonizing, tried to introduce items like,

> *Oh, the captain had a one-eyed mate,*
> *he loved him like a brother,*
> *and every night at half-past eight*
> *they buggered one another,*

but the boys, though they never actually asked him to shettup, would not join in and gradually Duddy's voice died. On other nights, when the boys went on midnight swims or to drink beer in Val Morin, Duddy was not invited.

Duddy, alone among the boys, was not rattled by the heat and the hurry, the quarrels and the sometimes spiteful squalor, of the kitchen. The gift of a bottle of rum insured the cook's good-will – Duddy had no trouble getting his orders. In fact he was so quick in the dining room that after two weeks Mr Rubin gave him three extra tables. This seemed to antagonize the other boys even more and, provoked by Irwin Shubert, they began to ride Duddy hard.

'It's the cretinous little money-grubbers like Kravitz that cause anti-semitism,' Irwin told the boys.

Irwin Shubert was nineteen. A tall bronzed boy with curly black hair, sleepy black eyes, and a mouth too lavish for his face. Persistently bored and with a tendency to smile knowledgeably, an insider sworn to silence, he seldom lifted his voice above a liquid whisper. His father was one of the most famous criminal lawyers in the province and it was said that Irwin promised to be even more brilliant. He kept his books locked in a suitcase. He owned a marriage manual and a copy of Kraft-Ebbing, but his prize was an enormous, profusely illustrated medical volume that was actually restricted to members of the profession. All these books Irwin feigned to approach with scientific disinterest, but Duddy was not fooled. He recognized the hoard as a creep's equivalent of his own library, beginning with *Gasoline Alley Gang Bang*, through *Kitty* to Tiffany Thayer's *Three Musketeers*, and he recommended some reading to Irwin.

'*God's Little Acre*,' he said, 'that's the horniest.'

He made this suggestion on his second day at the hotel and thereby also alienated Irwin. Duddy couldn't understand this. For, at the beginning, Irwin fascinated him. He claimed to be able to hypnotize people and he told dandy stories about women and whips and boy-scout masters. Duddy didn't believe any of the stories: he always laughed, in fact, and that infuriated Irwin still more. 'You're great,' he'd tell Irwin. 'Jeez, you know more hot stuff . . .'

Irwin began to bait Duddy when the other boys were there.

'Next time you intend to practise self-abuse, David, would you be good enough to lock the toilet door?'

Another time it was, 'Tell me, David, is it true that you and Yvette are cohabiting?'

Yvette was the second floor chambermaid.

'I'm told she's wild about *soixante-neuf*. But take care, child. She's got gonorrhea.'

'Don't worry. I wouldn't touch her with a ten-foot pole.'

Yet another day it was, 'Would you do us all a favour,' Irwin asked, flicking Duddy hard enough with a towel to make him wince, 'and take a bath. You stink.'

'How would you like to hold this for a while?'

The splash of laughter that followed then, and at other times, Duddy at first mistook for approval of his wit. Some of the other boys, like Donald Levitt, seemed fond of him. Bernie Altman had once invited Duddy to join him for a beer and said that when he graduated from McGill he was going to to go Israel. Then one morning Bernie discovered ten dollars missing from his wallet.

'*I'm* missing fifteen,' Irwin said.

'But we all went to Val Morin last night,' Donald said. 'It must be an outsider.'

'David didn't come with us,' Irwin said.

'I'd better check again,' Bernie said, 'Maybe I'm mistaken.'

'Sh,' Irwin said, 'here it comes. The Judas.'

For the first two weeks of the season Duddy and Irwin were separated in the dormitory by an empty bed, that's all. Irwin often stayed up late and read with a pocket flashlight. Around three o'clock one morning, when all the other boys were asleep, Duddy woke to see Irwin sitting up in bed with the flashlight and the enormous medical book. He took one look at Irwin's agonized face, saw the book and the other hand under the covers, and quickly guessed what was happening.

'Jeez.'

Irwin looked up, startled and pale. Duddy grinned, he winked, and gesturing enthusiastically, he said, 'Atta boy, Irwin. Whew! Pull!'

Irwin dropped his flashlight, he trembled. It seemed that he had begun to cry, but Duddy was not sure. The next morning, however, Irwin would not talk to him and the troubles that were to last all summer began.

Irwin spoke to Rubin's only daughter.

'Look, Linda, I don't want to cause any trouble. Don't say a word to your father either, because I don't want to get the Kravitz kid fired, but somebody's been stealing money from the boys in the dorm and I want to know if any guests are missing things.'

Sunday, with so many people checking out and new guests constantly arriving, was the most nerve-racking day of the week. At ten p.m., his work finally finished, Duddy went to collapse on his cot. He found a bottle of Scotch lying there with a note. The bottle, it seemed, was a gift from Mr Holstein who had left that morning without tipping him.

'Aren't you going to offer us a drink?' Irwin asked.

The other boys sat on their cots, heads drooping.

'I'd like to send the bottle to my grandfather. A gift like.'

'Oh, *it* has a grandfather,' Irwin said, getting glasses. 'Come on, child.'

'Let him keep it,' Donald said.

'Naw. Irwin's right. Let's all have a drink on me.'

Irwin quickly brought Duddy the glasses and he filled them one by one.

'Linda Rubin's got a crush on you,' Irwin said. 'Did you know that?'

'Aw.'

'Never mind. Hotel owners' daughters have fallen for poor boys before. Well, *à la vot* –' Irwin lifted the glass to his mouth, made a horrible face, and spilled its contents on Duddy. 'You filthy little swine,' he said, 'is this your idea of a joke?'

'Wha'?'

'Don't any of you touch your glasses. Do you know what this is?'

Duddy sniffed his glass and his face went white.

'I know we haven't exactly been friendly,' Irwin said, 'but if this is your idea of how to pay us back – Let's make him drink his, guys. He deserves it.'

The other boys, too whacked to fight or decide, began to file out.

'I came in and I found the bottle on the bed,' Duddy shouted. 'So help me God. You all saw. I came in and the bottle was on my bed.'

Irwin started after the others. 'You're lucky, Kravitz. They should have made you drink it. What a disgusting stunt.'

Shunned by the college boy waiters, Duddy began to investigate Ste Agathe on his own when he had time off.

Some sixty miles from Montreal, set high in the Laurentian

hills on the shore of a splendid blue lake, Ste Agathe des Monts had been made the middle-class Jewish community's own resort town many years ago. Here, as they prospered, the Jews came from Outremont to build summer cottages and hotels and children's camps. Here, as in the winter in Montreal, they lived largely with their neighbours. Friends and relatives bought plots of land and built their cottages and boat houses competitively, but side by side. There were still some pockets of Gentile resistance, it's true. Neither of the two hotels that were still in their hands admitted Jews but that, like the British raj who still lingered on the Malabar Coast, was not so discomforting as it was touchingly defiant. For even as they played croquet and sipped their gin and tonics behind protecting pines they could not miss the loud, swarthy parade outside. The short husbands with their outrageously patterned sports shirts arm in arm with purring wives too obviously full for slacks, the bawling kids with tripledecker icecream cones, the squealing teenagers, and the trailing grandfather with his beard and black hat. They could not step out of their enclaves and avoid the speeding cars with wolfcall horns. The lake was out of the question. Sailboats and canoes had no chance against speedboats, spilling over with relatives and leaving behind a wash of empty Pepsi bottles. Even the most secluded part of the lake was not proof against the floating popsicle wrapper, and the moonlight canoe trip ran the risk of being run down by a Cuckoo Kaplan-led expedition to the island. Boatloads full of honeymooners and office girls and haberdashery salesmen singing, to the tune of *Onward, Christian Soldiers*,

> *Onward, Rubin's boarders,*
> *Onward, to the shore,*
> *With sour cream and latkas,*
> *We're staying two weeks more.*

Rubin's was not the only Jewish resort in Ste Agathe, either. There were many others. But Rubin had, in the shape of Cuckoo Kaplan, Ste Agathe's undisputed number one comic.

'Cuckoo may be a Montreal boy,' Rubin said, 'but he's no shnook. He's played nightclubs in the States.'

Cuckoo was billed as Montreal's Own Danny Kaye and his name and jokes often figured in *Mel West's What's What*. Short and wiry, with a frantic, itchy face, Cuckoo was ubiquitous. At breakfast he'd pop up from under a table to crack an egg on a bald man's head and at midnight he'd suddenly race through the dance hall in a gay nineties bathing suit and dive through a window into the lake. He always had a surprise for lunch too. Once he'd chase the cook through the dining room with a meat cleaver and later in the week chances were he'd hold up two falsies, saying he had found them on the beach, and ask the owner to claim them. Aside from organizing games when it rained and his regular nightly act – his Romeo and Juliet Capelovitch skit was a knockout – Cuckoo had some special routines for the winter season and was good at getting publicity. He got his picture in the paper on the first sub-zero day of winter by sawing a hole in the ice and taking a dip. For this annual picture, with Rubin's Hotel Lac des Sables prominent in the background, Cuckoo wore an hilarious wig, blackened two front teeth, and put on a long black woollen bathing suit. Once, after his annual dip, he was in bed with a fever for two weeks.

Cuckoo's father couldn't understand him. 'What is it with you, Chaim? For a lousy ninety dollars a week,' he said, 'to make a fool of yourself in front of all those strangers.'

But Cuckoo was not without hope. He had once been held over for three weeks in a nightclub in Buffalo and another time he had stopped the show at the Pink Elephant in New Jersey. Each year on his vacation he went to New York and walked from one agent's office to another with a large folio under his arm. Meanwhile, he was adored in Ste Agathe. Guests from all the other hotels came to Rubin's on Saturday night to catch his act.

Duddy, too, was most impressed with Cuckoo and he used to bring him breakfast in bed. Cuckoo, who was familiar with Max the Hack by name, gave Duddy bit parts in two of his skits. He could see that the boy was lonely and he didn't mind when he came to his room late at night to talk.

The bed in the hot, smoke-filled little room was always unmade. Usually the breakfast tray was still on the floor and there were cigarette butts and soiled laundry and empty rye bottles everywhere. Duddy usually cleared a space for himself on the floor and Cuckoo, reduced to his underwear, curled like a coiled spring on a corner of the bed with a glass in his hand, mindless of the cigarette ashes he dropped on the sheets.

Duddy told Cuckoo about some of his business ideas.

Next summer, he thought, he might try to set up in the movie rental business. All he needed was a truck, a projector, and a *goy* to run the camera, and with a good movie, playing a different resort each night, he would rake in no fortune, but . . . Another idea he had was to make colour movies of weddings and *bar-mitzvahs*. There might be a gold mine in this, he told Cuckoo, and he was thinking of calling himself Dudley Kane Productions. Who knows, but if the idea caught on, five-six years from now he might be able to make a feature-length comedy right here in Montreal, starring Cuckoo Kaplan. But, to begin with, he needed that truck and projector and a *goy* to operate it. Maybe the Boy Wonder who was an intimate of his father would stake him. Duddy said that he would see about that in the autumn.

The rye helped to calm Cuckoo. Gradually he stopped scratching his head and, if Duddy stayed long enough, he sometimes tried out one of his new routines on him. But first he'd say, 'You've got to be honest with me. I want to know exactly what you think. I can take it.'

Duddy was flattered by the try-outs in the small bedroom and every one of Cuckoo's routines made him howl.

'You kill me, Cuckoo. My sides hurt me, honest.'

When Cuckoo was depressed after playing to a hostile house cn a Saturday night Duddy would hurry to his bedroom with a pitcher of ice-cubes and sandwiches. 'Look,' he'd say, 'you think it was always such a breeze for Danny Kaye when he was playing the borscht circuit?' On and on Duddy would talk while Cuckoo consumed rye with alarming haste. When Cuckoo replied at last, he'd say in a slurred voice, 'That's show biz, I guess. That's show biz.' It was his favourite expression.

'You know something, kid, my trouble is I've got the wrong face for a comic. People take one look at Danny Kaye or Lou Costello and right off they howl. I have to work too hard. They take one look at my kisser and they want to buy me a sandwich or help me find a girl.'

Cuckoo took lots of vitamin pills and he ate sparingly. Many times after a show that only went over so-so he was sick to his stomach. Then, perched on his bed ready for instant flight, wiping his thin chest with a towel, he would wait until he felt sufficiently settled inside to start drinking again. On one night like that he told Duddy, 'I'm going to be famous one day. I'm going to be very famous. And I'll never forget you.'

Something else about Cuckoo was that he too hated Irwin Shubert.

One night after the show Irwin phoned Cuckoo to say he was in the bar at le Coq d'Or, twelve miles away, with a Broadway producer on vacation who was looking for fresh faces for his latest musical. Irwin's manner was so urgent, so sincere, that Cuckoo hurried right over there. While Irwin and the producer went through a couple of bottles of champagne he did his Romeo and Juliet Capelovitch act twice and his James Cagney *bar-mitzvah* speech. 'Can you dance?' the producer asked. Cuckoo danced. 'Let's hear you sing something?' Cuckoo sang. The producer ordered more champagne. 'Let's see the Capelo-vitch routine again. If you're not to tired, I mean?' Cuckoo obliged. 'Thanks a million,' the producer said, and he got up and left the bar.

'Where's he going?' Cuckoo asked, out of breath.

'He wants to talk to me privately,' Irwin said. 'You wait here.'

Cuckoo waited an hour, he waited two hours, he waited until closing time and then he was given a bill for two dinners and a whole evening's drinking. It came to nearly thirty dollars. Only a couple of afternoons later he overheard Irwin say to one of the guests. 'Not only is he the most puerile comedian I've ever seen, he's also the most gullible. The other night Jerry and I were stuck with a big bill at the Coq d'Or so I phoned Cuckoo and . . .'

The story spread. People smiled at Cuckoo and slapped him on the back. 'Hey, how'd you like to meet a producer tonight?' So Cuckoo took to waiting for Irwin on the beach. Then, once his back was turned, Cuckoo would wink at the others, lick his index finger and wet his eyebrows with it, and walk off saucily. That was usually good for a laugh, but Duddy warned him against it one night. 'They say he and Rubin's daughter are going to get hitched. They go riding together a lot. So watch it, eh?'

Yet another business idea Duddy told Cuckoo about was his plan for a Ste Agathe newspaper. There were nine hotels in town, he said, and each one must have a list as long as your arm of addresses for all over the States. Wouldn't it be smart publicity for them to keep Americans in touch, to remind them out of season about Ste Agathe and the swell times they had had there? And think, too, of the possible advertisers who would want to reach American tourists passing through Montreal. Nightclubs, department stores, hotels, restaurants. Jeez, everybody. The newspaper could organize beauty contests and regattas and fight racial prejudice. This was an idea that could work. Duddy was convinced of it and he told Cuckoo that he would like him to write a funny column for the newspaper. He thought he might call it the *Laurentian Liner*, because it would travel everywhere, and Cuckoo agreed the name was a catchy one. Duddy said he would speak to the Boy Wonder about it in the autumn.

Duddy had been putting money in the bank since he was eleven and in his first month at Rubin's he had earned nearly three hundred dollars in tips, but what he needed was a real stake.

At night, lying exhausted on his cot, Duddy realized how little money he had in big business terms and he dreamed about his future. He knew what he wanted, and that was to own his own land and to be rich, a somebody, but he was not sure of the smartest way to go about it. He was confident. But there had been other comers before him. South America, for instance, could no longer be discovered. It had been found. Toni Home Permanent had been invented. Another guy had already thought up Kleenex. But there was something out there, like let's say the atom bomb formula before it had been discovered, and Duddy dreamed that he would find it and make his fortune. He had his heroes. There was the stranger who had walked into the Coca Cola Company before it had made its name and said, 'I'll write down two words on a piece of paper, and if you use my idea I want a partnership in the company.' The two words were 'Bottle it'. Don't forget, either, the man who saved that salmon company from bankruptcy with the slogan, *this salmon is guaranteed not to turn pink in the can.* There was the founder of the *Reader's Digest* – he'd made his pile too. The man who thought up the super-market must have been another shnook of a small grocer once. There was a day when even the Boy Wonder gathered and sold streetcar transfers. Sure, everyone had to make a start, but it was getting late. Duddy was already seven-teen and a half and sure as hell he didn't want to wait on tables for the rest of his life. He needed a stake. When he got back to Montreal in the autumn he would speak to his father and go to see the Boy Wonder.

'I'm not,' he once told Cuckoo, 'the kind of a jerk who walks around deaf and dumb. I keep my eyes peeled.' And already Duddy had plenty of ideas. He had even had letterheads printed – Dudley Kane, Sales Agent – and every week he marked the advertising section of the Sunday edition of the *New York Times* for novelties, bargains, and possible agencies. That was a hint he had picked up from Mr Cohen, whose family was staying at Rubin's for the entire summer.

Duddy watched all the businessmen who came to the hotel. He made sure they got to know him too, and that they made no mistake about his being a waiter. That was temporary. He watched the way they avoided their wives and the sun and sat around playing poker and talking about the market and the boom in real estate. Most of them ate too much and took pills. One, a Mr Farber, had summoned Duddy to his table on his first day at the hotel and torn a hundred dollar bill in two and given Duddy half of it. 'We're here for the season,' he had said, 'and we want snappy service. You give it to us and the other half of this note is yours. O.K. kid?'

Duddy replied to several advertisements in the *Times*. He was, at one time, interested in a new soap that was guaranteed not to sting the eyes. Duddy dreamed, he planned, he lay awake nights smoking, and meanwhile Irwin continued to torment him. One night a bottle of ketchup was emptied on his sheets and another he discovered a dead mouse in his serving jacket pocket.

The other waiters began to feel badly. 'Aw, lay off,' Bernie Altman said. Another night Donald Levitt said, 'Take it easy, Irwin. I'm warning you. He's had enough.'

But Irwin couldn't stop and Duddy began to retaliate. When Irwin started to mock him in the dormitory with the others there, Duddy would begin to improvise songs.

> *Hauling away,*
> *there I lay,*
> *hauling away.*

Another went,

> Take yourself in hand,
> said the sailor to his mate,
> because in this world
> a guy's gotta learn to hold his own.

Chapter Twelve

With the coming of July, the hottest and most gruelling month of the season, the waiters were soon too drained for midnight jaunts to Val Morin. They rose listlessly at seven to set their tables and squeeze fruit juices for breakfast and once the last breakfast had been served, say ten-thirty, it was necessary to set the tables again for lunch. The brawls in the kitchen quickened and the competition for tips got fiercer. After lunch, if the boys had no cutlery to polish, they were usually off duty for two hours and all of them either slept on the beach or in the darkened dormitory. Not Duddy, however. He hung around the card tables and picked up additional tips running errands for the players.

'There's nothing that little fiend wouldn't do for a dollar,' Irwin told Linda, 'and that's how I'm going to teach him a lesson. I've got it all figured out.'

It was a long hot summer and soon a misplaced toothpaste tube or a borrowed towel was enough to set one boy violently against another. The dormitory over the dance hall had a corrugated tin roof and there were nights when it was too stuffy to sleep. Bernie Altman lost seven pounds and circles swelled under Donald Levitt's eyes, but Duddy showed no signs of fatigue. One afternoon, however, he felt faint and instead of waiting on the card players he searched for a place to rest. He didn't dare go to the beach because he was a lousy swimmer and Irwin was certainly there, anyway, and he would ridicule his thin white body again, making the girls laugh. The garden was no use because he would surely be asked to fetch a handbag from a third floor bedroom or search for a misplaced pair of sunglasses. So Duddy wandered round the back of the hotel and sat down on a rock. It was so different here from the beach or the main entrance with its flower beds and multicoloured umbrellas and manicured lawns. Flies buzzed round a heap of garbage pails, and sheets and towels flapped on a dozen different lines that ran from the fire escapes to numerous poles. A group of chambermaids and kitchen helpers, permanent staff, sat on the fire escape. Dull, motionless, their eyelids heavy, they smoked in silence. Yvette waved, another girl smiled wearily, and Duddy waved back, but he didn't join them. He returned the next afternoon, however, and the afternoon after that, and each time he sat nearer to the drained, expressionless group on the fire escape. On Sunday afternoon, he brought six bottles of ice-cold beer with him, laid them on the steps, shrugged his shoulders, and walked off to his rock again. Yvette went over to him.

'Is the beer for us?'

'Let's not make a fuss, eh? I got some big tips today, that's all.'

'You're very nice. Thanks.'

'Aw.'

'Won't you join us?'

'I've got to get back,' he said, 'see you,' and he hurried off, embarrassed, to the dormitory. He found Irwin going through his suitcase there. 'Hey!'

'Somebody stole my watch.'

'Keep away from my stuff or you'll get this,' Duddy said, making a fist. 'You'll get this right in the kisser.'

A couple of afternoons later Irwin rushed into the dormitory. 'Do you know what Duddy told Linda this afternoon?' he asked the boys. 'Some fantastic story about a brother Bradley who owns a ranch in Arizona.'

'So?'

'I happen to know he only has one brother. He's in pre-med, I think.'

'Alright. He lied. Big deal.'

'He's taking Linda out tonight,' Irwin said in his liquid whisper.

'What?'

When Duddy entered the dormitory a half hour later the boys watched apprehensively as he shaved and shined his shoes. Bernie Altman would have liked to warn him that something was up, but Irwin was there, and it was impossible.

Duddy was pleased, but he felt jumpy too. He didn't know much about broads, though naturally there had been lots of rumours and reports. Of Flora Lubin, for instance, he had heard it said, 'That one likes it the Greek way,' but watching Flora walk down the street with her schoolbooks held to her breast Duddy couldn't imagine it. Neither could he credit another report, this one about Grepsy Segal's big sister, that, as A.D. put it, she jerks away for dear life every night. (A girl couldn't anyway, she didn't have a tool.)

Through the years Duddy had collected lots of injunctions about broads, and the handling thereof. War Assets safes are not safe. Tell them anything but never put it in writing. 'Talk, talk, talk, but no matter what they say there's only one thing they really want.' Don't give your correct name and address unless it's really necessary. The hottest are redheads and the easiest single ones over twenty-seven. 'A good thing is to start with tickling the back of the neck. That kills them. It's a scientific fact.' Gin excites them. Horseback riding gives them hot pants too. Cherries are trouble, but married ones miss it something terrible. 'Jewish girls like it just as much as *shiksas*. More, maybe. *I* know.'

Sure, Duddy thought, sure, sure, maybe it was all on the legit, but applying it was another thing. A guy could get his face slapped, or worse.

There were various approaches, of course. He had learned some at the hotel. Paddy Schwartz, the bachelor who came to Rubin's every summer for a two month stay, had a crack at all the goods under forty-five. 'If nine say no,' he told Duddy 'then maybe the tenth will be agreeable. The thing is to keep in there pitching.' Paddy was tall and dark with greying curly hair, but Duddy was disheartened to discover that his private approaches were never nearly so dashing as his public style. After filling his filly of the night, that's what he called them, with drink he'd say he had a bum ticker and had been given only six months to live. Then, his eyes filled with tears, he'd add that the filly was the most beautiful he had ever met, and was she going to send him to his maker without a night of love? Ed Planter, the furrier in 408, pursued the single ones, the office girls, but only after it had become clear to them that the vacation was ending with no marriage candidate around. He'd take them out, spending lavishly, and then back outside the single room at the hotel he'd say, 'I had a little dream about you last night, honey. I dreamt that you were nice to me, *very* nice to me, and I made you a gift of a little fur jacket to keep you warm in winter here . . . and here . . . and here.'

Duddy knew that there were many techniques and he had had some experience himself. There had been that afternoon he had got Birdie Lyman's brassiere half off when the goddam movie had suddenly ended, and once with a Belmont Park pick-up he'd had everything but. Still, he was scared.

'Yvette's got a real lust for you,' Cuckoo told him one night. 'Why don't you do something about it? You could bring her here if you wanted . . .'

'Aw. Yvette. Those are a dime a dozen.'

But Linda was something else. Soft, curvy, and nifty enough for one of those snazzy fashion magazines, she seemed just about the most assured girl Duddy had ever met. She had been to Mexico and New York and sometimes she used words that made Duddy blush. Her cigarette holder, acquired on a trip to Europe, was made of real elephant tusk. At night in the recreation hall she seldom danced but usually sat at the bar joking with Irwin and Paddy and other favourites. Every afternoon she went riding and Duddy had often seen her starting down the dirt road to the stables, beating her whip against her boot. Linda was nineteen and the daughter of an hotel owner – she was maybe an inch and some taller than he was too – and Duddy couldn't understand why she wanted to go out with him. He'd been leading Thunder back to the stables when he had run into her.

'Day off today?'

'Yeah.'

'Buy me a drink?'

'Wha'?'

'I'm thirsty.'

'Sure. Sure thing.'

He took her to the Laurentide Icecream Bar.

'No,' she said. 'A *drink*.'

It was not even dark yet.

'Let's go to the Chalet,' she said.

The bartender there greeted her warmly. Luckily Duddy had

lots of money on him because she drank quickly. Not beer, either.

'Well, Duddy, how do you like shovelling food into the greedy mouths of the *nouveaux-riches*?'

'Your father is a very decent man to work for,' Duddy said earnestly. He couldn't understand why she looked so amused.

'Why?'

'Jeez. I dunno. I mean . . .'

'Did you know that he pinches all the chambermaids' little bums?'

'Maybe we oughta go?'

'No. Let's have another. Hey, Jerry. Two more on the rocks.' Turning to Duddy again, she laughed. 'You shouldn't let Irwin pick on you like that. You ought to talk back to him.'

'I'm not scared. I keep quiet, but I've got my reasons.'

'Is that so?'

There was that amused smile again. He didn't like it.

'Yeah.'

'Like what?'

'Well,' he said, feeling a little dizzy, 'I don't really have to work as a waiter, you know. My father's in the transport business. But I'm making a study of the hotel business like.'

'Shouldn't I warn my father that he's harbouring a future competitor in the dormitory?'

Duddy laughed. He was pleased. 'Hey, have you ever read *God's Little Acre*?'

Duddy figured if she had, and admitted it, there might be something doing. But she didn't reply.

'I'm not much of a reader, really, but my Uncle Benjy has read millions of books. Hard-covered ones. My brother Lennie is gonna be a doctor.'

'What are you going to be?'

Without thinking, he said, 'I'm gonna get me some land one of these days. A man without land is nothing.'

He told her about his brother Bradley and that the Boy Wonder, an intimate of his father's, was willing to back him in any line he chose.

'Why don't you take me dancing tonight?'

Duddy drank three cups of black coffee and took a swim to clear his head before he returned to the dormitory. Irwin, lying on the bed, made him nervous – Linda was supposed to be *his* girl – and Duddy couldn't understand why the others watched him so apprehensively while he dressed. Duddy took half an hour combing his hair into a pompadour with the help of lots of brilliantine. He selected from among his shirts a new one with red and black checks and the tie he chose was white with a black and blue pattern of golf balls and clubs. His green sports jacket had wide shoulders, a one-button roll, and brown checks. A crease had been sewn into his grey flannel trousers. He wore two-tone shoes.

Bernie Altman looked hard at Irwin and stopped Duddy as he was going out. 'Listen,' he said, 'I'll lend you my suit if you like.'

'Jeez, that's nice of you, Bernie. I'm going dancing tonight. But this is the first chance I've had to wear this jacket. A heavy date, you know. Thanks anyway.'

Irwin choked his laughter with his pillow.

'Look, Duddy, I – Oh, what's the use? Have a good time.'

Outside, Linda leaned on the horn of her father's station wagon. Duddy ran.

'You're a son-of-a-bitch, Irwin. A real son-of-a-bitch.'

'Did I pick those clothes for him?'

'Why is she going out with Duddy?'

'Yeah, what have you two cooked up?' Donald asked.

Duddy and Linda drove to the Hilltop Lodge, the resort with the best band, and ordered Scotch on the rocks. Many of the bright young people there waved and two or three raised their eyebrows when they saw that Linda was with Duddy. 'We're engaged,' Linda said. 'He uses Ponds.'

Duddy danced with her three or four times. She was O.K. on the slow ones, but when the band played something hot, Duddy switched to his free-swinging FFHS tea dance style and all at once the floor was cleared and everyone stood around watching. At first this seemed to delight Linda, she laughed a lot, but the second time round she quit on Duddy in the middle of a dance. Once, during a slow number, he held her too close.

'Please,' she said.

'This is called a "Y" dance,' Duddy said. But she didn't get the joke.

Linda invited three others to their table and Duddy ordered

drinks for them. Melvin Lerner, a dentistry student, held hands with Jewel Freed. They were both working at Camp Forest Land. The other man was bearded and somewhat older than the others; he was thirty maybe. Peter Butler lived in Ste Agathe all year round, he had built his own house on a secluded part of the lake.

'Peter's a painter,' Linda said to Duddy.

'Inside or outside?'

'That's good,' Peter said. 'That's very good.' He slapped his knees again and again.

Duddy looked puzzled.

'He's not joking,' Linda said. 'Peter's not a house painter, Duddy. He paints pictures. Peter is a non-figurative painter.'

'Like Norman Rockwell,' Peter said, laughing some more.

'*Touché*,' Linda said, and she ordered another round of drinks.

'What do you do?' Melvin asked Duddy.

'He's making a study of the hotel business like,' Linda said.

Peter and Linda danced two slow numbers together and when Duddy looked up again they were gone. An hour later Linda returned alone, her face flushed and bits of dead leaves stuck to her dress. 'I need a drink,' she said, 'A big one.'

'Maybe we oughta go. I've got to be up at seven tomorrow.'

'One for the road.'

So Duddy ordered another round. Maybe it was the liquor – he was certainly not used to it – but all at once it seemed to him that Linda had changed. Her voice softened and she began to ask him lots of questions about his plans for the future. She was not ridiculing him any more, he was sure of that, and he was no longer afraid of her. From time to time the room swayed around him and he was glad he wasn't the one who would have to drive home. But dizzy as he was, he felt fine. He no longer heard all her remarks, however, because he was thinking that hotel owner's daughters had fallen for poor boys before and, given a shot at it, there were lots of improvements he could make at Rubin's. There was the *Laurentian Liner* too.

'Well, Duddy, are you game?'

The room rocked.

'Tell me if you don't want to. I won't be angry. Maybe Irwin would . . .'

84

'No, no. I'll do it.'

'It'll give you a good start on your stake.'

She helped him outside and into the station wagon. His head rolling and jerking loose each time they hit a bump Duddy tried, he tried hard, to remember what he had agreed to. He had told some lies about himself and the Boy Wonder, they had talked about the gambling house he ran, and the conversation had come round to roulette. Duddy pretended to be an expert and Linda just happened to own a wheel. Then, what? He told her he had already earned more than four hundred dollars in tips and Linda said that was plenty. Plenty? Plenty for him to act as banker for the roulette game they were going to run in the re-creation hall beginning at one a.m. Sunday night. Wouldn't her father object? No, not if ten per cent of each win went into a box for the Jewish National Fund. He couldn't lose – there was that too. She told him so. He might even come out a few hundred dollars ahead.

'Can you make it upstairs yourself?'

'Sure.'

'Aren't you going to kiss Linda before you go?'

'Mm.'

Chapter Thirteen

That was Wednesday, and in the three days to go before the game Duddy began to fear for his money. 'Sure you could win,' Cuckoo said, 'but you could lose too. If I were you I wouldn't do it.' But if he was afraid for his money neither did he want Linda to think that he'd welsh on a promise. She was so sweet to him these days. At night in the recreation hall she sometimes called him over to join her for a drink. Still, he thought, maybe I ought to speak to her. I work hard for my money and I need it. Then people began to stop him in the lobby or on the beach.

'I'll be there, kid,' Paddy said.

Farber slapped him on the back and winked. 'Count me in,' he said.

Mr Cohen stopped him outside the gym. 'Is it O.K. if I bring along a couple of pals?'

The Boy Wonder, Duddy thought, would not chicken out in a situation like this. He would be cool. But Duddy couldn't sleep Friday night and he was ashamed to go and tell Cuckoo again that he was scared. He wouldn't want Linda or Irwin to know that, either. It was so nice, too. Suddenly people looking at him, smiling. He no longer had to go round to the back of the hotel to sit with the kitchen help and chambermaids for companionship. Aw, the hell, Duddy figured out that if the bank ever dropped below one hundred dollars he would stop the game, but he withdrew three hundred just in case. Linda took him aside on Saturday afternoon. 'Maybe we'd better call it off,' she said. 'You might lose.'

'You said I couldn't lose.'

'I said, I said. How do I know?'

'I'm not calling it off. I can't. All those people. Jeez.'

Cuckoo pleaded with him once more. 'But what if you lose, Duddy?'

'Simple,' Duddy said. 'If I lose I drown myself. That's show biz.'

On Sunday night the boys in Artie Bloom's band, who were in on the story, broke up early and everyone pretended to be going off to bed or somewhere else. The lights in the recreation hall were turned out and the front door was locked. Fifteen minutes later some of the lights were turned on again and a side door was opened. The players began to arrive. Duddy set up the table and announced the odds in a failing voice. He would pay thirty to one on a full number and the top bet allowed was fifty cents. That would pay fifteen dollars, one-fifty of which would go into the JNF box. Linda, who was helping him, began to sell change. Farber bought five dollars worth and Mr Cohen asked for ten. Once Duddy had counted forty players in the hall he asked for the door to be shut.

'Don't worry,' Linda said. 'The more players, the more money on the board, the better it is for the bank.'

But Duddy insisted.

'I'll only take ten dollars worth for a start,' Irwin said.

Duddy looked sharply at Linda and it seemed to him that she was even more frightened than he was. 'O.K.,' he said. 'Place your bets.'

Duddy counted at least thirty dollars on the first run. Jeez, he thought. His hands shaky, he was just about to spin the wheel when a voice in the darkness shouted, 'Nobody leave. This is a raid.'

'Wha'?'

'My men have got the place surrounded. No funny stuff, please.'

A spotlight was turned on and revealed was Cuckoo Kaplan in a Keystone cop costume. His nightstick was made of rubber and the height he shook it at made all the women laugh.

'You're a dirty pig, Cuckoo.'

'Some cop.'

Duddy shut his eyes and spun the wheel and number thirty-two came up. Nobody was on it. He paid off even money on two blacks, that's all.

'Come on, Cuckoo. Gimme a number. I'll place a bet for you. Quick.'

Cuckoo took off his shoe, reached into an outlandishly

patched sock, and pulled out a dollar bill. 'Rubin just gave me an advance on next year's salary. He's crying in the kitchen right now.'

'Cuckoo!'

'Put the works on number six for me, but I can't look.'

After an hour of play Duddy was ahead more than two hundred dollars. 'I'll tell you what,' he said. 'Lots of you seem to be losing. I'm no chiseller. From now on you can bet a dollar on a number if you want.'

That's when Irwin changed another twenty-five dollars and sat down at the table and began to play in earnest. His bets seemed to follow no apparent pattern. On each spin of the wheel he placed a dollar on numbers fifteen, six, thirty-two, three, and twelve, and it was only the next morning when he looked closely at the wheel that Duddy realized these numbers ran together there. Irwin won, he didn't win on each spin, but whenever one of his numbers came up he collected thirty dollars and twice if his number repeated. Others, riding his streak of luck, began to bet with him, and once Duddy had to pay off three different people on number three. That cost him ninety dollars, not counting the side and corner bets.

'Don't worry,' Irwin said. 'David's father is in the transport business. He doesn't *really* have to work as a waiter.'

Duddy turned to Linda, his look astonished.

'His brother Bradley is a big rancher in Arizona,' Irwin said. 'All David has to do is wire him for more money.'

'It's getting late,' Mrs Faber said.

Ed Planter yawned and stretched.

'Don't go,' Duddy said. 'Not yet, please. Give me a chance to win some of my money back.'

Farber saw that Duddy was extremely pale.

'Don't worry, kid,' Mr Cohen said. 'Your luck will change.'

But Duddy's luck didn't change, it got worse, and nobody at the table joked any more. The men could see that the boy's cheeks were burning hot, his eyes were red, and his shirt adhered to his back. When Duddy paid out on a number his hands shook.

Cuckoo pulled Irwin aside. 'It's your wheel, you bastard. I found out.'

'Really?'

88

'Do you know how hard that kid works for his money?'

Irwin tried to turn away, but Cuckoo seized him by the arm. 'I'm going to speak to Rubin,' he said. 'First thing tomorrow morning I'm going to talk to him.'

'Linda and I are going to be engaged,' Irwin said. 'Rubin is very pleased about that. I thought maybe you'd like to know.'

'Come on,' Duddy said. 'Place your bets. Let's not waste time.'

The men at the table were tired and wanted to go to bed, but they were also ashamed of winning so much money from a seventeen-year-old boy and they began to play recklessly, trying to lose. It was no use.

'We want to see you upstairs later, Irwin,' Bernie Altman said.

On the next spin Duddy went broke and he had to close the game.

'That's show biz,' Irwin said. 'Right, Cuckoo?'

The men filed out without looking at Duddy, but Linda stayed on after the others had gone.

'Thanks,' Duddy said. 'Thanks a lot.'

'How much did you lose?'

'Everything. Three hundred dollars.' Duddy began to scream. 'You said I couldn't lose. You told me it was impossible for me to lose.'

'I'm sorry, Duddy. I had no idea that – '

'Aw, go to hell. Just go to hell please.' He gave the wheel a shove, knocking it over, and rushed outside. Once on the beach he could no longer quell his stomach. Duddy was sick. He sat on a rock, holding his head in his hands, and he began to sob bitterly.

'Hey,' Cuckoo shouted, entering the lobby, 'has anybody here seen Duddy?'

'No.'

'He still hasn't shown up at the dorm,' Bernie said. 'It's more than an hour now . . .'

'What's going on here?' Rubin demanded. 'I'm the boss here.'

Duddy clenched his teeth and pulled his hair until it hurt. 'God damn it to hell,' he said. Some stake. Six weeks of hard work and not a cent to show for it. He was back where he'd started from. Worse. He was probably a laughing-stock too. Jeez, he thought. 'God damn you.'

Some scraping on the sand disturbed him and Duddy hid behind a rock. He recognized Cuckoo's voice.

'Somebody saw him run towards the beach. There's no telling what he might do.'

Linda said something he couldn't make out and Cuckoo's reply was lost in the wind. Then he heard Linda say, 'I knew it was his wheel, but I never thought . . .'

Footsteps approached from another direction. Somebody had a flashlight.

'Duddy!'

Let them think I've drowned, he thought. It would serve them right. He had seen a drowned woman once at Shawbridge, and the thought of his own face bloated like that – Irwin hanging for it, the bastard, and his father maybe feeling sorry he hadn't treated him as well as Lennie – made a hot lump in Duddy's throat. He began to sob again.

'Duddy!'

There was a dip of oars and a rippling in the water. A boat had started out.

'Hal-lo! Duddy!'

Scampering barefooted across the sand, Duddy broke for the protecting woods. He heard Rubin's gruff voice, 'That little bastard, I'll kill him. There was a drowning at the Hilltop Lodge once and the next day there weren't two guests left at the hotel. If this got into the papers it could ruin . . .'

Duddy was seized by an uncontrollable fit of laughter. He rolled over in the grass, biting his arm to muffle the noise.

'. . . send for the cops?'

Next came Rubin's voice. 'Oh, no you don't. No cops. That little bastard, I'll choke him to death.'

Duddy came out on a dirt road on the other side of the woods and started back into Ste Agathe. Three times he stopped, his laughter immense. The thought of them searching for him all through the night and Irwin certainly catching shit galore almost made him forget the three hundred dollars. Almost, but not quite.

Pyjama-clad guests drifted down into the lobby one by one.

'I wouldn't like to be in your shoes, Rubin.'

'How could you let a seventeen-year-old kid lose all his tips in a roulette game?'

'I knew nothing about it. I swear I – '

'Save it for the reporters tomorrow. When they drag the kid out of the lake – '

'Bite your tongue,' Rubin shouted.

'The poor kid.'

'Next season it's the Hilltop Lodge for me,' Mrs Dunsky said.

'Me too,' Mrs Faber said.

Rubin reminded his guests that there had been a case of ptomaine poisoning at the Hilltop Lodge last year.

'You think your food goes down so good, Rubin? Around the corner at the drugstore bicarbonate sales are booming.'

'We're doing everything humanly possible,' Rubin said. 'All the boys are out searching.'

'The bottom of the lake?'

The guests stared accusingly at Rubin. 'Why don't you all go to sleep?' he said.

'In a hotel where tragedy has just struck?'

'Tomorrow,' Paddy said, 'you can change the name from the Hotel Lac des Sables to Rubin's Haunted Hotel.'

'Already it's beginning to feel spooky in here. Hey, open up the bar, Rubin.'

'Yeah, we could do with some salami sandwiches too. This is going to be a long night.'

'All right,' Rubin said. 'All right.'

Circling back over the highway Duddy re-entered Ste Agathe through those streets, remote from the lake, where the French-Canadians lived. His legs ached from the long hike; he was starved and searched for an open restaurant. He found a French-Canadian chip place open on the edge of town. Yvette was there.

'Duddy!'

Duddy didn't realize it, but his clothing was muddy and he had ripped his shirt in the bushes.

'Were you in a fight?'

He sat down and told her, between explosions of laughter, what had happened. Yvette felt rotten about the three hundred dollars, but when he got to the part about Rubin she began to laugh too.

'Have something else?'

Duddy had already consumed three hotdogs and two orders of chips.

'I think they want to close,' he said. 'Why don't we go for a walk?'

Avoiding the main streets and the lakeshore, or anywhere he might run into a searching party, they started out together holding hands. She led him towards the railroad tracks as the stars started to fade and light began to spread across the sky. Duddy saw for the first time the part of Ste Agathe where the poorer French-Canadians lived and the summer residents and tourists never came. The unpainted houses had been washed grey by the wind and the rain. Roosters crowed in yards littered with junk and small hopeless vegetable patches and Duddy was reminded of his grandfather and St Dominique Street, and he promised himself to send the old man a postcard tomorrow. There were faded Robin Hood Flour signs on some walls and here and there a barn roof or window had been healed with a tin Sweet Caporal sign.

'This way,' Yvette said.

Crossing the tracks they came out on a rocky slope on the edge of the mountain. The dew soon soaked through Duddy's shoes and trouser bottoms. His body ached. The excitement of the game and search past, he longed for his bed, but Yvette led him deeper into the field. Down a bumpy hill and up the other side on to a flat table of a rock. There she made him rest.

'It's so nice to see you lie still for once,' she said.

'Wha'?'

'You're always running or jumping or scratching . . .'

Duddy was surprised and flattered to discover that anyone cared enough to watch him so closely. 'I like you,' he said.

'Do you think I'm pretty?'

'Sure. Sure thing.'

He edged closer to her and, to his surprise, she didn't withdraw. Duddy fondled a breast tentatively. She kissed him, forcing his mouth open.

'Listen, Yvette, I haven't got a . . .'

But she didn't care. Jeez, he thought, if the guys could see me now.

'You're my speed, Yvette. You're for me.'

Duddy and Yvette returned to Ste Agathe by another route,

separating before they reached the lakeshore. Yvette kissed him on the cheek. 'You work too hard,' she said. 'There's nothing but bones . . .'

'Aw.'

She told him that she was off on Wednesday afternoon.

'Let's go swimming,' he said.

It was almost nine when Duddy entered the lobby of the Hotel Lac des Sables and the guests were beginning to come down for breakfast.

'Duddy!'

'It's the Kravitz boy. He's back.'

Guests came rushing out of the dining room and smiled, still clutching orange juices or slices of toast. Linda embraced Duddy in front of everybody. 'Boy,' she said, 'am I glad to see you!'

Rubin slapped him on the back. 'You little bastard,' he said. 'You lousy little bastard.' But even he smiled and Duddy could see that he hadn't shaved yet. Probably he'd been up all night.

'Are you O.K.?' Bernie asked.

The guests cheered when he entered the dining room.

'Don't worry,' Mr Cohen said with a meaningful wink. 'Everything's going to work out fine.'

Duddy looked puzzled.

'He can take the next two days off,' Rubin announced in a booming voice. There was some applause. 'But no complaints please if the service is slow. Duddy's my top man in the dining room.'

'*If* the service is slow. Is that what the man said?'

After breakfast Duddy went to the dormitory. He had only just sat down on the bed to rest when Bernie and Donald came in. They had brought Irwin with them. 'He has something for you,' Bernie said severely.

Irwin smiled.

'Give it to him.'

'I want to tell you how thrilled I am,' Irwin said, 'that you didn't drown. I was so worried.'

'Give it to him right now, please.'

Irwin handed over his winnings. It was just short of three hundred dollars. 'I intended to return the money anyway,' he said.

'Nobody's going to know about this, Duddy,' Bernie said, 'so don't worry.'

'They were afraid you might be too proud to take the money,' Irwin said. 'Isn't that amusing?'

'Shettup, Irwin.'

'You cheated me. You arranged it all with Linda and the wheel was crooked. I hope you had a good laugh.'

'The wheel wasn't crooked.'

'Cheaters never prosper,' Duddy said. 'I hope this'll be a good lesson for you. I hope you'll profit from it in the future.'

That night a delegation comprised of Farber, Mr Cohen, and Paddy invited Duddy to have a drink with them in the recreation hall. Mr Cohen, ever since he had winked meaningfully at Duddy, had been an awfully busy man. All morning and most of the afternoon he had waylaid guests in the lobby and on the beach and even – once the word had got out – in their rooms. 'Think of what the poor kid must be going through,' he'd say for a starter.

'It's my fault maybe.'

'Look,' he'd say, 'if you can afford a month here you can afford this. Would it be better to spend the money on doctors?'

Everyone smiled at the delegation when they sat down at the bar with Duddy. Mr Cohen held out a large envelope. 'We want a promise from you first,' he said.

'Wha'?'

'How much did you lose last night?'

'Three hundred bucks, but – '

'No buts, Duddy. You've got to promise us no more roulette. Finished.'

'Sure.'

He handed Duddy the envelope. 'It's from all the guests together. A hundred and forty-two contributors.'

'I don't get it.'

'I may have given more than Farber but we're not saying. Twenty dollars is the same as five,' Mr Cohen said, looking hard at Farber. 'It's the spirit that counts.'

'I don't know what to say. I mean . . .' Duddy pressed the envelope, testing it for thickness and substance. '. . . well, thanks . . .'

'You'd better go to sleep now. You must be tired.'

Duddy rushed upstairs, emptied the envelope on his bed, and started to count the money. There was close to five hundred dollars in the envelope. Duddy laughed, he shouted. He rolled over on the floor and did a couple of somersaults.

'Hi.'

It was Linda.

'I had no idea Irwin was going to bet that much. Honestly I didn't.'

With all your college education, he thought, what are you? A couple of crooks. 'Sure,' he said tightly.

'Do you really think we were after your money?'

Will you go, please, he thought. I work for your father but that doesn't mean I have to talk to you.

'I've broken with Irwin.'

'Congratulations.'

'It was a bad joke. I'm sorry. But I had no idea – '

' – that the wheel was crooked?'

'The wheel wasn't crooked. But it's only a toy and it's an old one. It has certain tendencies. Irwin knew them.'

Duddy shrugged. *Ver gerharget*, he thought.

'I thought you went out with me because you liked me. Boy, was I ever a sucker. That night at the Hilltop Lodge must have cost me twenty bucks.'

'You want the money back?'

'You think I'm dirt,' he said, 'don't you?'

Look at me, he thought, take a good look because maybe I'm dirt now. Maybe I've never been to Paris and I don't know a painter from a horse's ass. I can't play tennis like the other guys here, but I don't go around spilling ketchup in other guy's beds either. I don't trick guys into crazy promises when they're drunk. I don't speak dirty like you either. You make fun of your father. You don't like him. Tough shit. But he sends you to Europe and Mexico and who pays for those drinks in the afternoon? You're sorry for making a fool out of me. Gee whiz, my heart bleeds. Take a good look, you dirty bitch. Maybe I'm dirt today. That bastard of a black marketeer Cohen can give me twenty bucks and a lecture about gambling and feel good for a whole week. But you listen here, kiddo. It's not always going to be like this. If you want to bet on something then bet on me. I'm going to be a somebody and that's for sure.

'Did you laugh,' he shouted, 'tell me, did you laugh when I told you about my plans for the future? I'll bet you and Irwin split your sides.'

She flushed.

'Thank you,' he said. 'Thanks a lot.'

'You have no right to be angry. I kept my promise,' Linda said, indicating the money on the bed. 'I said you couldn't lose and you didn't.'

'And something else,' Duddy screamed, stepped between her and the money. 'He's not in the transport business.'

'What?'

'My father.'

She looked puzzled.

'He's a hack and he picks up extra money pimping. My father's a pimp. Now beat it. Scram,' He ran after her. 'Go tell Irwin. Hurry. That ought to be good for a laugh. My old man's a lousy pimp.'

Duddy slammed the door after Linda and the next morning he gave Rubin his notice. Since it was the height of the season, however, he agreed to stay on for another week if he was given a room of his own – any room – and did not have to eat with the other waiters. Duddy was the quickest boy in the dining room and Rubin agreed. He hoped Duddy would stay the season.

Chapter Fourteen

On Wednesday afternoon Duddy met Yvette at one of the rear entrances to the hotel.

'Wow.'

Yvette had black hair and large black eyes. A pretty girl even in her maid's uniform, today she wore a straw hat with a wide brim and a white linen dress and little white shoes.

'C'mon,' Duddy said. 'I'll get one of the boats.'

'No. We're going somewhere special. Another lake.'

Duddy looked pained and he wondered if she realized that he was ashamed of being seen with her on the lake.

'Do you like my dress?'

'You're a knockout.'

Yvette took his arm. 'I don't have to be back until nine,' she said. 'What about you?'

'I'm off until tomorrow breakfast. What's in the basket?'

'You'll see.'

Yvette led him across the railroad tracks again and up the rocky slope. They started up a narrow path over the mountain.

'Jeez. I thought we were going swimming.'

'You'll see.'

On top of the mountain she took a bottle of beer out of the basket and shared it with Duddy. He tried to pull her to him. 'No,' she said. 'Not yet.'

They came down on the other side of the mountain and walked through a field of corn and a wide, hilly cow pasture. They crossed some disused tracks, hopped from rock to rock over a swirling creek, climbed a wooden fence and crawled under a barbed wire one, and entered a thick wood. An hour later they emerged from the woods and started up a gentle green rise. On a shelf of level land near the hilltop Yvette stopped and pulled

T – D.K. – D

Duddy down on the grass with her. 'You close your eyes and rest,' she said.

When he woke he saw a roast chicken and bread and beer and pickles spread on a white tablecloth on the grass. They were both famished and ate quickly. Yvette rolled over into his arms and Duddy eagerly began to undo the buttons down the back of her dress.

'Have you got your suit on?' she asked.

'No.'

'Me neither. We don't need it here.'

Swimming in the nude, he thought, may be O.K. at night, but – 'Are we going to walk naked to the lake?'

Yvette laughed. He kissed her and began to pull tensely at her dress.

'The lake's right here,' she said.

'Wha'?'

Duddy jumped up impatiently, abandoning her on the grass with her dress half off. 'Where?'

'Go to the top of the hill.'

Duddy climbed the rest of the rise. 'For Christ's sake,' he said. 'God.'

Yvette embraced him from behind, pulling out his shirt and loosening his belt.

'This is really – For Christ's sake!'

Duddy's heart began to pound. Yvette was undressing him, she bit his neck, but Duddy hardly noticed. He stepped absently out of his trousers. Before him spread a still blue lake and on the other side a forest of pine trees. There was not one house on the lake. Some cows grazed on the meadow near the shore and over the next hill there was a cornfield and a silo. There were no other signs of life or ownership or construction. Duddy cracked his knuckles, he beat his fist into the palm of his open hand again and again.

'It's beautiful, isn't it?'

Her voice startled him. He had come to think he was alone.

'What's wrong?' she asked quickly.

'Beautiful?' Duddy laughed wildly. He broke rudely free of her embrace and raced down the hill and plunged into the lake.

'Wait. I'm coming.'

But he ignored her. She watched as he swam out and dived

down to the bottom time after time. Once or twice he stayed down long enough to worry her.

'Duddy, that's all. Come back.'

Once more he plunged to the bottom, nearer the shore this time. When he broke to the surface again there were scratches on his forehead and chest. 'The bottom's fine. There are rocks here and there that'll have to be cleared, that's all,' he said, stepping out of the water.

Yvette failed to understand. 'You stayed in too long,' she said. He trembled. His lips were purple, his teeth were chattering. Yvette began to rub him fiercely with a towel. 'Will you stand still for just *one* minute, please,' she said.

'Have you ever brought anyone else here before?'

His expression alarmed her.

'Answer me!'

'You're jealous,' she said.

He stiffened against her embrace.

'That's nice,' she said softly. 'I'm glad.'

Duddy realized that they were both nude and for the first time he was embarrassed.

'You fool,' he shouted. 'You little fool. I'm not jealous. But you've got to tell me. I want the truth. Have you ever been here with anyone from the hotel?'

'No.'

'But you've come here before?'

'Yes.'

'Many times?'

'Yes.'

'God damn it.'

'You don't understand. Not with . . . men. We used to come here to swim when we were kids.'

'Oh. Oh, I see.'

He began to walk up and down, scratching his arms.

'What's wrong, Duddy?'

'How far is it to the road?'

'About half a mile, maybe more.'

'Can you see the lake from there?'

'No.'

He started to pace again.

'Are you angry with me?'

'Listen,' he said, 'you mustn't tell anyone – absolutely nobody – that we came here today.'

'But we haven't done anything wrong?'

'Jeez. What can I do to make you understand?'

Yvette waited.

'Just promise me that, will you? You'll tell nobody we came here and you will never bring anybody else here.'

'Why?'

Duddy took a deep breath. He shook his head. 'If you promise me that I'll give you fifty dollars.'

Yvette turned and ran up the hill. Duddy took off after her. He watched sullen and afraid as she hurried into her clothes. 'Are you cold?' he asked hopefully.

'I'm going.'

'Why? It's still early.'

'I don't like you any more. I don't want your stinking money.'

He tried to take her in his arms but she pushed him away. 'Jeez, Yvette. I'm sorry. I'm – I'm just so excited, that's all. Don't go. Please don't go. I need your help.'

Yvette hesitated.

'Please . . .'

'You wouldn't be ashamed if you had come here with Linda. You'd never offer her money, either.'

'Oh, Yvette. Yvette. You don't understand. Let's go back and look at the lake again.'

The lowering sun blazed behind the mountain. He's all skin and bones, she thought, and she picked up his shirt and trousers. 'Take these,' she said. 'You mustn't catch a chill.'

Duddy made love quickly to Yvette by the shore.

'I feel so good,' she said. 'Do you feel good?'

He could watch the lake over her shoulder and in his mind's eye it was not only already his but the children's camp and the hotel were already going up. On the far side there was a farm reserved for his grandfather.

'I've never felt better.'

'Do you like me? A little, even.'

'Sure. Sure thing.'

He would have to buy up the surrounding fields with infinite care. Guile was required. Otherwise prices would surely sky-rocket overnight. Yvette lit a cigarette for him and Duddy decided where he would put the camp play field. The land there is as flat as a pool table, he thought. It's a natural. His heart began to pound again and he laughed more happily than he had ever laughed before.

'What's so funny?'

'Wha'?'

'You were laughing.'

Once the land was his, and he would get it if it took him twenty years, he could raise money for construction by incorporating the project and selling shares. He would never surrender control, of course.

'Do you trust me, Yvette?'

'Yes.'

'I want to buy this lake.'

She didn't laugh.

'I'm going to build a children's camp and a hotel here. I want to make a town. Ste Agathe is getting very crowded and five years from now people will be looking for other places to go.'

'That's true.'

'A man without land is nobody,' he said.

Yvette felt that his forehead was hot and she made a pillow for him out of a towel.

'If the wrong person saw this place he might get the same idea. That's why you mustn't tell anyone we came here or bring anybody else here. Who owns the land, Yvette?'

Brault owned a third of it, maybe. She wasn't sure about the rest. Brault was a hard man to deal with.

'So am I,' Duddy said. 'And this land is mine.'

He told her about the Boy Wonder, and how he would have to ask him for a stake. He explained that he did not have more than two thousand dollars saved and it might take him several years to buy up all the land surrounding the lake and she must help him. The farmers would be wary of a young Jew, they might jack up prices or even refuse to sell, but another French-Canadian would not be suspect. He was too young to marry, he explained calmly, and in any event he might have to marry a rich woman if he could get one, but if she helped him he would always look after her and she would get a share in the profits. He had to return to Montreal tomorrow and get started but before he left he would leave her money to cover the preliminary costs of inquiries, notaries, and anything else that might come up. He said he'd keep in close touch with her and come to Ste Agathe whenever he could manage it.

'I've got nearly three hundred dollars in the bank,' Yvette said, 'if it's of any help.'

They talked a lot longer and had to return by the road, it was too dark to attempt the woods or climb the mountain, and they did not get back to the hotel until two a.m. Yvette went right to bed, but Duddy saw a light in Cuckoo's room and he went to see him.

'*Gevalt!* What's happened to you?'

Duddy's trousers were caked with mud. He felt hot and sweaty, but he didn't realize that his eyes were swollen and his cheeks were burning red.

'You're sick,' Cuckoo said.

'Gwan.'

'Where in the hell have you been all night?'

Feverish but happy Duddy could not hold back his fantastic find. He told Cuckoo about the lake, though not where it was and, pledging him to secrecy, he swore that there would be a job for him.

'Sure, sure. But I think you'd better take a couple of aspirins and get right into bed.'

Duddy fainted and had to be carried into his room, but the next morning he was gone before anyone was up.

'Somebody saw Yvette with him at the station,' Cuckoo told Linda at the bar the same night.

'Were he and Yvette – ?'

'She's crazy about him.'

'Obviously I underestimated him.'

'He didn't even say good-bye to me.'

'Me neither. Let's face it, Cuckoo, he's a twisty one and a little liar too.' Linda chuckled. 'Among other things he pretended to me that he was an intimate of Jerry Dingleman's.'

Cuckoo was surprised. He thought everyone knew that when she was in Montreal Linda went to all of the Boy Wonder's parties.

'He's probably knocked up Yvette,' Linda said, 'and that's why he's skipped town like that.'

'Well, that's show biz,' Cuckoo said. 'But you couldn't beat Duddy for a dreamer.'

'Don't I know it? He thinks he's going to make millions.'

'I'm worried, though. He seemed so sick like last night. I don't mean the fever. I mean sick in the head. He went on and on about some lake he'd found and how he was going to build a whole town on it.'

'No kidding?'

'Isn't that terrible? I mean isn't it awful that a bright kid like that should have to live on pipe-dreams?'

'Listen, Cuckoo, are you sure about Duddy and Yvette? I couldn't care less, but . . .'

'I'm telling you. She was crazy about him from the start.'

Linda got up. 'I wonder if he left his address with my father.'

'You want to see him again?'

'Don't be absurd,' she said sharply. 'But if he got Yvette into a jam I'm not going to let him get away with it.'

Cuckoo remained at the bar.

'The same poison again?'

'Reet you are,' Cuckoo said. Maybe, he thought, I shouldn't have mentioned the lake. He had promised Duddy – Aw, it was all too crazy. Cuckoo turned around on his stool. The guests looked bored. Maybe a quiz game, he thought, or a dance contest. Here comes Rubin.

'I was just going to get the show on the road,' Cuckoo said.

Part Two

Chapter One

Max always had his breakfast at Eddy's Cigar & Soda. His usual fare was a salami sandwich and a Pepsi.

'Kee-rist,' Debrofsky said. 'According to Parsley's column the Dodgers are going to draft Bridges.'

'What's that got to do with the Jewish problem?' Max asked, hoping for a laugh and not getting one.

'Hey, look who's here!'

'Duddy!'

Duddy dropped his kitbag and ran to his father and embraced him.

'Hey, easy there,' Max said, breaking free. 'Take care for my *kishkas*.'

'Where's your sunburn, for Christ's sake? Two months in the mountains and you're still as white as a sheet.'

'Aw.'

'He's taller,' Eddy said, placing a coffee before Duddy. 'He musta shot up at least three inches.'

Max ruffled his boy's hair. 'You're right, Eddy. I have to reach up now. It seems only a week ago I had to bend down to . . . Hey, what are you doing here, anyway? Were you fired?'

'I quit.'

'You're sure there was no trouble? You're not holding anything back.'

'Jeez.'

'You don't look too hot. Are you sick?'

'I've got a fever.'

'Come on,' Max said, getting up, 'I'll take you home.'

Duddy leaned back in the car with his eyes closed. There were beads of sweat on his forehead. 'Why didn't you answer any of my letters?' he asked.

'Oh, you know me. I'm not one for the letters.'

But Duddy remembered that when Lennie had worked as a camp councillor one summer his father had written every week. He had driven out to visit him twice. 'How's Lennie?'

'Plugging away as usual. Anatomy's the big killer, you know.'

'Yeah.'

'His nerves are all shot. Lennie's not like you or me, you know. Those bright guys are never physically strong. Your Uncle Benjy is sending him to Cape Cod for a couple of weeks' rest.'

'That's nice. How's the *zeyda*?'

'The same. Still strong as a horse and digging away in that back yard. He brought me round some radishes last week and they were so bitter you could die. I had to eat them but. The old bastard sat there with me all the time, and do you know what? Afterwards he says to me, "Those are terrible radishes, Max. How could you eat them? I tried one and had to spit it out."'

Duddy laughed. 'Did he ask about me?'

'He sure did. The old man's crazy about you. I swear it.'

Lennie was home. He was in the bedroom, dressing to go out. 'Duddy,' he shouted, 'how are you?'

'Can't complain.'

'Look at him, Daddy. He'll soon be taller than me.'

Duddy punched Lennie lightly on the shoulder. His brother replied with a left to the belly and Duddy, suddenly pale, had to sit down.

'What's wrong?' Lennie asked.

'Nothing. A cold, that's all.'

'He's getting right into bed,' Max said.

'Where are you off to so early, Lennie?'

'Tennis.'

'He's got a new girl. Style? *Style.*'

'Hell,' Lennie said quickly, 'I forgot to get some money from Benjy yesterday. Listen, Duddy, can you lend me ten bucks until tomorrow?'

Duddy handed him three tens. 'I was going to get you a gift, but I didn't have the time. So you get it yourself now. O.K.?'

'Well, thanks a lot!'

'Skip it.'

'Have a good time, Lennie.' Max waited until he heard the

front door shut. 'I'm so glad when he takes his nose out of those books and gets some fresh air for once.'

'He looks pretty sunburnt to me,' Duddy said. 'What's happened to Riva?'

'Gone with the wind, I guess. He hangs out with a new bunch now. Most of them aren't Jewish and maybe they drink more than they should, but what the hell. They're all college kids and they come from good families.'

'And the girl?' Duddy asked, taking his clothes off.

'A knockout from Westmount. A blondie too.'

'Is it serious?'

'Serious? She's a *shiksa*.'

'I think I'll try and sleep now. But wake me up when you come in. I've got some important things I want to talk over with you. Oh, I almost forgot,' he said, rising, 'I bought you half a dozen sports shirts in Ste Agathe. One of them is handwoven.' Duddy started for his kitbag.

'Never mind. Get into bed. You can give them to me tonight.'

'Sure. Sure thing.'

Max had only been gone a moment when Duddy began to cry. Maybe it was the fever, maybe it was his bed and the room he shared with Lennie again, but Duddy wept long and brokenly before he finally fell asleep. He woke the next afternoon with a foul taste in his mouth, but the fever was gone. There wasn't much to eat in the kitchen. Duddy heated a tin of chicken soup and broke an egg into it. Afterwards he felt better, a little woozy, perhaps, but good enough to go out. Duddy found his grandfather bent over the last in the shoe repair shop. '*Zeyda*, it's me.'

The old man rose and stroked Duddy's cheek. 'You've been home two days,' he said.

'I was sick. I was in bed. *Zeyda*,' he said. 'I've found some land. It's in the country.'

Simcha smiled, he made a deprecating gesture with his hand. 'Lie to an old man,' he said.

'No. I'm serious.' He told his grandfather about the lake. 'The greenest field is reserved for you. For a farm like.'

Simcha looked shrewdly at Duddy. He nodded his head. 'You're bigger,' he said, 'and the pimples are gone. My grandson is going to be handsome.'

'A somebody,' Duddy said.

'I'll make tea,' Simcha said, and he looked Duddy up and down again, his delight undisguised. 'What a change in you. My God.'

The little baby-fat there had been in Duddy's face was gone. He was taller, more broad, and he had no more need to encourage a beard. The boyish craftiness in his eyes had been displaced by tough adult resolution. He was able to sit still longer and he seemed calm and confident. Like his grandfather he now gave the appearance of a man who held plenty in reserve. Duddy didn't chew his nails any more, either. Unknowingly emulating his grandfather he had taken to sitting with his big broad-palmed hands gripping his knees. He held his head high, if a little to one side. But not quite eighteen years old, he was practically a chain-smoker. His fingers were dark with nicotine.

'I brought you something,' Duddy said, placing a package on the counter.

'You don't have to bring me gifts.'

'I want to.'

Simcha undid the brown package, carefully rolling up the string again and putting it in a drawer. There was a pair of blue overalls, a couple of dozen seed packages, and a pair of gardening shears.

'For the farm.'

Simcha folded the brown wrapping paper in four and put it in another drawer.

'If you don't like it I can take it back. I kept the bills.'

'Let's have a drink,' Simcha said, and from under the counter he brought out a bottle of cognac. 'You pour it in your tea. That makes you warm here, Duddel. Watch me.'

That night Duddy waited up for his father. He was alone in the house; Lennie had gone out in the afternoon to play tennis and still hadn't come home. When Max came in Duddy made him some scrambled eggs and coffee.

'About a half hour ago,' Max said, 'two guys stop me and ask to be driven out to Dorval. I keep a lead pipe behind me under the seat special for such jokers. Last week they rolled one of the Diamond drivers. The damn fool tried to fight with them and got fifteen stitches in the head for his trouble. Where's Lennie?'

'He's not home yet.'

'It's almost two o'clock.' Max took off his shirt and got his back-scratcher out of the kitchen drawer. 'Hey, did I tell you about last week? The cops caught this young punk from Griffintown trying to steal the radio out of Debrofsky's new Dodge. That would have made the fifth one swiped in a month. Anyway, the cops took the kid into the can and broke his arm. Boy, did he ever yell.'

'Why didn't they just pull him in?'

'They say that's no use. They get off too easy. This way they said he won't be swiping radios for another few months at least. Listen, they oughta know what they're doing ... Aw, *that's* the spot. You want to borrow it for a minute?' he asked, offering Duddy the scratcher.

'No.'

'Where in the hell's Lennie? I don't like this.'

'Daddy, I want you to take me to the Boy Wonder tomorrow. I have to speak to him.'

'Pardon me while I clean the wax out of my ears.'

'What's wrong?'

'What do you mean you want to speak to him? You're a kid.'

'You always promised you'd take me to him.'

'When you were ready. Don't forget. I always said when you were ready. Max the Hack is no welsher.'

'I'm ready, Daddy.'

'Ask around. Go ahead. Never in my life have I welshed on a promise.'

'I have to see him important.'

'Oh, there's trouble coming. I can smell it.'

'No trouble. There's a deal I want to speak to him about.'

'A deal! Do you think the Wonder waits to hear from *pishers* of eighteen for deals?'

'I want you to take me there tomorrow.'

'Impossible. He's in Florida.'

'When does he get back?'

'In two weeks, they say. But with him you never know. I remember once,' Max began, 'when the Boy Wonder flew to Paris, France, just for the weekend. It was a Friday afternoon and – '

'I know that story.'

Max looked hurt.

'As soon as he gets back I want you to take me to him.'

'What about? A job.'

'I can't say.'

'I'll take you to him under two conditions. One, you must be ready. Two, you have to tell me why first.'

'If you don't take me I'll go myself.'

'And embarrass me?'

'Why are you always afraid I'm going to embarrass you?'

'Don't shout at me,' Max said, making a fist. 'When I lose my temper I lose my temper.'

'I remember,' Duddy said acidly.

'You shouldn't have said that. You have no right to bring that up again.'

Duddy glared at him. He started to say something, but the doorbell rang and rang. Somebody was leaning against the bell. 'I'll go,' Duddy said. It was Lennie, and he was dead drunk. 'Daddy's sitting up in the kitchen. He mustn't see you like this.'

'Gotta get t'bed.'

'Listen,' Duddy said, shaking him, 'you wait here. I'll be right out. Jeez.'

In the kitchen Duddy said, 'It was the wrong address. A lush. Go to bed, Daddy.'

'Where are you going?'

'For a walk.'

'I'm going to wait up for Lennie.'

'If I were you I'd go to bed.'

Duddy found Lennie sitting outside on the next door steps, his head hanging between his shoulders. 'It's terrible,' Lennie said. 'Terrible.'

'Gwan. You're drunk, that's all. Here. Grab on. I'll take you round through the lane and we'll climb in the window.'

'It could ruin me for life.'

'What?'

'So there wouldn't be a doctor in the family. Who cares?'

'*What did you say?*'

Lennie grinned. He rocked to and fro.

'What did you say about no doctor in the family?'

'Why, it's Duddy Kravitz, the kid who once cornered the comic book market on St Urbain Street.'

'Awright. *Very* funny. Now tell me what's going to ruin your life.'

'I'm gonna be sick.'

Duddy supported him. He held his forehead. 'Better?' he asked.

'Bed.'

'Lennie, listen to me. Lennie! Listen. Are you listening? I want you to tell me if you're in trouble. This is no joke.'

Lennie burped. 'Whoops,' he said.

'I'm going to keep you standing here. No bed. Until you tell me – '

Lennie squinted, he swayed, and he brought Duddy into focus once more. 'I've fallen behind in my studies,' he said. 'Too much tennis. Anatomy's the big killer, you know.'

'Is that all?' Duddy asked, releasing him. 'You sure?'

'Sure I'm sure.' Lennie pretended to be conducting an orchestra. He sang, 'We are little black sheep – '

'Shettup,' Duddy said quickly.

'What?'

'I don't care for that song, that's all. C'mon. We're going home.'

Duddy got him in the back window and into bed without much trouble. His father was no longer in the kitchen, but the light was on in his bedroom.

'Daddy?'

'Lennie?'

'He just got in. He's in bed asleep already. I thought I'd tell you.'

Lennie woke when Duddy entered the room. 'Thanks,' he said. 'Thanks a lot.'

'Aw.'

'Want to know something? I think Uncle Benjy is a pain in the ass.'

Duddy laughed.

'He stinks. UNCLE BENJY IS A BIG STINKER!'

'Quiet,' Duddy said warmly, 'you'll wake Daddy.'

'Did you know he was impotent?'

'Wha'?'

'He can't have babies. He can't even – '

'You oughtn't to say that. He's been very good to you.'

'He'll kill me. If he finds out he'll . . .'

'What did you say?'

'Nothing. Thanks, Duddy. Thanks a lot.'

'Let's go to sleep, eh?'

'I just want to say thanks.'

'O.K.'

'Thanks a lot.'

'Jeez.'

'Thank *you* very much. *Merci.*'

'For Christ's sake, let's go to sleep.'

'Night.'

'Good night.'

'And thanks. Thanks a lot.'

Duddy pulled the blankets over his head.

He waited two weeks before he approached Max again about the Boy Wonder. 'He's back,' Duddy said. 'I know that for a fact.'

'Listen, Duddy, he dropped a fortune in Florida. They say he's in a black mood.'

'I'll take my chances. Speak to him for me tomorrow.'

'Tomorrow's Friday.'

'Yeah, and the day after that's Saturday. So what?'

'First thing next week I'm going to speak to him. That's a promise.'

Chapter Two

Duddy was not idle while he waited for his father to introduce him to the Boy Wonder. The morning his fever had gone he began to size things up. He figured he would need at least fifteen thousand dollars down for the land he wanted (he'd have to sign mortgages for the balance) and no job advertised in the *Star* would bring him in that kind of dough, not in twenty years. He had to make a killing. A real killing. But these things just don't fall into a guy's lap, he thought, and meanwhile it would be wise to bring in as much money as he could whatever way possible. You've got to start operating, he told himself. It's getting late.

But where does a guy start, he thought. Where and how?

He read enviously about the real estate boom in Toronto and of men who had bought land as farms and sold it at twenty to thirty cents a square foot two months later. Other guys had gone prospecting for uranium in Labrador and come back with a mint. Television, he had heard, was the coming thing. Dealers had already made a fortune in the States. Duddy got an appointment with the representative of a big American firm and tried to get an agency, but the man, obviously amused, asked Duddy how much selling experience he had had, what his education was, did he own a car and how much capital was he willing to invest in stock. He told Duddy that he was too young and advised him to try for something smaller. 'You can't run before you learn how to walk,' he said. So Duddy grew a moustache and began to take the *Reader's Digest* and work hard on How To Increase Your Word Power. He also came to an arrangement with his father about the taxi. While Max slept Duddy drove.

Duddy drove at night and during the day he got a job selling liquid soap and toilet supplies to factories. For this work he had to have a car of his own and here Debrofsky helped out. He took

Duddy to his son-in-law's used car lot and got him a '46 Chevvie cheap and on excellent terms. While Debrofsky was bargaining Duddy visited the clothing factory next door and got a medium-sized order for soap and paper towels. He usually slept from four to six and at a quarter to seven he drove down to Wellington College, where he was taking a course in business administration. He joined the cine-club at Wellington and that's where he met Peter John Friar, the distinguished director of documentary films. Mr Friar had come to Wellington to speak on 'Italian Neo-Realism What Next?'. He had a lot to say against Hollywood (it was a soul-killing place, he said) and he seemed to be against something called the witch-hunt, but Duddy wasn't sure. Mr Friar had a difficult British accent and he spoke softly. There was a question period after he was finished and Mr Friar was asked point-blank did he think Houston had gone permanently commercial and what had become of Sir Arthur Elton? Afterwards Duddy pulled him aside. 'I'm going into the film business here myself soon and there's something I'd like to talk over with you,' he said.

Mr Friar checked his smile. Irving Thalberg, he remembered, had been only twenty-two when he took over MGM, and besides the most surprising people had money in Canada. 'Why don't we have a drink together?' he said.

They went to a bar around the corner and Mr Friar immediately ordered a double gin and tonic.

'Your talk was a pleasure,' Duddy said. 'It was very educational.'

'Jolly decent of you to say so.'

Duddy hesitated. The palms of his hands began to sweat. 'I hope you like it here. Montreal,' he said, 'is the world's largest inland seaport.'

Mr Friar lifted his glass and gave Duddy an encouraging smile. 'Cheers.'

Peter John Friar was a small, pear-shaped man with a massive head and a fidgety red face. His greying hair was thin but dishevelled and there were little deposits of dandruff on his coat collar. He seemed especially fond of stroking his greying Van Dyke beard, knitting his fierce eyebrows, and – squinting against the smoke of a cigarette burnt perilously close to his lips – nodding as he said 'Mm. Mm-hmm.' He wore a green tweed suit and a shirt with a stiff collar. Duddy figured him for forty forty-five and something of a lush maybe. He had those kind of jerky hands and the heavily veined nose.

'Have another on me,' Mr Friar said.

'No thanks. But you go right ahead.'

Duddy wanted to ask Mr Friar for advice, but lots of drinks were consumed before he got a chance to say anything. Mr Friar, stammering a little, told him about the documentary he made for an oil company in Venezuela. It had been shown at the Edinburgh Festival and had won a prize in Turkey, but even though he had directed it his name was not actually on the picture for a dark reason he only hinted at. Mr Friar had come to Canada from Mexico to work for the National Film Board, actually, but he was having trouble again because he was a left-winger. An outspoken one. Temporarily, he said, he was at liberty. 'Grierson,' he said, 'is madly determined for me to come to Ottawa, but . . .'

'Jeez,' Duddy said, 'I feel a bit embarrassed now to bother such a BTO with my plans.'

'Dear me. Why?'

'Naw. You wouldn't like it. They're what you called . . . commercial.'

'Let's have another. But this one's on me, old chap.'

Duddy said there was plenty of money around these days. He told him about his idea to make films of weddings and *bar-mitzvahs*.

'A splendid notion.'

But that, Duddy said, would only be a beginning. He wanted to investigate the whole field of industrial films and one day he hoped to make real features. He had under contract, in fact, Canada's leading comedian, and next week he was going to meet a potential big backer. 'Listen,' Duddy said, 'I'm no shnook. I can see you're a very sensitive man. I know you couldn't care less about making films of weddings and *bar-mitzvahs* but if you could help me with advice about equipment and costs I would certainly appreciate it. I'd be willing to show my appreciation too.'

Mr Friar waved his hands in protest. 'Have you any interested clients?' he asked.

'I have two orders in hand,' he said, 'and a long list of weddings and *bar-mitzvahs* that are coming up soon. I spent some time in the hotel business and I know lots of people in Outremont. All I need is to get started.' Duddy leaned back in his chair with his hands resting on his knees.

'I just might be interested. You see,' Mr Friar said, 'it so happens that for years I have been absorbed in folklore and tribal customs in every shape and form. I'm not unfamiliar with Hebraic rituals, you know. Your people have suffered so much. The lore is rich.'

'Wha'?'

'The record of a wedding or *bar-mitzvah* needn't be crassly commercial. We could concentrate on the symbolism inherent to the ceremony.'

'They'd have to be in colour. That would be a big selling point.'

'I say,' Mr Friar said, 'there's one thing I like to warn every producer about before I start on a project. I demand a completely free hand. I will tolerate no interference with my artistic integrity.'

'I don't know a camera lens from a horse's ass, so stop worrying. But look, Mr Friar, I've got a feeling that the important thing about this kind of movie is not the symbolism like, but to get as many relatives and friends into it as humanly poss –'

'That,' Mr Friar said, 'is exactly what I mean,' and he leaped up and started out of the bar.

'Hey, wait a minute,' Duddy shouted, starting after him. The waiter stepped in front of Duddy. '*You* wait a minute, buster.'

The bill came to eight dollars. Duddy paid it and hurried outside.

'Have you ever got a temper. Jeez.'

'In my day, Kravitz, I've thrown more than one bloody producer off a set.'

'No kidding?'

'If I could only learn to be as obsequious as Hitchcock I wouldn't be where I am today.'

Duddy could see that Mr Friar's eyes were red. He took his arm.

'I have no home,' Mr Friar said. 'I'm a vagabond.'

'Listen, I'm starved. Why don't we go in here and grab a smoked meat? My treat.'

'I'm going back to my flat.'

'Where is it? I'll walk you.'

'You are tenacious, Kravitz, aren't you?'

'Aw.'

'I'd really like to be alone now. Sorry, old chap.'

'Aren't you interested in my project any more?'

Mr Friar hesitated. He swayed a little. 'Tell you what, Kravitz. You come to my flat tomorrow at four. We can talk some more then.' He gave Duddy his address and shook hands with him. '*Hasta mañana*,' he said.

'Sure thing.'

Mr Friar lived in an apartment on Stanley Street and Duddy was there promptly at four the next afternoon. He had brought a bottle of Booth's Dry Gin with him. There was no bell on the door and Duddy had to knock again and again.

'*Avante*.'

Mr Friar was in the nude, his fallen belly thick with curly grey hair.

'Hiya!'

Every drawer in the living-room-cum-bedroom was open and dripping underwear or shirtsleeves. One wall was completely covered with bull-fighting posters.

'It's not my flat, actually. It belongs to Gilchrist. He was my fag at Winchester. A proper bastard. Well, Kravitz, sit down.'

Mr Friar freed a couple of glasses from the pile of pots and pans in the sink, wiped the lipstick off one with the corner of his sheet, and poured two drinks. He knocked all the magazines off the coffee table with a scythe-like sweep of a hairy leg and set down a tray of ice-cubes beside the bottle.

'Cheers,' Duddy said quickly.

'*Prosit*.'

But Duddy continued to stare. Mr Friar sighed, retrieved an old *New Yorker* from the floor, and covered his genitals with it.

Duddy began to talk quickly, before Mr Friar could begin on his reminiscences once more. He told him that he had no equipment and not the vaguest notion of the production costs of a *bar-mitzvah* picture. Mr Friar, speaking frankly, could be of invaluable service to him. Duddy explained that he was the one with the connections and it was he who would risk his capital on equipment. 'But you're the guy with the know-how,' he said, and he offered Mr Friar one-third of all the profits. 'We can help each other,' he said. 'And if you don't trust me the books will be open to you any time you like.'

'Your glass is empty.' Mr Friar poured two stiff drinks.

'*Prosit*,' Duddy said quickly.

'Chin-chin.'

Mr Friar told Duddy that he was not interested in money. All he wanted was enough to keep him and a guarantee of non-interference.

'You've got a deal,' Duddy said.

'One moment, please. There's another stipulation. I won't be bound by any contract. I'm a vagabond, Kravitz. I've got the mark of Cain on my forehead. I must be free to get up and go at any time.'

And then Mr Friar became very businesslike. He told Duddy that to begin with they ought to buy their own camera but rent everything else they needed. He said that he knew lots of people at the Film Board in Ottawa and he was sure that they would let him edit and process the film there. That, he said, would be a substantial saving. He told Duddy he'd need five hundred dollars down towards equipment and he asked for an advance of one hundred dollars against personal expenses.

'Agreed.'

'Let me refresh your drink.'

Duddy told Mr Friar that he had his eye on an office in the Empire Building. First thing tomorrow morning he would put down a deposit on it. He would have DUDLEY KANE ENTER-PRISES printed on the glazed glass door and, since the Empire Building was in the Monarch exchange area anyway, he would pay a little, if necessary, to get a phone number that spelt MOVIES and then he could advertise 'Dial MOVIES' in all the newspapers.

'Brilliant.'

Another thing, Duddy added, is that he wanted Mr Friar to give him a write-up on his past work and stuff. He hoped to get a story in the *Star* and maybe a paragraph in Mel West's What's What.

After a few more drinks Duddy could see that Mr Friar's eyes were red again and he began to worry.

'I should have followed my brother into the FO,' Mr Friar

said. 'Winchester and King's did me no good in Hollywood. I couldn't speak Yiddish.'

'Jeez.'

Mr Friar wiped his eyes and poured himself another drink, straight gin this time. 'It's no good, Kravitz. I can't do this to you. You're young. I have no right to ruin what promises to be a brilliant career even before it's begun.'

Duddy looked puzzled.

'I'm afraid I've been concealing something from you, old chap. I'm a communist.'

'So?'

'I believe in the brotherhood of man.'

'Me too,' Duddy said forcefully. 'Do unto your neighbour . . . Aw, you know.'

'I am a card-holder,' Mr Friar said in a booming voice. He stood up and the *New Yorker* dropped to the floor. 'I tell you that here but no committee could drag it out of me with wild horses. Do you realize what that means?' Mr Friar touched Duddy's knee. He lowered his voice. 'I fled the United States one step ahead of the FBI. I'm on the blacklist.'

'No kidding!'

'I *must be*. I've never attempted to conceal my beliefs.'

'So?'

'Don't you see, Kravitz? I will not direct again without a credit. But if you hire me it's likely that you'll never be able to work in Hollywood. Don't hesitate. I'll understand perfectly if you want to call the deal off.'

'We're partners, Mr Friar. Shake.'

Duddy saw Mr Friar daily after that, but the next time he came he only brought a half bottle of gin. On Monday he moved into his office. He took out a subscription to *Variety* and, quickly adapting himself to the idiom of the trade, learned to think of himself as an 'indie'. Duddy waited until the paragraph he wanted had appeared in Mel West's column before he went to see Mr Cohen about his son's *bar-mitzvah*. He had kept putting the visit off because if Mr Cohen was not interested he was in trouble. Mr Friar was anxious to get started. 'You told me you had two orders,' he said.

'Sure. Sure thing.'

If Mr Cohen didn't bite Duddy would be in bad trouble. The

Office cost him a hundred dollars a month and, added to that, there was the price of standard office equipment. He had to give up driving the taxi when Max was off. One night he had just avoided getting Farber for a fare. He could not approach people as a budding businessman by day and take their tips by night. Duddy carried on selling liquid soap and other factory supplies, but that didn't bring in a hell of a lot. He continued to pursue his father about the Boy Wonder, and soothing Mr Friar consumed lots of his time. He kept in close touch with Yvette, too. A week after he had returned to Montreal she sent him a large envelope by registered mail. It was a map of Lac St Pierre with all the bordering fields sub-divided into farms and listing the land owners. Duddy was relieved to find that they were all French-Canadians. Farmers, probably. The largest land owner was a man named Cote, and Brault, the man Yvette had spoken of, owned a good-sized pasture round the bend of the lake. Duddy hid the map under his mattress. Later he transferred it to his office, where he kept it locked in a desk drawer. A week after it had arrived the map was already greasy from too much handling. Sometimes Duddy would wake at two in the morning, drive down to his office, and study the map until he could no longer keep his eyes open.

Yvette had sent a letter with the map. A notary she trusted had estimated that the land had a market value of four to five hundred dollars an arpent and if Duddy wanted all of it and could pay the price he needed twenty thousand dollars cash. He would have to assume mortgages for the balance – probably another thirty thousand dollars. He could pay these mortgages off over the next five to ten years, at five per cent interest, if he were lucky. But the notary also said that the land was good for nothing better than a pasture. If somebody was foolhardy enough to want to invest in a development of summer cottages there then he'd better count on buttering up more than one member of the town council to get them to bring in electricity and sewers. The half-owner of one large farm was in an insane asylum. Her brother couldn't sell until she died. Two other farms were owned by a fierce nationalist who would sell to nobody but another French-Canadian. Yvette also wrote that the notary said it would cost thousands of dollars to build on the land. In a postscript she added that Duddy, in any event, was still a minor and that made for other difficulties. It's true that he could legally own land. But a minor couldn't enter into most contracts without being assisted by his tutor, unless the purchase and sale of land was his business. So it would be best to have somebody act for him. His father, perhaps.

Two days later another large envelope came. Maybe Yvette felt she had been too discouraging. Anyway, this one contained sixteen photographs of the lake that Yvette had taken herself. Duddy drove up to Ste Agathe that Friday night and took Yvette to a bar where they would not be seen. 'I think I'm going to be fired,' she said. 'Linda's taken a dislike to me. She finds fault with everything I do.'

Duddy tried to change the subject, but Yvette persisted. 'She asked me a lot of questions about us one afternoon. I pretended not to understand what she was talking about and that made her angry.'

'About us?'

'She likes you. You needn't look so pleased.'

'Who gives a damn?' Duddy told Yvette about Mr Friar. He said that he wanted her to quit the hotel anyway, and learn to type and take shorthand because any day now he was going to need her in Montreal. He had to have somebody he could trust in the office. He had thought that would please Yvette and he could not understand why it only made her angrier.

'What makes you think I want to go to Montreal to work for you?'

'Why not?' he said. 'Jeez,' and he made a mental note to bring her a gift next time he drove out.

'You're too sure of yourself,' Yvette said.

'Aw.'

A day before Duddy was supposed to see Mr Cohen about the *bar-mitzvah* picture Yvette phoned. She called early in the morning and he was startled when she told him that she was actually waiting for him in a drugstore around the corner. Duddy hurried down there.

'Brault wants to sell right away.'

'Wha'?'

She told him that Brault's wife had died and he was going to move to Nova Scotia to live with his son. He wanted to sell out for cash and just as quickly as possible. Yvette had gone out with the notary and offered him four hundred and fifty dollars an arpent; half cash. That came to thirty-two hundred dollars down; he had accepted, and Yvette had put down a deposit of two hundred and fifty dollars. 'If you can give me a cheque for the rest,' she said, 'I can be back in Ste Agathe before the banks close.'

Duddy began to bite his nails.

'What's wrong? I thought you'd be pleased. Look,' she said, 'there were two other people interested. I had to act quickly. Maybe we could have got it for less, but – '

'No. The price is O.K.'

'The land will have to go on my name. You're still a minor. Is that what's bothering you?'

'How long have we got to pay the balance?'

'Three weeks. Haven't you got the money, Duddy? You told me you had nearly three thousand dollars in the bank. You mustn't lie to me.'

He told her what the camera and other equipment had cost and that he had rented an office. He had six hundred dollars left in the bank, maybe less. He would need money for film too.

'Sell the car,' she said.

Duddy laughed. 'The car isn't even paid for. Look, don't worry. We've got three weeks and I'll raise the rest of the money even if I have to kill somebody for it.'

But Duddy was obviously worried himself. He drove her back to Ste Agathe and all the way there he hardly spoke.

'Stay the night with me,' she said.

'I can't, I have to see that bastard Cohen at nine tomorrow morning.'

'You don't have to make excuses.'

'Oh, for Christ's sake.'

Duddy couldn't sleep. He smoked one cigarette after another. Lennie hadn't come home again, he had told Max he was spending the night at a friend's house. Duddy knew better, but he didn't care. All he could think of was that if he was Lennie and needed three thousand dollars he'd only have to say pretty please Uncle Benjy. Son-of-a-bitch, Duddy thought. If he was Lennie he'd probably even be able to get the money from the old man. But for him there was not a hope. Max would say he was too young and too dumb to buy land. He wasn't even proud that Duddy had an office. 'Go ahead,' he had said. 'Throw your money away. It'll teach you a good lesson.' His grandfather might have that much money. He'd lend it to him too. But Duddy had promised him a farm and he wasn't going to go crawling to Simcha for the money to buy it with no matter what.

Duddy didn't fall asleep until shortly after seven and he was late for his appointment with Mr Cohen.

'Sure. That's right, Duddy. My Bernie's going to be *bar-mitzvah* in three weeks' time. I'm sorry I couldn't ask you to the dinner, but ... well, you know. At second cousins we put a stop to it. Listen, come to the ceremony anyway and have a schnapps.'

Duddy showed him the write-up in the *Star* and the paragraph from Mel West's column. He told him that when Farber's daughter got married he was making a movie of it. He went on and on hopefully about Mr Friar, and how lucky he was to have such a talented director. 'All my productions will be in colour. A lasting record like,' he said. 'For your grandchildren and their grandchildren after them.'

'It's O.K. for Farber. His girl's marrying into the Gordons. They can afford it.'

'You say that without even asking me a price. I'll bet you think it would cost you something like three thousand dollars for the movie.'

'What? Are you crazy? Do you know how much it's costing me just for the catering?'

'You see. But it wouldn't cost that much. I can make you a top-notch movie for two thousand dollars.'

'The boy's mad.'

'But on one condition only. You mustn't say a word to Farber about the price we made. It's a special.'

'Look, when I want to see a movie I can go to the Loew's for ninety cents. My Bernie's a fine kid, but he's no Gary Cooper. I'm sorry, Duddy.'

'Alright. No hard feelings. I just felt that since Bernie is such a good friend of the Seigal boy and I'm doing that *bar-mitzvah* in December – '

'That cheapskate Seigal is paying you two thousand dollars for a movie?'

'He should live so long I'd make him such a price. Well, I'd better go. I've got another appointment at eleven.'

'Alright, smart guy. Sit down. Come on. Sit down. You're trembling like a leaf anyway. There, that's better. I oughta slap your face.'

'Wha'?'

'I happen to know that you're not making a movie for Seigal. O.K.?'

'Are you calling me a liar?' Duddy demanded in his boldest voice.

'Sit down. Stop jumping around. Boy, some kid you are. Now, for a starter, how do I even know that a kid who's still wet . . . wet? . . . *soaking* behind the ears can make a movie?'

'Mr Friar is a very experienced director.'

'Sure. He's Louis B. Mayer himself. Duddy, Duddy, what's he doing here making *bar-mitzvah* pictures with . . . with a boy?'

Duddy flushed.

'Have you got lots of money invested?'

'Enough.'

'Oi.'

'It's going to work. It's a great idea.'

Mr Cohen sent out for coffee. 'O.K., Duddy, we'll see. I want you to tell me straight how much it would cost you to make a colour movie of the *bar-mitzvah*.'

Duddy asked for a pencil and paper. 'About nine hundred to a thousand,' he said at last.

'Lies. You lie through your ears, Duddy. O.K., your costs are six hundred dollars let's say.'

'But – '

'Shettup! I'd like to see you get a start and I'll make you a deal. You go ahead and make me a film of Bernie's *bar-mitzvah*. If I like it I'll give you a thousand dollars for it. If not you can go and burn it.'

Duddy took a deep breath.

'Before you answer remember I should have thrown you out of the office for lying to me. Think too of the prestige you'd get. The first production for Cohen. I could bring you in a lot of trade. But it's a gamble, Duddy. I'm a harsh critic. There are many academy award winners I didn't like and if I don't care for the picture . . .'

'I can make you a black-and-white for twelve hundred dollars.'

'Get out of here.'

'Look, Mr Cohen, this is a real production. I have to pay for the editing and the script and – '

'All right. Twelve hundred. But colour, Duddy. And only if I like it. Come here. We'll shake on it. What a liar you are. Wow!' Mr Cohen pinched his cheek. 'If you're going to see Seigal now about his boy's *bar-mitzvah* you have my permission to say you're making one for me. Tell him I'm paying you two thousand. He can phone me if he wants. But listen Duddy, he's not like me. Don't trust him. Get five hundred down and the rest in writing. Such a liar. Wow!'

Duddy drove for fifteen minutes before he figured out that he had no advance and nothing in writing from Mr Cohen. The film would cost him at least five hundred dollars – more, when you consider the work and time it would take – and there was no guarantee of a return on his investment. That lousy bastard, Duddy thought, and he makes it sound like he was doing me a favour. He went to see Seigal at home and his wife talked him into letting Duddy make the picture. Seigal paid an advance of two hundred and fifty dollars and signed an agreement to pay fifteen hundred in all if he liked the film and another six hundred even if he didn't want it. It was a mistake to see Cohen at the office, Duddy thought afterwards. You've got to get them at home with the wife and boy there.

He phoned Yvette and told her he was sending her a cheque for three hundred dollars in the morning. He said he was making the movie for Mr Cohen, but he didn't tell her that if Mr Cohen didn't like it there was no deal. He was so happy about Seigal, too, that he didn't realize until he got home that the Seigal *bar-mitzvah* was six weeks off and even if he got paid right away it would be too late. He still had to raise twenty-five hundred dollars to pay Brault and twenty days was all the time he had. In the next three days Duddy visited eight potential clients. They were interested. Nobody showed him the door exactly, but first they wanted to see one of his productions.

'You can't blame them,' Duddy told Mr Friar. 'We'll have to rent a screening room or something for the Cohen picture. I want to send out lots of tickets.'

'When's the *bar-mitzvah*?' Mr Friar asked.

'Two weeks from Saturday,' Duddy said, rubbing his face with his hands.

'I'd like to start looking at some of the locations tomorrow.'

'Wha'?'

'Can you take me to the synagogue?'

'Yeah, sure.'

'I say, old chap, you do look down in the mouth. Haven't you been eating?'

'Sure. Sure I have.' Jeez, he thought, even if Cohen likes the picture that money will be too late too.

'We've got to hit them with something unusual right in the first frame. Have you ever seen Franju's *Sang des Bêtes*?'

'I don't think so.'

'It was a documentary, old chap. A great one. We could do worse than to use it for our model.'

'It's got to be good, Mr Friar. Better than good, or I'm dead.'

Mr Friar could see that Duddy was depressed. He gave him his most genial smile. 'Come on, old chap, I'm going to take you out for a drink. But this time it's definitely on me.' In the bar Mr Friar tried to amuse him with scandalous stories about celebrities, but Duddy didn't even smile once.

'I want you to think about that picture, Mr Friar. I want you to think about it night and day. It's got to be great.'

Mr Friar assured him that he kept a notebook by his bed and marked down all his creative ideas, even if he had to get up at three a.m. to do it. 'I'm thinking of the part when the boy is up there reading his chapter from the Torah. I see a slow dissolve into the boy's racial memory. We could begin with the pain of the baby's circumcision and – '

Duddy jerked awake. 'Hey, you can't show a kid's pecker in this picture. There are going to be women and children there.'

'Remember,' Mr Friar said severely. 'No artistic interference.'

'Right now I can see myself waiting on tables again.'

'Let's have another,' Mr Friar said.

They had one more and then Duddy called for the waiter and paid the bill. Outside, Mr Friar was not as loquacious as usual. He seemed self-absorbed.

'Thanks a lot for the drinks, Mr Friar.'

'Don't mention it. *À demain.*'

Chapter Three

Duddy was exhausted. I'll sleep in tomorrow morning, he thought. I need the rest. But he woke with a scream at three a.m. from a dream that was to become a recurrent nightmare. Bulldozers, somebody else's surveyors, carpenters and plumbers roared and hammered and shouted over the land round Lac St Pierre. Irwin Shubert held an enormous plan in his hands. He smiled thinly.

'Waaa . . .'

Somebody shook him. 'Duddy, wake up! Duddy! It's me. Lennie.'

Max rushed into the room. 'What's going on here?'

'It's Duddy. He had a nightmare.'

'You O.K.? You want a coke or something? Tea?'

'Listen, Duddy. Listen closely. I want you to try to remember everything about your dream.' Lennie grabbed a pencil and paper. 'Anything that comes into your head you tell me. I'll analyse it for you.'

'Jeez.'

'Go ahead. Tell him.'

'I dreamt I was screwing this broad,' Duddy said.

'That's my boy.'

'Were there any doors? Did you have to go through passages to get to her? What made you – '

'There was a bed like. Her cans were something out of this world . . .'

'Oh, for Christ's sake,' Lennie said, putting his pencil and paper away.

'What'sa matter?' Max asked. 'Aren't you interested in that kind of dream? Go ahead. Duddy. I'm listening.'

'Are you making tea?'

They couldn't get to sleep again. Max and Lennie sat at the

kitchen table and Duddy made one of his huge and intricate omelettes.

'I don't get it,' Max said, getting out his back-scratcher. 'If you were in bed with this broad why did you scream?'

'She bit my toe.'

'Even if you didn't dream that,' Lennie said. 'It's a very significant remark.'

'Hey,' Max said, 'what did you put in this omelette?'

'It's great,' Lennie said. 'Duddy makes the best omelette this side of the Rio Grande.'

Lennie said that yesterday in the operating theatre he had seen a baby delivered for the first time. He described it for them and said that three students had fainted. Max made both his boys laugh with his story of the drunken American who had got into his taxi and asked to be taken to where the king lived. He wanted to see the palace. 'Can you beat that?' Max asked.

Duddy's imitation of Mr Friar brought tears to Lennie's eyes.

'You know what,' Max said, thumping the table. 'I'm taking Sunday off. We're going out for a drive and a first-class feed. The three of us.'

'Atta boy.'

'I'm sorry,' Lennie said, 'but I've got a date.'

'Can't you break it?'

'Not a chance.'

'Well,' Max said, 'maybe next Sunday. We don't see enough of each other. I'm your father. You're supposed to come to me with your problems.'

Lennie frowned. 'I'd better turn in,' he said. 'I've got an early class tomorrow.'

'You go to bed too, Duddy. I'm going to sit up for a bit.'

'I'll sit with you; 'night, Lennie.' Duddy made more tea.

'Do you know anything about Lennie that I should know?'

'No. Why?'

'There's something funny going on.'

'Aw. It's your imagination.' Duddy started to tell him about his adventures as an 'indie', but Max wasn't interested. 'Daddy, have you ever thought of getting married again?'

'*What?*'

'Jeez. Don't get angry. I thought maybe you were lonely like.'

'Nobody could ever replace your mother for me,' Max said

sternly. 'You're a funny kid. I can't figure you. Out of left-field you come running with the craziest questions.'

'I don't remember her very well. I was only six when she . . .'

'You missed out on plenty, brother. Plenty. Minnie was some wife.'

There was a picture in the living-room of Max and Minnie on their wedding day. He wore a top hat and her face was in the shadow of a white veil. But her smile was tender, forgiving. It looked to Duddy as if she had probably used to laugh a lot. He could remember her laugh, come to think of it. Something rolling, turning over dark and deep and endless, and with it hugs and gooey kisses and a whiff of onions. He remembered too that Max had held him pinned down to the bed once, saying over and over again, 'Easy, kid, easy,' while Minnie had applied argyrol drops to his nose. Once more Duddy was tempted to ask his father if Minnie had liked him, but he couldn't bring himself to risk it.

'Omelettes weren't coming out of our ears in those days,' Max said. 'I used to come home after work and for a starter there'd usually be chopped liver and what gefilte fish she made! Ask Debrofsky. Ask your Uncle Benjy even. He was crazy about Minnie. You'd be surprised how often he used to come here in the old days. We used to sit around the dining-room table after dinner on a Friday night cracking nuts and waiting for the eleven o'clock news. Your mother used to keep up with all the radio programmes. On Monday night we'd sit together in the living-room, me with my books on electrical studies and Minnie making cookies with one ear open in case you should start bawling your head off, and together we'd listen to the Lux Radio Theatre. That's still an excellent programme, but without Minnie . . . We used to play parcheesi a lot, too, and Chinese checkers, and if I had the boys round for a poker game they loved it. Minnie would make us *latkas* or open up some herring she'd pickled herself and the boys were so happy that when she came round to collect for a raffle for the new synagogue or something nobody ever made a smart remark. The boys,' he said, his voice filled with marvel, 'would even buy up a whole book just because it was Minnie, and a dollar was a dollar in those days.

'Montreal wasn't what it is now, you know. For kids these days everything's a breeze. I remember when the snow in winter

T – D.K. – E

was often piled higher than a man on the streets. There was a time back there when they had horses to pull the streetcars. (That's why even today they say horse-power and measure an engine's strength by it.) Hell, they tell me that new rabbi in Outremont, Goldstone I think his name is, runs a sort of marriage clinic where he gives sex talks. In my day all you had to do was mention the word sex to a rabbi and you'd get a clap on the ear that would last you a week. Look at you,' he said, his anger rising, 'eighteen years old and driving a car of your own already. My father never even bought me a bicycle. O.K., I didn't pay for your car, but I could have you know.' Max paused, searching Duddy's face for scepticism. But Duddy merely grinned. 'Boy, if I got into half as much trouble at school as you did the zeyda would have taken off his belt to me. Aw, kids these days. Softies.' Max replaced his back scratcher in the kitchen drawer and got up and yawned. 'Why don't we turn in?'

'Tell me more about Maw.'

'Some other night.'

'O.K., I'll just do the dishes and then – '

'The noise'd wake Lennie. They'll keep. C'mon to bed. Hey,' Max said, 'I almost forgot. The Boy Wonder will see you at eleven-thirty tomorrow.'

'Jeez. No kidding?'

'A promise is a promise.'

Duddy embraced Max. He punched him softly on the shoulder.

'Just be punctual,' Max said, 'and don't make trouble,' and he started for his bedroom.

'One minute. That means I'm ready doesn't it, Daddy? That means you think I'm like O.K. now.'

'Don't make trouble. That's all I ask. This is a special favour the Wonder is doing me.'

'I won't make trouble, Daddy. You'll be proud.'

Chapter Four

Jerry Dingleman, known to many as the Boy Wonder since Mel West had done a complete column on him, was a man with many offices. His most impressive office was on the top floor of his gambling establishment on the other side of the river, but on Wednesday mornings he did business in a poky little office off the Tico-Tico dance floor. The Boy Wonder was only a St Urbain Street boy to begin with, he remembered well his own early hardships, and he liked to lend a helping hand. Time was precious, however, and so he limited his consideration of favours to Wednesdays. Wednesday was known to his inner circle as Schnorrer's Day and from ten to four the supplicants came and went. Third cousins once removed and just off the train from Winnipeg came. Chorines too old even for the streets tried him, and crackpot inventors who claimed to have been at FFHS with him came at least once a month. Cops who wanted to borrow against the pay-off and side-men too far hooked to ever play again were among the Schnorrer's Day regulars. The collector from the Liberal Party and aged lushes with lice crawling over their faces sat in the same stiff-backed chair opposite the Wonder's maplewood desk. When the Jewish General Hospital went out on a building campaign it sent a representative too.

The Boy Wonder was a God-fearing man and he didn't smoke or drive his car or place bets on the Sabbath. His father had spent ten years in prison and his Uncle Joe had been shot down on the street during the bad days, but Jerry Dingleman had never been involved even indirectly in any bloodshed or spent a day behind bars. Not before the time of his personal trouble, anyway.

His legs were twisted and useless. At the age of twenty-eight the Boy Wonder had been struck by polio and when he got out of bed many months later he could only walk with the help of crutches. He never once spoke about his illness but there were lots of stories about it. Mel West had printed the one about the insurance policy. The Wonder, it seems, had carried a polio policy worth fifty thousand dollars and, according to West, when the doctors told him he would never walk again the Wonder had replied with a tough smile, 'Yeah, but I beat Lloyd's. I never lose a bet.' This led West to compare Dingleman with FDR and the Boy Wonder barred him from his clubs for two years.

The story nobody ever mentioned to his face had to do with the girl. There were many versions. But about several facts there could be no question. Before his illness Jerry Dingleman had been engaged to Olive Brucker and two weeks afterwards she had sailed for Europe alone. There was some dispute about who had broken the engagement, but there was no argument over whether or not the two young people had been in love.

'You must never repeat this. Not a word of it,' was how Max always began the Wonder-Olive story, 'but you should have seen the Wonder in those days. Handsome? *Handsome*. He had a smile that melted the rubber bands in the girls' panties left, right, and centre. For good looks he could have wiped the floor with Clark Gable or any other star. You take your pick. And Olive? A knockout! If old man Brucker wasn't so stinking with cash, if it wasn't that she needed money like I need a headache, she could have raked in plenty as a model. When she walked down St Catherine Street it was enough to stop the traffic ... Only the Wonder was always by her side and the guys stepped on the gas quick again, let me tell you. They were inseparable. Not only that but they looked so right together that complete strangers would take one look and smile, they felt so good inside.

'That son-of-a-bitch Brucker should only live long enough to choke to death on razor-blades. They say it was the Wonder who called it off because he didn't want her stuck with a cripple. But that's a dirty lie. The old scum-bag, may his stocks fall through the bottom of a graph tomorrow and his balls float in sulphuric acid the day after, he was the one. He packed her off to Europe before she could say Jack Robinson.'

Some other facts were beyond dispute too. Polio wrought immense physical changes in Jerry Dingleman. At thirty he was no longer a handsome man. His shoulders and chest developed enormously and his legs dwindled to thin bony sticks. He put on lots of weight. Everywhere he went the Boy Wonder huffed and puffed and had to wipe the sweat from the back of his rolled hairy neck with a handkerchief. The bony head suddenly seemed massive. The grey inquisitor's eyes, whether hidden behind dark glasses – an affectation he abhorred – or flashing under rimless ones, unfailingly led people to look over his shoulder or down at the floor. His curly black hair had dried. The mouth began to turn down sharply at the corners. But the most noticeable and unexplained change was in the flesh of his face. After his illness it turned red and wet and shiny. His teeth, however, remained as white as ever and his smile was still unnervingly fresh.

The smile that somehow retained an aura of innocence made those who feared or disliked the Boy Wonder resent him all the more. A man, they said, after a certain age, is responsible for his face, and following that they always brought up in a whisper the riddle of the Wonder's sex life since his personal trouble. He was still capable. But some insisted he was now indefatigable and others said that he had picked up some dirty specialties. There was the question of the girls in and out of his apartment three-four at a time, a rumour of incredible films imported from Europe, books of photographs, and amazing statues. Nobody really knew. It was intriguing, that's all.

But people did know what had happened to Olive – and it was a dirty shame. She had gone through three husbands, two she had divorced and one had committed suicide. All of them had been handsome and, they said, had looked a lot like the Wonder before his personal trouble. Olive darted to and fro between Montreal, New York, Paris, and the Riviera. She usually looked potted and there were some who said you don't get like that on booze: it was something else. Olive never stayed in Montreal for more than three weeks at a time, but each visit spawned a multitude of scandalous stories. Murray Gold swore that he had seen her come running out of the Wonder's apartment building one wintry night with a bloody nose and no shoes. She was not allowed into the gambling house on the other side of the river or any of his restaurants or night spots. Olive, they said, had a head-shrinker in New York that cost fifty bucks a crack. The same people said that although he wouldn't see her in Montreal the Wonder visited her in New York. It was Dingleman, they said, who got her out of Bellevue that time.

But little was known for certain about the Boy Wonder's activities. Only a favoured few, not counting the girls, ever actually got inside his apartment, and even on Schnorrer's Day his visitors had to pass Mickey 'The Mauler' Shub before they were allowed inside the poky little office.

Shub, another FFHS graduate, had in his prime been rated number one challenger for the welterweight crown in *Ring* magazine. He had fought lots of bouts in Madison Square Garden in the days before television when a fight there drew maybe twenty thousand fans. People in the know said that had he been handled right, if he hadn't got mixed up with gamblers, Shub could have been World Champion. He had the stuff. He also fought too long, and his two comeback attempts were disastrous. The last time out Ike Williams had knocked him silly in three rounds. So naturally Shub came to see Jerry Dingleman. He said he wanted to cash in while he still had a name and open up a fancy tailor shop right in the downtown area. His father and his younger brother would do the cutting for him. The Boy Wonder backed him, but the tailor shop developed into more of a hangout than a business. Shub's father, for instance, seldom got a chance to use the cutting table because it was generally in use for poker. The occasions when it was free he just had enough time to scrub it clean of smoked meat fat and pickle juice before another game got started or some friend in a hurry came in with a girl and the old man was sent on a long message. After the tailor shop failed Dingleman hired Shub to be his chauffeur and all-round personal assistant.

Shub was a pale, shuffle-shouldered man with little puzzled eyes and a huge spread of shapeless nose. From time to time he was fuzzy in the head and had to stay home. When Shub wasn't looking there were some guys who liked to suddenly bang a fist on the table. This unfailingly made Shub leap to his feet, assuming his famous stance, and the guys would look at each other and laugh. Bang, bang, bang, the fist would come crashing down again. Then while they still had him on the go, some guy was sure to shout in his ear, 'Ike Williams.'

'Yeah, how long did you last against Williams?'

'. . . fifteen rounds . . .'

'*Three*, you bastard, *three*.'

But nobody ever got funny with him when the Boy Wonder was around and there were times when Shub got his own back too. 'On Schnorrer's Day,' Murray Gold once said, 'Dingleman sits like God in that office and this one, a regular St Peter, stands outside with the keys.' When one of his tormentors showed up for a loan Shub always kept him waiting.

Shub, however, had no grudge against Duddy and he did not keep him waiting. 'What's your name, kid?'

'Kravitz.'

Duddy sat down beside an embarrassed man with a brief case on his lap and watched as Shub slipped inside the office.

'The Kravitz boy is here,' Shub said.

'Who?'

'Don't you remember, Mr Dingleman? The taxi driver's kid. He was here to ask you about him a few days ago.'

'Oh, I remember. Listen, take him to see Charlie. Say I said he should start him as a bus-boy and see how he does. Will you send Kennedy in, please?'

Shub told Mr Kennedy to step inside and turned to Duddy. 'You've made it, kid. We're going to take you on as a bus-boy right here at the Tico-Tico. Isn't that something?'

'There must be some mistake. Did you tell him it was Kravitz? Duddy Kravitz.'

'Look, you've got to start somewhere. If you're O.K. Charlie'll be giving you some tables of your own in no time. C'mon.'

'Isn't Mr Dingleman even going to see me?'

'He's a very busy man, you know.'

'But I'm no waiter. Didn't you tell him that I was Max Kravitz's boy?'

'Sure I did. Let's go, kid. Come on.'

Duddy turned pale. 'I'm not moving,' he said. 'I'm staying right here until he comes out.'

The office door opened and Mr Kennedy stepped out. He looked shaken. 'By this afternoon,' Dingleman shouted after him.

'I'll try my best, Jerry. That's all I can do.'

Duddy slipped past Shub into the office. 'I'm Max's boy,' he began. 'Duddy Kravitz. There must be some mistake. I – '

'What's this?'

Shub grabbed Duddy quickly from behind. 'I'm sorry, Mr Dingleman.'

'I'm no shnook,' Duddy shouted. 'I don't need your help to become a lousy waiter.'

'Let him go.'

Duddy rubbed his shoulder where Shub had held him.

'Are you in the habit of barging into other people's offices, sonny?'

'My father said we had an appointment.' Duddy whipped out his newspaper clippings. 'I'd like you to look at these, please, sir.'

Dingleman grimaced.

'We can help each other,' Duddy said.

He laughed. 'Another time, sonny.'

The phone rang. 'Get it, Mickey. If it's New York I'm here.'

'Won't you even look at them? One's from Mel West's column.'

'Are you still here?'

'It's New York, Mr Dingleman.'

Dingleman wiped his face with a handkerchief and held the receiver to his breast. 'I'll see you next Wednesday, sonny.'

'Oh, sonny yourself you big fat lump of – '

Shub gripped Duddy's collar with one hand and the seat of his pants with the other and lifted him out of the office.

'He's still got my clippings,' Duddy said.

'Are you looking for real trouble?'

Duddy picked up his coat and ran to the door. 'Tell him he can go and kiss my ass,' he shouted on the run.

Shub started after him.

'Mickey! MICKEY!'

'I'm coming. I'm here.'

Dingleman wiped his neck and spat into his handkerchief. 'Where's that boy gone to?'

'He beat it.'

'Get the car. I want to see him right away. Wait. Tell Shirley to book two sleepers on tonight's train to New York. Tell her to phone Kennedy's office and remind him that I said *this* afternoon.'

Chapter Five

Duddy had to wait a half hour before Max turned up at Eddy's, but he was no calmer when his father entered the store with a smile.

'Hi, Duddy. How'd you make out?'

'You lousy liar. Afraid I'd embarrass *you*, were you?'

The other taxi drivers began to file out. Only Walsh stayed. He had three free games coming to him on the pinball machine.

'An intimate of the Boy Wonder? Hah! He doesn't know you from a hole in the ground.'

'Duddy, please. Not here. The other guys – '

'All those stories. Ever since I was a kid. How could you let me build on it when I need a stake so badly right now?'

'Easy. Easy, kid.'

'Couldn't you have told me the truth? Do you think I would have cared? It's the time wasted and the hopes. It's – how could you do this to me?'

'Do what? You talk so fast I can't keep up with you, You asked me to get an appointment and you got one. Right? *Right.* You think any *shnunk* can walk in off the street and see the Wonder just like that?'

'Oh, no. No sir. Not just like that. You said some dirty things to me.'

'Yeah,' Duddy said in a small voice.

'Take them back.'

'I take them back.'

'There. Isn't that better than yelling at the old man?'

But Duddy stiffened when Max tried to ruffle his hair. 'I'm a big boy now,' he said.

'O.K. Sure.'

A car stopped outside and Shub opened the door for Jerry

Dingleman. 'Max Kravitz,' Dingleman said, smiling his freshest smile, 'how are you?'

'Mr Dingleman!' Max grinned broadly and gave Duddy a poke. 'Hey, Eddy, Eddy quick! Would you like a drink?'

'No thanks. Hullo Duddy.'

'A sandwich maybe?'

'I'm on a diet.'

'A coffee?'

'Stop begging him.'

'You shettup. I'm your father and you shettup. Mr Dingleman and I are old pals. Isn't that right?'

Dingleman nodded. 'Here,' he said, handing Duddy his clippings. 'That's an intriguing idea you have there. I'd like to talk to you about it.'

'You don't say?'

'Be polite,' Max said, gritting his teeth. 'Talk nice.'

'I have to go to New York tonight. We can talk on the train.'

'Wha'?'

'You heard what the man said.'

'We'll only be gone three days. I'll handle your fare and expenses and something more. Mr Shub can't come with me. Can you drive a car?'

'Sure he can, Mr Dingleman.'

'I don't get it.'

Max stepped in front of Duddy. 'What time do you want him at the station, Mr Dingleman?'

'Ten.'

'He'll be there.'

'One minute.' That would mean leaving Mr Friar on his own for a few days. He could do plenty of damage.

'He'll be there with bells on,' Max said.

Dingleman left and the other taxi drivers hurried back into the store.

'No questions,' Max said, making a sweeping gesture with his arm. 'I'm not free to talk.'

Debrofsky ordered a lean on rye.

'Jerry's taking Duddy to New York tonight. More I can't say.'

Shub missed two traffic lights running.

'What's wrong, Mickey?'

'Nuttin'.'

But Shub was concerned. It was true that Mr Dingleman's hunches had always worked out right before, but –

'Don't worry,' Dingleman said. 'The boy is innocent. He's perfect.'

Dingleman didn't turn up at Central Station until a minute before departure time. He smiled absently at Duddy and led him into the club car. 'Here,' he said, handing him a one hundred dollar bill. 'Order anything you want. I'm going to sleep. We can talk tomorrow.' But the next morning at breakfast in the hotel Dingleman did not say a word to Duddy. He read the market reports in the *Times*.

'It's nice here,' Duddy said. 'I've never been to New York before like.'

Dingleman lowered his newspaper. 'I'm going to be tied up all day,' he said. 'Why don't you see the sights?'

'Didn't you want me to drive you around or something?'

'Not today.'

Duddy bit his lip. 'What do you want me here for?' he asked.

'Meet me in the lobby at seven-thirty. We're going to a play together tonight. Afterwards I'd like to talk to you about your film company. It sounds fascinating.'

Duddy went to see the Rockettes at Radio City Music Hall. He visited the planetarium, he sent postcards to his father, Lennie, and Yvette, and he wandered up and down Broadway until his legs ached. He got to Lindy's on time but Dingleman was more than three-quarters of an hour late. 'Did you enjoy yourself today?' he asked.

'Yes. Thank you.'

'Good.'

There were some new books lying on the taxi seat beside Dingleman. One was by somebody called Waugh and two others, Duddy observed gleefully, were in French with plain covers.

'Have you ever read *God's Little Acre*?' Duddy asked.

Dingleman laughed. He squeezed Duddy's knee. 'Here we are,' he said, 'I hope you'll like the play. It was very difficult for me to get tickets.'

There were no movie stars in it. Some bit players. Duddy recognized Lee J. Cobb from the movie with William Holden about the boxer and the violin. He thought he had seen the

Kennedy guy before too, but he couldn't remember in what movie. The play went on and on with people shouting and using dirty language. The jokes were from hunger and there was only one sexy scene, but the broad in it was old and not much to look at. A big deal, he thought.

'Did you like it?'

'It had a lot to say about life,' Duddy said.

At supper Duddy began to talk uneasily about his film company and gathering courage with the wine he gave away more than he had intended. Dingleman asked him more and more questions, and at first Duddy took this for genuine interest, but each reply made him laugh harder and when Duddy told him about Mr Friar Dingleman slapped the table again and again and said, 'That's too much. Too much.'

'What I'm really looking for is a silent partner. An investor.'

'I'm sure you'll find one. Let's get out of here. We're invited to a party.'

The party started off to be a bore for Duddy. There was lots to drink, it's true, the view of the river from the window was A-1, and three or four of the broads there he wouldn't have tossed out of bed on a cold night, but for a long time nobody spoke to him. He could have been a piece of wood for all they seemed to care. Two o'clock came, it was soon after three, and nobody even bothered to turn the lights out. New guests were still arriving, in fact. Then, all at once, Dingleman summoned Duddy to his crowded corner and he became the centre of attention. 'Tell them what you thought of the play,' Dingleman said.

He did.

'Isn't he the end?' a girl said.

She was, Duddy noticed, as flat as a board. The jerk with her was introduced to him as a painter and Duddy, winking at Dingleman, asked, 'Inside or outside?'

Dingleman explained that Duddy was a movie producer. A vital new Canadian talent. 'Tell them about Mr Friar,' he said.

Duddy's imitation of Mr Friar went over bigger than anything Cuckoo Kaplan had ever done. Dingleman laughed so hard he had to keep wiping his neck.

'Jerry,' a woman said, approaching timidly. 'Don't be angry. They told me you'd be here, Jerry.'

Dingleman's smile shut like a purse. 'Get me my coat, Duddy.'

'Jerry. I've got to have some. Please.'

An embarrassed man tried to lead the woman away but she wouldn't be pushed. 'Jerry,' she said. 'I'll go crazy. Please, Jerry.'

'You're a tramp,' he said so that nobody else could hear. And puffing, his face red and shiny, he started for the door where Duddy waited with his coat. From behind he heard her empty, foolish laughter. 'It's like a scissors,' he heard her tell somebody. 'When he walks on those four legs it's just like a scissors.'

Duddy hailed a taxi.

'We're not going to the hotel,' Dingleman said. 'Tell him to take us to Harry's on Seventh Avenue.'

Dingleman consumed one cup of coffee after another.

'Shouldn't we get back to the hotel? Aren't you sleepy?'

'Why are you so crazy to make money?'

Duddy was startled. He stiffened. 'I want to get me some land,' he said. 'A man without land is nobody.'

Dingleman grasped that the boy was repeating somebody else's platitude, and he laughed in his face.

'I wish you'd stop laughing at me. I'm not that stupid. And while we're at it why did you lug me all the way down to New York? For a joke?'

'I know your uncle. Benjamin Kravitz. He's a childish man. I don't like him.'

'Maybe he doesn't like you either.'

'Maybe. But you like me.'

'What makes you so sure?'

'There's something wrong. A mistake somewhere when a boy your age is already pursuing money like he had a hot poker up his ass.'

'Look, do I stick my nose into your business?'

'Come. Let's go for a walk.'

'Wha'?'

'I can walk further than most men. Don't worry. Come on.'

He could not only walk further but he walked faster. Duddy was half-asleep. He yawned again and again. 'How's about a little rest?' he asked.

'This bench here?'

Duddy slumped on the bench, holding his head in his hands. 'Couldn't we go back to the hotel now?'

'Quiet.'

When Duddy looked up again he caught Dingleman unawares. Something had happened to him. His neck had contracted. The massive head had rolled uselessly to one side and the piercing eyes were shut. I don't have to stay here with him, Duddy thought. There's no law that says I can't go back to the hotel.

'Sit down.'

'I wasn't going anywhere,' Duddy said.

'Come. We're going to sleep.'

But in the taxi Dingleman had some instructions for Duddy. 'Remember that woman at the party? I want you to go into the lobby and see if she's there.'

She wasn't there. Duddy also walked ahead to Dingleman's room, but she wasn't waiting outside there either.

'Come in and have a drink with me.'

'I'm tired.'

'You can sleep in tomorrow.'

Duddy accepted a straight scotch. The phone rang. It rang and rang. 'Aren't you going to answer it?'

'You're right for once. If not I'll never get any sleep.' He picked up the receiver and, without waiting to hear who was on the other end, said, 'I'm sorry. I'm not giving you any more.' There was a pause. 'That's right. I brought him down from Montreal with me. I've picked up with boys now ... No. Absolutely no more.' Dingleman turned to Duddy intending to ask for his drink, but Duddy was already by his side with it. 'My,' Dingleman said, 'aren't you ambitious?'

Duddy retreated.

'Look,' Dingleman said into the phone, 'no more. And don't try to phone me here again because I'm telling them not to put any more calls through. Good night.' He hung up. 'O.K. You can go to sleep now.'

By morning Dingleman's mood had altered again. He was very businesslike. 'Be packed and ready by eight. We're leaving tonight.'

'I thought we were staying three days?'

'There's been a change in plans. Look, I'm sorry, I thought

I'd really need you down here, but things didn't work out that way. I'm going to pay you for the trip anyway. Oh, one minute. There *is* something you can do for me. I want you to take this suitcase with your luggage.'

Duddy wandered in and out of Broadway restaurants all afternoon and shortly after four he made a business contact. He met a young man who had been in the pinball machine business. Recently, however, the mayor had come down hard on machines – they were illegal, in fact – and he was stuck with ten of them in his basement. They cost three-fifty each new, he said. Duddy was in a giddy mood. He'd wasted two days on a crazy trip. Probably Dingleman would give him fifty bucks for his trouble. No more. 'I'll tell you what,' Duddy told the young man, 'if you can get those machines across the border, I don't care how and I don't care when, I'll give you a hundred bucks apiece for them.' The young man's name was Virgil. Duddy left him his card.

Dingleman was waiting for him at the station. 'I'm not going to sit with you on the train, Duddy. As a matter of fact when I leave you here you don't know me until we get to Montreal. I may have to get off at the border on some business. If that's the case don't worry. You don't even know me. Understand?' Dingleman dug into his pocket. 'Here's five hundred and fifty dollars. The fifty is for all the little things you did for me here and the five is a loan. I wish it could be more, but . . . Oh, I almost forgot. Here are the keys to the suitcase and a list of what's in it. Just in case they ask you to open it at customs. If I'm not on the train when we get to Montreal Mr Shub will be waiting for you at the station. You can give him the case.'

Duddy counted the money, put it away, and read the list for the suitcase. 'Two shirts, two boxes of chocolate, a tin of imported cookies, and a pound of coffee. There are no other items to declare.'

Jeez, Duddy thought. What in the hell's going on here?

He was scared, but it was too late. He couldn't return the suitcase to Dingleman now. I could throw it out of the window, he thought as the train started. I can pretend it's not mine. Aw, he thought, there's probably nothing in it. He's a funny guy and this is his idea of a joke. Duddy closed his eyes and tried to think about his land. He'd saved fifty of the first hundred

Dingleman had given him and so that made six altogether for two days' work. Another nineteen and he'd own Brault's land. Another nineteen, jeez. There was less than three weeks left. Maybe he could squeeze two-fifty out of Cohen? A fat chance.

'Anything to declare, son?'

'A couple of shirts, that's all. Oh, and a tin of imported cookies for my Auntie Ida and a carton of cigarettes.'

The Inspector didn't even bother to look inside the suitcase. Duddy, relieved, looked outside and saw Dingleman standing on the platform. Two men were talking to him. One of them wore a policeman's uniform. The train started up again, but Duddy didn't wave. He waited another ten minutes and locked himself in the toilet with the suitcase. But Dingleman had told the truth. Aside from the items mentioned on the list there was nothing in the suitcase but soiled laundry. Duddy felt in all the side pockets, he tried the case for a false bottom, he slipped his hand between all the shirts and shook out each soiled sock carefully. Jeez, he thought, and he went through the suitcase again. This time he noticed that although the cookie and chocolate boxes were all secured with gift wrappings the coffee tin was not sealed. He opened it. But what he was looking for – 'hot' gems – he didn't find. There was no coffee in the tin, but the white sweet-smelling dust inside meant nothing to him. He salted away some of it in an envelope, though, just in case. Probably, he thought, the jewels or diamonds are individually wrapped inside each chocolate. Boy, he thought, that would be something. But he didn't dare open either of the boxes for fear he'd never get the wrappings on right again.

Shub met him at the station.

'Jerry got off at the border. He told me to give you this suit-case.'

'Thanks. You're a good kid.'

When Dingleman got into town that night Shub was waiting for him in his apartment. 'The coffee tin was open,' he said.

'It's O.K. I opened it.'

'I thought you weren't going to let her have any more?'

'Get me Kennedy on the phone, please. I want to speak to him right away.'

Chapter Six

The Cohen boy's *bar-mitzvah* was a big affair in a modern synagogue. The synagogue in fact was so modern that it was not called a synagogue any more. It was called a Temple. Duddy had never seen anything like it in his life. There was a choir and an organ and a parking lot next door. The men not only did not wear hats but they sat together with the women. All these things were forbidden by traditional Jewish law, but those who attended the Temple were so-called reform Jews and they had modernized the law to suit life in America. The Temple prayer services were conducted in English by Rabbi Harvey Goldstone, M.A., and Cantor 'Sonny' Brown. Aside from his weekly sermon, the marriage clinic, the Sunday school, and so on, the Rabbi, a most energetic man, was very active in the community at large. He was a fervent supporter of Jewish and Gentile Brotherhood, and a man who unfailingly offered his time to radio stations as a spokesman for the Jewish point of view on subjects that ranged from 'Does Israel Mean Divided Loyalties?' to 'The Jewish Attitude to Household Pets'. He also wrote articles for magazines and a weekly column of religious comfort for the *Tely*. There was a big demand for Rabbi Goldstone as a public speaker and he always made sure to send copies of his speeches to all the newspapers and radio stations.

Mr Cohen, who was on the Temple executive, was one of the Rabbi's most enthusiastic supporters, but there were some who did not approve. He was, as one magazine writer had put it, a controversial figure.

'The few times I stepped inside there,' Dingleman once said, 'I felt like a Jesuit in a whorehouse.'

But Mr Cohen, Farber, and other leaders of the community all took seats at the temple for the High Holidays on, as Mr Cohen said, the forty-yard line. The Rabbi was extremely popular with the young-marrieds and that, their parents felt, was important. Otherwise, some said with justice, the children would never learn about their Jewish heritage.

Another dissenter was Uncle Benjy. 'There used to be,' he said, 'some dignity in being against the synagogue. With a severe orthodox rabbi there were things to quarrel about. There was some pleasure. But this cream-puff of a synagogue, this religious drugstore, you might as well spend your life being against the *Reader's Digest*. They've taken all the mystery out of religion.'

At the *bar-mitzvah* Mr Cohen had trouble with his father. The old rag peddler was, he feared, stumbling on the edge of senility. He still clung to his cold-water flat on St Dominique Street and was a fierce follower of a Chassidic rabbi there. He had never been to the Temple before. Naturally he would not drive on the Sabbath and so that morning he had got up at six and walked more than five miles to make sure to be on time for the first prayers. As Mr Friar stood by with his camera to get the three generations together Mr Cohen and his son came down the outside steps to greet the old man. The old man stumbled. 'Where's the synagogue?' he asked.

'This is it, Paw. This is the Temple.'

The old man looked up at the oak doors and the magnificent stained glass windows. 'It's a church,' he said, retreating.

'It's the Temple, Paw. This is where Bernie is going to be *bar-mitzvah*.'

'Would the old chap lead him up the steps by the hand?' Mr Friar asked.

'Shettup,' Duddy said.

The old man retreated down another step.

'This is the *shul*, Paw. Come on.'

'It's a church.'

Mr Cohen laughed nervously. 'Paw, for Christ's sake!' And he led the old man forcefully up the steps, 'Stop sniffling. This isn't a funeral.'

Inside, the services began. 'Turn to page forty-one in your prayer books, please,' Rabbi Goldstone said. 'Blessed is the Lord, Our Father . . .'

The elder Cohen began to sniffle again.

'Isn't he sweet,' somebody said.

'Bernie's the only grandchild.'

Following the *bar-mitzvah* ceremony, Rabbi Goldstone began his sermon. 'This,' he said, 'is National Sports Week.' He spoke on Jewish Athletes – From Bar Kochva to Hank Greenberg. Afterwards he had some announcements to make. He reminded the congregation that if they took a look at the race horse chart displayed in the hall they would see that 'Jewish History' was trailing 'Dramatics Night' by five lengths. He hoped that more people would attend the next lecture. The concealed organ began to play and the Rabbi, his voice quivering, read off an anniversary list of members of the congregation who over the years had departed for the great beyond. He began to read the Mourner's Prayer as Mr Friar, his camera held to his eye, tip-toed nearer for a medium close shot.

The elder Cohen had begun to weep again when the first chord had been struck on the organ and Mr Cohen had had to take him outside. 'You lied to me,' he said to his son. 'It is a church.'

Duddy approached with a glass of water. 'You go inside,' he said to Mr Cohen. Mr Cohen hesitated. 'Go ahead,' Duddy said, 'I'll stay with him.'

'Thanks.'

Duddy spoke Yiddish to the old man. 'I'm Simcha Kravitz's grandson,' he said.

'Simcha's grandson and you come here?'

'Some circus, isn't it? Come,' he said, 'we'll go and sit in the sun for a bit.'

Linda Rubin came to the *bar-mitzvah*. So did Irwin. 'Well,' he said, 'look who's here. Sammy Glick.'

'All right,' Linda said sharply.

Duddy introduced Cuckoo Kaplan to Mr Friar and Cuckoo did some clowning for the camera. 'You've got a natural talent,' Mr Friar said.

Duddy apologized to Cuckoo because he couldn't pay him for being in the movie.

'That's show biz,' Cuckoo said.

At the reception that night Duddy danced with Linda once. 'If Yvette knew she'd be jealous,' Linda said.

'Aw.'

'Am I going to be invited to see your movie?'

'Sure.'

But in the days that followed Duddy began to doubt that there ever would be a movie. Mr Friar was depressed. His best roll of film had been over-exposed. It was useless. The light in the Temple was, he said, a disaster. 'I say, old chap, couldn't we restage the *haftorah* sequence?' he asked.

'You're crazy,' Duddy said.

Mr Friar went to Ottawa to develop the film at the National Film Board and when Duddy met him at the station three days later Mr Friar was very happy indeed. 'John thinks this is my greatest film,' he said. 'You ought to see the rushes, Kravitz. Splendid!' But Duddy was not allowed to see the rushes. Night and day Mr Friar worked in secret on the cutting and editing. Duddy pleaded with him. 'Can't I see something? One reel. A half of a reel, even.' But Mr Friar was adamant. 'If I was Eisenstein you wouldn't talk to me like that. You'd have confidence. You must be fair to me, Kravitz. Wait for the finished product.'

Meanwhile Mr Cohen phoned every morning. 'Well?' he asked.

'Soon, Mr Cohen. Very soon.'

Duddy, still trying to meet the Brault property deadline, was out early every day pushing liquid soap and toilet supplies. He began to drive his father's taxi during off-hours again. Then he had a stroke of luck. Brault accepted a further payment of a thousand dollars and agreed to wait one more month for the final payment. 'Everything,' Duddy told Yvette, 'depends on Mr Friar. If the movie's O.K. we're in. If not . . .'

'Duddy, you look terrible. Look at the circles under your eyes. You've got to stop driving that taxi and get some sleep at night.'

Three weeks after the *bar-mitzvah* Mr Friar was ready. He arranged a private screening for Duddy and Yvette. 'I'm beginning to think we'd be making a grave error if we sold this film to Mr Cohen. It's a prize-winner, Kravitz. I'm sure we could get distribution for it.'

'Will you turn out the goddam lights and let me see it, please?'

Duddy didn't say a word all through the screening, but afterwards he was sick to his stomach.

'It's not that bad,' Yvette said. 'Things could be done to it.'

'You think we'd be making a mistake?' Duddy said. 'Jeez. I could sell Mr Cohen a dead horse easier than this pile of – '

'If you so much as cut it by one single frame,' Mr Friar said, 'then my name goes off the film.'

Duddy began to laugh. So did Yvette.

'Timothy suggested we try it at Cannes.'

'Jeez,' Duddy said. 'Everyone's going to be there. But everyone. The invitations are all out.'

Duddy took to his bed for two days. He refused to see anyone.

'I'm so worried,' Yvette said.

Mr Friar kissed her hand. 'You have a Renaissance profile,' he said.

'He won't even answer the phone. Oh, Mr Friar, please!' she said, removing his hand.

'If there were only world enough and time, my love . . .'

'I'm going to try his number once more,' Yvette said.

But Duddy was out. On the third day he had decided that he could no longer put off seeing Mr Cohen. He went to his house this time. 'Ah,' Mr Cohen said, 'the producer is here.'

'Have you got the movie with you?' Bernie asked.

Mrs Cohen poured him a glass of plum brandy. 'If you don't mind,' she said, 'there are a few more names I'd like to add to the guest list.'

'I've got some bad news for you. I'm cancelling the screening. Tomorrow morning my secretary will call everyone to tell them the show's off.'

'Aw, gee whiz.'

'Is it that bad?' Mr Cohen asked.

'It's great. We're going to enter it in the Cannes Festival.'

'I don't understand,' Mrs Cohen said.

'You won't like it. It's what we call *avant-garde*.'

'Watch it,' Mr Cohen said, 'this is where he begins to lie. Right before your eyes the price is going up.'

Duddy smiled at Mrs Cohen. 'I suppose what you expected was an ordinary movie with shots of all the relatives and friends . . . well, you know what I mean. But Mr Friar is an artist. His creation is something else entirely.'

'Can't we see it, Maw?'

'Aren't you taking a lot for granted, young man? Don't you think my husband and I can appreciate artistic quality when we see it?'

'Don't fall into his trap,' Mr Cohen said.

Duddy turned to Mr Cohen. 'I'll let you in on a secret,' he said. He told him that Mr Friar had been a big director, but he had had to leave Hollywood because of the witch-hunt. That's the only reason why he was in Montreal fiddling with small films. He wanted to make his name and get in on the ground floor of the Canadian film industry, so to speak. Turning to Mrs Cohen, he added, 'Please don't repeat this, but if not for Senator McCarthy I wouldn't have been able to hire a man as big as Friar for less than five thousand dollars. Not that he isn't costing me plenty as it is.'

Mr Cohen started to say something, but his wife glared at him. She smiled at Duddy. 'But why can't we see the movie? I don't understand.'

'It's different. It's shocking.'

'Oh, really now!'

'Mr Friar has produced a small screen gem in the tradition of *Citizen Kane* and Franju's *Sang des Bêtes*.'

'How can we cancel all the invitations at this late date? We insist on seeing it.'

Duddy hesitated. He stared reflectively at the floor. 'All right,' he said, 'but don't say I didn't warn you first.'

Mr Cohen laughed. 'Don't believe a word he says, Gertie. It's good. It must be very good. Otherwise he wouldn't be here talking it down. But, listen here, Kravitz, not a penny more than I promised. Wow! What a liar!'

Duddy gulped down his plum brandy. 'I'm not selling,' he said. 'That's something else. You can see it, but . . .'

'Hey,' Mr Cohen said, 'hey there. Are you getting tough with an old friend?'

'I want it, Daddy. I want the movie! Gee whiz, Maw.'

'You outsmarted yourself, Mr Cohen. You wouldn't give me an advance or put anything in writing.'

'Sam, what's the boy saying?'

'You gave me your word, Kravitz. A gentleman doesn't go back on his word.'

Bernie began to cry.

'You can't blame him, Mrs Cohen. He didn't want to take too big a chance on a young boy just starting out.'

'Alright,' Mr Cohen said hoarsely, 'just how much do you want for the film?'

'Money isn't the question.'

'Such a liar! My God, never in my life – Will you stop crying please? Take him out of here, Gertie.'

'I'm not going.'

'Well, Kravitz, I'm waiting to hear your price. Gangster!'

Duddy hesitated.

'Please,' Mrs Cohen said.

'I can't sell outright. I'd still want to enter it in the festival.'

'Of course,' Mrs Cohen said warmly.

'We can't talk here,' Mr Cohen said. 'Come up to my bed-room.'

But Duddy wouldn't budge. 'For fifteen hundred dollars,' he said, 'I'll give you an excellent colour print. But you'd have to sign away all rights to a percentage of the profits on Canadian theatre distribution.'

'What's that? Come again, please?'

'We're going to distribute it as a short to Canadian theatres.'

'Gee whiz.'

'For twenty-five hundred dollars in all I'll make you a silent partner. I'd cut you in for twenty per cent of the net theatre profits. My lawyers could draw up the agreement. But remem-ber, it's a gamble. This is an art film, not one of those crassly commercial items.'

'Would my husband's name appear anywhere?'

'We could list him in the credits as a co-producer with Dudley Kane enterprises.'

Mr Cohen smiled for the first time. 'A boy from the boys,' he said, 'that's what you are.'

'Maybe you'd like to think it over first.'

'Sam.'

'Alright. O.K. I'll write him a cheque right now.' Mr Cohen looked at Duddy and laughed. 'Look at him. He's shaking.'

After Duddy had left with the cheque Mr Cohen said, 'I could have got it for less if you and Bernie hadn't been there.'

'Then why are you smiling?'

'Because yesterday I spoke to Dave in Toronto. He's with Columbia of Canada now and he told me a screen short is worth up to twenty thousand dollars. I could have got it for less, it's true, but in the end it still won't have cost me a cent for the colour print. And think of the publicity. It must be terrific,

151

you know. Otherwise he wouldn't have talked it down like that. He's still got a lot to learn, that boy.'

Duddy met Yvette at a quarter to ten the next morning. He told her what had happened while they waited for the bank to open. 'But that's wonderful,' she said.

'Yeah, sure, until they see the damn thing. Then the law-suits start. And nobody in town will ever want me to make a movie for them again.'

'Maybe they'll like it.'

'Are you kidding? Listen, I'm taking cash for this cheque. Pay Brault and put the rest in your account. If they sue I'll go into bankruptcy.'

'All right.'

'I hope the cheque's still good. Maybe he's stopped payment on it.'

*

THE SCREENING

DUDLEY KANE ENTERPRISES
with M. Cohen, Inc., Metal Merchants
presents
A Peter John Friar Production
HAPPY BAR-MITZVAH, BERNIE!
executive producer d. kravitz
directed, written, and narrated by
j.p. friar
additional dialogue by
rabbi harvey goldstone, m.a.

'So far so good.'

'Would you mind taking off your hat please, Elsie?'

'Sh.'

1. *A close-shot of an aged finger leading a thirteen year old boy's hand over the Hebrew letters of a prayer book.*
2. *Grandfather Cohen is seated at the dining-room table with Bernard, teaching him the tunes of the Torah.*

NARRATOR: *Older than the banks of the Nile, not so cruel as the circumcision rite of the Zulus, and even more intricate than a snowflake is the bar-mitzvah . . .*

'Hey, what's that he said about niggers being clipped? I thought – '

' – comparative religion. I take it at McGill.'

'Comparative *what*? I'll give you such a *schoss*.'

3.   *In the synagogue Bernard stands looking at the Holy Ark. His reaction.*

CHOIR: *Hear O Israel the Lord is Our God the Lord is One.*

4.   *Grandfather Cohen, wearing a prayer shawl, hands the Torah to Mr Cohen who passes it to his son.*

NARRATOR: *From generation to generation, for years before the birth of Christ . . .*

'Hsssssss . . .'

'O.K., smart guy. Shettup!'

NARRATOR: *. . . the rule of law has been passed from hand to hand among the Chosen People. Something priceless, something cherished . . .*

'Like a Chinchilla.'

'One more crack out of you, Arnie,' Mr Cohen said, 'and out you go.'

In the darkness Duddy smiled, relieved.

NARRATOR: *. . . a thing of beauty and a joy forever.*

5.   *The wrappings come off and Mr. Cohen holds the Torah aloft.*

CHOIR: [RECITES IN HEBREW] *In the beginning God created heaven and earth . . .*

6.   *Camera closes in on Torah.*

NARRATOR: *. . . In the beginning there was the Word . . . There was Abraham, Isaac, and Jacob . . . There was Moses . . .*
      AS CHOIR HUMS IN BACKGROUND
          King David . . . Judas Macabee . . .
               CHOIR TO CLIMAX
        . . . and, in our own time, Leon Trotsky . . .

'What's that?'

'His *bar-mitzvah* I would have liked to have seen. Trotsky!'

NARRATOR: *. . . in all those years, the Hebrews, whipped like sand by the cruel winds of oppression, have survived by the word . . . the law . . .*

7.   *A close-shot of a baby being circumcised.*

'Lock the doors. Here comes the dirty part.'

'Shame on you.'

'Awright, Sarah. O.K. You've seen one before. You don't have to pretend you're not looking.'

NARRATOR: ... *and through the centuries the eight-day-old Hebrew babe has been welcomed into the race with blood.*

  TOM-TOMS BEAT IN BACKGROUND. HEIGHTENING

8. [MONTAGE] *Lightning. African tribal dance. Jungle fire. Stukas diving. A jitterbug contest speeded up. Slaughtering of a cow. Fireworks against a night sky. More African dancing. Torrents of rain. An advertisement for Maiden-Form bras upsidedown. Blood splashing against glass. A lion roars.*

'Wow!'

'Are you alright, *Zeyda*?'

    DRUMS TO CLIMAX. OUT.

9. *A slow dissolve to close-up of Bernard Cohen's shining morning face.*

NARRATOR: *This is the story of one such Hebrew babe, and how at the age of thirteen he was at last accepted as an adult member of his tribe.*

'If you don't feel well, *zeyda*, I'll get you a glass of water.'

NARRATOR: *This is the story of the bar-mitzvah of Bernard son of Moses . . . . . .*

10. *A smiling Rabbi Goldstone leads Bernard up the aisle of the Temple. In the background second-cousins and school-mates wave and smile at the camera.*

'Good,' Duddy said. 'Excellent.' He had asked Mr Friar to work Rabbi Goldstone into every possible shot.

'Look, there I am! Did you see me, Mommy?'

'You see Harry there picking his nose? If he'd known the camera – '

'A big joke!'

11. *As Bernard and Rabbi Goldstone reach the prayer stand.*

NARRATOR: *As solemn as the Aztec sacrifice, more mysterious than Helen's face, is the pregnant moment, the meeting of time past and time present, when the priest and his initiate each ho'mat.*

Rabbi Goldstone coughed. 'That means priest in the figurative sense.'

'He's gone too far,' Duddy whispered to Yvette. 'Jeez.'

CHOIR: [SINGING IN HEBREW] *Blessed is the Lord our God, Father of Abraham, Isaac, and Jacob . . .*

'There, *zeyda*, isn't that nice?'

'Oh, leave him alone, Henry.'

'Leave him alone? I think he's had another stroke.'

12. *As Bernard says his blessings over the Torah the camera pans around the Temple. Aunt Sadie giggles shyly. Ten-year-old Manny Schwartz crosses his eyes and sticks out his tongue. Grandfather Cohen looks severe. Mr Cohen wipes what just might be a tear from his eye. Uncle Ernie whispers into a man's ear. The man grins widely.*

13. *A close shot of Bernard saying his blessings. The camera moves in slowly on his eyes.*

BRING IN TOM-TOMS AGAIN.

14. *Cut to a close shot of circumcision again.*

'It's not me,' Bernie shouted .'Honest, guys.'

'Atta boy.'

'Do you think this'll have a bad effect on the children?'

'Never mind the children. I've got such a pain there now you'd think it was me up there.'

15. *Résumé shot of Bernard saying his Haftorah.*

NARRATOR: *The young Hebrew, now a fully accepted member of his tribe, is instructed in the ways of the world by his religious adviser.*

16. *A two-shot of Rabbi Goldstone and Bernard.*

NARRATOR: *'Beginning today,' the Rabbi tells him, 'you are old enough to be responsible for your own sins. Your father no longer takes them on his shoulders.'*

AS CHOIR HUMS ELGAR'S 'POMP AND CIRCUMSTANCE'

17. *Camera pans round Temple again. Cutting back again and again to Bernard and the Rabbi.*

SUPERIMPOSE KIPLING'S 'IF' OVER THE ABOVE

NARRATOR: *'Today you are a man, Bernard son of Moses.'*

18. *[MONTAGE] Lightning. Close-shot of head of Michelangelo's statue of David. Cartoon of a Thurber husband. African tribal dance. Close-shot of a venereal disease warning in a public urinal.*

'*Zeyda*, one minute.'
'You'd better go with him, Henry.'

*Soldiers marching speeded up. Circumcision close-up again.
Upside down shot of a hand on a woman's breast.*

'Hey,' Arnie shouted, 'can you use a new casting director,
Kravitz?'
'Haven't you any appreciation for the finer things?'
'Hoo-haw.'
Duddy bit his hand. The sweat rolled down his forehead.
'This is meant to be serious, Arnie. Oh, he's such a fool.'

*A lion roars. Close-shot of Bernard's left eye. A pair of
black panties catch fire. Lightning. African tribal dance.*
NARRATOR: *Today you are a man and your family and friends
have come to celebrate.*
GIUSEPPI DI STEFANO SINGS DRINKING SONG FROM
LA TRAVIATA.
19. *Close shot of hands pouring a large scotch.*
20. *Cut to general shots of guests at Temple kiddush.*

'There I am!'
'Look at Sammy, stuffing his big fat face as usual.'
'There I am *again*!'
'What took you so long, Henry?'
'Did I miss anything?'
'Aw. Where's the *zeyda*?'
'He's sitting outside in the car. Hey, was that me?'
'I'd like to see this part again later, please.'
'Second the motion.'

NARRATOR: *Those who couldn't come sent telegrams.*
21. *Hold a shot of telegrams pinned against green background.*
AS CHOIR HUMS AULD LANG SYNE
NARRATOR: 'HAPPY BAR-MITZVAH, BERNIE. BEST UNCLE
HERBY' . . . 'MAY YOUR LIFE BE HAPPY AND SUCCESS-
FUL. THE SHAPIRO BROTHERS AND MYRNA.' . . . BEST
WISHES FOR HEALTH, HAPPINESS, AND SUCCESS FROM
THE WINNIPEG BRANCH OF THE COHENS . . . SURPRISE
PARCEL FOLLOWS.' . . . 'MY HEART GOES OUT TO YOU
AND YOURS TODAY. MYER.' . . .

'You notice Lou sent only a Greetings Telegram? You get a
special rate.'

'He's had a bad year, that's all. Lay off, Molly.'

'A bad year! He comes from your side of the family, you mean.'

NARRATOR: *Those who came did not come empty-handed.*

'Try it some time.'

22. *They came with tributes for the boy who had come of age.
Camera pans over a table laden with gifts. Revealed are
four Parker 51 sets, an electric razor, a portable record
player . . .*

'Murray got the player wholesale through his brother-in-law.'

> *. . . three toilet sets, two copies of Tom Sawyer, five
> subscriptions to the National Geographic Magazine, a
> movie projector, a fishing rod and other angling equipment,
> three cameras, a season's ticket to hockey games at the
> Forum, a set of phylacteries and a prayer shawl, a rubber
> dinghy, a savings account book open at a first deposit of
> five hundred dollars, six sport shirts, an elaborate chemistry
> set, a pile of fifty silver dollars in a velvet-lined box, at
> least ten credit slips (worth from twenty to a hundred
> dollars each) for Eaton's and Morgan's, two sets of H. G.
> Wells's Outline of History.*
>
> AS CHOIR SINGS 'HAPPY BIRTHDAY, BERNIE!'

23. *Hold a shot of numerous cheques pinned to a board. Spin it.*

'Dave's cheque is only for twenty-five bucks. Do you know
how much business he gets out of Cohen every year?'

'If it had been Lou you would have said he had a bad year.
Admit it.'

'Hey, Bernie,' Arnie yelled, 'how many of those cheques
bounced? You can tell us.'

'I was grateful for all of them,' Bernie said, 'large or small.
It's the thought that counts with me.'

'Isn't he sweet?'

'Sure,' Arnie said, 'but he could have told me that before.'

24. *A shot of Rabbi Goldstone's study. Bernard sits in an
enormous leather chair and the Rabbi paces up and down,
talking to him.*

NARRATOR: *But that afternoon, in the good Rabbi's study, the
young Hebrew learns that there are more exalted things in this*

157

*world besides material possessions, he is told something of the
tragic history of his race, how they were exploited by the ancient
Egyptian imperialists, how reactionary dictators from Nehru to
Hitler persecuted them in order to divert the working-classes
from the true cause of their sorrows, he learns – like Candide –
that all is not for the best in the best of all possible worlds.*

AS AL JOLSON SINGS 'ELI, ELI'

25. *Rabbi Goldstone leads Bernard to the window and stands
behind him, his hands resting on the lad's shoulders.*

'Five'll get you ten that right now he's asking Bernie to remind his father that the Temple building campaign is lagging
behind schedule.'

Rabbi Goldstone coughed loudly.

NARRATOR (RECITES): '*I am a Jew: hath not a Jew eyes? Hath
not a Jew hands, organs, dimensions, senses, affections, passions,
fed with the same food, hurt with the same weapons, subject to
the same diseases, healed by the same oils, warmed and cooled
by the same winter and summer as a Christian is? If you prick
him does he not bleed?*

26. *Rabbi Goldstone autographs a copy of his book, Why I'm
Glad To Be A Jew, and hands it to Bernard.*

27. *Hold a close-shot of the book.*

From there the movie went on to record the merry-making and
odd touching interludes at the dinner and dance. Relatives and
friends saw themselves eating, drinking, and dancing. Uncles
and aunts at the tables waved at the camera, the kids made funny
faces, and the old people sat stonily. Cuckoo Kaplan did a soft-
shoe dance on the head table. As the camera closed in on the
dancers Henry pretended to be seducing Morrie Applebaum's
wife. Mr Cohen had a word with the band leader and the first
kazatchka was played. Timidly the old people joined hands and
began to dance around in a circle. Mr Cohen and some spirited
others joined in the second one. Duddy noticed some intruders
at the sandwich table. He did not know them by name or sight,
but remembering, he recognized that they were FFHS boys
and he smiled a little. The camera panned lovingly about fish
and jugs and animals modelled out of ice. It closed in and swallowed the bursting trumpeter. Guests were picked up again,
some reeling and others bad-tempered, waiting for taxis and
husbands to come round with the car outside the temple.

And Mr Cohen, sitting in the first row with his legs open like an inverted nutcracker to accommodate his sunken belly, thought, it's worth it, every last cent or what's money for, it's cheap at any price to have captured my family and friends and foolish rabbi. He reached for Gertie's hand and thought I'd better not kiss Bernie. It would embarrass him.

AS CHOIR SINGS HALLELUJAH CHORUS

74. *Rear-view long shot. Mr Cohen and Bernard standing before the offices of M. Cohen, Inc., Metal Merchants.*

FADE OUT

Nobody spoke. Duddy began to bite his fingernails and Yvette pulled his hand away and held it.

'A most edifying experience,' Rabbi Goldstone said. 'A work of art.'

Everybody began to speak at once.

'Thank you very much, indeed,' Mr Friar said. 'Unfortunately the best parts were left on the cutting room floor.'

'Play it again.'

'Yeah!'

Chapter Seven

When Duddy came home he found out about Lennie.

'What do you mean he's gone?' Duddy asked.

Max could hardly speak. He paced up and down the kitchen. 'His clothes are gone. Every drawer in the bedroom is empty. Here's the note. Read it yourself.'

Duddy took the note.

> I'll get in touch with you as soon as I can, but I'm not going back to Medical School. I'm sorry. Please forgive me.
>
> Leonard

'That explains a lot,' Duddy said. 'What do you think, Uncle Benjy?'

Uncle Benjy poured himself another drink. Standing behind his older brother Max gestured urgently to tell Duddy not to question him. He was looped.

'I can't understand it,' Uncle Benjy said. 'You'd think he would have got in touch with me whatever it was.'

'*I'm* the father.'

'Jeez. Are we going to have a family quarrel at a time like this?'

Uncle Benjy looked sharply at Duddy. 'I haven't seen you in a long time,' he said. 'You've changed.'

'He's in business for himself. An operator.'

'I heard.'

'You wait. He'll burn his fingers.'

Duddy lit a cigarette off his butt. 'How's Auntie Ida?' he asked.

Max made more urgent gestures. He grimaced.

'She left for Florida this morning. I'm your uncle, you know. You shouldn't hold a grudge. Bygones are bygones.'

'Sure thing.'

'O.K.' Uncle Benjy emptied his glass. 'If that's how you feel.'

'What's between you?' Max asked. 'How come I never know what goes on around here?'

Duddy sighed.

'Don't look at me like that,' Max said. 'I'll brain you.'

'Easy, Daddy. Easy. What's the name of Lennie's girl?'

'We phoned,' Uncle Benjy said. 'She's sick in bed. I spoke to the father.'

'Have you tried his friends?'

'Nobody knows from nothing.'

'I think you both ought to go to bed,' Duddy said. 'We can't do anything at this hour. I'll get up early tomorrow and start seeing his friends. Somebody will know something.'

'Look who's in charge,' Uncle Benjy said.

'Do you expect me to sleep at a time like this?'

'I sure do. Would you like me to drive you home, Uncle Benjy?'

'I'll call a taxi. He's right, Max. We ought to get some sleep.'

'It's easy for you to talk. He's my son but. His blood is my blood.'

'Daddy, for Christ's sake!'

'Maybe I never had lots of money to give him. I don't talk very fine either. But he's my son and maybe he's lying dead in a ditch right now.'

'Daddy. Easy, Daddy.' Duddy held his father close. 'He's been studying too hard, that's all. I'm sure he's all right.'

'I never tried to take him away from you, Max. I was only trying to help out.'

'I've got feelings. You'd be surprised.'

Uncle Benjy phoned for a taxi.

'Come on, Daddy. You get into bed and I'll bring you some tea.'

'You think it's easy to bring up two boys without a wife?'

'We'll find him tomorrow,' Duddy said, pulling back the bedspread. 'I'm sure.'

'Good night,' Uncle Benjy said. 'Let's keep in close touch.'

'I'm sorry,' Max said, 'but you know me. When I lose my temper I lose my temper.'

Uncle Benjy nodded. Duddy touched his father's head.

'Good night, Duddel.'

'I'll call you as soon as there's any news.'

Duddy made tea. But when he was ready to serve it his father had fallen asleep, so Duddy shut the bedroom door softly and sat down at the kitchen table. 'At a time like this,' he said aloud, 'just when everything is beginning to move. That's what you call luck.'

After the screening of *Happy Bar-Mitzvah, Bernie!* Duddy had felt so marvellous that he had invited Mr Friar and Yvette out. 'We'll go to Ruby Foo's,' he said.

Some of the people who had been at the screening were already there. 'There's young Kravitz himself,' somebody said.

'That's the director. He's English. I'll tell you something Gertie told me about him, but you must promise not to repeat it.'

Duddy waved.

'Congratulations, kid.'

'A fine job.'

Duddy couldn't see Linda anywhere. She hadn't even come up to him after the screening. The hell with her, he thought. He introduced Mr Friar to people here and there. Yvette waited to one side.

'We've got a table for you now, sir.'

'A bottle of champagne,' Duddy said. 'The best.'

He told Yvette that after the screening he had been offered enough wedding and *bar-mitzvah* contracts to carry them through into January with an estimated gross of eight maybe ten thousand dollars. Not only that, he added when Mr Friar went to spend a penny, but he had had a long chat with Grossman, the owner of Camp Forest Land, and next summer Duddy was going to make a film there. He had offered Grossman such a cut-rate price that the poor bastard couldn't afford to turn him down. That meant, Duddy said, that he would have an opportunity to see the camp from the inside. The information he'd gather about costs, prices, staff, and the handling of kids would be invaluable to him. He'd also get an address list of all the kids there so that they could be invited to the screening. Grossman was a crap-artist. He didn't suspect a thing. 'What's wrong?' Duddy asked. 'You're in a bad mood.'

Yvette didn't reply.

'Tonight of all nights. Hey, *garçon*. More champagne.'
Yvette laughed. 'That's my girl. Here's Mr Friar.' Duddy filled
all the glasses. '*Prosit*.'

'Here's looking at you.'

'Hey, Mr Friar, remember that first night? You know, after
the lecture. You weren't angry when you walked out of the bar.
You just didn't want to get stuck with the bill.'

'It seems to me I paid for the drinks that night.'

'And every other night. Aw, you're a great guy. I don't know
what I'd do without you. Or you too, Yvette.'

'Thanks.'

'Order anything you want. The sky's the limit. Jeez, does this
stuff ever make you wanna piss. Excuse me a minute.'

'It's the first door to the left, old chap.'

'Thanks, old chap.'

'Not the most delicate boy in the world, is he, Yvette?'

'Maybe not.'

'But not without his charms, I'm sure.'

'Let's order. I'm starved.'

'He'll never marry you.'

'Let's not start on that again, please.'

'A Hebrew never marries outside his own race. I'd marry you.
I'm mad for you.'

'He's your friend. He admires you. And I'm supposed to be
his girl.'

'He didn't even introduce you to anyone here.'

'You don't miss a thing,' Yvette said coldly.

'He's callow. His manners are unbelievably *gauche*. Why, he
hasn't the first notion of how to treat a woman. What on earth
do you see in him?'

'Plenty. Here he comes. Please be sweet, John. He's so happy
tonight.'

'Yvette,' Duddy said, 'I've just made an important decision.
I've decided to get an apartment of my own.'

'Earth-shaking.'

'What's eating him?'

'He's teasing. Sit down, Duddy.'

'Did I say anything wrong, Mr Friar? Are you angry because
I kidded you about that first night before? Jeez. You're my best
friend. You can have as much to drink as you want.'

'*Merci mille fois.*'

'Where would I be without him?'

'That's enough, Duddy,' Yvette said.

Duddy gulped down another glass of champagne. 'Know something, Yvette. We ought to find a dame for Mr Friar. We're supposed to be his friends like. I'm sure it's no fun for him always tagging along like this.'

'I think we'd better order,' Yvette said.

At a time like this, Duddy thought, just when I need every minute I can spare for the business I have to start chasing around after Lennie. Jeez, he thought, what if he *is* in trouble? Maybe it's something serious. Duddy was kept awake considering all the catastrophes that could have happened to his brother. Yvette will help me, he thought. We'll find him all right.

Lennie was nervy, it was true – sensitive – even as a kid the smallest things used to upset him. He was only six years older than Duddy and there had been a time when they had been real pals. There had been that summer when Duddy had still been at the Talmud Torah and Max had taken a cottage with the Debrofskys. Shawbridge, with that river like coffee that had been left standing, was no hell, but Duddy had had fun there. Together he and Lennie had built shacks on the mountain and made field telephones out of empty oil cans and yards of carefully waxed string. When the other guys complained about Duddy always coming with them, saying things like what do we need the kid with us for, Lennie always stuck up for him. 'Duddy's my kid brother,' he'd say. 'Where I goes he goes.'

It had changed, of course. When Lennie was in tenth grade at FFHS the brothers no longer saw so much of each other. But Duddy still took pride in all of Lennie's achievements.

'Rank one again,' he'd say. 'You're a genius, Lennie. Congrats.'

They still shared the same bedroom. Duddy's side was thick with pennants and airplane models he had made and Lennie's side was laden with gifts from Uncle Benjy, the Books of Knowledge and the Harvard Classics. Lennie used to tell him about his talks with Uncle Benjy. 'He wants me to be the kind of doctor that's a helper to the poor. He says I shouldn't worry if I can't get into medical school at McGill because of the anti-semitism there. Because he'll send me to Queens or Switzerland. Anywhere. He's becoming a boozer, you know. After he'd had a lot he held me so tight I got scared. You're going to have to be my *kaddish*, he said. I don't get it. Half the time he talks against religion and then when he's drunk he goes and says a thing like that.'

Once Lennie entered McGill he was no longer amused when Duddy reported things like, 'Boy, have I ever got a bone on tonight.'

He still told Duddy about Uncle Benjy, but his tone had changed. 'You mustn't tell him I've joined Hillel. He says it's a reactionary organization with a ghetto mentality.'

'What did you say to that?'

'Nothing. You think I'm crazy?'

Occasionally Lennie would revert to the intimacy of their younger days together. 'Boy,' he told Duddy once, 'did I ever have a time at the Oneg Shabat tonight! That Riva Kaplan. I mean I never thought a Jewish girl . . .'

'It's going up,' Duddy said.

Lennie laughed. 'Her house in Outremont has about six telephones. I'm taking her to the Arts Ball. Uncle Benjy is lending me his car.'

'Let's stay up and talk all night. I'll make us an omelette.'

Then when Duddy bragged about his brother one night it turned out that one of the girls at the dance was a cousin of Riva's. She knew all about Lennie and he had never mentioned that he had a brother. He wasn't a St Urbain Street boy either. He lived on Cote St Catherine Road. That was Uncle Benjy's address. But there were still things that Lennie liked to share with him. There had been, for instance, a brief but burning conversion to socialism. A time when he had begun to see a lot of Uncle Benjy again and had tried to make a convert of Duddy.

'Are you aware that during the depression tons of oranges were being dumped into the Pacific to keep prices up while people in New York were starving?'

But once he had entered medical school Lennie had no more time for politics. He studied continuously, his headaches worsened, and he became very short-tempered.

I've got to find him, Duddy thought. After all those years of study he can't throw in the sponge just like that.

He woke when he heard Max drop the frying pan on the kitchen floor. 'I thought you were getting up early this morning,' Max said, 'to start looking for him.'

Duddy stretched. His eyes were puffed.

'Did I ever have a night,' Max said.

'Don't worry. I'll phone you at Eddy's the minute I find out anything.'

Chapter Eight

Duddy phoned Yvette to tell her about Lennie. 'That means I won't be in today,' he said.

Yvette said she'd like to go to Ste Agathe for a couple of days. The notary wanted to see her and it was her brother's birthday tomorrow.

'Sure thing. Just call the telephone answering service before you go. If you're short there must be at least thirty bucks in the petty cash.'

'I can live on my salary,' Yvette said in that special cold voice.

Those dames, Duddy thought, there's no need for them to tell you when they've got the curse. 'Have a nice trip,' he said, and hanging up he added, '*Ver gerharget.*'

College kids, Duddy discovered, do not get up too early. He loitered longer than an hour in Hillel House before he saw a familiar face. It was nice there, but he couldn't relax, he was worried that he was sitting in somebody else's chair or that his fly might be undone. Some girls in cashmere sweaters drifted in and there was a sweet-looking boy with a pipe. Duddy began to whistle and one of the girls raised an eyebrow. 'It's from *Carmen*,' Duddy said, clearing his throat. Then he saw Riva. She wore a McGill blazer. 'Riva,' he said, 'I've got to speak to you for a minute.'

Riva looked surprised.

'I'm Lennie Kravitz's kid brother. Remember?' Duddy explained that Lennie was home sick in bed. Nothing serious, mind you, but his father was worried, and Duddy wanted to know if she had noticed anything odd about him recently. 'Bothering him like.'

'We move in different circles these days.'

Riva, he gathered, was going to Tel Aviv to teach school once she graduated from McGill. 'That's a fine ambition,' he said, 'but what about Lennie?'

'He's become an assimilationist.'

'Wha'?'

'You never see him at Hillel any more. Jewish boys and girls aren't good enough for him. It's a disgrace, honestly. Every time they take him into one of their frat houses he practically licks their boots.'

Riva was late for Eng. 1 and had to run. She couldn't meet him later, either. She was busy.

'Duddy! Duddy Kravitz!'

'Bernie!'

'Boy, is it ever good to see you.'

'Yeah,' Duddy said. 'No kidding?'

'You're a big business success. I've heard all about you. Congratulations.'

'Aw.'

'Never mind. One day I'll be saying I knew him when.'

'*You'll* be saying that? Gwan. You're getting a real education. You're going to be an architect.'

'What are you doing here?'

Duddy repeated the story he had told Riva. He said he was anxious to find out anything he could about Lennie's life at McGill.

'Well,' Bernie said, 'I knew I'd never get to that sociology class. Come around the corner with me. We'll have a coffee.'

They joked for a while about the old days at the hotel before Bernie got serious. 'Look,' he said, 'I don't want to interfere. Lennie minds his own business and he's entitled to choose his own friends.'

'Give,' Duddy said.

Bernie told Duddy that Lennie had a rep for being a plugger. He had never been very popular but nobody had really disliked him, either. He had hardly been noticed, in fact, until he began to take out Riva. She was a popular number, a bit flighty, and soon Lennie was seen at parties with her everywhere. 'He was crazy about her,' Bernie said. 'Unfortunately Riva liked to dance close with all the boys and she wasn't beyond a little friendly necking, if you caught her in the right mood. Lennie didn't go for that. He began to cut in on all of Riva's dances. Once, at a party I was at, he caught her fooling around with one of the guys in the upstairs hall and later I found him sitting on the steps outside. He'd been crying. His nerves were all shot. I really think that guy studies too hard.'

'Anatomy's the big killer,' Duddy said.

'Anyway things went from bad to worse and one night they had a fight at a party. He was hysterical. I think it was just after the mid-terms and he looked like he hadn't slept for weeks . . . Well, he called her lots of ugly names. Everybody was there and he yelled things at her he shouldn't have.'

'Like what?'

'Maybe I shouldn't be telling you all this, Duddy . . . Well, you know . . .'

'He isn't sick in bed. He's run away from home.' Duddy told him about the note. 'Like what?' he asked.

'Like Outremont whore. Daughter of a war-profiteer. Well, you know. The works. Up to that point everyone was on his side. But you know it wasn't Riva's fault that he was so serious about her. She's flighty. I told you that. But she's got a good sense of humour and everybody likes her. You want the gory details?'

'Yeah.'

'She slapped his face. Then Lennie began to call everyone in the room dirty names. Well, you know. We weren't such bigshots just because we had cars and he was as good as any of us . . . He tried to pick a fight with Shelby Horne and then he took a poke at me. Christ, he's even skinnier than you are. I could have laid him flat with one whack. Anyway we got him home – What are you going to do, Duddy? Have you any idea where he's gone to?'

'Not yet.'

'Only three Jewish kids got into med in his year. A lot of people are expecting him to get the medal. Christ.'

'Tell me the rest, Bernie. I'm sure there's more.'

'Well, you know, he dropped out of sight for a while. Then the next thing I'd heard he'd picked up with the Joe-college bunch. The football crowd. Well, you know, drink chug-a-lug and all that.

'Listen, everyone's entitled to enjoy themselves the way they want. It's not for me, that's all. They're mostly rich kids, Duddy. *Goys*. Some of them live in Westmount but most come from out of town and have rooms in the frat houses. They run sports cars and get the prettiest girls. Well, you know, the campus beauty queens. I don't know how Lennie ever got mixed up with them. I can understand about Irwin Shubert, but – '

'Irwin! That bastard.'

'He's the only other Jew in their crowd. It costs plenty to keep up with them, and I don't know where Lennie got the money.'

'There was a broad, wasn't there? A blonde.'

'Sandra Calder? That's something else that used to puzzle me. I've seen her around a lot with Lennie recently, but she's really Andy Simpson's girl. Everybody knows that. Andy's made the Olympic hockey team.'

Duddy got up.

'What are you going to do?' Bernie asked.

'First I'm going to see the girl. She's sick at home. What I want to find out is if she's sick like I said Lennie was sick. Maybe they eloped?'

Bernie whistled. 'If they eloped you can stop worrying. Old man Calder is a millionaire. He's on the board of governors at McGill.'

Westmount was where the truly rich lived in stone mansions driven like stakes into the shoulder of the mountain. The higher you climbed up splendid tree-lined streets the thicker the ivy, the more massive the mansion, and the more important the men inside. Mr Calder's place was almost at the top. 'Jeez,' Duddy said aloud, getting out of his car. He had been in Westmount before in the taxi but usually at night and never this high up. Below, the city and the river hummed obligingly under a still cloud of factory fumes. What a site for a restaurant, Duddy thought. Looking up at the Calder house again he wondered what the bastard did with all those rooms. Maybe he's got eighteen kids, he thought. A Catholic like.

'Yes.'

The butler was a British movie sprung to life.

'I'd like to see Sandra.'

The butler told him that she was indisposed.

'It's important. I'm one of her best friends.'

'I'm sorry, but the doctor's with her right now. If you'd like to leave a message . . .'

Duddy thought of slipping the butler a fin. That, he thought, is what the Falcon would have done.

'Is there any message?' the butler asked sharply.

Duddy retreated a step. 'Naw. Thanks anyway. I'll call again.'

As the door closed gently on him Duddy began to curse himself. What's the matter with me, he thought. I should have insisted. There was a Bentley parked in the driveway. An Austin-Healey too. The third car had a doctor's licence plate on it. Well, that proves something anyway, Duddy thought, and he drove off.

The office was lonely without Yvette. Duddy locked the door and got out a map of Lac St Pierre. Twice already he had filled in with red crayon the land that had used to belong to Brault. His land. He started to go over it with the crayon again when the phone rang.

'I thought you were out looking for Lennie?'

'I just got in this minute, Daddy. There's no news yet. I'm seeing more people tonight but.'

Seigal phoned. 'About the movie,' he said, 'the *goy* was here again today to look over the house. Not only did he drink up all my Johnny Walker, but he tried to get my Selma to sit on his lap. She's only seventeen.'

'Artists are like children' Duddy said.

'It was black label. The best. He wrote a dirty poem to her too. It's called, quote, Advice to Virgins to Make Much of Time, unquote. It –'

'That verse might be worth a lot of money some day,' Duddy said. 'If I were you I'd hold on to it.' But he promised to be there next time Mr Friar came.

Duddy met Bernie at nine and they went to the bar where the students gathered. At one table boys and girls drank beer and sang and at another a long thin Negro sat with a girl who wore slacks. The girl had dirty fingernails.

'Steve,' Bernie said, 'this is Duddy Kravitz. He's Lennie's brother. Steve takes a lot of classes with Lennie.'

'What happened to Lennie today?'

'He's at home sick. Nothing serious, mind you.'

'Just a nervous breakdown,' Steve said.

'That's a joke, Duddy,' Bernie said.

'A joke? We've had two already this term. Three others have dropped out.'

'He's teasing you,' Bernie said.

'Is it Leonard *Kravitz* you're talking about?' the girl asked.

'Yeah. Why?'

'He's a suicidal type, isn't he, Steve?'

'Oh, you're a pair,' Bernie said. 'A real pair.'

'Did he say we're a pair?'

'I think so. One minute I'll ask him. Did you say we're a pair?'

'His brother's sick. Can't you see he's worried?'

'I think what he's trying to say is that this guy's brother is sick.'

'The pair type?'

'I'm not sure. One minute. Bernard, you were saying –'

'Oh, *that's* Bernard. I thought Bernard had committed suicide.'

'Come on, Duddy,' Bernie said, and he hurried him outside. They got into the car and drove off. Duddy didn't speak. He chain-smoked.

'You're driving very fast,' Bernie said.

'I think I'd better take you home, Bernie.' What a time for Yvette to be away, he thought. The bitch. 'I'm going home too. My father must be worried sick by this time.' Duddy thanked Bernie for all he'd done and promised to ring him as soon as he had any news. 'Good or bad,' he said morosely.

'Maybe he's home right now,' Bernie said.

But Lennie wasn't there.

'Where in the hell have you been all this time?' Max asked.

'At the movies. O.K.?'

'Oh, you're in that kind of mood. That's all I need.' Max pulled his back-scratcher out of the drawer. 'How the *zeyda* found out about all this I'll never know. But he wants you to call him tomorrow. My word he won't take.'

'I need some coffee.'

'O.K. Sit down before you fall down. You're white as a sheet. Boy, have you ever got a lousy build. Why don't you ever use my weight-lifts any more?'

'Tomorrow.'

'A guy's got to keep in shape, you know. This world is full of shits. When you meet one and he gives you a shove you want to be strong enough to shove him back. Right?'

'Right.'

'O.K.,' Max said, 'now tell me what you found out today.'

Duddy omitted the part about suicide. He didn't say anything about Lennie's fight with Riva, either.

'That Altman sounds like a prince of a fella,' Max said.

'He sure is. Oh, another thing. They expect Lennie to win the medal. A lot of people think he'll come first.'

'Wouldn't that be something?'

'Don't worry, Daddy. We'll find him and he'll go back to school.'

'Maybe Lennie'll turn out to be the guy who finds the cure for cancer.'

'Another Pasteur.'

'Bigger. Wow, the cure for cancer.'

Duddy rose and rubbed his eyes. 'Tomorrow I'm going to try to see the Calder girl again. There's also this Andy Simpson guy.'

'That would be a big thing for the Jews. One of ours finding the cancer-cure. Aw, they'd still make us trouble.'

'I'd better call Uncle Benjy before I go to sleep. I promised.'

'Don't waste your time. He's asleep on the sofa in the living-room. Benjy's going to be a real catch for the AA one of these days. He can go through a bottle of scotch quicker than I can drink a Pepsi.'

'What kind of signals were you trying to give me last night?'

'One minute.' Max tip-toed into the hall and shut the living-room door. 'It would be a good idea if you did not mention Auntie Ida to him for a while.'

'Why?'

'She was supposed to stay here for two months. She only got here yesterday afternoon, you know. They had a big row right off and, wham, she left for Florida again the same night.'

'You think she asked him for a divorce?'

'Maybe. I dunno. Imagine not being able to get it up. Ever, I mean.'

'I'm dead, Daddy. I'm going to sleep.'

'He can't even get into the States any more. That's what he gets for being such a smart guy.'

'Wha'?'

'Listen, there wasn't a petition invented that Uncle Benjy didn't sign in triplicate. They don't want commies there these days. You blame them?'

'Good night. Go to sleep, Daddy.'

Duddy lay on his bed with his eyes open. The police would have reported it, he thought. *What if he jumped in the canal?* A body could stay under for two-three days. Oh, no, Duddy thought, please. You're crazy. Suddenly Duddy decided to phone Yvette. What would he say, but? Make up something about the office. I'll tell her I can't find the keys to the desk, he thought. It would be so nice to speak to her.

'Do you mind if I come in?'

'Naw. Sit down, Uncle Benjy.'

Duddy repeated the story he had told his father. 'I'm going to try to see the girl tomorrow,' he said.

'You're holding something back. I'm not your father. I want to know all the facts.'

Duddy jerked awake. 'Why don't you lay off my father for a change? It hasn't been easy for him all alone since my mother died.'

'He told you that?' Uncle Benjy asked, smiling a little.

'Never mind.'

A car slowed down outside. Duddy rushed to the window, but it passed.

'Do you think he's committed suicide?'

'Shettup,' Duddy said.

'I see. It's been eating you too.'

'Lennie hasn't committed suicide. He's not the type.'

'There's no such thing as the type. You'd be surprised at the people . . .'

Aunt Ida, Duddy thought. She's tried it, I'm sure. Duddy searched his uncle's fat funny face in the darkness. The heavy bloodshot eyes returned the look coldly. 'You were saying?' he asked.

'It's a possibility. Let's face it.'

'He took all his clothes,' Duddy said.

'That's true.'

Duddy yawned.

'You want to sleep. I'll go.'

'What were you trying to tell me about my mother before?'

'Nothing. Good night.'

'He couldn't have killed himself. It's impossible.'

'I hope so, *Duddele*.'

'Good night.'

'When I was a boy in your *zeyda's* house,' Uncle Benjy said, 'I used to say my prayers before I went to sleep. He used to come in and listen and then he'd kiss me. That was a long time ago.'

'Why are you such a boozer, Uncle Benjy?'

'Good night and God bless you.'

Uncle Benjy lurched towards the door. Outside, he belched.

Chapter Nine

At ten the next morning Duddy came charging out of a bottom-less sleep, unsure of his surroundings but prepared for instant struggle, the alibi for a crime unremembered already half-born, panting, scratching, and ready to bolt if necessary. He shook his head, recognized his own room and sighed gratefully. Staggering out of his bedroom he tripped over a set of dumb-bells that had been left before his door and stubbed his toe badly. His father had left a note for him on the kitchen table.

> Remember, the world is full of shits. *Exercise!*
> Soon as you hear something phone me at Eddy's.
> Pop

Duddy ate breakfast around the corner at Moe's and read Dink Carroll in the *Gazette*. Next he turned to the financial page.

'Look what's worried about the market,' Moe said. 'Only last year if he came in here it was to steal cigarettes.'

Duddy ignored the remark and turned to the 'apartments to let' column.

'One year the nose is running,' Moe said, 'and the next they buy a jockstrap for eighty-nine cents and you can't say a word to them any more.'

Duddy marked off some of the more interesting ads. He graded the apartments available like movies in the Tely, giving one place on Tupper Street three stars. 'Another coffee please, sonny,' he said to Moe.

'It talks,' Moe said.

Duddy turned to Fitz's column. It's no use, he thought, I can't stall here all morning. I've got to get in to see that girl somehow. Duddy tossed a quarter on the counter. 'There you are, old chap,' he said.

Duddy took the longest route to Westmount, just as if he was driving the Dodge and had an out-of-town fare in the back. He blessed every red light, too, but eventually he got there. A maid answered the door.

'I've got an urgent message for Miss Sandra Calder,' Duddy said.

'I'm sorry, but – '

Duddy forced his way into the hall.

'Edgar,' the maid called. 'Edgar.'

A blonde girl in a kimono came through a glass door. 'Is it for me, Doris?'

The butler came through another door wiping his chin with a napkin.

'I'm Lennie's brother.'

The blonde girl lifted a hand to her cheek. 'Let him in,' she said.

'Miss Sandra your father said you were to have no visitors,' Edgar said.

'He won't be back for hours. Come inside.'

''Scuse me, Ed,' Duddy said, stepping past the butler, and he followed Sandra through an enormous dining-room with panelled walls into the breakfast room. Sandra poured him coffee, but she didn't speak until the maid had gone. 'How's Leonard?'

'Oh, fine. Just fine.'

'You have the same mouth. Otherwise there's not much of a resemblance.'

'So they tell me.'

'Did he send you?'

'Sure thing.'

'Tell him Daddy doesn't know. Dr Westcott promised not to tell him.'

'Is that so?'

'But he's going to try his best to find out who did it and when he does, brother, he's threatened everything but a lynching. Look, tell Leonard not to worry, because now that I'm all right I think I can talk Dr Westcott into keeping his mouth shut. Why don't you say anything?'

'Aw.'

'You think I'm not being fair to Leonard. You think I'm using him.'

She's going to cry, Duddy thought. 'Easy,' he said.

'Everything's going to work out. Tell him that, please. Dr Westcott's furious right now, but I can handle him. He adores me. What's wrong?'

Duddy bit his fingernail.

'*What is it?*'

'Lennie didn't send me. I don't even know where he is.'

'What?'

'Give me his address. I've got to see him.'

'No!'

'Listen here –'

'Oh, God, what did I tell you? How could you lie to me like that?'

Duddy grabbed her by the wrist. 'I want his address,' he said.

'I can't give it to you. I promised.'

'You promised,' he shouted. 'You think I care what you promised?'

'I can't do it.'

'He left a note saying he was going to quit medical school. Do you know how much sweat and struggle has gone into making Lennie –'

'But he needn't quit. I'll handle Dr Westcott.'

'Give me his address. Come on.'

She shook her head violently and tried to break free of him.

'You see this fist,' he said. 'Honest to God . . .'

'Edgar!'

Duddy let her go. 'O.K.,' he said, 'I'm sitting here until daddy-waddy comes. I'm going to tell him Dr Westcott knows something he doesn't know. O.K.?'

'You're terrible.'

Ver gerharget, he thought. *Platz*.

'That would just about ruin Leonard.'

'Give me his address.'

Edgar came. 'It's all right,' Sandra said. 'I found what I wanted.'

Duddy waited until he'd gone again. 'Look,' he said, 'all I want is to see him. Why should I do Lennie harm? He's my brother.'

'No. I can't.'

'Will you stop the water-works, please?'

'I can't give you his address.'

'I'm not a busy man. I'll just wait here until your father comes.'

Ten minutes passed. Sandra lit a cigarette. 'I'm not going to talk to you any more,' she said. 'I'm going to ignore you.'

'Don't make *me* cry,' Duddy said.

'I'm going up to my room.'

There was a pause. 'Well,' Duddy asked, 'what's keeping you?'

'Aren't you going?'

'I'm waiting here for your father. I told you that.'

'If I gave you his address would you promise not to make any trouble?'

'Give me his address. Come on.'

Sandra wrote out the address and led him through the dining-room again.

'You could fit a bowling alley into here. Jeez.'

'I don't even know your name. All you told me is that you're his brother.'

'Dudley. I'm in the film business. An indie.'

'I beg your pardon?'

'An independant producer,' he said, handing her his card. 'Hey, you must know a lot of debutantes like . . .'

Sandra was still absorbed by his card.

'Listen,' Duddy said, 'have you ever heard of John Peter Friar?' He told her about him. 'We could do a top-notch picture on a coming-out party. A record for your grandkiddies and their grandkiddies after them.'

Sandra smiled.

'Don't lose that card. You get us a job in Westmount and there'll be something in it for you. I'm no piker, you know.'

'Do I look as if I need the money?'

'I never met a pretty girl yet who couldn't use a few extra bucks for a nice dress.'

'Tell Leonard not to worry.'

'Can do,' Duddy said. 'Cheerio.'

Chapter Ten

Max was out. Duddy phoned Yvette and his grandfather and Uncle Benjy and when he returned to the office he called his father again. 'He's in Toronto.'

'What in the hell's he doing there?'

'A fling. He's been studying too hard, that's all. I'm leaving on the four o'clock train. I'm too tired to drive.'

'Maybe I oughta go with you?'

'Ixnay.'

'He's awright? You're not kidding me?'

'I'll bring him home tomorrow as good as new.'

'You're a good kid.'

'Sure.'

Max phoned back two minutes later. 'Listen, is Uncle Benjy going with you?'

'No. Certainly not.'

'Awright. Hey, one minute. Has Lennie got a broad with him there?'

'A dozen maybe. If they're any good I'll bring one home for you.'

'Hey, I'm your father. Don't forget that. There should be respect.'

Duddy laughed.

'I mean that,' Max said.

'That's not why I'm laughing. I'm laughing because I feel good. Cheerio.'

Duddy phoned Bernie and then he rang Mr Friar. He told him he had to go to Toronto for a couple of days. There were some things he wanted to discuss with him first, however, and they arranged to meet for a drink.

'First off,' Duddy said, 'keep your hands off Seigal's girl. He's on to you. Here's a list of suggestions for the movie.'

'I told you when I started, Kravitz, that I will tolerate no artistic interference.'

'They're only suggestions. You can throw them out if you want to. Do you need any money?'

Mr Friar began to stammer. 'Here.' Duddy gave him a hundred dollars. 'Oh, before I forget. Yvette will be back at seven. Take her out for a good dinner, Mr Friar. I'd really appreciate that.'

'Doesn't the competition worry you?'

Duddy's face brightened. 'Gwan.' He clapped Mr Friar on the back. 'You're old enough to be her father.'

'What a charming boy you are!'

'I'm going to miss my train,' Duddy said.

'Wait. There's something I want to ask you. In some ways you're just about the shrewdest bastard I've ever met yet I happen to know that you're buying land under Yvette's name.'

Duddy set down his bag.

'Don't worry. She didn't tell me. I couldn't help overhearing.'

'So?'

'Doesn't it worry you having the deeds under her name?'

'A friend is a friend. You've got to trust somebody . . . Jeez, I've gotta run.' But Duddy stopped short at the door. 'Hey,' he shouted, 'I've got a seat in the club car. *Style?* Style.'

Mr Friar lifted his glass to him. 'Cheers,' he said.

'I'd trust you too,' Duddy shouted. '*Prosit*,' And he ran off.

Duddy got into Toronto at ten-thirty. He had never been there before and he had no hotel reservation. Imagine, he thought, if my grandfather had had another ten bucks in his pocket when he came to Canada I would have been born here. I would never have gone to FFHS or found Lac St Pierre. He took the address Sandra had given him out of his pocket again. A number on Church Street. That tells me a lot, he thought. But Duddy was in an excellent mood. He had never travelled so far on his own before and the excitement of the club car was still with him. At least eight guys had exchanged cards with him. I'm good at making contacts, he thought. One of the men who had sat with him in the diner, the grey-haired one, was going all the way to Chicago. He was with Massey-Harris. 'The market is hard this year,' he told Duddy. Another guy in the diner, this one very nice, had told him, 'I like doing business with the people of your race. I've never had any trouble with them.'

'Good of you to say so.'

The last man to make up their dinner party was a jovial Westerner. Ed Brody was stopping off in Toronto for the Grey Cup Finals. 'Are we ever going to give those Argos a licking,' he said. 'Christ Almighty.'

They discussed the communist menace.

'If I were Truman,' the grey-haired one said, 'I'd pull out of the UN. It's just a glorified debating society.'

'You've got a point there,' Duddy said.

Duddy had no trouble getting a taxi outside the station. The address was a door over a chinese laundry. This is worse than St Urbain Street, he thought. There was a 'room to let' sign and a bowl of paper flowers in the bay window alongside. He rang three times before the landlady came. 'I'm looking for Leonard Kravitz.'

'Never heard of him.'

'He's my brother. We've got the same mouth.'

'Isn't that nice for you?'

Duddy showed her a picture. 'I know he's staying here,' he said.

'Are you calling me a liar?'

'You're a fine lady. Anybody can see that.'

The landlady began to tap her foot. 'Have you got a search warrant?'

'Listen. Listen here. I go to the movies too. I'm not a cop. I'm his brother. Lennie! Hey, Lennie! *Lennie!*'

A door opened on the third floor.

'It's me. Duddy!'

'Duddy!'

Duddy pushed the landlady aside and took the stairs two at a time. The whole lousy house was permeated with *goy*-smell. Bacon grease. The way they can live, Duddy thought. Jeez.

'How did you find me?'

'Me and Bulldog Drummond went to different schools together. Aw,' Duddy said, grabbing his brother, punching and hugging him, 'Sandra gave me your address. I had to twist her arm to get it but.'

'You went there?' Lennie asked, breaking free.

'Yeah. Come on inside and close the door. I'll bet your landlady's standing down there and listening to every word. Look at you. Wow!'

Lennie needed a shave. He'd lost weight too. 'I'm all right,' he said. 'I can take care of myself.'

'Sure. Who said no? Now let's get out of here.'

'I'm not going home. I can't. I'm finished at medical school.'

'Look, I'm starved. We can't talk in this dump. Is there anywhere near here where we can get a good smoked meat?'

They went to a restaurant on Yonge Street. 'Well,' Duddy asked, 'is it good to see me?'

'Nothing will make me go back.'

'What happened?'

'Nothing.'

'Why'd you run away then?'

'I felt like it.'

'Great! Now that you've brought me up to date I can go home.'

'I'm going to get a job here. Tell Daddy I'm O.K.'

'You tell him yourself. Daddy wants you to be a doctor. That's his dream of a life-time.'

'Everybody wants me to be a doctor. What about what I want? Look, even if I wanted to I couldn't go back to medical school.'

'Why?'

'I can't say. I gave my word.'

'No kidding?'

'And if Uncle Benjy doesn't like it he can go to hell.'

'I'll tell him that. I'll tell him Lennie took all that money from you over the years just to prove how much he hated you. What's the diff, I'll say, you've got lots of kids of your own. It isn't as if you put your heart into educating Lennie . . . Daddy is something else. All the other drivers know he's a big liar anyway. They won't be surprised when you don't turn out a doctor.'

'Will you leave me alone please?'

'I'll tell Daddy you're getting a job here as a shipper. There's a big future for you. I'll tell him he doesn't have to pimp for Josette any more so that he can give you gifts like Uncle Benjy.'

'What?'

'Any more messages for home?'

'I'm getting one of my headaches,' Lennie said.

'Tell me why you can't go back to medical school even if you wanted to.'

'I've given my word of honour. I'm sworn to silence.'

'What are you? A boy scout?'

'I'm a gentleman.'

'Come again. This ear is blocked.'

'You think just because I wasn't born in Westmount I can't be a gentleman?'

'Ah,' Duddy said.

'You think just because some of our people made buckets during the war and others, like Uncle Benjy's pals, wouldn't think twice about handing over war secrets to Russia, that I still can't be a gentleman?'

'I've got it. You're an anti-semite.'

'O.K. I'm an anti-semite. I prefer the company of Gentiles.'

'You don't mind my sitting here, I hope?'

'You asked me, I told you.'

'I mean you're not scared of being contaminated?'

'No.'

'Good. Because I've got a message for you. Sandra says not to worry. Her father doesn't know and Dr Westcott promised not to tell him.'

'That's fine. Thanks.'

'But she also told me that Dr Westcott is going to try his best to find out who did it and that when he does there's going to be a lynching. I'm looking at the leading candidate.'

'I see.'

'You don't look so good, Lennie. Headache?'

'Lay off.'

'What is it her father doesn't know?'

'I can't say.'

'You're a gentleman.'

'Lay – off – please.'

'You're a chicken, that's what you are.'

'Ssh. People are beginning to look at us.'

'You want me to tell you what happened? You performed an abortion on that girl.'

'Let's get out of here,' Lennie said. 'Quick.'

They went back to Lennie's room.

'Can we talk tomorrow?' Lennie said. 'My head is splitting.'

'You're twenty-four years old. Don't you know better than to go bareback?'

'Please,' Lennie said.

'We'll start from the beginning. You tell me everything right from the beginning.'

'What's the use, Duddy? Nothing can be done.'

'That night you came home drunk. When you said "it could ruin me for life". That's when you first found out she was pregnant, isn't it?'

Lennie didn't reply.

'Come on Lennie, please. I want to help.'

Lennie told him about the party where he had quarrelled with Riva. 'She's no better than a whore,' he said. 'You should have been there. Boy, did I ever tell her off.'

'I heard.'

He had run into Irwin Shubert a few days later and they had had a long intimate chat. Irwin, he said, was one of the most intelligent people he had ever met, and he had no use for the Hillel bunch either. 'They inhabit a psychological ghetto,' he had said, 'and dare not step outside of it because they're afraid of being rejected.' He had offered to take Lennie to a party the next night and that's where he met Sandra and Andy Simpson.

'This is the man I've been telling you about,' Irwin had said.

Sandra had smiled so warmly and Andy had clapped him on the back. 'Good to have you with us, kid.'

Andy's father, Lennie pointed out, was J. P. Simpson. *The* J. P. Simpson.

'*Mazel tov*,' Duddy said. 'Did Irwin seem to be a good friend of his?'

Irwin, it seemed, was very devoted to Andy. He was always fetching him drinks, he went down to watch him at hockey practices, and he was coaching him privately in English and history. Andy had to keep his marks up or he'd have to quit athletics. 'Andy liked me,' Lennie said, 'and so did Sandra. I could tell. I'm sensitive to that kind of thing and anyway Irwin took me aside once and as much as told me that Sandra had a crush on me. He was a bit drunk, you know, and he said he was glad he wasn't Andy. Sandra was supposed to be Andy's girl.

Anyway there were lots of parties and after that I was invited to every single one of them. What a swell bunch of characters, honestly, so generous and relaxed and happy. When they have a party or go to a restaurant nobody worries about making too much noise or attracting attention, if you know what I mean. They're just themselves and glad of it. Nothing scares them. They're not always plugging away either, worried about this, worried about that, frightened about the future. They have a good time. *They're young*. That's it. That's what I'm trying to say. I never had such a wonderful time in my life. Honestly, Duddy. If there wasn't a party I'd meet Irwin and Andy and we'd go and drink together in the Maritime Bar in the Ritz. Sometimes we'd pick up Sandra and a couple of other girls and we'd drive all the way out to Ste Adèle to eat. Just like that, Duddy. And Irwin knows so much about food, you know. He knows all the . . . em . . . *exciting* wines too. There were times, it's true, when he and Sandra would bicker about this and that, but – '

'Bicker about what?'

'Oh, you know the kind of thing. Everyone's had too much to drink and Sandra would say something like, I'm seeing Andy tomorrow night, do you mind? It was nothing really. The next day it would be forgotten.'

'Yeah? Keep talking.'

'They're such a great crowd, Duddy. You must understand that. I never dreamt I'd have such a swell time. They knew I was Jewish too. I told them. *I* wasn't going to hide it. I'm glad I didn't either because it didn't make any difference. Nobody minded.'

Then Lennie had noticed that Andy was in bad shape. He drank an awful lot. 'Even for him,' Lennie said. Irwin took Lennie aside and explained why Andy was drinking so much and how Lennie could help.

'You mean it wasn't even you who knocked her up? Jeez, now I've heard everything.'

'Do you want to hear the rest of the story or not?'

'A gentleman. Is that what you said you were? I've got news for you, brother. You're the Number 1 Sucker of All-Time.'

'You *would* look at things like that. You have no code of honour, Duddy. That's your trouble.'

'Wha'?'

'What's in it for me, that's your philosophy. I knew you'd never understand.'

'Tell me the rest, please. Come on.'

Irwin had told Lennie that Sandra was pregnant, that much was true, and he had asked Lennie if he would perform the abortion. Andrew, he said, knew nothing about their conversation, he would never ask such a favour of Lennie. 'But I know you're not a frightened little hebe,' Irwin had said. 'I know you'll come through.'

Lennie had said absolutely no. It was too big a risk, he couldn't do it, and that's the night he had come home drunk. 'The way he looked at me,' Lennie said, 'I knew I was through. I'd never see any of them again.'

'So what,' Duddy said. 'A big deal.'

'And I was right,' Lennie continued, 'because after that I began to see less and less of Sandra, Andy, and their crowd.' Irwin still drank with him from time to time. Lapsing into that liquid whisper of his, he'd say things like, 'I hear there's an Oneg Shabbat at Hillel tonight. Why don't you go?' He told Lennie that he was right not to take the risk. Friendships only went so far, a man had his career to think of.

'Then he'd be off to one of their parties,' Lennie said, 'and I'd be left sitting there. It was terrible. I never felt so bad in my life. Listen, Duddy, those people were my friends. I never really had friends before. She's so pretty, you know. All I could think of was her crying and Andy saying what can you expect, he's a Jew and he's afraid.'

'Why couldn't she go to Dr Westcott for the abortion?'

'Don't be ridiculous, Duddy.'

'You want to know something? I know Irwin. I know that bastard inside out and I'll put down a hundred bucks against your ten that before he ever brought you around he told Andy you'd do the abortion.'

'There you go again. You suspect everybody. Nobody's decent in your book. They like me, Duddy. They're my friends.'

'Don't shout.'

'You don't like Irwin because he used psychology to show you up for a money-crazy kid at the hotel. I know all about that.'

'I hope you didn't take my side.'

187

'You deserved what you got. You're greedy. I'm saying that to your face.'

'O.K. Skip it. Let's get on with the story. The rest, please.'

'I phoned Irwin and said I would do it and the arrangements were made. Why he got so jumpy right in the middle of it I'll never know. I could have handled it, I swear it, but Irwin saw the blood and went crazy. Sandra got hysterical. "Irwin wants to kill me," she said over and over again. "He wants to kill me." And the next thing I knew Irwin had dashed out to call Dr Westcott.'

'I don't get it.'

Lennie explained that the phone call had been made anonymously. The three boys had waited in the hall until Dr Westcott had come and then they had slipped outside. Sandra had naturally refused to tell Dr Westcott who had started the abortion.

'So what are you doing here?' Duddy asked. 'What are you so scared of?'

'He's sure to find out eventually. And when he does it's the end of me. I'll be thrown out of medical school.'

'You're goddam right he's sure to find out. Because from what I know about Irwin and from what I hear about this Andy bastard all he has to do is ask.'

'They'd never say a word.'

'Sure.' Duddy rose and cracked his knuckles. 'It must be three o'clock,' he said. 'How's your headache?'

'Right now it's not so bad. Look, Duddy, I'm sorry. I know Daddy will feel terrible. But what can I do?'

'Bernie Altman says you had an excellent chance of winning the medal.'

'Lay off. Please, Duddy.'

'Let's go to sleep. I've got some business to do here to-morrow.' Duddy began to undress. 'Look, I want you to think hard. I want you to think hard and tell me the truth. Do you still want to be a doctor?'

'What does it matter what I want?'

'Answer me. Jeez.'

'Yes.'

'O.K. Which side of the bed do you want? Good Lord! What

lumps, old chap. How does that old *fershtunkene tuchos*-head rent these rooms?'

Duddy fell asleep instantly, but not Lennie. Lennie turned on his side and stared at the wall. Duddy huddled close to him, embracing Lennie's waist. Twice Lennie moved away, embarrassed and uncomfortable, but each time Duddy pulled tighter to him again. Duddy snored. His body was seized by sudden jerks in his sleep.

'Lennie?'

It was five a.m. maybe.

'What is it?'

'Talk to me about Maw. Tell me about her.'

'In the morning.'

'Did she . . . well, like me?'

'You were her kid.'

'That's not what I meant.'

'Tomorrow. O.K.? And will you stop hugging me, please.'

'I'm freezing, you jerk. What are you so scared of? I'm no homo.'

Duddy was gone before Lennie woke the next morning. There were several independent film companies in Toronto, outfits that made industrial films, and Duddy, pretending to be a Diamond T Trucks representative, checked them all on prices. He also visited Columbia and Paramount to inquire about the price of films for semi-private distribution and to pick up catalogues. He was exhausted by the time he came round to pick up Lennie.

'Well,' he said, 'I've got the train tickets. We leave at four.'

'What are you going to do?'

'I'm going to see Calder and tell him the whole story.'

'Are you crazy?'

'No. But I'm not a gentleman either.'

'I won't let you do it.'

'I'm not asking your permission.'

'It would mean the loss of all my self-respect, Duddy. It's not honourable.'

'How would you like to hold this for a while?'

'If you go and tell Calder I did it I'm sure to be kicked out. He could send me to prison.'

'We'll have to take that chance. There's no other way of being sure.'

'I'm not going there with you.'

'I didn't expect you to.'

'Don't do it to me, Duddy. Please don't go there and tell them. Sandra would . . .'

'I'll say you don't know I'm doing it.'

'When Irwin finds out – Well, there goes my summer in Maine.'

'Wha'?'

'Irwin's taking a cottage in Maine this summer with some of the crowd. I was invited.'

Uncle Benjy, Duddy remembered, couldn't get into the States. He was a communist. 'Listen, Lennie, there's no other way. Calder's sure to find out some time. I've got to see him first.'

'What'll we tell Daddy?'

'You were studying too hard and you went on a fling. That's the story.'

'Maybe if I just stayed here for a while Westcott wouldn't find out anything. Maybe it would all blow over.'

'Have any other medical students who have been seen at parties with Sandra Calder taken it on the lam to Toronto recently?'

Duddy slept on the train. He didn't wake until they reached the outskirts of the city. 'Look,' he said as they pulled into Central Station, 'snow. The first snow. Aw, come on, Lennie. Buck up.'

'Yeah.'

'There's Daddy.'

'Taxi,' Max shouted. 'Taxi, sir.' He embraced Lennie.'Oh, Duddy, your girl has been calling all day. She says to go right to the office.'

'Me and Frank Buck,' Duddy said, 'we bring 'em back alive,' and he punched his father lightly on the shoulder. 'See you later, old chap.' Duddy ran, he jumped, grabbing for the falling snow, opening his mouth to swallow some.

'Some kid,' Max said.

Duddy took a taxi, watching the snow and the rush of lights outside, searching for lookers among the window-shoppers, gazing at their legs and in his mind's eye stripping the juicier ones down to black lace panties. Boy, he thought impatiently, am I ever in the mood.

Yvette was excited. 'Duquette's willing to sell,' she said.

Duddy unlocked the desk and got the map out and saw that Duquette owned a considerable amount of lake frontage on the side opposite Brault.

'The sister in the asylum died. He's got a clear title now.'

'How much?'

'Four hundred and twenty-five dollars an arpent. Twenty-five hundred dollars down.' There was no rush this time. The notary said there were no other potential buyers.

'Let's try to knock him down to sixty-five. Tell the notary we'll hand over the works in cash if he'll take sixty.'

'Have you got twenty-five hundred dollars?'

'Not quite. But I can get it,' he said, picking up the phone. 'Oh, I brought Lennie back. He was in Toronto.'

'Why did he run away?'

'Aw, he knocked up a *shiksa*. A girl, I mean. Whoops . . . Hello, Mr Seigal? Kravitz here. Listen, I'm going to need another five hundred in advance on the film – What? Oh, I see. Sure that's O.K. Good. See you soon. No, don't worry. It'll make *Happy Bar-Mitzvah, Bernie* look sick. I promise.' He hung up. 'Seigal says he gave five hundred dollars on account to Mr Friar this morning. Friar asked him for it. He gave him a receipt. Have you seen Friar today?'

'No.'

Duddy looked closely at Yvette. 'We need a couch in here,' he said hoarsely. 'We oughta have a couch.' He let Mr Friar's number ring and ring. There was no answer. 'He's probably asleep. Stop looking so worried, please. He needed money for film or something, that's all.' Duddy hung up and told Yvette that he wanted her to find him an apartment downtown. 'I also want you to get me subscriptions to *Fortune*, *Time*, *Life* and – There's another one, but I forget. We also ought to get some stills to hang on the walls. The bigger the better . . . Come here a minute,' he said, taking her hand and guiding it. 'Some flag-pole, eh? A regular Rock of Gibraltar.'

Yvette wanted to wait, but Duddy insisted, and they made love on the carpet.

'I don't get it,' Duddy said. 'Imagine guys getting married and tying themselves down to one single broad for a whole life-time when there's just so much stuff around.'

'People fall in love,' Yvette said. 'It happens.'

'Planes crash too,' Duddy said. 'Listen, I've got an important letter to write. We'll eat soon. O.K.?'

She didn't answer and Duddy began to type.

TO WHOM IT MAY CONCERN:

It has come to my attention that one Irwin Shubert intends to rent a cottage in Maine this summer. It is therefore my painful duty to inform you that the aforementioned Shubert is well-known for his communistic beliefs on the McGill campus. He is known far and wide for sticking up for un-Americans like Henry Wallace, Paul Robeson, and Fred Rose, and I hardly think he would be a desirable guest in the fine State of Maine. I don't understand why he is going (unless it is to do some dirty work for the commies) because the aforementioned Shubert is always propagandizing against the United States, saying how it is run by Wall Street and they are fascists and started the Korean War.

PATRIOTIC CITIZEN

PS. It is my firmly held conviction that the abovementioned Schubert is also a sexual pervert. This is a heart-break to his family but I thought you ought to know as these are dangerous times.

Duddy handed Yvette the letter. 'Check the spelling,' he said, 'and first thing tomorrow send copies to Senator McCarthy, the FBI, and the principal of McGill. I also want you to take out subscriptions for Irwin to the *Tribune* and any other commie papers you can think of. Pay for them in cash. O.K., let's go eat. I'm starved.'

Chapter Eleven

Hugh Thomas Calder had not made the family fortune, his father had done that, but he administered it with conservative good sense. His financial operations lacked panache, he avoided the big gamble, but steadily, unobtrusively he made money with his father's money. *Time* had called him 'bland, brilliant Hugh Thomas Calder', but that, he supposed, was because he said very little, and so people being what they were, put him down for a thinker. That wasn't the case. Most things he had to say were, he felt, rather asinine, usually he was bored, and so he seldom spoke unless he was asked a direct question. Mr Calder was a widower, and grateful for it. He enjoyed living alone. Well, not quite alone. For there was Sandra. When Sandra had been fourteen he had looked at her and realized that she would grow up to be the true rich bitch, but he didn't care. Why not, he had thought. There's certainly money enough for it, and it's time somebody enjoyed it.

Hugh Thomas Calder did not pine for power, he had had his father's fortune thrust on him. He abhorred the stale atmosphere of board rooms and committees and clubs, but there was nothing else he really wanted to do. He was not a frustrated artist or farmer. Neither did he see himself as a political candidate. A mere fifty and still mildly handsome, Calder was not altogether without enthusiasms. They were short-lived, however. He had collected pictures by young Canadian artists for a time, the non-figurative kind of stuff, and then one day he looked at them all together, gave them away, and never bought another one. He had tried an analyst once, a little German refugee with sour breath, and he had invented the most extravagant dreams for his sake, but the German had been more interested in his opinions on the market and Calder had dropped him. He had once been intrigued with a girl who sang in a nightclub under the name of

Carole – she complained endlessly about the conditions of her work – and one evening he asked her, 'I wonder what you would do if you were suddenly given five thousand dollars out of nowhere.'

'Oh,' was all she said, and he made out the cheque right there.

Carole had seemed such a spirited girl that he had hoped she would do something wild. What she did was quit her job and bring her sister and mother in from the country and open up a hat shop.

There had been other and, when he reflected on it, more shameful little experiments with money. Once, at the Chantecler in Ste Adèle, a hundred dollar bill had accidentally dropped to the bottom of a urinal when he had hurriedly reached for his handkerchief. Calder hadn't retrieved the soaking note. He had returned to the bar and sat there staring at the toilet door for some time. After four other men with all of whom he had a nodding acquaintance had been inside Calder went to the toilet again. The hundred dollar bill was gone. Back in the bar again Calder examined each of the four men severely, trying to guess who had stooped for the note. He thought of announcing his loss, he wanted badly to humiliate whoever had done it, and that depressed him. But the shocking part of it – for him anyway – was that following the first accidental loss he had, while staying at smart resorts, two or three times purposely repeated the procedure and then sat where he could keep an eye on the toilet door. Each time he would try to guess the man who had stooped. It was shortly after he began this that he paid his first visit to the little German analyst.

Hugh Thomas Calder disliked Dr Westcott intensely. He knew Sandra was not suffering from a mere nervous upset and that Westcott knew more than he was saying and – what's more – was aching to be asked about it. Calder was going to deny him that pleasure. Sandra was, to his mind, a shallow little bitch and unless it was absolutely necessary for him to know he'd much rather not get involved in what was bound to be sordid. So he was displeased and in a most unreceptive mood when Edgar came to tell him that there was a young gentleman who insisted on seeing him alone.

'What does he look like?'

Edgar described him as a thin, shifty boy. He wore pointed

patent-leather shoes. 'He was here once before, Sir. To see Miss Sandra.'

'I see. Send him in, please.'

When Duddy entered the living-room Hugh Thomas Calder rose with studied weariness from his armchair and put on his glasses to have a better look.

'It's about Sandra,' Duddy said quickly. 'She hasn't got a cold. She was knocked up.'

Calder removed his glasses. He stared. 'Are you an abortionist?' he asked.

'Me! Are you crazy? Oh, I'm sorry.'

'Let me guess, then. You're a blackmailer.'

'Hey, one minute. I'm a respectable businessman.' He handed Mr Calder his card. 'I'm in the motion picture business.'

'I see. Are you sure you wouldn't like to sit down? Now, are you a blackmailer?'

'Jeez.' There was a pause. 'Could I have a drink, please? I mean is that rude for me to ask . . .?'

Mr Calder went to the bar and poured two whiskies and soda. 'You were saying?'

'Lennie's not going to be the fall-guy, see. I've got friends.'

'I'm sure you have, but – '

'He's a cinch to win the medal. You're on the board of governors and you can help.'

'I'm afraid I don't understand.'

'O.K. Sure. But one thing I want to get straight first. Lennie doesn't know I'm here. He'd kill me if he found out.'

'Lennie?'

'He's my brother.'

Duddy told him about the bungled abortion.

'But they could have killed her,' Mr Calder said. 'Why didn't she come to me?'

'They're kids,' Duddy said. 'I've seen quite a bit of them in the last week and if you'll pardon me they don't know from their ass to their elbow.'

'Perhaps you're right. But what do you want from me?'

'This Dr Westcott can make trouble. He can get Lennie expelled.'

'Don't you think he ought to be expelled?'

'No sir. I'm speaking candidly.'

'Give me one good reason why not.'

'Oh, let's not talk like that please. They took advantage of him like.'

'Don't you think he might at least have waited until he got his degree before he started to perform illegal operations?'

'O.K., he made a mistake. Why should he be the fall-guy but? Why should your daughter and Andy Simpson get off and Lennie be expelled?'

'I think they all ought to be thrown off the campus.'

'Wow.'

'I'm trying to be fair.'

'Sure. Sure you are. Sandra's expelled and she comes home to this Yankee Stadium here and for all I know she can sleep in a different bedroom every night. That Andy Simpson goes home and sits on his ass until his father croaks and he inherits enough money to choke ten horses. But what about my brother,' Duddy shouted, approaching Calder, 'what happens to him? He becomes a taxi-driver. He gets a job in a candy store. Do you know what went in to getting that guy into medical school?'

'Why didn't he think of that before?'

'Maybe he did. But he's a poor boy and he never met up with ladies and gentlemen before. Present company excepted.'

'That's not a good enough excuse.'

'And what happens to my father? He dies of a broken heart. Thank you.'

'I'm sorry.'

'He's sorry. Hah! Look it wasn't even Lennie who knocked her up. He never once touched her. Is that how you people pay off favours?'

Mr Calder didn't reply.

'All you have to do is tell Westcott to shettup. When he finds out, I mean. Meanwhile he doesn't even know it was Lennie.'

'Why should I use my influence to conceal a criminal act?'

'What are you? A lawyer.'

'Are you very fond of your brother?'

'He's my brother,' Duddy said, annoyed. 'You know.'

'How old are you?'

'Almost nineteen.'

'Good God!'

'What's the matter?'

'Couldn't your brother have come here to see me himself?'

'He doesn't know I'm here.'

'Nonsense.'

'O.K., so he knows. Lennie's very sensitive. He gets head-aches. Coming here was my idea anyway. Be a sport, Mr Calder. Don't make trouble.'

'Why shouldn't I?'

'You'd feel better to see him expelled, ruined for life?'

'No.'

'O.K.,' Duddy said, 'then it's settled. You'll speak to Westcott and – '

'Wait a minute, please.'

'I thought you said – '

'Tell me how a boy your age gets into the film business. I'm interested.'

Duddy told him about Mr Friar, Yvette, and *Happy Bar-Mitzvah, Bernie*. Each time he made Mr Calder laugh he felt easier, more hopeful, but it was difficult for him to tell if he was really making progress. Mr Calder resisted each attempt to bring the conversation back to Lennie's future.

'And what about you,' Mr Calder asked. 'Why didn't you go to the university?'

Duddy guffawed. 'I'm not the type, I guess.'

'Are you positive?'

'I come from the school of hard knocks.'

'And what do you want out of life? Money.'

'I want land. A man without land is nothing. Listen, about Lennie – '

'I still see no reason why he shouldn't be expelled.'

'Just this once, Mr Calder, couldn't you – Well, he's a good boy. Really he is. And he's worked so hard like. Studying and studying . . .'

'If he was such a good boy he wouldn't have allowed you to come here to speak for him. He would have come himself.'

'What do you want? Blood? He has to go back to McGill. He has to see Sandra and Andy and all those other rich stinkers every day. How could he come here?'

'It would have been awkward. I understand, but – '

'Have a heart.'

Mr Calder smiled.

'Maybe some day I'll be able to return the favour. I've got friends, you know.'

'Oh.'

'You heard of the Boy Wonder?'

Mr Calder waited.

'Only the other weekend the Wonder and I went down to New York together for the weekend. Just like that.'

'What on earth is the Boy Wonder?'

'Jerry Dingle – the *Boy Wonder*. You mean you never heard of him?' What, Duddy thought, if the truly powerful people in the city knew nothing about the Wonder? Could it be that Dingleman was only famous on St Urbain Street? 'You're sure you never heard of him?'

'Absolutely.'

'Jeez. I thought everybody–Look, Mr Calder, give Lennie a chance and I swear I'll never forget it. I'm only small beans right now, but one day . . . well,' Duddy said, 'you know the old saying. Mighty oaks from little acorns grow.'

Mr Calder laughed. He refilled his glass. 'Very well,' he said at last, 'I'll speak to Dr Westcott.'

'Shake on it?' Duddy asked, jumping up.

'Is he waiting outside?'

'No. He's at home.'

'Well, you can tell him for me that he's lucky to have you for a brother.'

'Aw. You'd be surprised at some of the things I've done in my time.'

'I wouldn't.'

'I'd like to show my appreciation, Mr Calder. I'd like to send you a gift, but – Jeez, what does a guy like you need?' Usually, Duddy knew, it was safe to send a *goy* booze, but Calder owned a distillery. 'I've got it. You name your favourite charity and I'll send them fifty bucks. A token like.'

'That won't be necessary, Kravitz, but why don't you come and see me again?'

'Wha'?'

'Phone me,' Mr Calder said. 'We could have dinner together.'

Chapter Twelve

'Crook!' It was Mr Cohen on the phone. 'Rotten stinker!'

Mr Cohen had shown *Happy Bar-Mitzvah, Bernie* to Dave Stewart in Toronto and Dave, who was with Columbia, had walked out in the middle of the first reel. 'Amateur night in Dixie,' he had said. But Mr Cohen was the least of Duddy's worries.

Mr Friar had disappeared. He had not removed his belongings from his apartment, but for three nights running he did not show up there. Duddy and Yvette phoned the police and all the hospitals. They went from nightclub to nightclub.

'You'll never see that five hundred dollars again,' Yvette said.

'The hell with the money. The day after tomorrow is the Seigal *bar-mitzvah*. What am I going to do for a camera man?'

'He's probably back in England by now.'

'Do you think,' Duddy asked, 'if I studied up on it that I could learn how to shoot a film before Saturday morning?'

On Friday afternoon Duddy moved into his apartment on Tupper Street. 'This is the berries,' he said. There were two rooms, a kitchen, and a tiled bathroom. Duddy tried the shower, he poked his head inside the fridge. 'It still stinks of *chazer-fleish* in here,' he said.

'What?' Yvette asked.

'*Goy*-stink. We oughta rub the walls down with chicken fat before I move in.'

Yvette's one-room apartment was in the basement of the same building. 'I can come up and cook for you,' she said.

'That's my girl Friday,' Duddy said, goosing her.

'Stop that.'

'Jeez. Have you got the curse again?'

'Maybe I'm not going to have my period this month. Maybe I'm pregnant.'

'Congrats. Come on. We'd better start checking through the bars for Friar again.'

'One minute. What would you do if I *was* pregnant?'

'I've got just the guy to fix you. A real pro. My brother Lennie.'

They went from bar to bar. They tried the taverns. Duddy showed Mr Friar's picture to the hat check girls in at least ten night clubs. The head waiter at Rockhead's had seen him about an hour earlier and Duddy's spirit lifted. 'Was he sloshed?' Duddy asked.

'Are you kidding, buster?'

They found him in the Algiers at two in the morning. He was snoozing.

'Ah, Kravitz, come to collect your pound of flesh, I suppose?'

'I'm surprised at you, Friar. We've got to go to a *bar-mitzvah* tomorrow morning.'

Yvette began to go through his pockets.

'Kravitz, I have never in my life held up a production. I always turn up on the floor. Apologize.'

'Would it make you feel better if I kissed your ass for you? Come on. Let's go.'

Yvette cursed. 'A hundred and twenty-two dollars. That's all he's got left.'

They took him to Duddy's flat and put him under the shower. Yvette fed him cup after cup of black coffee.

'I've sold my soul to the Hebrews. Shame on me,' Mr Friar said, slapping himself on the cheek. 'Shame, shame.'

'More coffee, Yvette.'

'I was supposed to be a second Eisenstein. What happened?'

'You're a very gifted man. Everybody says so. Isn't that right, Yvette?'

'My essays on the cinema in *Isis* used to be widely quoted. Everyone expected me to . . . I'd like a drink, please.'

'Ha ha.'

'Kravitz, you can't treat me like this.'

'Listen, Friar, tomorrow night you can have all the booze you want on me. But right now you're going to sleep. We have to be up at eight. That gives you four hours and you're going to need every one of them. Come on.'

Duddy led him into the bedroom. Mr Friar protested feebly, he spluttered, and then he fell asleep.

'You'd better get some sleep too, Yvette. Hey, one minute. You haven't really got one in the oven? You were only kidding me, weren't you?'

'Yes, I was only kidding.'

'Good. See you at eight. Eight sharp.'

Mr Friar arrived punctually at the synagogue, but he was in no condition to shoot a movie. He also discovered too soon exactly where the liquor was kept. He was most reassuring, however. 'Don't fret, Kravitz. I can shoot this kind of thing with my eyes closed.'

'You are, you bastard!'

Duddy, on his side, tried to comfort Seigal. 'He's not drunk,' he said. 'He gets dizzy spells. Malaria.'

But during Mr Friar's four day absence in Ottawa Duddy took to biting his fingernails again. 'I'll kill him, Yvette. If he ruins this film I'll break every bone in his body.'

'I can't stand seeing you like this any more,' Yvette said. 'You're making a nervous wreck of me too.'

'A friend in need,' Duddy said. 'Aw.'

Yvette went to Ste Agathe for the weekend. Left on his own, Duddy phoned Mr Calder. What can I lose, he figured. He hangs up, that's all.

'What a pleasant surprise,' Mr Calder said.

They had dinner together at Drury's and Duddy discovered that Mr Calder had recently bought the controlling shares in a well-known stove and refrigerator factory just outside of Montreal. 'I've driven past there many times on my way out to the mountains,' Duddy said. 'There was sure lots of scrap in the yard.'

Mr Calder said he was going to dismantle the old foundry and put up an enormous new plant. When the bill came Duddy covered it with his hand and said, 'Your money's no good here, Mr Calder.'

Duddy phoned Mr Cohen when he got home. 'It's Kravitz,' he said.

'Do you know what time it is?'

'Don't hang up. This is important. I've got a deal for you maybe.'

'God help me.'

'I just got in from dinner. I was out with Hugh Thomas Calder.'

'Liar!'

'I'm not lying, Mr Cohen.' He told him about the foundry. 'Would you be interested in picking up the scrap there every week?'

'Are you crazy? He'd never give it to a Jew.'

'If I can get it for you what's in it for me?'

They finally settled on a twelve and a half per cent commission.

'Listen,' Mr Cohen said, 'maybe I ought to go and see him myself. He wouldn't want to deal with a kid like you.'

'Oh, no?'

'You really know him?'

'I'll call you next week to say when you can pick up the first load.'

'Some kid. Some operator you are.'

Yvette returned in the morning. 'Now you've gone and done it,' she said. 'The notary spoke to Duquette and he's accepted our cash offer. Have you got two thousand dollars, please?'

'Don't worry. I'll get it.'

'The papers are being drawn up. We've got until next Friday.'

Duddy took the map out of the desk and looked at it. He rubbed his hands together. 'Next is Cote. He's got a big farm.'

'We haven't even got Duquette's land yet.'

'Don't worry. Worrying's my department.' Duddy grinned. 'Give me your hand a minute,' he said.

'Oh, go to hell please. I haven't even had breakfast yet.'

Mr Friar arrived in the afternoon. 'It's an unmitigated disaster,' he said soberly.

They drove right down to the screening room to look at the movie. Outside, it was snowing. Christmas decorations were going up in all the department store windows.

'Oi. *Shicker*-head. *Mamzer*,' Duddy shouted. 'Did you do this to me on purpose, Friar?'

A headless Bobby Seigal read his *Haftorah*, a grotesquely over-exposed rabbi delivered his speech cut off at the eyes, and relatives walked down the synagogue steps at a thirty degree angle. 'Oh, no. No,' Duddy said.

'We'll have to refund Mr Seigal his money,' Yvette said.

'Yeah. Where do I get it?'

'The land will have to wait.'

'When do you start on the Farber wedding?' Duddy asked Mr Friar.

'I was supposed to start yesterday but they won't give me any more film on credit.'

'Jeez.'

'The chap's going round with the bill tomorrow afternoon. We owe him rather a lot, actually.'

'Listen to me, Friar. You've got lots of other footage on Bobby. Can anything be done to save this movie in the editing? I don't care if it only lasts twenty minutes.'

'It would take a genius.'

'That's the spirit,' Duddy said.

'Duddy,' Yvette said, 'you're going too far this time. You can't show this film. Nobody will ever give you another job.'

'*Ver gerharget*. Now you listen to me, Friar. Make me some of those dopey montages. Anything. I don't care if you have to stay up night and day but I want this movie put into shape, you hear. Now when can you have it for me?'

'Two weeks, perhaps.'

'Ten days. I'm going to stick with you. I'm not going to let you out of my sight.'

Duddy drove back to the office with Yvette.

'The two-fifty advance,' he said, 'we spent. Friar blew the other five hundred. Where would I get the money to refund Seigal? Let Friar work on it and I'll give the whole thing to Seigal for fifteen hundred. That way we'll get something back at least.'

'He'll never make that film any good. You're making a mistake, Duddy.'

'Oh, will you shettup please. You're giving me a headache.'

Yvette stopped the car. 'I'm getting out right here,' she said.

'All right, I'm sorry. I beg your pardon. Tonight I'll buy you some flowers. Come on. Let's get to the office.'

They owed the film supply company nine hundred dollars. Another payment was due on the car and there were the office and apartment rentals to be settled. His bank account was overdrawn a hundred and sixty-seven dollars. Duddy seized on the phone bill. 'Who,' he shouted, 'called Ste Agathe three times last week?'

'My brother's sick. One call was to the notary.'

'It's cheaper after six o'clock or didn't you know that?' Duddy sent out for coffee. 'When do they start the heating in this building,' he shouted, giving the radiator a swift kick, 'on January first?'

'What are you going to do?'

'I'm going to get that land, Yvette. I have to take each bit of it as it comes. Do you realize how prices will sky-rocket when they find out we're after the whole lake? What are you looking at?'

'You. I'm wondering how long you can keep this up before you fall flat on your face.'

'That reminds me.' He phoned Lennie. 'Hey, you know those pills you told me some of the guys take before exams? Yeah, benzedrine. Can you get me some tonight? I'll pick them up on my way home. Thanks.' Next Duddy phoned Mr Calder.

'Mr Calder is in Washington,' Edgar said. 'He is not expected back for at least a week.'

Duddy hung up. 'That's a bad break,' he said. He picked up the receiver again and replaced it. No, he thought, Cohen won't give me anything in advance without definite word. 'Will you stop staring at me, please.'

'Would your Uncle Benjy lend you any money?'

'I'd drop dead before I gave him the pleasure.'

The coffee arrived. 'Charge it,' Duddy said. 'Listen, Yvette, when the guy comes about the bill tomorrow I'm in Washington. I'm there with Hugh Thomas Calder. You can't say about what. Hush-hush. But you *can* say I'm thinking of getting my film direct from Toronto. O.K.?'

'I'll try it,' she said.

'Forty-five hundred dollars, Jeez. Hey, maybe if I mentioned Calder's name the bank manager . . .'

There was a knock at the door. Duddy leaped out of his seat. 'A parking ticket,' he shouted. 'I knew it. How many times did I tell you not to let me park in a one-hour zone?'

'Take it easy, Duddy. You mustn't get so excited.'

Yvette opened the door.

'Hiya.'

A skinny young man with a crew-cut and a long lopsided face, his hands stuffed into the pockets of an old army windbreaker like a child's into jam jars, smiled ecstatically at Duddy. 'Long time no see,' he said.

Duddy gave Yvette a baffled look. 'Yeah,' he said. 'Sure.'

'Everything's O.K.,' the long loose-boned man said. 'Getting 'em over the border was a breeze.'

'It was . . .?'

'You're not happy to see me,' the man said and all at once his expression was so melancholy that Duddy feared the flesh would melt and the bones collapse with a rattle to the floor.

'Oh, no! No!' Duddy flung his arms in the air. 'It can't be. It's Virgil.'

Virgil nodded, he beamed, ducking his head as if to avoid an affectionate slap.

Duddy looked at Yvette and groaned. 'How did you ever find me?' he asked.

'You left me your card, remember? "DIAL MOVIES". I thought I'd come straight up, though.' He searched Duddy's face for displeasure. 'I find telephone conversations highly unsatisfactory.'

'Sure thing.'

'What's going on, please?'

Duddy explained in a failing voice that he had met Virgil in New York when he had been there with Dingleman. He had told Virgil that he would pay him a hundred dollars each for his pinball machines any time he could get them over the border.

'Em, Virgil, did you bring all ten of them?'

Virgil grinned enthusiastically.

'A thousand dollars,' Yvette said.

'They're worth three-fifty each new in the States. More here.'

'All you have to do is sell them,' Yvette said.

'Sure. That's right,' Duddy said, excited. 'All I have to do is sell them. Let's say at – Well, we'll discuss that later. Where are they Virgil?'

They were hidden under a tarpaulin about twenty miles from the border.

'O.K. Let's go. Come on, Yvette.'

'At this hour?'

'We'll need two cars. I can pick up my father's taxi.'

They picked up the Dodge on St Urbain Street.

'O.K., Virgil, we'll follow you.'

The morning's snow had melted and frozen, the roads were slippery, and there was a high wind. Duddy didn't have any tyre-chains and his heater didn't work. Yvette did up the top button of his coat and snuggled close to him.

'I couldn't tell you while he was there,' Duddy said, 'but I think we can get two-fifty apiece for them from the hotels in Ste Agathe.'

Yvette closed her eyes. She shivered. 'That boy looks like a lunatic to me,' she said.

'I figure if we get them packed in the cars by two-thirty we can be in Ste Agathe by six-seven o'clock.'

'You mean we're going to drive all the way out to Ste Agathe tonight?'

'Reach into my jacket pocket. Yeah, that one. Lennie got me the pills. Give me one, will you?'

Yvette stared at the bottle. There was no label. 'I don't want you to take one,' she said. 'I'm afraid.'

'I should fall asleep at the wheel. Is that what you want?'

'Duddy, please, you mustn't . . .'

'Heads-up, guys. Here come the water-works.'

'You won't be happy until you kill yourself.'

'Gimme the pill, please. O.K., now listen. I'm not going to kill myself. But I'm going to get that land, see. All of it. It's going to be mine.'

'Duddy, even if you ever did raise enough money for all the land . . . what then? The price of the land is nothing compared to how much money you'd need to develop it.'

'Don't worry. I've thought of that. Just let me buy up all that land first. You wait, Yvette. You wait and see.'

'Oh, what's the use?'

'Listen, can we stay at your place tonight? Virgil and I can sleep on the hall floor or something. Wha'?'

'I'd better take you to a hotel.'

'O.K. Skip it. You go to sleep.'

Yvette took a pill. 'I'd better stay up,' she said. 'Just in case.'

Chapter Thirteen

After covering a hundred and fifty miles, the last forty-five
through heavy snow, they finally reached Ste Agathe. Yvette
got Duddy and Virgil a double room at the St Vincent Hotel
and muttered something about sleeping in all day. Duddy, too
tired to drive any more, put her in a taxi. One of his ears,
he was sure, was frozen, and his eyes were bloodshot. There
was a ringing inside his head.

'A bed,' he said, entering the room. He pulled off his
trousers and flopped on it. 'Good night, Virgil.'

'One minute. There's something I ought to tell you.'

Duddy mumbled something inaudible through his pillow.
Virgil shook him awake. 'Mr Kravitz,' he said.

'Mm?'

'I'm an epileptic.'

'Wha'?' Duddy rolled over on the bed and groaned. 'Go
away, Virgil. It's not true.'

'I can't help it. That's the way I was born.'

Duddy sat up and rubbed his eyes. 'You mean you're really
an epileptic?'

Virgil nodded. He grinned.

'Jeez.' *Ver gerharget* twice, he thought. All the world's
ranking crap-artists, how do they find me? 'You got a cigarette?
Thanks. What happens . . . well, if you have a fit like?'

'Oh, don't worry about a thing, Mr Kravitz. I don't make
much noise.'

'You don't?'

Virgil grinned.

'Well, there's always a silver lining.'

'It's not easy to be an epileptic. You'd be surprised how
many people are prejudiced against us.'

'Listen, if you have a fit – I mean just in case. No offence, eh? Am I supposed to put a spoon down your mouth or . .'

'Naw. Don't worry about a thing. Sometimes I have fits in my sleep and I don't even know about it until I wake up in the morning.'

'Oh.'

'Yeah, then I can tell by looking in the mirror. My tongue gets cut.'

'Do you . . . em . . . have these fits in your sleep very often?'

A couple of times a week. They're not very severe.'

'Is that so?'

'You know, Mr Kravitz, life is no bowl of cherries for a guy like me.'

'You don't say?'

'Who would take a chance on me as a waiter?'

How would you like to kiss my ass, Duddy thought.

'Or a driver?'

Jeez, Duddy thought, I'd better not let him drive the Dodge back to Montreal. A crack-up, that's all I need.

'We're a persecuted minority. Like the Jews and the Negroes.'

'Yes, I guess that *is* one way of looking at it.' Duddy lit another cigarette off his butt. Who can sleep, anyway, he thought, with this one in the room. God help us.

'Only you have Bnai Brith to fight for you and the Negroes have the NAACP. We have nobody. We're all alone.'

'It's a shame, Virgil. A real shame.'

'Even the queers are getting organized now. No offence – '

'*What do you mean no offence?*'

'Well, I don't know you very well, Mr Kravitz, and you did ask for a double room – '

'Just don't get any stupid ideas,' Duddy said, pulling his blankets tighter around him.

'Anyway, like I was saying, even the queers now have organizations to fight for them.'

'Is that so?'

'You know, Mr Kravitz, you're a Jew and wherever you go other Jews will help you. I'm not speaking against that. I think it's swell. Why, you could turn up tomorrow in Kansas City or Rome or – well maybe not Tokyo. But my point is other Jews there will lend a helping hand. You're sort of international.

With the fags it's like that too. You know, they have their special little faggoty nightclubs in every city. But epileptics? No. Nothing. A lot of them, *plenty*, won't own up to it, that's why. You think there's shame attached to being an epileptic?'

'Certainly not.'

'Some of the greatest men in the world were epileptics.'

'No kidding?'

'Julius Caesar.'

'Yeah?'

'Jesus Christ, even. Dostoievski. Charlie Chaplin.'

'Charlie Chaplin is a Jew,' Duddy said snidely.

'A guy can be both, you know.'

'Jeez.'

'That's why I started out in the pinball machine business in the Bronx, you know. Nobody would hire me so I had to go into business for myself.'

'Necessity is the mother of all invention,' Duddy said.

'Those are true words, but look where it got me. Even with the thousand dollars I'm getting from you I will have lost almost all my savings.'

'That's show biz,' Duddy said. Cuckoo, he thought warmly. I'll call him tomorrow. 'Shouldn't we try to get some sleep?' he asked.

'My life ambition, Mr Kravitz, is to organize the epileptics of the world. I'd like to be their Sister Kenny.'

'That would be something, Virgil.'

Virgil's voice took on the vibrations of a platform speaker's. 'Why aren't we covered by the Fair Employment Act?' he demanded.

'Why don't we get some sleep?'

'I like you, Mr Kravitz. Do you like me?'

'Yeah, sure thing, Virgil.'

'Why?'

'Couldn't I tell you in the morning?'

'You're not just saying it are you? You do like me.'

'I think you're a prince of a fella.'

'Thanks. So many people are prejudiced against us, **you** know.'

'Good night, Virgie.'

'We're going to be buddies. Real buddies. I can tell.'

Sure, Duddy thought. You bet. He got up and turned out the light.

'What does Yvette think of me? Be frank.'

'Jeez, Virgie. She didn't say.'

'I like her. She's got qualities.'

Duddy pretended to be snoring.

'I've got a theory about women, you know. Mr Kravitz?'

'Mm?'

'I've got a theory about women. It always works too. There are three types of women. The Berthe-type, the Matilde-type, and the – '

'Virgil?'

'Yeah?'

'*I* would like to sleep now. *I* am very tired. *I* must be up in four hours. *I* am saying good night. Good night.'

Virgil leaped out of bed. 'It's almost light,' he said. 'It's snowing. I love snow.'

Duddy woke with a hacking cough at nine-thirty. The room was freezing. He stumbled over to the sink, splashed cold water on his face, and took another benzedrine pill.

'Good morning,' Virgil shouted. 'A happy day in store, I hope.'

Duddy moaned.

'I want to see all the sights.'

Virgil leaned close to the mirror and stuck out his tongue. Duddy stared at him and remembered and suddenly froze.

'Are you O.K.?'

'Not a scratch,' Virgil said. 'Look, everything's covered with snow outside.' He began to dress hastily. 'I want to be the first person to walk in it. The first in the world.'

It took three days of lies, threats, pandering, cajoling, insult and the ultimate appeal to avarice to sell the pinball machines, but sell them he did. All but one of them. He went to Rubin's first and told him that the Hilltop Lodge had already bought one. 'Why,' he said to Rubin, 'pay rent to some jerk in Montreal – why split the take – on this junky old model when for two hundred and fifty bucks I can supply you with the latest machine?'

'You know how long I can get for receiving stolen goods?'

Duddy assured him that he owned the machines. He had a receipt. 'Look,' he said, 'six months from now you do a switch with the Hilltop Lodge and the Hilltop Lodge changes with the Chalet. I've got ten machines. You keep rotating them.'

'I'd like to think about it.'

'All right. I'll tell you what. I'll guarantee to buy the machine back from you one year from today for a hundred dollars. Right off you start with a profit. Don't you see?' Duddy put his arm around Virgil. 'I brought Mr Roseboro all the way in from New York special to install and service the machines. He's an expert.'

'That's a falsehood,' Virgil said.

'Ah ha ha,' Duddy said. 'Would you mind waiting outside in the car, please?'

After he had sold the first four machines Duddy dumped the rest with comparative ease. They went for an average of two hundred and twenty-five dollars and he was paid in cash for all but three of them.

'Well,' Duddy said to Yvette, 'I've got the money for the notary now.'

'What about the bills in Montreal? And you have to give Virgil his thousand dollars.'

'Sure. Don't worry.'

Yvette took to Virgil and showed him all the sights in and around Ste Agathe. Once or twice Duddy came out of an hotel after making a sale and found Yvette and Virgil laughing together in the car. 'Hey,' he asked, 'what gives between you two?'

'Virgil wanted to know if you had a wife and children. He thought you were thirty-five at least.'

'Very funny.'

'*I* thought it was funny.'

'You'd make a very good parent, Mr Kravitz. I observe people and I can tell.'

'Let's get moving, please.'

Duddy was almost always bad-tempered in Ste Agathe. Yvette put it down to the benzedrine pills, but she didn't like it. Their second night there she moved out of her house and into a single room in the St Vincent Hotel.

'Virgil and I are going to the movies tonight. Want to come?'

'No.'

'Do you mind if I go?'

'Listen,' Duddy said, 'I'll tell you what. I'll take over your single room and you can move in with Virgil.'

'I don't have to go to the movies. I can stay here with you.'

'Go ahead. Enjoy yourself.'

Once they had gone, Duddy got into the car and drove as near as he could to Lac St Pierre. He had to walk the last three-quarters of a mile through deep snow. The drifts were soft and often, between rocks, he sunk in up to his knees. But it gave him quite a lift to see his land in winter. A thin scalp of ice protected the lake and all his fields glittered white and purple and gold under the setting sun. All except the pine trees were bare. It must be pretty in autumn, he thought, when all the leaves are changing colours. Duddy saw where he would put up the hotel and decided that he would not have to clear the wood all in one shot. It's lovely, he thought, and lots of those pine trees I can peddle at Christmas-time.

Duddy trudged up and down through the snow with an owner's sharp eye for fire hazards and signs of mischief. He tried the ice on the lake with his foot. It cracked. He urinated into a snow bank, writing his name. It's my land, he thought. But the wind began to cut quicker across the fields, suddenly the sun went out like a light, it was dark, and Duddy began to shiver. Jeez, he thought, why didn't I leave the car lights on? He buttoned up his collar and began to strike matches. Duddy was able to trace his footsteps until the snow began to fall again, and then he was in bad trouble. He circled round and round, his teeth chattered, and twice he began to run. He ran and ran to no purpose until he collapsed panting in the snow. His feet burned from the cold, his eyes felt as if they were stuffed with sand, and he began to think what in the hell am I doing lost in a blizzard, a Jewish boy? Moses, he recalled from *Bible Comics*, died without ever reaching the Promised Land, but *I've* got my future to think of. He tripped, he fell time and again, his nostrils stuck together. If God pulls me through, he thought, I'll give up screwing for two weeks. Smoked meats too. When he finally stumbled on the car, shortly after two, he'd run out of cigarettes and matches. The car wouldn't start. Duddy sat in the back seat and wept, blowing on his hands. Eventually, because it was too cold to sit there any more, he started back into Ste Agathe. It was nearly four o'clock when he reached the hotel. Yvette and Virgil were waiting up for him in the double room.

'Duddy!' She embraced him. She felt his forehead. 'It's a furnace,' she said. 'I'll call the doctor right away.'

'No doctors, please. Get me a basin of hot water for my feet. There's a bottle of scotch in the top drawer. Get me that too.'

'I'm calling the doctor.'

'Sure. Go ahead. He puts me in bed for a week and I don't sell the rest of the machines.' Duddy drank the scotch neat. He also took three aspirins. 'I'll sweat it out tonight,' he said. 'Tomorrow I'll be good as new.'

'You're remarkable, Mr Kravitz. You have a great fighting spirit.'

'Will you shut your face, please? Good night.'

Each morning at nine o'clock Duddy phoned Mr Friar. 'Well, how goes the battle?'

'I'm working on it, Kravitz. I'm not giving up.'

Wherever he went Duddy took the movie catalogues he had picked up in Toronto. He made deals with four hotels to supply them with movies one night a week. Six, he figured, was his break-even point, and anything over a profit. With a run of the resorts between Shawbridge and Ste Agathe he hoped to work up to two showings a night, fourteen rentals a week, by the summertime. The children's camps could be worked during the afternoons, and that would bring in even more. Duddy didn't forget his soap and toilet supply order book either. He earned enough on this to pay his hotel bill and get his car out of the garage.

When they started back for Montreal on Thursday afternoon Yvette got into the Dodge with Virgil. 'Hey,' Duddy said, 'you come with me.'

'I thought I'd keep Virgil company. You're in such a bad mood anyway.'

Virgil rubbed the back of his neck. He blushed. 'I'd like to assure you, Mr Kravitz, that I have no carnal designs on Yvette.'

'Come on,' Duddy said, grabbing Yvette's arm. 'Get in the car.'

They found Max at Eddy's and he was furious. 'Who do you

think you are,' he said, 'that you can run off with my car for three days? Just like that.'

'I phoned you,' Duddy said. 'I told you it was important.'

'I've got a living to earn. Smart guy! Operator!'

'I'll pay you for the use of the car, Daddy.'

But Max walked away from Duddy and the proffered fifty dollars. He stood by the window and saw Yvette talking to Virgil outside. 'Some kid,' he said, turning to Debrofsky, 'he's got his own apartment now and a *shiksa* to go with. You dirty pig!'

'Yvette is my Girl Friday.'

'I hope you get the clap. That would teach you a lesson,' Max shouted.

'He's a healthy kid,' Debrofsky said. 'A girl's good for him.'

'It's all glandular,' Eddy said. 'At his age –'

'I'm worried about his future,' Max said.

'Don't worry. I'm not getting hitched.'

Duddy ordered six smoked meats and some pickles to take out. Max sat down at the bar and sucked a sugar cube. 'You don't look so hot, Duddy,' he said.

'I'm all right, Daddy.'

'I haven't even seen your apartment yet. I wasn't invited.'

'Come tomorrow night with Lennie. We'll all go to dinner.'

'Don't try to get around me,' Max said. 'If there's anything wrong with the Dodge I'm holding you responsible. When you took it there wasn't the smallest rattle.'

'He should live so long,' Debrofsky said.

'Oh, I want to speak to you.' Duddy took Debrofsky aside and they whispered together for a minute.

'What going on?' Max asked.

'You take it into the garage, Daddy. Send me the bill.'

Duddy and Virgil and Yvette went back to the apartment and ate there. Virgil helped Duddy carry the one pinball machine that was left upstairs and they set it up in the living-room.

'High score for a dollar,' Duddy said.

Mr Friar came over and Duddy opened a bottle of gin.

'What an intriguing machine,' Mr Friar said.

Duddy, a practised hand at shaking, coaxing, and pushing, won twelve dollars on high score.

After Mr Friar had gone back to work, Virgil asked, 'Can I sleep here tonight, Mr Kravitz. I've got a sleeping bag.'

'Let me refresh your drink, Virgie,' Duddy said. 'I've got business to talk with you.'

'I'm staying,' Yvette said.

'Sure.'

Virgil grinned. He waited.

'How would you like to stay here and go to work for me, Virgie?'

'Duddy,' Yvette said, 'that would be wonderful!'

'Well, Virgie?'

'You mean you'd give a guy like me a job. I mean knowing –' He noticed Yvette watching him and averted his eyes. 'Well, you know . . .'

'I could trust you. That's the most important thing with me.'

'What do you want him to do?' Yvette asked.

Duddy explained that he was expanding into the distribution side of the movie business. Yvette could book the rentals. But he needed a man on the road to show the movies, somebody trustworthy and presentable: Virgil. In summer, probably, he would have an assistant.

'But I don't know how to work a projector,' Virgil said.

'That's something a four-year-old kid could learn in a week. Don't worry.'

Yvette kissed Duddy on the cheek. 'I'm sorry if I was sharp with you in Ste Agathe,' she said.

'You'll never regret this, Mr Kravitz. I'll work so hard.'

'There's only one thing. I need a man with a truck.'

'Oh.'

'You know. A small panel job.'

'I see.'

'What's the matter with you two? That's no problem. Look, Virgie, I owe you a thousand bucks. Right? Right.'

'Duddy,' Yvette began apprehensively. But he looked at her sharply and she sat down again.

'What would you say if for that thousand bucks I could put my hands on just the truck for you?'

'Could you, Mr Kravitz?'

'I spoke to Debrofsky at Eddy's. His brother-in-law has a used-car lot and there he's got a '49 Chevvie. A half ton job. It's in beautiful shape and he wants twelve-fifty for it. But if you were interested, Virgie, and willing to pay cash, I think I could swing it for a thousand.'

Virgil's eyes filled with excitement. 'When could you know definitely?' he asked, his fists clenched.

Yvette started for the door.

'What's wrong?'

'Go to hell,' she said, and she slammed the door after her.

'Maybe you ought to sleep on it, Virgie. I don't want to push you.'

'Imagine. You'd give a guy like me a job. You'd trust me.'

'I'll give you sixty bucks a week to start, Virgie, and of course I'll handle all the gas bills and stuff. You'd have to put the company name on the truck though.'

'Dial Movies?'

'Yeah.'

'It would be a genuine honour, Mr Kravitz.'

'O.K., Virgie, I'll see about the truck first thing tomorrow morning. Now if you'll excuse me for a minute . . . I want to see Yvette.'

Duddy poured himself another drink and took it with him to Yvette's apartment. She sat on the sofa in her nightgown.

'O.K., what's got into you?'

'I've seen you do lots of dishonest things, Duddy, but never in my life did I expect you to cheat a boy like Virgil.'

'Cheat. I'm a cheater? Wow!'

'How much are you paying for the truck?'

'It's a gift. From Debrofsky's son-in-law to me. I'm getting it for nothing.'

'You are getting it for nothing. The company is, anyway.'

'I'm smart. Can I help it?'

'You can't do this to Virgil.'

'What am I doing? Twisting his arms. I take a boy in off the streets and give him a job and –'

'Please, Duddy, I'm not Mr Cohen.'

Duddy sat down beside her on the sofa and tried to kiss her. 'I'm in the mood,' he said.

'I never thought you were such a bastard,' she said, moving away.

'Hey, one minute. What's with you and this Virgil?'

'I like him. I think he's sweet.'

'Is that all? Are you sure?'

Yvette laughed. 'Is that why you wouldn't let me drive back to Montreal with him?'

'He's an epileptic. I wouldn't let you drive with him because I was afraid of an accident. I think of your welfare, you know. You'd be surprised. What's wrong now?'

'You're not lying to me, Duddy? He is an . . . an epileptic?'

Duddy told her how Virgil had kept him up all night at the hotel. 'There, aren't you sorry now? You thought I was trying to swindle him when all the time I was being a big help to him. I'm taking a chance on the boy. I like him.'

'I ought to slap your face.'

'What did I do now?'

'Do you mean to say that knowing how grateful he'd be for a job – any job – you managed to swindle him out of his thousand dollars? Oh, Duddy.'

'Swindle. The truck will be registered under his name. I'm paying his sixty-five bucks a week too. *While I train him.* Where could he earn that kind of dough?'

'How much are you paying for the truck? Tell me the truth.'

'I'm a humanitarian. I took such a chance on a boy like that and this is the thank you I get.'

'Chance? Do you think he could have a fit while he was driving the truck?'

'Why not?'

'You mustn't let him do it, Duddy. You have to stop him.'

'I'm exaggerating,' Duddy said, sighing. 'He can tell when they're coming on. All he has to do is pull over to the kerb.'

'Are you sure?'

'Yeah,' he said wearily.

'I'll never forgive you if anything happens to him. I swear it.'

'What's so special about Virgie?'

'I told you. I like him.'

'Is that why you moved into the hotel the second night,' he began to shout, 'when you could have stayed at your place for nothing?'

'I had a fight with my family.'

'Oh. About what?'

'Never mind.'

'About what, please?'

'My brother found out I'm living with you.'

'Which brother? Jean-Paul? That anti-semite! That *shicker*!'

'I won't be able to see my parents again.'

'Oh, gee. I'm sorry.' He took her hand. 'Really, Yvette.'

'Duddy, I'm very tired. I want to go to sleep. I know that truck isn't costing you more than five or six hundred dollars. I want you to return the rest of the money to Virgil.'

'Listen, listen, the cat's pissin'.'

'I'm not coming into the office until you do that.'

'That does it,' Duddy said. 'I was just on the verge of giving him a couple of hundred dollars . . . just to make you feel good. But I won't be threatened, you hear?'

'Do as you like. But just remember what I said.'

Duddy leaped up. 'You're fired,' he said, 'and that's final.'

He took the steps back to his own apartment two at a time and poured himself another drink. Virgil was laying out his sleeping bag on the floor. 'Listen,' Duddy said, 'I'm giving you sixty-five bucks a week. Not sixty.'

'Gee.'

'He hasn't even worked for me one day and he's got a raise. Oh, that bitch.' Duddy picked up an enormous book. 'What in the hell is this?'

'A rhyming dictionary, Mr Kravitz. I'm a poet.'

'He's a poet.'

'I wrote two sonnets for Yvette in Ste Agathe.'

Duddy put down his drink. 'I'd like to see them, please,' he said.

'She has them. She wanted to keep them.'

'Turn your back for one minute. That's all you need.'

'I beg your pardon, Mr Kravitz?'

'You want to play high score again?'

'Whatever you say.'

'We'll play for five dollars this time.'

'Gee whiz, that's a lot of money.'

Duddy was ahead on the fifth ball when he shook the machine too avidly and tilted it. 'Here,' he said, handing Virgil the five dollars.

'Oh, I couldn't take it, Mr Kravitz. I'd feel so guilty.'

'For Christ's sake!'

'You work so hard for your money.'

'A gambling debt is a gambling debt. Tomorrow you'd better find yourself a room.'

'Are you angry with me, Mr Kravitz?'

'No. I'm not angry.' He picked up the dictionary again. 'A poet, eh?'

'I've got a very good name for a poet. Virgil was the most famous poet of olden times. He wrote in Latin.'

'You read a lot?'

'Whenever I can.'

'Well, I read a lot too. I'm no dope. You ever read *God's Little Acre*?'

'No.'

'You get a copy. I recommend it highly.' Duddy began to pace. Twice he ran to the door and opened it. 'I thought I heard somebody.' That bitch, he thought. 'Well, let's see a sample of your work.'

Virgil jumped up, dug into his kitbag, and handed Duddy a page. Duddy read the poem and handed it back to Virgil, smiling broadly. 'It doesn't even rhyme,' he said. 'A poet.'

'Modern poetry isn't supposed to. This is a blank verse.'

'Wha'?'

'I'm a follower of Kenneth Patchen.'

Virgil told him about Patchen. He said he was great.

'Get me a copy of his book. I'd like to read it. Excuse me a minute.'

Duddy ran downstairs and listened at the door. He heard Yvette in the kitchen. 'Can I come in?' he shouted.

The kitchen light went out.

'Try to be ready at eighty-thirty. I want to get down to the office early tomorrow.'

Again there was no reply and Duddy went upstairs to sleep. Yvette did not come into the office the next morning or the morning after. Duddy sent flowers, but they came back: so did the chocolates. Meanwhile he discovered that Yvette was seeing Virgil every evening. Duddy worked late with Mr Friar every night and helped to get the Seigal movie into presentable shape. When he got in early one morning he told Virgil, 'Tell Yvette I'm drinking too much. Say I look terrible.'

'I don't mean to intrude, Mr Kravitz, but I understand the

two of you have had a disagreement. I put in a good word for you whenever I can.'

A week went by. Ten days. Duddy called Virgil into the office. 'Look,' he said, 'a funny thing happened. Debrofsky's brother-in-law made a mistake. The truck only cost seven-fifty.' He handed Virgil a cheque for the difference. 'I'm afraid it's post-dated,' he said. 'But if you wait a couple of weeks . . .'

Yvette returned to work the next morning.

'I want you to go to Ste Agathe,' Duddy said. 'I've got the money for Duquette.'

She put out her hand for the keys.

'I've got nothing to do this afternoon. Maybe I'll tag along for the drive.'

'If you like.'

Back in Montreal again they drove straight to the office. Duddy had lots of letters to dictate. But first he took out the map and red crayon and coloured in the land that had used to belong to Duquette.

'I own nearly half of it now. Well, more than a third anyway. Six months it took me. That's all. Well, what do you say? What's your opinion of Duddy Kravitz now?'

Part Three

Chapter One

Duddy's winter was exceptionally prosperous; and happy too. Mr Friar had succeeded in making something of the Seigal *bar-mitzvah* movie and Duddy had picked up a small profit, although he let it go at a reduced price. He did extremely well, too, with his third *bar-mitzvah* movie and two about weddings. He hired a girl to help Yvette. Making commercial films for television, it seemed to Duddy, might turn out to be even more profitable than – as he called them – his 'social featurettes'. He began to think in terms of large offices with a studio of his own and he made several trips to Toronto to find out what he could about industrial films and the profits to be made there. Meanwhile, on the distribution side, he was breaking even, better sometimes, and building up lots of good-will. Whenever it was possible he showed films free of charge at, for instance, a Knights of Pythias evening for under-privileged kids or any charity event in Ste Agathe. He was determined to make friends with the mayor there and he succeeded. He rented his films by the week and Virgil's salary had to be paid anyway. Lots of his free showings got him mentions in *Mel West's What's What*, and once he got a whole paragraph to himself. It read:

AND MONTREALERS WITH A HEART: Up-and-coming cine-man Duddy Kravitz informs me he's rarin' to show movies free any time, anywhere, if the cause is worthy . . . Kravitz, soon to celebrate his first year in show biz, has three original productions under his belt already, and his plans for the future include a feature-length comedy production with Ourtown's Cuckoo Kaplan . . . *Howdy dood it?* 'I work eighteen hours a day,' he says, 'And if I drive my staff hard they know I've always got my shnozolla to the grindstone too.' How old is he? Nineteen! *So don't let any socialist sad-sacks tell you it's no longer possible to go from rags-to-riches in this country* . . . Born and bred on St Urbain

Street, Duddy was working as waiter not many moons ago . .
REMINDER: For those free films DIAL MOVIES.

Virgil never found a room. He stayed on in the apartment – he
was on the road three or four days a week anyway – and Duddy
got to enjoy having him there. With his second week's salary
Virgil bought Duddy a record player, and he never returned from
a trip to the Laurentians without flowers or a box of chocolates
for Yvette and a trick cigarette lighter or maybe a book for
Duddy. Only twice during the first month did he waken with a
bruised and bloody mouth.

One of Virgil's poems was published in *Attack!*, a mimeographed magazine published by some fighting young followers
of Ezra Pound. It was called 'Himmler has only got one ball'.

'At least this one rhymes,' Duddy said, 'but why don't you
try something longer. You know, with a story.'

Virgil had met the editor of *Attack!*, a fierce man with a
broken nose, at Duddy's apartment soon after it had become a
gathering place for Bohemians. That came about through
Duddy's acquisition of the record-player and his discovery that
he was a music lover. Duddy bought Beethoven's nine sym-
phonies on long playing records and listened to them in order.
He kept a date stamp and ink pad next to his records and each
time he listened to one of them he stamped the date on the album.
He also began to collect Schubert and Mozart and Brahms and
that's how he ran into Hersh, his old FFHS schoolmate. Hersh
had come into the record store to collect an extremely rare
African war chant record he had ordered some months before.

'For Christ's sake,' Duddy shouted. 'Hersh, of all people.'

Hersh wore his hair long. He had grown a beard.

'Hey,' Duddy said, punching him on the shoulder, 'where's
your violin and the cup, eh?'

But Hersh made a sour face.

'I was only kidding,' Duddy said.

Hersh, who had campaigned against the seven cent chocolate
bar and come second in the province and won a scholarship to
McGill, had quit the university. Duddy was astonished. 'Jeez,'
he said.

He was no longer short, he'd lost his squint, but he was still
somewhat pimply. Hersh had grown up to be a big, chunky
man with a long severe head and enormous black eyes. 'There

was no sense in staying on,' he said. 'I had no intention of becoming the apogee of the Jewish bourgeois dream. Namely a doctor or a lawyer.'

'Aha,' Duddy said.

'I think I've succeeded in purging myself of the ghetto mentality.'

Duddy took Hersh to his apartment for a drink.

'A writer,' Duddy said. 'Can you beat that? How are you doing?'

'Writing isn't a career. It's a vocation. I'm not in it for the money.'

'No offence. Publish anything?'

Hersh quickly told him what he thought about editors. He said his writing wasn't commercial. He pointed out that he didn't get the usual printed rejection slips, but personal notes from editors, always asking if they could see more of his work.

'Sure,' Duddy said, 'but have you published anything?'

'No.'

'Well, some people hit it off right away. Others struggle for years. I'm sure you'll be famous. I'll bet you'll be another Ellery Queen.'

'I don't write detective stories.'

Hersh told him that he was going to Paris in the autumn.

'A St Urbain Street boy. Isn't that something. Boy, I understand that the dames there . . .'

'That's a cliché. It isn't true.'

Duddy grinned. 'Hoo-haw,' he said, and he poured Hersh another drink. 'It's so good to see you. We ought to have reunions like. When I think of all the swell characters I used to know at FFHS. Hey, remember the time that lush-head MacPherson accused me of killing his wife?'

'He's in an asylum.'

'Wha'?'

'He's in Verdun.'

'That's show biz, I guess,' Duddy said, flushing.

'I think I'd better be off. Thanks for the drink.'

'Aw, come on. Sit down.'

'Why pretend we're friends, Duddy? We hated each other at school.'

Virgil arrived and Duddy sent him out for some smoked

meat and more liquor. 'Virgie's a poet. He writes blank verse. Like Patchen.'

'Do you read Patchen?'

'Sure.'

'He's a minor talent.'

'No kidding?'

Yvette came and Hersh decided to stay. He had a date, though.

'Tell the broad to come here,' Duddy said.

The girl came and brought two others with her. Mr Friar arrived. One of Hersh's friends got on the phone and by ten-thirty there were twelve people in the apartment, including the fierce editor of *Attack!* Duddy sent Virgil out for more booze and began a high score competition on the pinball machine. When the party finally broke up at two a.m. or thereabouts he shouted. 'Come again. Come any time.'

They did, too, and they brought still more friends. Yvette was amused. 'I never thought I'd see the day when you were played for a sucker. Maybe there's still hope for you.'

'Hersh is going to be another Tolstoi. Boy, are you ever a kill-joy.'

'All right,' Yvette said, 'but if you think I'm going to clean up his mess every night . . .'

'Intellectual stimulation is good for you,' Duddy said. 'I read in *Fortune* where nowadays many executives go to the university in the summer to read up on philosophy and shit like that. It broadens you.'

Virgil showed Yvette a book of poems by the editor of *Attack!* 'He signed it for me,' he said.

'He tried to sell me a copy too.'

'Jeez, Yvette, a poet's gotta live too. Have a heart.'

'Don't tell me you bought one off him?'

'What if I did?'

One or another of Hersh's crowd dropped in every night. Keiley was the noisiest and the most troublesome. He left burning cigarettes everywhere and when Yvette got angry with him he said, 'A man shouldn't be dominated by his possessions.' The hardest to get rid of, however, was the fierce editor of *Attack!* Blum never left until the last bottle was empty. Virgil adored him. After the others had gone he would sit on the floor and Blum would recite his latest poems to him in a booming voice. 'I can't understand it,' Blum said, 'when you think how well-known the other poets of my generation are . . . Spender and Dylan and George Barker . . . I can't understand it . . .'

When he had too much to drink and began to cry Blum reminded Duddy of Cuckoo Kaplan. Hersh didn't like Blum. 'An unsigned copy of his poems,' he said, 'is a collector's item.'

But Hersh only spoke hard or cynically when the others were around. Alone with Duddy he was a different sort of person. 'Watch out for some of the others,' he once warned Duddy. 'They don't understand your kind of generosity. They poke fun at you behind your back.'

Yvette agreed. 'They're taking advantage of you,' she said.

'Gwan. The trouble with you, Yvette, is you just can't understand people who are interested in the higher things.'

'Like what?'

'Man does not live by bread alone,' Duddy said.

It was a rare night when Duddy came home from the office and found nobody sitting in the apartment. He ran up enormous food and liquor bills but Hersh's crowd gave him more pleasure than he had ever had before. There were other guests too. Max and Lennie came occasionally and Bernie Altman was invited to dinner at least once a week. Duddy, taking him into his confidence one night, told him about Lac St Pierre, and with Yvette's help the two boys constructed a relief model of the area. That took them weeks of painstaking work on the floor with balsam wood, flour, paints and airplane glue while Yvette fed them sandwiches and coffee and outside the snow fell. There were fierce arguments too over the site of the camp dining-room and whether or not it was in good taste to have the boys' and girls' bunk houses laid out to spell D K. Bernie lent Duddy books by Mumford and spoke passionately to him about Le Corbusier but, though Duddy swore he would have no other architect design Lac St. Pierre, he still felt that some of Bernie's designs were a little too unusual.

'You're being too arty-farty. Buck Rogers won't be sending his kids to my camp but Mr Cohen might, if you get what I mean?'

During the winter Duddy purchased two more small lots on

the lake. Yvette enjoyed the evenings with Bernie enormously – it was good to have Duddy home and happy for a change instead of pursuing deals – but she was also frightened. More and more it began to look as if one day he would actually own all the land surrounding Lac St Pierre and what then, she thought. How in the world would he ever raise the thousands and thousands of dollars needed to develop the area? Impossible, she thought, and the day he discovered it would be dreadful.

Virgil didn't agree. 'Duddy can do anything,' he said.

'You think so?'

'I love him.'

Duddy saw other friends too. He was careful to keep up his contact with Hugh Thomas Calder and he had reason to believe he was making a hit there until the evening he brought up the scrap deal with Cohen. This seemed to displease Mr Calder even though Duddy, speaking on Cohen's behalf, offered him two-fifty more a ton than he had been getting up to now.

'I suppose,' Mr Calder said, pushing his plate away, 'that I should have expected something like this from you. I had hoped we were friends.'

'Sure we are,' Duddy had replied, flushing. 'But friends help each other.'

'Certainly.'

'Aren't you getting more for the scrap than you got before? Mr Cohen will do nicely, that's true. This deal is to your mutual advantage.'

'I expect,' Mr Calder had said, 'that you're earning a good commission on this?'

Something had risen in Duddy's stomach. His eyes filled. 'I look after myself,' he had said. 'Why not?'

'Why not, indeed?'

'Listen, Mr Calder, the truth of the matter is it's not the money. The commission I get from Cohen is more trouble than it's worth. My plate is full, as they say. But I'm in your debt because of what you did for Lennie. Speaking frankly, I also happen to know that your reputation in the Jewish community is nothing to shout about. There are even some people who say you're a lousy anti-semite. That's crazy, *I* know. But public opinion counts for plenty in this day and age, a man like you needs the good-will of all sectors of the community, and that's why I put myself out to push through the Cohen deal. It's a good thing for word to get out that you're not against doing business with people of my faith.'

The deal had gone through, but a month had passed before Duddy had seen Mr Calder again and this time he was much cooler.

White men, Duddy thought. *Ver gerharget*. With them you just didn't make deals. You had to diddle. They were like those girls you had to discuss God or the Book-of-the-Month with so all the time they could pretend not to know you had a hand up their skirt, but just try to take it away. Just try, buster. He's offended, Duddy thought, but he made the deal all the same. Two-fifty more a ton, sure. I suppose he wanted me to play golf with him for eighteen years first or something. I haven't got that much time to waste, he thought.

Time became an obsession with him and he was soon trying to do two and even three things at once. He kept self-improvement books beside him in the car to glance at when he stopped for a red light. He did exercises while he listened to his records and in bed with Yvette he memorized stuff from *How To Increase Your Word Power* while she went on and on about a scarey but horny dream she had had or some dumb story about her childhood. After his anger against Mr Calder had cooled he bought a set of golf clubs and an instruction book by Ben Hogan and practised whenever he could. One weekend when Yvette had gone to Ste Agathe to stay with an old friend and Mr Friar was out of town somewhere he invited Bernie round to teach him how to play bridge. That, he felt, was important too.

'Listen,' he said, 'what kind of a friend are you? You must know lots of nice Jewish girls in Outremont. Why don't you ever fix me up?'

'What about Yvette?' Bernie asked, embarrassed.

'Yvette? I could never marry her. She's my Girl Friday.'

'Does she know that?'

'It's one of the first things I ever told her.'

So Bernie arranged a double-date.

'Tell me something about this Marlene kid first,' Duddy asked.

She was pretty, a sweet girl, and studying sociology at

McGill. Bernie pleaded with Duddy to take it easy, though. She might neck a little, but no more.

'A bang I can get any time, Bernie. What's her father in?' Mr Cooper owned Cooper Knitting. He had no sons. 'That's for me,' Duddy said.

But he had a lousy time, so did Marlene, and for Bernie it was an awful evening. Duddy behaved in a stiff, unnatural way, and he was embarrassingly aggressive about paying all the bills wherever they went. He insisted on discussing Shakespeare and Patchen with Marlene and whether or not Canada would be wise to pull out of the UN. 'She's a very refined girl,' Duddy whispered to Bernie at one point. 'I think she goes for me too. But help me, for Christ's sake. I'll dance the next one with Charlotte and you build me up to her while I'm gone. O.K.?'

But while Duddy was gone Bernie had to pacify Marlene. 'I'm sorry,' he said, 'I don't understand what's got into him tonight.'

'What a drip! He told me Cooper Knitting turned out some of the finest sweaters on the market. He wanted me to tell my father that.'

Marlene wouldn't go out with him again. There were other girls, but few of them would see him twice.

'Do you think I'm ugly?' Duddy asked Virgil once. 'Be objective.'

'There's so much character in your face.'

'I think so too, you know. I just can't understand . . .'

He couldn't understand, but he was relieved too. I've got plenty of time to find myself a rich wife, he thought. Meanwhile, with Yvette, he could be himself. She came from a poor family too and she knew that a guy's underwear got dirty sometimes and didn't look disgusted if you scratched your balls absently while you read *Life* on the living-room floor. It was true that she didn't have class like Marlene or some of those other Outremont broads but he didn't have to watch himself with her every minute, just in case he did something vulgar. With those rich girls probably a guy couldn't even read in the toilet. He didn't know, not for sure, but that's how it looked to him anyway. She'll have to have *lots* of money, he thought.

During that winter when Duddy prospered and made so many new friends he did not have much time for his family.

He kept his eye on Lennie, however, and whenever he was in the vicinity of Eddy's he dropped in to see if his father was there.

'Look who's here,' Eddy would say, 'Montreal's own Cecil B. Demille-nik,'

Eddy's hair was beginning to fall out.

'Where's Debrofsky?'

'Retired to the pastures. Like Whirlaway.'

Max was depressed. 'It's not like it used to be,' he said.

'Don't worry, Daddy. You'll be able to retire soon too. Lennie and me will look after you.'

'I don't like the way you're living. I don't approve. I'm beginning to see I should have given you more of a religious upbringing.'

Then one day Duddy ran into Uncle Benjy on the street. 'Jeez,' he said, 'I hardly recognized you. Have you ever lost weight.'

'An operation. Luckily it was only an ulcer. Well, Duddel, how are you?'

'Can't complain.'

'And your grandfather?'

'I haven't seen him in weeks. But I'm going to visit him tomorrow afternoon, that's definite.'

But first Duddy phoned Lennie. 'Listen,' he said, 'what's with Uncle Benjy? He looks terrible.'

'Auntie Ida left him for good.'

'Wha'?'

'She wants a divorce. There's another man. Somebody she met in Miami.'

What a family, Duddy thought, what a bunch we are.

'I guess it should have been expected,' Lennie said. 'You know.'

'Is that how come he's so skinny all of a sudden?'

Lennie hesitated.

'Tell me,' Duddy shouted.

'Daddy's here,' Lennie whispered. 'I can't talk.'

Duddy found his grandfather seated next to the Quebec heater in the shoe repair shop. 'I won't beat around the bush,' Duddy said.

'Good.'

'Maybe it's not in my place, *Zeyda*, but don't you think

whatever it is you have against Uncle Benjy it's time to forgive and forget?'

'How can I go and see him now?'

'But you used to be so close. Can't you let bygones be bygones?'

'Your Uncle Benjy is no idiot and he knows me very well. If I went to see him all of a sudden he'd understand right away why.' Simcha put the kettle on top of the Quebec heater and brought the bottle out. 'All I'd have to do is ring his bell and he'd know it was no ulcer.'

'Does Auntie Ida know?'

'She's in New York.'

'With the other man?'

Simcha nodded. 'Somebody should tell her. She has a right to know.'

'Yeah.'

'Benjy can't even get into the States any more. They say he's a communist.'

'Guess who goes? Shit.'

Simcha served him tea and brandy. 'You have to be very, very careful because if she does come back with you he mustn't suspect why. Your Uncle Benjy is a proud man.'

'There's no love lost between us. You know that, I hope.'

'You don't understand each other.'

'I worked for him once,' Duddy said.

'We're a small family, Duddele.'

'I didn't say I wasn't going, did I? It's just that he'd do anything for Lennie and he's always made fun of me and my ambitions. I'm living with a *shiksa*,' Duddy said.

'I know.'

Duddy rose. 'They're lots of scientists working on it,' he said. Maybe they'll find a cure for it before . . .'

'Maybe.'

Outside, the spring thaw had begun. Driving past the mountain Duddy saw clumps of dirty yellow grass thrusting through the snow. There were no more skiers and the streets were black with slush. Stopping for a red light Duddy was taken aback to see Linda Rubin seated with Jerry Dingleman in the back of his Cadillac. Duddy averted his eyes, hoping Linda wouldn't see him. He felt like sleeping, that's what, and for the first time in weeks he hoped there would be nobody in the apartment when he got there.

'Hullo?'

No answer. But Duddy had no sooner stripped down to his shorts when the doorbell rang.

'It's Yvette. Let me in, Duddy.'

He opened the door. 'Listen,' he said, 'I'm getting into the bath. Mix a couple of drinks and come in.'

Yvette brought one of the kitchen chairs with her. 'Here,' she said, 'take a long swallow and prepare yourself for a shock. Friar's run off.'

'Are you sure he's not off on a drunk somewhere?'

'He's gone for good this time. He took the cameras with him.'

'Jeez. I thought he was so happy working for me.'

Yvette laughed.

'A big joke. We've got the Hershorn wedding coming up in two weeks.'

'We'll have to hire Reyburn full-time, that's all.'

Reyburn had worked on the last two films. Duddy didn't like him. 'Let's try to find somebody else,' he said.

'There isn't enough time.'

'Did you say he took the cameras?'

'The insurance will cover that.'

'What a bastard. He didn't even say good-bye to me.'

'He left because he was in love with me.'

'Look,' Duddy said, 'it floats.'

'He asked me to marry him.'

'Are you kidding. He was my friend. I liked him.'

'What's that got to do with it?'

'Aw, you're crazy. He wasn't in love with you.'

Yvette threw her drink in Duddy's face.

'What in the hell's going on here?' he asked. But Yvette rushed out of the bathroom and by the time Duddy had wrapped a towel around himself, he heard the outside door of the apartment slam. Virgil had arrived, he was typing at the table by the window. 'When are you going to find yourself a room?' Duddy shouted.

Virgil flushed.

'Oh, what's the use? Were you writing a poem? I mean I hope I'm not disturbing you or something.'

'I was writing a letter to my father. You know what I said, Mr Kravitz?'

'No, I don't know what you said, Mr Kravitz, and I don't give a shit either.'

'I wrote him that one day you'd be as big a hero to epileptics as Branch Rickey is to the Negroes.'

'Come again, please?'

'Look at it this way, Mr Kravitz. Before Branch Rickey hired Jackie Robinson – '

'Come here, Virgie. We're going to play high score. For twenty dollars but.'

'Gee whiz, Mr Kravitz, I couldn't take any more of your money. I'd feel – '

'For Christ's sake!'

'You're upset. Is it something Yvette said?'

'Why don't you just kiss my ass and die!'

Duddy gulped down his drink, secured the towel round his waist, and ran down to Yvette's apartment. She was lying on the bed with a book.

'Are we not having dinner tonight?' he asked.

No answer.

'We're not speaking, I see.'

Yvette turned her back to him and Duddy stuck out his tongue and made an obscene gesture. Turning around she almost caught him. Duddy lifted his hand quickly to his mouth and coughed twice delicately.

'Did it ever occur to you,' Yvette asked, 'that you're still under-age and all the deeds are made out in my name?'

'What is this? Traitors' night on Tupper Street? I'm hungry. Make dinner.'

'Go to hell.'

'Now, is that a way to talk?'

'Are *you* going to teach *me* manners?'

'Listen, I just got an idea. Why don't you move upstairs and Virgil move down here? Living this way is crazy.'

'Are you trying to cut expenses?'

'Are you ever in a mood. Boy! Did Friar write you little poemsy-woemsies?'

'As a matter of fact, yes.'

'You're a real poet's delight, aren't you?'

'You don't know how to treat a woman. That's your trouble.'

'Aw, let's eat, eh? I'm starved.'

'He was in love with me, you know. It was nice.'

'I'm tickled for you.'

'Wouldn't you ever be surprised if I did get married one of these days?'

'Guys stop you on the street to propose left, right, and centre. Oh, Christ, I almost forgot. Get me a sleeper on the train to New York tomorrow night.'

'Why are you going to New York?'

Duddy told her about Uncle Benjy.

'Does it always have to be you?' she asked.

'That's show biz, I guess.' Duddy stopped, his face went white. 'He's going to die, Yvette. Isn't that terrible?'

Chapter Two

His memories of Auntie Ida were jumbled. He recalled his lips touching one of the curly red locks when she held him tight for one of so many good-byes. Her ear had seemed enormous with waxy hairs inside. But she had the whitest, most delicate skin, and the only time she had taken him down the street for an ice-cream men had stopped to smile. He remembered the dizzying smell of violets that lingered in his grandfather's house after she'd gone. Taken to his uncle's house once he had stumbled on her in the soft pink bedroom. Ida had just emerged from her bath and she sat in a powder blue nothing before a mirror at a little table crammed with jars. The mirror had an elaborate white frame with armed cupids carved into each corner. The cupids, cheeks puffed, blew at Aunt Ida's reflection. Humming a tune, Aunt Ida picked up a tiny bottle, spilt something on the palm of her hand, and rubbed it into her calves and wrists and neck. There were two packed suitcases on her bed and a trunk on the floor. The sticker on the trunk read *Not Wanted on Voyage*.

That, Duddy figured, must have been twelve years ago, and he had not seen her since. There had been rumours and reports, however. 'She's here again,' Max would say, sitting stiffly in his best dark suit. 'I just come from there.' And turning to Lennie, he'd add, 'Is-payed again, the two of them.'

But there were always gifts delivered via Max. Crazy ones, too. A seashell, perhaps, or an elaborately tooled leather book cover. For his *bar-mitzvah* she had sent Duddy a small hand-woven carpet from Algiers. Rolling his eyes, Max had said, 'Come with me to the casbah, Pepele.'

Duddy couldn't remember what had happened to the carpet but he had made good use of another one of her gifts. This one had actually been sent to Lennie for his twenty-first birthday.

It was an enormous scroll with lots of Chinese writing running down it and a faded drawing of a man and a house and a lake and some trees.

'You can hardly make it out any more,' Max had said. 'She probably got it reduced.'

A certificate signed by somebody from the Louvre had come with the scroll. Lennie and Duddy, somewhat baffled, had taken it to How Lee, the laundry man. 'It's an old prayer,' he told them. 'It is a blessing on your house and everyone who visits there.'

Soon after he had moved into his own apartment Duddy had given Lennie twenty-five dollars for the scroll and had it cut up into place mats with bamboo frames.

She won't even recognize me after all these years, Duddy thought. This is crazy.

Her hotel was a small junky-looking place not so far from where Dingleman had taken him to that party on his last trip to New York. Duddy had been surprised, he had thought Uncle Benjy gave her a whopping allowance. A slender young man opened the door. He wore a T-shirt and blue jeans that seemed too small for him.

'I beg your pardon,' Duddy said. 'I'm looking for a Mrs Ida Kravitz.'

The man turned to a woman seated on a large sofa. 'There you are,' he said. 'I told you they'd send a boy over before three.'

Duddy looked at the woman and groped anxiously for a cigarette. There must be some mistake, he thought. He looked at the room number again.

'Ida thought you'd never get here,' the young man said.

The heavily made-up woman on the sofa was small and round and fat. She wore what he guessed from his experience of MGM musicals was a Mexican costume. A white crocheted blouse and a wide skirt of many colours. Beads dripped endlessly from her neck and when she rose with a small apprehensive smile there was a clack of bracelets. Her toe-nails were painted silver and the ring on her proffered hand swelled like a green sore. Her hair had been dyed black. Her eyebrows had been plucked and heightened, the eyes were smaller than he had remembered them, but he was sure now that it was she. There was the thick smell of roses and the luggage on the bed. A crust of torn labels obliterated the original *Not Wanted on Voyage*, but it was the same trunk.

'Auntie Ida?'

She held a hand to her throat.

'I'm Duddy. Your nephew like.'

The young man threw his hands up in the air. '*Ça, alors,*' he said.

'Uncle Benjy has cancer of the stomach. He's going to die.'

There was a lot to do. Ship reservations to Cannes had to be cancelled and sleepers reserved on the train to Montreal. There were disputes over luggage and many anguished telephone calls and puzzling telegrams, deliveries from the cleaners were late, pills and creams not available in Montreal had to be procured quickly and in large quantities, and only an hour before train-time Aunt Ida collapsed on the sofa and said she couldn't go.

'Isn't it just like Benjy,' she said, 'to get cancer just after I've finally made the break. Don't look so shocked. Psychology has proven that people can bring such diseases on themselves.'

'You mean he wants a cancer? That's crazy but.'

'Benjy has suffered from an overpowering death wish all his life. He wants his death to be my fault though. That's part of it.'

'Oh. Oh, I see.'

'But I'm no longer the guilt-ridden girl he used to know. If I go to him now I don't want there to be any hypocrisy about it. I want to be clear in my mind about motives.'

'He's your husband and he's dying. So?'

'I try to look at all my relationships honestly. I'm not going to him because I'm afraid he'd cut me off without a penny. He's too subtle a sadist for that. He'd want me to suffer.'

'You mean if he left you his money it would only be to make it harder for you?'

'That's right.'

'Jeez.'

'Your Uncle Benjy and I . . . Well, we never had a satisfactory horizontal relationship. I guess you know that?'

'Come again, please?'

'Our sex-life was never satisfactory to either partner.'

'Listen, we don't want to miss the train, do we?'

'Did you think he was impotent?'

'Well, I heard stories. You know how it is?'

'He was as capable as the next man. I can't have children.'

'Wha'?'

'I used to think there was something noble about Benjy. That he told his father he was impotent because he loved and wanted to protect me.'

'You mean Uncle Benjy can have babies?'

'But his relationship with his father was never what it appeared to be. The father-figure has dominated Benjy since he was a child. He was always afraid that if he did something wrong the old man's love would be withdrawn and he grew to hate him for it. So he hurt him the worst way he could. He told him he was impotent.'

'Maybe I'm stupid, but – '

'At the same time,' Aunt Ida continued, 'he was protecting himself. As long as he stayed with me there would be no children. Benjy never wanted a child. He wanted to be the child. (He always slept in the foetal position, you know.) He was scared stiff that if he had a child your grandfather's love would be projected on to it and he would be forced to cope for himself. Benjy has a castration complex.'

'Listen, he's got cancer. I don't know what complications there are, but – Please let's go. Auntie Ida?'

'I bet you think he's a socialist?'

'Who cares?'

'That's his technique of winning attention. He doesn't believe in it for a minute, but he's always wanted to shine and that's his way – If only he'd go to an analyst. I'd be so pleased if he'd learn to live with himself.'

'He's dying,' Duddy said, 'so what's the point?'

'Are you sure? He could have all the symptoms of cancer and not have it, you know. It could be psychosomatic. There are lots of case histories . . .'

'Do you really think so? I mean there's a chance he hasn't got it?'

'It wouldn't surprise me.'

Pretending to be fascinated by what she had to say and all the while coaxing her with drinks, Duddy somehow managed to get her downstairs and into a taxi and on to the train.

'The human personality is like an iceberg,' Aunt Ida said. 'Nine-tenths of it remains submerged.'

Ver gerharget, Duddy thought, slumping beside her on the train at last, and ordering more drinks.

'You think he's been wonderful, don't you, when all these years have really been a torture to me. Doctor after doctor after doctor he sent me to, and afterwards he'd always say it's all right, dear, never mind, it's not your fault. Why wouldn't he leave me if he wanted a child so badly? He hasn't got a mistress either. He never had one. He couldn't do that to me, he said, and then he'd forgive me all my little affairs. I understand, he'd say, it's all right, darling, and he'd send me to still another doctor . . . *He was trying to murder me with guilt.* Your Uncle Benjy is the next thing to a psychopath.'

Duddy patted her hand. 'Aw, you're only saying that,' he said. 'Deep down you love him. In your heart of hearts I'm sure – '

'We could have adopted a child and been happy together. But no, he wouldn't have it. He knew of another doctor.' She began to weep. 'He won't be happy until I'm a raving lunatic and he'll make me one yet.'

'Look,' Duddy said, 'we're passing the Hudson River!'

'The few times I came home and tried to make a fresh start he wouldn't let me do a thing around the house. At first,' she said, blowing her nose, 'when we were still happy together, I thought it was because he was so kind. He used to kiss my hands and tell me how pretty and white they were and how he didn't want them soiled.'

'No kidding,' Duddy said, grinning. 'Uncle Benjy said that?'

'While all the time he was already plotting my mental destruction.'

'Oh. Oh, I see.'

'He wouldn't let me cook or wash the floors or do the laundry because he wanted me to feel inadequate. He succeeded too.'

'Hey,' Duddy asked, 'did you see *Gaslight*?'

'The more he martyred himself the happier he was.'

'Joseph Cotten was in it. I forget who played the wife.'

'What?'

'Skip it. Never mind.'

Nothing could surprise him by then, so that when after a few more drinks the conversation turned dirty he was not shocked. Aunt Ida confessed that if their horizontal relationship had been a failure then she was not blameless. There had been her own problem of penis envy, for instance, and this she illustrated with some smutty stories about her childhood. Uncle Benjy, she said, was an oral fetishist, and when she explained that for him he blushed and quickly ordered another drink. Then she turned her attentions on Duddy and, hoping to distract her, he talked about Yvette.

'The Oedipus,' Aunt Ida said.

'Wha'?'

'Your mother was taken from you when you were young and all your life you will be searching for a woman to replace her. All boys want to have sexual relations with their mothers,' she said.

'Hey,' Duddy said, 'enough's enough.'

'Don't tell me you're a prude?'

'My mother's been dead for years. I don't want her talked about like that.'

'You see. I hit a vulnerable spot. That's why you lost your temper.'

'Oh, for Christ's sake!'

Eventually she fell asleep and began to snore. Tears had wrecked her make-up. Duddy lifted her glass gently out of her hand and stared at her and thought, what can Uncle Benjy see in her? But the more he reflected on it the smaller was his comprehension. Imagine, he thought, she's the one who can't have kids and now he's dying.

Breakfast together was trying. Her hands shook, she looked very old – silly, even, with all the fresh make-up – and Duddy understood that she was afraid. 'Listen,' he said, 'there's one thing. Uncle Benjy doesn't know he's got cancer. He's got to think you came back because you wanted to.'

'Come with me to the house.'

'Are you crazy? He doesn't even know I went to New York to get you.'

'I can't go. He knows about Larry and he'll make fun of me. An old woman with a gigolo.'

'You're not old. Why, one man on the train asked me if you were my sister.'

'I'm afraid of him. I'm afraid of how he'll look at me. You have no idea how pretty I used to be.'

'He's dying, Auntie Ida. Please . . .'

Uncle Benjy summoned Duddy to his house three days later. He lived on Mount Royal Boulevard, above Park Avenue and overlooking the mountain. The house, built according to Uncle Benjy's specifications, represented his idea of how an English gentleman lived. The dominant room, *his* room, was the library and this was severely furnished. There was also an enormous glassed-in sunporch looking out on the garden and the central feature of the living-room was a fireplace of immense proportions. His basement was 'unfinished', and here he kept his stores of hard liquor and wines. There were four bedrooms and a nursery. On the living-room walls Uncle Benjy had hung prints and engravings and maps of nineteenth century England. His collected edition of Dickens he had had bound in morocco leather and kept on a special shelf handy to his bed. Uncle Benjy wore his ornate silk dressing-gown and smoked a cigar. 'Sit down and don't stare, please. I know I'm getting thinner. I suppose you expect me to thank you for bringing her back?'

'Will you leave me alone, please?'

'I know what I've got so we won't pretend. I knew before she came back. The day they let me out of the hospital I knew.'

'I'm sorry, Uncle Benjy. But – well, where there's life there's – '

'Oh, shettup! Did she fill your head with foolish talk on the train?'

Duddy shrugged.

'Don't let me ever catch you making fun of her. I'm warning you. Now there are some favours I have to ask. Why are you smiling?'

'Don't you find it funny?'

'I have lots of money.'

'I know,' Duddy said.

'If you'll give up those vulgar movies you're making and take over the factory you can have fifty per cent. The rest is hers.'

'I've got other ambitions.'

'You can make more running my factory and you like money so much.'

'Why can't Manny run it for her?'

'Manny's a fool.'

'You mean I'm not a fool? Thank you, Uncle Benjy. Thanks a lot. I thought you were the only one in the world with brains.'

'Why do you hate me so much?'

'I worked for you once. Remember?'

'How long will you hold a grudge, Duddel?' he asked, smiling.

'You think it's funny. Everything about me's funny. I'm a regular laughing stock. You know, as a kid I always liked Auntie Ida. But I remember when you used to come to the house you always brought a surprise for Lennie. I could have been born dead as much as you cared.'

'Let's not pretend. Everybody has his favourites. There was always the *zeyda* to bring you surprises. He'd never hear a bad word said against you.'

'Why,' Duddy asked, 'did you try?'

'You've developed quite a *chuzpah* since I last saw you. You have money in the bank, I suppose.'

'Why did you send for me?'

'A man should arrange his affairs.'

'Well, if you can't trust Manny to run the factory you'd better sell out. I'm not interested.'

'What is it about us, Duddel, that we can't sit together for five minutes without a quarrel? I really brought you here to say thanks. I'm grateful for what you've done. Aw, what's the use? We bring out the worst in each other.'

'We don't pretend but.'

'That's true. I wonder what will become of you, Duddel. Well . . .'

'I'll never be a doctor, that's for sure.'

'Now why did you say that?'

'Because Lennie never wanted to be a doctor either. You forced him.'

'I did my best for that boy.'

'You sure did, Uncle Benjy.'

'If I'd left it to your father to bring him up he'd be driving a taxi today.'

'I don't like the way you talk about my father. I never have.'

'I'll be generous. Max is not very bright. I can't change that with my talk one way or another.'

'You're very bright and nobody likes you. I'm sorry, Uncle Benjy. I say things I don't mean. It's just you make me so sore sometimes . . .'

'We eat each other up, Duddel. That's life. Take Ida. I know what you think of her. I know what everyone thinks . . . But she wasn't always such a foolish woman. She was once so lovely that – I'm not apologizing for her to you. You understand that? It's just – Well, I won't be sorry to die. I'm leaving lots of money. There's some for you too.'

'Jeez.'

'I thought we didn't pretend?'

'Why didn't you ever have time for me?'

'Because you're a *pusherke*. A little Jew-boy on the make. Guys like you make me sick and ashamed.'

'You lousy, intelligent people! You lying sons-of-bitches with your books and your socialism and your sneers. You give me one long pain in the ass. You think I never read a book? I've read books. I've got friends now who read them by the ton. A big deal. What's so special in them? They all make fun of guys like me. *Pusherkes*. What a bunch you are! What a pack of crap-artists! Writing and reading books that make fun of people like me. Guys who want to get somewhere. If you're so concerned, how come in real life you never have time for me? It's easy for you to sit here and ridicule and make superior little jokes because you know more than me, but what about a helping hand? When did you ever put yourself out one inch for me? Never. It's the same with all you intelligent people. Except Hersh maybe. He's different. You never take your hand out of your pockets to a guy like me except when it's got a knife in it. You think I should be running after something else besides money? Good. Tell me what. Tell me, you bastard. I want some land, Uncle Benjy. I'm going to own my own place one day. King of the castle, that's me. And there won't be any superior *drecks* there to laugh at me or run me off. That's just about the size of it.'

'You're such a nervy kid. My God, Duddel, you're even touchier than Lennie and I never realized it. Take care. Take my advice and take care.'

'I don't want your advice.'

'You don't want anything from me. Come to think of it, you're the only one in the family who never came here to ask for something. My God, it never occured to me before. You're the only one. Duddel I've been unfair to you.'

'I can never tell if you're joking. There's such a tricky business in your voice, if you know what I mean?'

'I'm not joking. Lennie, your father, all of Ida's family, nobody has ever come to visit me without the hand outstretched. Except you. Now isn't that something?'

'There was lots of times I needed help.'

Uncle Benjy waited.

'No sir. I wouldn't come to you.'

'You're hurting me. You know that?'

'I'm sorry.'

There was a knock at the door. 'That's for me. It's the doctor.' Duddy rose.

'Would you come again?' Uncle Benjy asked.

Duddy rubbed the back of his head.

'Sometimes. When you're free.'

'Sure.'

But Uncle Benjy knew he wouldn't come. 'Was I that bad to you when you worked for me?' he asked.

'You were my uncle,' Duddy shouted, 'and I thought it was the right thing to tell you the *goy* was stealing from you. I'm no squealer. I wanted you to like me. You treated me like dirt.'

The doctor knocked again.

'You always looked for the bad side with me,' Duddy said.

'I wish I'd made more time for you. God help me but I wish I'd seen what your *zeyda* saw.'

The door opened. 'May I come in, please?' the doctor said.

Without thinking Duddy seized the doctor. 'Don't let him die,' he shouted. 'He's my uncle.' And then embarrassed he fled the house.

'I'm sorry,' the doctor said, 'I didn't realize I was interrupting.'

Uncle Benjy went to the window and watched Duddy leap into his car and drive off. Run, run, always running, he thought, he can't even walk to his car. 'What kind of pills did you bring me today?'

'You mustn't be so cynical, Benjy.'

'I can't stand pain, Harry. As soon as it starts for real I want the morphine. Lots of it.'

He won't come again, Uncle Benjy thought. I don't deserve it either.

'Benjy, please. What did the boy say to you? You're so excited.'

'We're a very emotional family. Come back later, please.'

'Is there anything I can do?'

'Yes. Go away, please,' Uncle Benjy said, turning his face away quickly.

Chapter Three

Yvette brought him the news.

'Virgil's been in an accident. The truck went into a tree outside St Jerome. They had to use blow torches to get him out.'

Just when everything seemed to be going right, Duddy thought. Son-of-a-bitch.

With the coming of summer there was the promise of two wedding movies and the camp featurette to be made for Grossman. The distribution side of Dudley Kane Enterprises had begun to show a nice profit too. Duddy had just been considering making a bid for more land at Lac St Pierre when Yvette had come into his office.

'Where is he?'

'At the neuro. They brought him in at one last night.'

It had taken them nearly ninety minutes to free Virgil from the cab of the Chevvie. Luckily he had been unconscious most of the time. But his injuries had been so severe, he had lost so much blood, that the ambulance driver had taken his time driving back to Montreal. 'This guy's had it anyway,' he said.

Five ribs were broken, his skull had been fractured in two places, and his spine had been severed near the base, but Virgil survived the crucial first night. Duddy and Yvette found him in the public ward. He was only semi-conscious. His head had been shaved and bandaged, both eyes were blackened, and he was held in a huge plaster cast. Virgil's face was grey. A tube coming from an overturned bottle ran into an arm that was yellowish and twitching. He's going to die, Duddy thought, and, his stomach rising, he took out a handkerchief and wiped his mouth.

Virgil's eyelids flickered, he smiled faintly. He had recognized them. Yvette began to sob quietly.

'I think we'd better go,' Duddy said, taking her arm.

'Don't touch me.'

'You can stay longer tomorrow,' the doctor said.

Who are you trying to kid, Duddy thought, and outside the ward he excused himself. He swayed dizzily over a wash bowl for a while, but he wasn't sick. Duddy splashed cold water on his face, wiped his eyes, and went to look for the doctor and Yvette. The doctor was gone.

'He says Virgil will never walk again. His spine was smashed.'

'Let's get out of here, please.'

'It has something to do with torn nerves and the spinal fluids. I couldn't understand everything he said.'

He led her outside. They sat in the car together and smoked.

'I'll take care of him for the rest of his life,' Duddy said. 'He'll never want for anything. I swear it.'

'It'll be months and months before he gets out of bed. Then it's a wheelchair for the rest of his life. If he pulls through, that is.'

'Alright, Yvette. O.K. He's my friend too.'

'They lose all sense of feeling below the hips. They can't control their bowels and they don't know when they're urinating.'

Duddy slumped forward with his forehead pressed against the wheel. He stared at the clutch.

'I want you to know all the details. You're not going to get off easy.'

I wish I'd never met him, Duddy thought. I hope he dies and I never have to see him again. 'You're taking a lot for granted,' he said. 'How do you know he had a fit? Accidents happen every day.'

'Their legs get thinner and thinner. Like dry sticks. They could break them twenty times and they wouldn't know and it wouldn't heal. The circulation is practically dead.'

'He was happy to get the job. I didn't force it on him.'

'You knew it was dangerous. I warned you.'

'Crossing the street is dangerous. You've got to live. A guy takes chances.'

'There's no getting around it. You're to blame.'

Only a week before, what with the summer season coming on, Duddy had considered hiring a man to work with Virgil. But after so many months the distribution side was just beginning

246

to show a profit and Duddy had decided to hold back on the assistant until July first, when things would really be moving up north.

'I'll take care of him. Anything he wants.'

But he knew what Yvette was thinking. Virgil's fits had begun again when Duddy had asked him to move downstairs into Yvette's apartment. He had understood, he said, that Duddy and Yvette wanted to be together, but he no longer ate with them every night he was in town and Duddy and Yvette sometimes went off to dinner or to the movies without him. He understood, he had said, but the fits began again.

'We were entitled to some privacy,' Duddy said, 'weren't we?'

'You always treated him like your personal message boy.'

'Look, I happen to like Virgie.'

'You like me and that doesn't stop you from behaving like . . . well, like you owned me.'

'Oh,' he said, relieved, 'we're going to start on that, are we?'

'No, Duddy. We're not.'

But when they got back to the apartment she gathered her bedclothes together. 'I'd rather sleep downstairs,' she said.

'Would you like to marry me?' Duddy asked.

Yvette smiled.

'We could get married,' he said. 'You know.'

'Are you beginning to worry that the deeds are in my name?'

Duddy slapped her hard across the face. 'Get out of here,' he shouted.

Yvette didn't come into the office the next morning or the morning after. She sat by Virgil's bedside. Duddy drove out to St Jerome to take a look at the truck. It was a complete loss and – according to the lawyer – once the insurance company established that Virgil was an epileptic he wouldn't collect a cent. The projector, miraculously, was not badly damaged and the sound equipment could be easily repaired. Duddy had dug the playing schedule out of the battered glove compartment, ripped off the bloody cover, and shoved it into his pocket.

The lawyer told him. 'He can sue you, you know. He's got a case.'

'Aw.'

'He can sue you for everything you've got.'

'He's a friend.'

'Get him to sign a release. I'll make up a letter for you.'

'You must be crazy! I can hardly bring myself to go to the hospital.'

'Don't look at me like that. You hired me to protect you and that's what I'm doing.'

'I can't do it. Let him sue me, better.'

Duddy began to interview replacements for Virgil but he didn't like anyone he saw and finally decided to rent a truck and do the job himself in the meantime. He was short of cash and in no mood to chase around after deals or sit in the office. Reyburn was hired full-time to work on the Hershorn wedding. He was competent, and not really such a bad guy, but Duddy was forever finding fault with him. 'That's not how Friar would have done it,' he'd say. Without Yvette the office was a bore. Going out on the road, doing Virgil's job, was the only peace he knew those days, and heading back for Montreal at two in the morning he always drove as fast as he could, sure that Yvette would be home when he got there. He never left the apartment for even a package of cigarettes without leaving a 'BACK IN 5 MIN' note tacked on the door. Often he woke in the middle of the night, thinking he had heard her on the stairs, but he did not go down to her apartment, and he waited for more than two weeks before he phoned her. 'As long as you're still drawing a salary,' he said, 'you might show up in the office once in a blue moon,' and he hung up.

Yvette came upstairs. 'You might go and see him,' she said.

'I phone the hospital every morning. They tell me he's doing fine.'

'He's not out of the woods yet. They're worried about the fracture. There's a sliver of bone that – '

'Awright.'

'He asks about you every day. He thinks you're angry he smashed up the truck and that's why you won't come.'

'Let's not waste time,' Duddy said. 'Here's a box of matches. You poke them under my fingernails and light them one at a time. Go ahead.'

'I don't feel sorry for you.'

Duddy poured himself a drink. 'Did he have a – '

'He had a fit. Yes. It was brought on by fatigue.'

Duddy began to play the pinball machine. He won three free games.

'I want you to go to the hospital tomorrow.'

'When can I expect you back at the office?'

'I'm not coming back. You can stop my salary right away. I'll consider the last two weeks as my notice.'

'What are you going to do?'

'As soon as possible I'm going to take Virgil to Ste Agathe. I'll get a job there and I'll take care of him.'

'You make me laugh. Have you any idea how much money it's going to take to look after him? The doctor's bills alone –'

'I'll manage.'

'How? On a chambermaid's salary? *I'm* looking after Virgie. He's going to have the best care. Anything he wants.'

'It's all settled. I'm sorry, Duddy.'

'What about me? You said you loved me.'

'Looking after Virgil will be a full-time job.'

'Couldn't we look after him together?'

'I don't think so.'

'You've got a martyr-complex. Do you know that?'

'If you start shouting I'm going to leave.'

'I'm a realist but. I know you inside out. You're gonna look after a cripple for the rest of your life? You're no nun, let's face it. You like it as much as I do.'

'There are times when I wonder what I ever saw in you.'

'You do, eh? Well I'll tell you. You know what you saw in me? You saw a young guy who was going to make it. You saw a pretty good life ahead. Don't look at me like that either. Let's be frank. If not for me you might have been a lousy chamber-maid for the rest of your life. Don't! You try to slap me and I'll kick your teeth in. ''Sometimes I wonder what I saw in you.'' Don't make me laugh.'

'We had some good times together, Duddy. Don't spoil it. I prefer to remember that.'

'You want my handkerchief?'

'I'll speak to the notary. The deeds can be transferred to your father's name until you come of age.'

'You think the business is going to fall apart without you?'

'I never said that.'

'Well, there were lots of things you did pretty bad in that

office. You couldn't add your way out of a paper bag and it takes a magician to read your handwriting. You know what? I'll tell you what. I'm going to get myself a really experienced secretary. *A girl who can spell*. Somebody real pretty. Boy, am I ever going to start having a good time.'

'Are you finished?'

'Shettup!'

'I want you to go and see Virgil tomorrow. I won't be there. You won't have to see me.'

'I wish Virgie was dead. Get out,' he hollered. 'Get out, please.'

Chapter Four

Duddy didn't go to see Virgil the next morning. He put an advertisement in the *Star* and began to interview girls to fill Yvette's job. He hired the cutest one, but she left after a week because she couldn't abide his language. He hired another one, a kid just out of school, began a desultory affair, and fired her when her period started eight days later. The third girl was highly experienced. She wanted desperately to put the office in order and went in for bullshit like inter-office memos (rockets, she called them) and asked Duddy so many questions he couldn't answer that he fired her too. Four days of the week he was on the road, showing movies. He was not getting much sleep again and Lennie got him more benzedrine pills. Every Friday he sent Virgil his cheque and every Monday morning it was back on his desk, the envelope unopened. We'll see, he thought. She's proud, but they can't hold out forever.

By the end of June the hotels had filled for the summer and Duddy's playing schedule required him to be on the road all week. He kept Virgil's sleeping bag in the back of the truck and slept in the fields and on the beaches to save money and hoping to catch pneumonia or be bitten by a snake. He'd go for days without shaving and was seldom seen in a clean shirt. If anyone remarked on his appearance he'd smirk and say something rude. He looked for fights everywhere and by mid-June he had already lost three clients. Even so, his schedule was a gruelling one, enough to keep two men busy, and there were times when he forgot to take a pill and fell asleep at the wheel. He drove recklessly too. The hell with it, he thought.

'You look like a bum,' Max said to him one day at Eddy's.

'A big deal.'

'Business isn't so hot? I knew you'd get your fingers burnt one day. I warned you.'

Reyburn did a surprisingly good job on the Hershorn wedding. His film was straight-forward, exactly the sort of thing Duddy had wanted and never had from Friar. But now he found it boring. He missed the crazy angle shots and montages and outlandish commentary.

'What's wrong?' Reyburn asked.

'Nothing.'

'Mr Hershorn is delighted.'

'Mr Hershorn doesn't know his ass from his elbow.'

'Look here, Kravitz, I don't think you're happy with me. I've been offered something in Toronto, but – '

'Take it. Goodbye.'

'You're a funny kid. I don't understand you.'

'I'm a comedian.'

It was crazy, he had the Camp Forest Land film coming up and he'd never find another cameraman in time. Duddy phoned Grossman and offered to return his advance.

'We've got a contract,' Grossman said, 'I promised all the parents that the kids would be in the movie . . .'

'My heart bleeds, Grossman.'

'A contract is a contract.'

'Sue me,' he said, hanging up.

He refused to show movies at Rugin's because he was afraid to see Linda again, but one night in Ste Agathe he ran into Cuckoo.

'Hey,' Cuckoo said, 'remember the old days, before you were a movie mogul? No time for your old pals now, eh?'

'I'm working day and night.'

'All work and no play. You know what they say? Hey, how would you like to see one of my new routines?'

Duddy went to Cuckoo's room. He couldn't get out of it.

'The band's playing Yiddish music, but eerie. There's a scream offstage. I come on in this leather jacket, see. I'm on a tricycle. I'm slouching. Did you see *The Wild Ones*?'

Duddy nodded.

'I'm on a tricycle, see. I've got a lollypop in my mouth and the number's called The Return of Moivyn Brandovitch or Mumbles The Macher. Wait till you hear the lyrics . . . I'm a vild von from vay – What 'sa matter? You dead.'

'Cuckoo, you're never going to make it. You're not good enough.'

Cuckoo staggered. He freed an imaginary dagger from his chest. '*Et tu, Brute*.'

'You're going to be playing this lousy hotel for the rest of your life.'

'Boy, have you ever changed. I've heard stories, but – '

'What kind of stories?'

'Stories.'

Duddy grabbed him. 'What kind of stories?'

'Yvette's back in town, living with some guy in a wheelchair. They say you took them both for every cent they had.'

'You little bastard.'

'Irwin's graduated, you know. He's got his law degree and he's been speaking to Yvette. It seems the guy never should have been allowed – '

Duddy shoved Cuckoo across the room. He collapsed on the floor there, shielding his face. 'Don't hit me on the nose,' he shrieked. 'Whatever you do don't touch my nose! The operation cost me – '

Duddy fled. That makes the second time this week I hit a guy, he thought, and he drove to Montreal that night, even though he had to be back in the mountains to show his first movie at two the next afternoon. Duddy got out his typewriter and made a pot of coffee. He wrote a long intricate letter to Hersh, saying how much he loved and missed Yvette, how Virgil's accident was destroying him and the business was in ruins, and ending with how he saw no reason why he shouldn't commit suicide. It was dawn by the time he finished. Duddy put the letter into an envelope addressed to Yvette and wrote another letter to her, this one shorter.

Dear Miss Durelle,

It appears my secretary sent a letter for you to Mr Hersh. Since I wrote you both at the same time Mr Hersh's letter must have gone into your envelope by mistake. Please don't open it. The letter to Mr Hersh is Personal & Confidential. I would appreciate it if you would return it to my office at your convenience. I hope you are well. I'm keeping very busy.

Sincerely,
Duddy

He mailed the long letter in the morning and held the shorter one back for a day, but both of them were returned to his office unopened.

At ten-thirty Monday morning the phone rang. It was Max. 'Your Uncle Benjy died at three o'clock this morning,' he said. 'He passed away in his sleep. He didn't suffer.'

Everyone from the factory came to the funeral and so did lots of buyers and competitors and old comrades. Duddy drove in the car that followed immediately behind the hearse with his grandfather, his father, his brother, and Auntie Ida.

'We're a small family,' Lennie said.

'But we stick together,' Max said. 'We're loyal.'

Duddy took his grandfather's hand and held it between his own.

'He couldn't have weighed more than a hundred pounds,' Simcha said.

Ida looked out of the window. Duddy could make out the stays beneath her black silk dress and he imagined the raw marked flesh underneath.

'It's about time either you or Lennie got hitched,' Max said. 'Paw here would like to see some grandchildren . . .'

'Shettup,' Duddy said.

'He waited by the window for you day after day,' Ida said.

'I came whenever I could,' Lennie said.

'She means Duddel,' Simcha said.

'Gwan,' Max said. 'He never had time for Duddy. Lennie was his favourite.'

'There's a letter he left for you,' Ida said. 'I've got it at home.'

'Sure thing,' Duddy said.

They drove in silence.

'He had his faults,' Max said.

Nobody answered.

'A better brother I couldn't have had. I'm just saying he had his faults.'

They finally turned on to the gravel road leading to the cemetery.

'I've got faults too,' Max said. 'I recognize it.'

Simcha watched without tears when they lowered the coffin into the earth. But when Duddy freed his hand from his grandfather he saw that the palm was cut and bleeding and he wrapped a handkerchief round it. '*Zeyda?*'

The old man was muttering something in Hebrew. A prayer.

'Where's my mother's stone?'

He pointed it out. Lennie was already standing there.

'He did so much for me, you know,' Lennie said. 'But I was always frightened of Uncle Benjy. There was something about him . . .'

'Easy. Take it easy, Lennie.'

'Towards the end, you know, I had a feeling he was making fun of me.'

'He loved you like a son. Everybody knows that. Let's go, eh?' But Duddy lingered to take a last look at his mother's stone. 'We're supposed to come here once a year, aren't we? This year let's try. We could come together.'

Duddy went home. They had heard about his uncle's death in the mountains so they didn't expect him with the movies, but his clients were annoyed because he didn't even bother to phone.

I'll get into bed, he thought, and never get out, not unless somebody comes for me. But nobody came and the heat made his head ache. He dreamt again about somebody else's bulldozers clearing his land. He saw himself horribly mutilated in a road accident. Yvette came to the hospital, but it was too late. The doctors led her away. 'He kept calling for someone,' they said. 'A girl named Yvette. He's left everything he owned in her name.' *Go ahead, cry your heart out, you lousy bitch.* In another dream he was an old man of forty, toothless, bald, a drunk, and he stopped at a big rich house to ask for a cup of coffee. Yvette answered the door wearing a mink coat. She recognized him and sank to her knees, but Duddy wouldn't stay, he freed himself from her embrace and limped away. 'I've got the mark of Cain on me,' he told her. He woke with a cry of anguish. His bed floated like a raft amid a wash of orange peels, last week's newspapers, cigarette butts, sticky glasses, and watery ice-cube trays. As the piercing sun sought him through a haze and a vulture circled predatorily, the sea lifted him on to an island. 'Where does the white man come from?' a girl asked. 'I think he's dying,' her brother observed. 'Bring me to your head man,' Duddy said. '*Capishe?*' Old, handsome, a scornful multimillionaire, presiding over a banquet table he heard whispering in the background.

'But why didn't he ever marry?'

'They say that when he was very young . . .'

Sometimes the phone rang and twice the door.

'Yvette?'

Anxiously she ripped open the telegram.

THE WAR DEPARTMENT REGRETS TO INFORM YOU THAT DUDLEY KRAVITZ FELL WHILE LEADING HIS MEN OUT OF A TRAP IN KOREA STOP HE HAS BEEN AWARDED THE VICTORIA CROSS STOP HE ASKED THAT THE MEDAL BE SENT TO YOU STOP

THE PRIME MINISTER

There were broads, an endless spill of beauty queens for him and Friar, the merry movie-makers, as they wandered from country to country, but at the Academy Award dinner there were those who saw through his mask of forced gaiety.

'He hates all women so, poor devil.'

'But what an appetite! The comings and goings from his house in one night. Jeez.'

A crowd gathered round the grizzled old lush who had expired on the Bowery pavement. Flies filled his battered face.

'Any identification?'

'Nothing in his pockets, except this.'

A faded photograph of Yvette.

'Let's get him down to the morgue quick. He's beginning to stink.'

On Fifth Avenue the hearse passed a Rolls Royce going in the opposite direction. Inside, Hugh Thomas Calder pressed a french-kiss on Yvette.

'Why are you crying, my sweet?'

'I don't know. I felt a chill just now.'

Aunt Ida's face loomed so large he had to avoid the hairy ear again. 'It's psychosomatic,' she said. 'He's no cripple. It's the only way he could get Yvette from you.'

'Wha'?'

'He's got a whang that makes yours look like a mosquito bite. She's crazy about him.'

A leering Mr MacPherson waited round every corner. 'You'll

go far, Kravitz. I told you you'd go far.' He tried to run, he wept for trying so hard, but his legs wouldn't work.

At home Irwin waited with a briefcase on his lap. 'We'll expect you in court first thing tomorrow morning.'

'But – '

Even a white wig failed to disguise the judge's red fussy face. Mr MacPherson's laughter squirted across the court room.

'*Please!*'

Duddy woke with a shriek. He staggered out of bed, tripping over a pitcher and spilling stale orange juice on the floor. He sat down at the kitchen table and filled a bowl with corn flakes. He poured the milk without looking and realized too late that it had curdled. Duddy knocked over the bowl with his fist and started for the bedroom again. He stepped into the spilt orange juice and for hours afterwards in bed he couldn't get his toes unstuck. He wept bitterly before he sank into a stupor again. I ought to get up, he thought, but he kept putting it off. I'd do it, he thought, if I could just get up and get out of here. But he'd have to brush his teeth, wash, wipe up the orange juice, clean out the fridge, do the dishes, shop – *shave, don't forget shave* – phone the office, and all for what? He fell asleep again and dreamt he saw Yvette in bed with another man. It could have been Bernie Altman, he wasn't sure, but she was certainly enjoying it. Duddy woke with a bone and pulled the sheet over his head. His toes were stuck together again. He sat up in bed, rummaged around for some empty cigarette boxes, and stuffed silver paper between each of his toes. I'd still get up, he thought, and do everything, but there's no toilet paper. Next time he woke the room was dark and outside it was raining hard. The thunder and lightning excited him, but after the storm the heat seemed even more oppressive. I'll wait here, he thought, until somebody comes with good news. But nobody came and when he woke again it was dawn. There was a mosquito in the room. Sliding his arm stealthily under the sheet he reached down for a newspaper, but orange juice had seeped through all the papers within reach. They were stuck to the floor. Duddy pulled his pillow over his head and began to concoct a delightful dream about Linda and himself going out horseback riding and getting caught in a storm. He got to the part where they take refuge in the barn quickly enough – and he was interrupted by the discovery that now his fingers were sticking together. Duddy tried wiping them on the sheets, he licked each finger dry with infinite care, but afterwards they still tended to stick together. His feet had begun to ache too. The silver paper had formed into hard balls and was cutting into the tender flesh. His mouth tasted stickily of stale orange juice. I was just going to get out of bed too, he thought, but I'm not going to get up just because of the orange juice. If I get up it will be because I want to get up. He fell asleep again, but he couldn't wangle his way back into the barn with Linda. That dream was lost. He lived through what he could remember of *The Maltese Falcon*, taking the part of Bogart. But when he got to the point where the police come to wake him up he could no longer remember the name of the actor who played the nasty cop. Regis Toomey was one, but the other . . . Duddy could see his face so clearly and he could remember him from *She Wore A Yellow Ribbon* and umpteen other movies, *but he couldn't remember his name* and that prevented him from continuing with the Falcon story. Five times he got to the point where the cops come to wake him up, once he almost had the name, and three times he tried to substitute other actors for whosits, but it didn't work. He woke again around noon, freed the silver paper pellets from his aching toes, and dozed off and dreamt that he had brushed his teeth, washed, wiped up the orange juice, cleaned the fridge, done the dishes – and woke to discover that he was still in bed and had to go to the toilet something terrible. He slept only fitfully now – two, three minutes at a time – and woke again from a dream that he had, indeed, gone to the toilet. He had a headache. He leapt out of bed and ran to the toilet. Quickly he urinated, soaked a towel in warm water, grabbed it, and got back into bed. He washed his sticky hand and both feet and triumphantly pulled the sheet over his head again when there came a pounding at the door. Go away, he thought. F— off. But the pounding persisted and he got out of bed to answer the door, stepping into the orange juice again. It was a registered letter for him. A large, serious-looking envelope.

'They're suing me,' he said.

'I beg your pardon?'

'What time is it, kid?'

'One thirty-two approximately.'

'Tuesday?'

'Thursday, Buster. Where have you been?'

The letter was from his Aunt Ida. Inside, in another large envelope, was the letter from his Uncle Benjy. Duddy laid it on the palm of his hand, trying it for weight. It's not a letter, he thought, it's a goddam book. He flung it on the pinball machine and turned on the shower. He drank cup after cup of black coffee and finally he went to the office. 'Any calls, doll?'

Creditors, cancelled orders, indignant clients. Hugh Thomas Calder had called twice.

'Get him on the line for me, please.'

Mr Calder wanted to know why Duddy hadn't called in such a long time. He suggested that they have dinner together that night. 'Can do,' Duddy said. He went to his house and they dined alone there.

'You're not in a very talkative mood tonight,' Mr Calder said.

'What do you want from me, Mr Calder?'

'I enjoy your company.'

'Come off it, I amuse you. That's what you mean.'

'You're a friend of mine. I take a fatherly interest in you.'

'Yeah,' Duddy said, 'then how come you never introduce me to any of your other friends?'

'They might not understand you.'

'You mean I might try to make a deal with them like I did with you over the scrap and that would embarrass you. I'm a little Jewish *pusherke*. Right?'

Mr Calder didn't answer.

'If I was a white man I wouldn't say that. You guys never say what's on your mind. It's not – well, polite. Right?'

'You're acting like a young man on the verge of a nervous breakdown.'

'Bullshit.'

'Is there anything I can do?'

'Would you excuse me if I went home? I don't feel well.'

But Duddy couldn't sit at home. The apartment was too depressing and he did not feel up to reading Uncle Benjy's letter. He went to the office and looked at his bills. The sum they added up to was terrifying. Duddy unlocked the desk and took out the map of Lac St Pierre. He found Yvette's first letter and the photographs of the lake. I'd like to see the day she ever got a job as a photographer, he thought. Boy. He sat there chewing on a pencil and trying to think of somebody he'd like to see. Bernie Altman was out of town, Hersh wasn't home. Duddy went to a bar around the corner. I wonder, he thought, if – objectively speaking – I could be blamed for the death of MacPherson's wife? I never even met her. He drove down to Waverly Street and parked outside Hersh's house. An hour, two hours, passed before he showed up.

'Hersh!'

'Hi, Duddy, how are you?'

Duddy began to cry.

'Hey, what's wrong?'

'Nothing. Get in, please.'

They drove to the nearest bar.

'How's Yvette these days?' Hersh asked.

'Aw. We're through, you know. We've had it.'

'That's too bad. I'm sorry to hear it.'

'They're a dime a dozen. Don't you get involved. Take my advice.'

'I'm sailing for Europe next Wednesday.'

Duddy's eyes filled. He had to blow his nose. 'I must be becoming an old lady,' he said. 'This afternoon I heard somebody say that the Dodger's lead had been cut to half a game and I burst into tears. Hey, did you ever see *The Maltese Falcon*?'

'Yeah.'

Duddy asked him if he could remember the name of the guy who had played the other cop. Regis Toomey was one.

'Ward Bond.'

'Ward Bond! That's it, *Ward Bond*.'

'Are you going to cry again?'

'Naw. I'm awright. Honest. Listen, there's something I want to ask you. I – About MacPherson. It's true, I made the phone call. His wife died, you know.'

'Look, we were kids then. How were you to know – '

'We used to phone them all the time, didn't we? All the guys did. *You never phoned*.'

'I was something of a sissy in those days.'

'Next Wednesday. Jeez. Will you write me, Hersh?'

'Sure.'

'Aw, you'll never write me.'

'Sure I will. I promise.'

'You're my only friend.'

'You don't look so hot, Duddy. Maybe you ought to see a doctor.'

'How was I to know that his wife would answer the phone?' he asked, his voice breaking.

'Let's go for a walk.'

'You'll never write me,' Duddy said. 'You'll forget all about me.'

'Come on, Duddy. Let's get out of here.'

'If I had known that his wife was going to get out of bed to answer the phone,' Duddy said, 'I never would have – Let me send you money when you're in Paris. Let me help you.'

'I'm your friend, Duddy. You don't have to give me money.'

'I'm going to write you every week. Even if you don't answer my letters.'

'You've got to calm down, Duddy. You've been working too hard.'

He gave Hersh a lift home. 'I'm going to come and see you there,' Duddy said. 'I can go to Paris too.'

'Sure. Why not?'

'You'd be embarrassed to see me there. All your friends in Paris will be intelligent Artists like.'

'Duddy. Listen, Duddy – '

But Duddy stepped on the gas and drove off.

'Duddy!'

Hersh pursued him for thirty or forty feet before he gave up. Duddy skidded around the corner, turned into St Urban Street and parked the car. He rested with his forehead pressed against the steering wheel and stared at the clutch.

Chapter Five

Lots of painful facts came to his attention the next morning at the office. He had ruined himself up north, nobody wanted him to show movies any more.

'You're not reliable.'

'Sure, you say you'll come. That's what you said last time.'

His bills, long overlooked, had reached insupportable proportions. There were enough lawyers' letters around for him to paper the walls with. There was no money coming in either. He had no prospects.

'There's only one thing to do,' his lawyer told him. 'Declare bankruptcy.'

'Wha'?'

'Have you any other assets?'

Duddy thought of the deeds Yvette held. 'No,' he said.

'You go bankrupt, that's all.'

'Listen, I'm not a failure. I don't want people – '

'People! Failure! Everyone's gone bankrupt at least twice. Think of it like a Purple Heart, that's all. There's no disgrace.'

'But – '

'Next year you go into business again. It's simple.'

'After all that work.'

But it was the only solution. So Duddy drove back to his office, gave the girl two weeks' notice, and cleared out his desk. Clearing out required several trips. For now that he was broke he did not omit to take the typewriter, all the office supplies including a dozen boxes of paper clips and the wastepaper basket and, naturally, his map of Lac St Pierre.

Twice during the week he picked up Uncle Benjy's letter, but he could not bring himself to read it. He began to sleep in until noon and go from one downtown movie to another. At night he usually hung around Eddy's.

'Here it comes,' Eddy would say, 'St Urbain Street's Nine-Day Wonder.' But he let Duddy have anything he wanted on credit. 'Until your ship comes in,' he'd say.

'I think you've got the sleeping sickness,' Max said. 'Listen, why don't you go to New York for a week. A vacation. Poppa pays.'

'Aw.'

'Go see the Wonder again. Maybe he'll put something your way?'

'On Schnorrer's Day?' Duddy asked.

'A word from the wise. Before a swelled head was bad enough, but now when you couldn't rub two cents together to save your life and you bum around like a haunted house – '

'Lay off, Max,' Eddy said.

Whenever one of the men wanted to knock off for an hour Duddy took over the taxi. That kept him in spending money. That, too, was how he happened to run into Mr Cohen one night.

'Duddy, it's you!'

'A big deal.'

'What are you doing driving a taxi? Look at you.'

'Where do you want to go, please?'

Mr Cohen got in beside him in the front seat. 'Look at you. Oi.'

'Is there a law against driving a taxi?'

'But you, Duddy. You? No, it can't be.'

'I went into bankruptcy.'

'Gangster. What did you clear on it?'

'I'm broke. Honest.'

Mr Cohen clacked his tongue. 'Come to the house,' he said. 'I want to speak to you.'

'I'll take you there, but I'm not going in.'

'You can't have a drink with me? The family's up north. I'm all alone.'

Once settled in the furnished basement Mr Cohen removed his shirt, pulled off his shoes, and started all the fans going. He stood behind the bar, looking at Duddy and clacking his tongue. 'Here,' he said, handing him a drink. 'Now tell me about it.'

'There's nothing to tell.'

'Are you going to start lying again? Don't you ever tell the truth?'

'I had some bad luck.'

'Who hasn't had some bad luck? Tell me what happened.'

'I'd rather not talk about it. O.K.?'

'You know what you look like in those old clothes? A communist. A potential menace.'

'Thanks.'

'I had such hopes for you, Duddy. I thought you'd go so far and look at you. A boy with your get-up-and-go.'

'Money isn't everything, Mr Cohen.'

'A real communist. Oi-oi. Gimme your glass.'

'I really should be going. I – '

'Gimme your glass I said. That's a good boy. Sure, money isn't everything. Who in the hell ever said it was? Duddy, I like you. Tell me what happened. Maybe I can help?'

'I don't think so.'

'Any time you want to come and work for me you name the salary. How's that? A girl. Is that the trouble?'

'Jeez.'

'Duddy, I've got a soft spot for you. You know the way I feel about you? If you told me right now that you wanted to shave and start out again in another business I'd finance you. That's the kind of confidence I have in you.'

'My driver was in an accident.'

'I heard.'

'He's crippled for life. It's my fault.'

'The hell it is!'

Duddy told him haltingly about Virgil.

'Duddy, it's not easy to earn a living. If you went out in the trade and asked about me there are lots of men who would tell you Cohen is a lousy son-of-a-bitch. You think I've never had troubles? You think you run a scrap yard for twenty-five years next September without accidents or law suits or under the table pay-offs or lies? There's not one successful businessman I know, Duddy, who hasn't got something locked in the closet. A fire, maybe. A quick bankruptcy, the swindling of a widow . . . funny business with a mortgage . . . a diddle with an insurance agent. It's either that or you go under, so decide right now. You're going to drive a taxi all your life or build a house like this and spend the winters in Miami.

'You know I once nearly went to jail, Duddy? I came this

close,' he said, 'but I had a partner and he wasn't as smart as me so he went to jail instead. He did two years for receiving stolen goods and all that time I took care of his wife. When he got out he yelled his head off at me. He picked up a knife to me, even. But I didn't feel bad because I know that if he'd been smarter than me I would have been the one to go to jail. Listen, Duddy, it's not all wine and honey in this world, but I've got a family and I take damned good care of them. My Bernie won't have to send his partner to jail. But he didn't land in this country with three words of English and fifty cents in his pocket, either, and there you are.'

'But he's crippled for life, Mr Cohen.'

'It's not your fault. Goddam it, I never thought you were such a softie.'

'It was dangerous to let him drive the truck.'

'Duddy, in my yard once there was an accident with the derrick and a *goy* got killed. The derrick was on it's last legs and I got it cheap. So? I was working night and day then like you. It was the best derrick I could afford. I'm no monster. I had bad dreams. I'll tell you this and I never said it not even to my wife before. I cried too. But you know what I thought to myself. Moishe – I thought to myself – your wife's got one in the oven. A boy maybe. When that boy grows up do you want him to have to stand under faulty derricks for a lousy thirty-five bucks a week? No. Then pull yourself together, Moishe, and stop being a woman. Make yourself hard.'

Mr Cohen told Duddy more stories that reflected badly on himself, he even exaggerated some, but Duddy didn't respond as he had hoped.

'Listen here, my young Mr Kravitz, you want to be a saint? Go to Israel and plant oranges on a *kibbutz*. I'll give you the fare with pleasure. Only I know you and I know two weeks after you landed you'd be scheming to corner the *schmaltz* herring market or something. We're two of a kind, you know. Listen, listen here. My attitude even to my oldest and dearest customer is this,' he said, making a throat-cutting gesture. 'If I thought he'd be good for half a cent more a ton I'd squeeze it out of him. A plague on all the *goyim*, that's my motto. The more money I make the better care I take of my own, the more I'm able to contribute to our hospital, the building of Israel, and other worthy causes. So a *goy* is crippled and you think you're to blame. Given the chance he would have crippled you,' he shouted, 'or thrown you into a furnace like six million others. You think I didn't lose relatives? I lost relatives.'

'Jeez,' Duddy said. 'Wait a minute. Virgie is no Nazi.'

'You're sure?'

'He's my friend.'

'They're all Nazis. You scrape down deep enough and you'll see. Up to here, Duddy,' he said, repeating his throat-cutting gesture. 'That's how I like to get them. Have another.'

'Cheers.'

'You want a helping hand? A loan until you get on your feet again?'

'No. But thanks just the same.'

'Duddy,' Mr Cohen said sternly, 'you won't find me plastered like this again in another five years. Take while I'm in an offering mood. I'm not the Red Cross that you can call at any emergency.'

'But I'm not sure what I want to do any more.'

'Well, whatever you want to do, don't stand under any faulty derricks for thirty-five bucks a week. That's how people get killed. Good night and good luck.'

After Duddy had gone Mr Cohen took his drink into the kitchen and got some more ice.

The *goy* had hollered, he had rolled his eyes, and it had taken him longer than an hour to die. The health inspector had cost him five hundred dollars, but the case had never come to court. Death by misadventure was how the coroner put it. And five weeks later the coroner had sent Mr Cohen a Christmas card and, terrified, Mr Cohen had phoned his lawyer.

'Don't lose sleep,' the lawyer said. 'Send him a case of scotch. The best there is.'

Mr Cohen still had the card. It was one of those religious ones, *Joyeux Noël* and a *Yoshka* on the cross. Some sense of humour they have, he thought.

It's a battlefield, he thought, it sure is. But you and I, Duddy, we're officers, and that makes it even harder. (Remember how Gregory Peck had to send his fliers out to die in *Twelve O'clock High*?) We're captains of our souls, so to speak, and they're the cabin boys. Cabin boys, poor kids, often get left standing on the burning deck, just like in that poem Bernie read me. It's a battlefield. I didn't make it (I wasn't asked). I've got to live, that's all.

Mr Cohen poured himself another drink. It had cost him fifty thousand dollars to build the house, his wife's dream, and the only room he could tolerate was the kitchen. Mr Cohen got up and looked in the fridge. With his wife up north for the summer he had a rest from that stinky new-style Chinese food, all those nuts and pineapple and not a chunk of meat anywhere as big as your toe-nail. With his wife away he was even able to keep a smoked meat in the fridge. There was nobody to lecture him about calories and stomach linings and fatty tissue around the heart. He made himself an enormous sandwich, leaned back, and let out a resounding burp.

It's my house, he thought, and I can do what I want here.

Duddy started to take his father's taxi out on a full shift. He usually started at six and drove until four in the morning. Most days he slept in until noon, went out for a bite, and came back to sit by the window in his apartment until it was time to work again. He still couldn't bring himself to read Uncle Benjy's letter and he avoided any place where he might run into old friends. The heat wave worsened and Duddy began to make do on one meal a day. He lost lots of weight. Nights when he couldn't sleep or woke from a dream of Virgil he played his pinball machine endlessly. He invented a league with eight teams and playing for each one of them in turn he kept track of the results and standings on a specially designed chart. He knew the machine extremely well, it would have been possible to cheat for his favourite team, but he was scrupulous about giving his best to each one. The machine had other uses too. If he wanted to go out for a drink, for instance, when he should have been trying to get some sleep, he would make an agreement with himself that if he hit five million on the machine – not an easy mark – he could go. Here he cheated sometimes. If he wanted to go out badly enough and the score on three balls was unpromising he'd tilt the machine accidentally, which entitled him to another game.

He played other games too. In one he was a blind man and had to find his way round the apartment with his eyes shut. He lost if he bumped into anything. There were penalties to be paid too, like sleeping without a pillow or cutting out smoked meat for two days at a time. The apartment was gradually filled with crossword puzzle magazines and he worked out a method for playing two-handed scrabble. He could roll dice for hour after hour and kept elaborate graphs to illustrate his imaginary winnings set against time invested, physical depreciation, and some even more esoteric data. The bookcase was soon crammed with the cheaper kind of paper backs and in each one he marked how many man-power hours it had taken him to read it. The results of his over-all paperback chart were gratifying. His reading speed per man-power hour showed a consistent tendency to improve.

One night, bored with his other games, he got out the model of Lac St Pierre and started a fire at the hotel. It was brought quickly under control, however, with a minimum loss of life, and he estimated the damage at approximately twenty thousand dollars. Luckily, he was covered with a good insurance policy.

Duddy discovered that he was broke four days before his rent came due. He didn't want to borrow from his father again, so he arranged to drive Miller's taxi during the day. Working day and night for seventy hours, catching a half hour's sleep here and there, he took in the necessary seventy-five dollars, staggered back into his apartment and collapsed on the bed. There was a letter for him from Ste Agathe. It wasn't from her, though. It was from Virgil.

Dear Duddy,

I hope this letter finds you in the best of health. I know that you are still angry at me or you would have come to see me by now. I am also aware of the fact that you've had a quarrel with Yvette. She didn't tell me about what but it would be tragic if the two of you severed relations. She doesn't know that I'm writing you. I must make that clear. But you must come to see her. I've never seen somebody so depressed. Come out soon, Duddy, *please*.

Sincerely yours,
Virgil

PS. Enclosed are two copies of my magazine. I'm looking forward to your frank opinion of same.
PPS. I miss you too.

Duddy picked up one of the magazines. It was mimeographed.

Chapter Six

THE CRUSADER

The Only Magazine in the World Published By Epileptics For Epileptics

Vol. 1 No. 2   September

Famous Health Handicappers Through History No. 2

A BIOGRAPHY OF JULIUS CAESAR

HERE LIES THE NOBLEST ROMAN OF THEM ALL

Julius Caesar was born in 100 BC and died of twenty-three dagger thrusts on March 15 44 BC. But between those dates he won
world-wide fame as a soldier, administrator, author, and emperor,
in spite of his health handicap. He was the author of several
Latin books, including The Conquest of Gaul, still a good seller
in the English translation. He is also the hero of a famous play
by Shakespeare, part fact and part fiction. This play was recently made into a movie with Marlon Brando heading the all-star
cast.

Life was no breeze for the young Julius, but from the day of
his birth until the day he met his untimely end he never once let
his health handicap stand in his way. Julius had been born an
epileptic and he was not ashamed of it. He had guts a-plenty.

Like Abe Lincoln, another great man, his beginnings were hum-
ble. There was no silver spoon in his mouth at birth. He came
up the hard way. First as a soldier and then as a politician. He
served in Spain, Germany, and other lands, making him very well
travelled before the air-age, broadening his mind, and therefore
making him fitter to rule. But his fantastic success story, his
amazing popularity with ordinary joes, naturally made smaller men
jealous and when he returned triumphant from Gaul they began to
plot against him. This plot, in fact, led to a civil war, and the
death of Caesar's old comrade, Pompey. It also resulted in Caesar's being appointed Dictator for life of the Holy Roman Empire,
quite a big honour. Unfortunately, only a month later - after
one of the dirtiest double-crosses of all time - he was stabbed
twenty-three times on the steps of the senate. One of the mur-
derers was his best friend, Brutus, and that's how the expression

'Et tu, Brute'[1] (meaning double-cross) has come into the English language.

Caesar, though always at odds with the Senate, was not the Hitler-type Shakespeare (also an anti-semite) made him out to be. He was always good to his mother and a faithful husband, too. He was also very good to his troops and centuries ahead of his time he introduced something like our own GI Bill. His books, according to scholars, were models of their kind, and the word 'honour' was often on his lips. Among other accomplishments he did lots for economic reconstruction and agrarian reform in old Italy. It's a dirty lie to say he was a tyrant. We have every reason to be proud. You too, Brutus.

Next issue: A Biography of Jos. V. Stalin

A SPECTRE IS HAUNTING EUROPE

THE CRUSADER

Editor & Publisher
    Virgil Roseboro

Business Manager
    Yvette Durelle

THE CRUSADER is a non-sectarian magazine with no political bias. Yearly subscription $2.00 No part of this periodical may be reproduced without consent of the publishers. All mss should be addressed to 8 Rue St. Paul, Ste Agathe des Monts, Que., Canada. A Self-addressed envelope should be enclosed.

YE OLDE EDITOR'S CORNER

UNITED WE STAND
    ---- DIVIDED WE FALL

IT'S time to get in there and start pitching, comrades. We've got to organise. We've got to take a leaf from the book of the negroes, Jews and the homosexuals. Let's not be too proud to learn from other minority groups. LET'S NOT BE SLOUCHS. If a Jew gets kicked out of an hotel the Bnai Brith hollers. If a negro is refused

(cont. p.3)

OUR READERS WRITE
Sweet (and Sour) Notes

Sir:
    Congratulations and good luck! Your first issue was great. Let's have more of those fighting editorials! Enclosed, please find two dollars for my subscription.
    Sincerely,
    Harvey S. Pignatano
    Houston, Texas
Thanks Harv. We'll try to keep up the good work — ED.

Sir:
    Until you started your moronic magazine the best thing about sufferers from epilepsy is they didn't band together against the world. Your sectarian rag is just about the biggest step backwards we can take! Next thing you'll want to elect an epileptic Pope, so people can say we have dual-loyalties too. If you mail me another copy it goes right into the ash can, like the last one.
    U.S. Marine Captain, Retd.
Check your history book, captain. We've had a Pope with a health handicap: Leo IX

Sir:
    Everyone in the asylum thinks your mag is the mostest. A couple of suggestions however. How about a special supplement for paraplegics? What about some pin-ups?
    The Guys of Ward Six
Watch for news of our Miss Health

a job the NCAAP goes to court. In Scandinavia the homosexuals were brave enough to organise and now they have laws to protect them. I'm not saying that, like the Jews, we need our own homeland or, like the queers, we want our own nightclubs. WE'RE BETTER MIXERS THAN ANY OF THEM. But look at what the Harlem Globe Trotters have done for their race. Everybody knows that Einstein was a Jew, F.D.R. a polio victim, and Marcel Proust a homosexual, but how many folks know that MacKenzie King, record-holding prime minister for the whole Empire, was born with a Health Handicap? (cont. p.4)

Handicap competition -- ED.
Sir:
    I have been going steady with a boy for six years. He is very nice. All my friends like him. I love him and want to marry him. But last Saturday eve at the church dance he had a fit in the middle of the dance floor and I'd be less than honest if I didn't admit I was _very_ embarrassed. I had no idea before the dance that he had a health handicap. What should I do? I'd still like to marry him, but I'm very fond of dancing too. What about our kids if we have any?
                        Very Upset
Turn to Verne Delaney's moving story on page 4 -- ED.

BOOKS
GLOOMY IS THE NIGHT By Derek. Marler. Stubbs. $3.50

You said it, Buster. The night I read this novel was the gloomiest I've spent in years.

    Here we go again, boys. We're back in Paris, on the Left Bank, with those crazy mixed-up kids. Has Marler's hero got problems? Sure. His next cheque from home may be overdue and meanwhile the world's going to pot. He hates everybody and he's just too, too sensitive to live. But Marler can write. Some of his dialogue just leaps off the page.

    A word of advice, Marler. How about giving us a novel about real people with real problems next time out? Hemingway was there before you, remember, and his hero had a bigger problem than mere Weltschmertz. Jake had a real health handicap.

    When, oh when will somebody give us a novel about epileptics? Not since The Idiot has anyone made a real stab at it and there's a subject big enough for any artist.
Rating: One Star

PEN-PALS CORNER, PERSONALS, CLASSIFIED ADS

          IN EVERLASTING MEMORY
                  OF
          MRS EDNA PLUNKETT

Break, break, break, at the foot
    of thy crags, oh sea,
But I would that my tongue could
    utter the thoughts that arise

      IN YOUR FAMILY AND FRIENDS

EDITORIAL (cont)

They all use publicity. We don't
And why not? Because we're not
organized yet. We don't meet
and form pressure groups. If the
communists can have an international SO CAN WE.
The Senator from New York is a
Jew and he speaks up for his
people. According to Senator
McCarthy there are plenty of
commies and homos in the State
Department. There must be some
epileptics too. WHY DON'T THEY
SPEAK UP FOR US? Are they ashamed? The hell with them, then.
We health handicappers want
legislation to protect us.

POLIO VICTIMS HAVE THE MARCH OF DIMES (AND WE DON'T BEGRUDGE 'EM IT)
-------BUT WHAT IN THE HELL IS BEING DONE FOR US?????

A Short Story with a Moral

A CHANGE OF HEART by Verne Delaney

"It's terrible," Mr Dermott exclaimed, "I just don't know what to
do."
Big, kindly old Jim Brody stuffed his pipe slowly. "Nothing can
be that bad" he laughed."Come closer to the fire.Tell us about it."
There were three of them seated round the fire in the old home-
stead. Outside the moon smiled down on the river. Clouds sailed to
and fro, blotting out the stars. The fish were jumping.
There was the visitor, Hugo Dermott, a fat fellow with beetle
brows. He was 52. There was old Jim Brody, who everyone in town
came to for advice. He was 60 maybe, but still straight as a ram-
rod. He looked so kind you'd think he couldn't harm a fly, but he
had a list of war decorations as long as your arm. The third man,
Rocky Holmes, was Jim's son-in-law. He was tall dark and handsome.
"Anything I can do?" Rocky grinned.
"Thanks, Rocky, but I don't think so," Mr Dermott answered, ret-
urning the young man's smile. What a fine lad, he thought.
"Darn it all," Jim said, "will you tell us what's ailing you?"
"It's about Lindy Lou."
Lindy Lou was Mr Dermott's only daughter, his pride and joy. She
was gorgeous with blonde hair and pear-shaped breasts and firm
thighs.
"She wants to marry Bill Handy and nothing I say will stop her."
"Ah, that would be Jake Handy's boy," Jim said. "They're good
folks. Why are you agin the match?"
"Bill's a fine fellow" Rocky said, his teeth set grimly.
"Sure," Mr Dermott snarled. "Oh, sure. But you know how fond I
am of Lindy Lou?"
"Bet your life I do," Jim smiled.
"Well," Mr Dermott said, gritting his teeth. "Bill Handy's an
epileptic."
The silence that fell was so thick you could cut it with a knife,
but Mr Dermott didn't notice that Rocky turned pale as a sheet.

"I'm not having my girl marry one of those shakers," Mr Dermott exclaimed. "I'd always hoped she'd hook a fine feller. Somebody like Rocky here."

Rocky rose to interrupt, but Jim stopped him. "Quiet, son. Easy does it." Turning to Mr Dermott he asked "Why are you agin epileptics.

"I've got nothing against them personally. I even like Bill. He's a quiet, hard-working lad, but Lindy Lou is my only daughter," he said, reddening. "I want grandchildren and - Look here, Jim, how'd you feel? I mean would you have let you girl marry an epileptic?"

Jim poked his pipe some before replying. "She did," he said with a twinkle in his eye.

"You mean---"

"That's right," Rocky said.

"For Pete's sake!"

Just then Jim's daughter Mary brought in handsome little Harold, hers and Rocky's two-year-old boy, for a goodnight buss from gramps.

"And the boy," Mr Dermott inquired nervously, "is he---"

"Right as rain," Jim replied.

Mr Dermott bust out in a big smile. "I want to invite you all to a wedding," he laughed. "I've just had a change of heart."

THE END

Chapter Seven

'You see,' Virgil said, 'it was a blessing in disguise. I'm glad you're not angry though. I mean well, remember I said you'd be remembered as the Branch Rickey like of the Health Handi-cappers? Well, what if Jackie Robinson had turned out to be a two hundred hitter? That's what I turned out to be, you know. A prize flop. But if not for the accident there'd be no *Crusader*. It might have taken me years and years to get going. See my point?'

'Sure, Virgie. Sure thing.'

There was a kind of flask attachment under the mattress of Virgil's bed and it was gradually filling with urine.

'You know what,' Virgil said. 'You get a life's subscription and a monthly "Dial Movies" ad free. How's that?'

'Oh, fine. Fine, Virgie.'

Yvette sat in a chair by the window. 'How are things at the office?'

'Oh, *comme-ci, comme-ça.*'

'Not that I care,' she said, 'but how's the new girl making out?'

'Can't complain.'

'I hope she can add and has a better handwriting than I had.'

'Jeez.'

'The *Crusader* doesn't look like much yet,' Virgil said. 'But it's a start.'

'It looks just swell to me, Virgie.'

'We've got eighty-five subscriptions all paid up. In a year, maybe, I'll be able to have it printed.'

'I sure hope so. Yvette?'

'Yes?'

'Well, why don't you say anything?'

She didn't answer.

'Are you all right?'

'That's a new dress she's wearing,' Virgil said. 'She made it herself.'

'It's very elegant,' Duddy said stiffly. 'Stylish.'

Yvette got up and left the room.

'Shit,' Duddy said, 'I'm always putting my foot in it.'

'Why didn't you bring some flowers?'

'Aw.'

'It's so good to see you. You're my buddy.'

Ver gerharget, Duddy thought. 'Listen,' he asked, lowering his voice, 'what does she do at night?'

'What do you mean?'

'You know.'

'I don't understand,'

'What's there to understand? It's a simple question.'

'Well, she goes out for walks . . .'

'Alone?'

'With her brother sometimes.'

'The little Hitler one?'

'Jean-Paul.'

'That's the one. What else?'

'She goes to the movies.'

'Has she ever been out all night? Quick, she's coming back.'

Yvette came in. 'Would you boys like some coffee?' she asked.

Duddy looked at his watch. 'Well,' he said, looking hopefully at Yvette, 'I guess I'd better be moving along . . .'

'Aw, stay some more.'

'I'd like to, Virgie, but it's getting on dinner time and . . . well . . .'

'Isn't he to stay for dinner, Yvette?'

'If he wants to.'

After dinner Duddy and Yvette sat together on the porch steps.

'He looks well,' Duddy said.

'He's been through a hard time.' She explained how after such an accident the focal point of the body's balance alters. Virgil had suffered severe headaches and dizzy spells. 'But starting next week he'll be able to spend all his afternoons in the wheelchair.'

'Isn't that something?' Duddy said.

Yvette sighed.

'You must be proud. I think you've worked miracles with him.'

'Please.' There was an edge to Yvette's voice.

'Well, *I'm* proud of you, that's all.'

Yvette rose abruptly.

'What have I done now?' Duddy asked.

'You look awful.'

'Thanks. It's getting late, you know.'

'A bag of bones.'

'That's me.'

'What's happened to your car? How come you drove up here in the taxi?'

'My car's in the garage.'

'You've stopped showing movies at the hotels. This is the best part of the season. Why?'

'I was spreading myself too thin. There are more lucrat – '

'Is that why your ads have stopped too?'

'Listen,' Duddy said, getting up, 'how would you like to kiss my ass?'

'Is business that bad?'

'I've gone into bankruptcy. I hope that makes you happy.'

'Oh, Duddy, I'm sorry. Really I – '

'Stop being so sorry. I didn't die. There's not a businessman in town who hasn't at least one bankruptcy in his pocket. I've got plans, you know.'

'Like what?'

'There are possibilities. Never mind. It's getting late, you know.'

'Are you driving the taxi again?'

'For two cents I'd wring your neck. One cent.'

'Have you missed me?'

'What do you care? You're having a pretty good time here.'

'Oh.'

'I hear things, you know.'

'Is that so?'

Duddy shrugged.

'I asked you a question. Have you missed me?'

'What's the diff, eh?'

'I missed you.'

'Oh, here come the water-works. Boy. It's late, you know.'

'I missed you so much.'

'This is an age of scientific wonders. You miss somebody so you pick up the phone to say hello. Three minutes for sixty-five cents. Nobody goes broke.'

Yvette laughed.

'It's getting late,' Duddy said.

'You've said that three times already.'

'Have I?'

'Why don't you just come out with it and ask me if you can stay?'

Duddy drove to Montreal the next morning, picked up his stuff, and returned to Ste Agathe by bus the same evening. Yvette met him at the station. 'Hey,' he said, 'did you see the paper? They raided Dingleman's joint. For real, though. There's going to be a trial.'

The house Yvette had rented for Virgil and herself was near the tracks, some distance from the lake. But there was a fine back yard and Duddy used to take out a blanket and lie in the sun there. Yvette had a good job, she was a lawyer's private secretary, and every day at five-thirty Duddy would wheel Virgil out to meet her. Duddy was thin and, it seemed to her, nervously spent. But in a week's time he was tanned, he had stopped biting his nails and he ate with appetite again. He was gradually losing his fear of Virgil too. At first Duddy had treated him cautiously, stiffly, like a bachelor with a newborn baby, but now he was beginning to joke with him. He no longer stared morosely at the urinal attached to the bed. Neither did Duddy moan or twitch in his sleep any more. But he avoided the lakeshore, the hotels or, indeed, any place where he might run into old friends or business associates. She knew that he had the map of Lac St Pierre locked in his suitcase and that occasionally he took it out to study, but he would not discuss it. Neither would he go swimming there with her. She had, at first, been pleased when he slept in every morning: he needed the rest. But when she discovered that he was sleeping in until noon and taking a nap before dinner she began to worry. She tried to joke about it. But he misunderstood. He snapped at her. 'O.K.,' he said, 'so you're the breadwinner. You work hard.'

That made it awkward to ask him about his plans for the

future. He was evasive. He'd say no more than, 'I've got plans. I'm just letting them jell, that's all.'

But what he thought was maybe I can just stay here, maybe everyone will forget me. He enjoyed it most when it rained and he could sit on the screen porch playing scrabble with Virgil or, still better, just staring glumly. Then one afternoon when he was going through his papers he stumbled on Uncle Benjy's letter. This time he read it.

The date doesn't matter

Dear Duddel,

I've lived fifty-four years and lots of terrible things have happened to me, but I didn't want to die. That's the kind of malarky you can hear on the radio any Sunday morning. But I didn't want to die and I'd like you to know that.

I wish there was some advice, even one lousy little pearl of wisdom, that I could hand down to you, but – It's not for lack of trying, Duddel. I have notebooks full of my clever sayings: don't worry.

Experience doesn't teach: it deforms.

Some Oscar Wilde I would have made, eh? Anyway, I've burnt the notebooks. I have no advice for you.

Wear rubbers in winter and don't go bareheaded in the sun. It's a good idea to brush your teeth twice a day. That, Duddel, is the sum of my knowledge, so this letter isn't to teach you how to live. It's a warning, Duddel. You're the head of the Kravitz family now whether you like it or not. It took me by surprise, you know. I thought it would be Lennie. He was the bright one, I thought. OK, I was wrong. Your *zeyda*, bless him, was too proud and I was too impatient. I hope you'll make less mistakes than we did. There's your father and Lennie and Ida and soon, I hope, there will be more. You've got to love them, Duddel. You've got to take them to your heart no matter what. They're the family remember, and to see only their faults (like I did) is to look at them like a stranger.

You lousy, intelligent people, that's what you said to me, and I haven't forgotten. I wasn't good to you, it's true. I never took time. I think I didn't like you because you're a throwback, Duddel. I'd look at you and remember my own days as a hungry salesman in the mountains and how I struggled for my first little factory. I'd look at you and see a busy, conniving little yid, and I was wrong because there was more, much more. But there's something you ought to know about me. Every year of my life I have looked back on the man I was the year before – the things I did and said – and I was ashamed. All my life I've ridiculed others, it's true, but I was the most ridiculous figure of all, wasn't I?

Note: Before you go any further you might as well know that I haven't left you a cent. Not a bean. The estate will be adminis-tered by Rosenblatt and there's money for Ida, a regular income, and enough to set Lennie up in practice. I've also left something for student scholarships (I haven't got a son, and my name has to live on somehow). What I have left you is my house on Mount Royal with the library and everything else in it. But that bequest is conditional, Duddel. You are not allowed to sell it. If you don't want to live in it with your family when you have one then it reverts to the estate and Rosenblatt will sell it.

Anyway, now that you know where you stand with the inheritance you can read on or not read on, just as you please.

There's more to you than mere money-lust, Duddy, but I'm afraid for you. You're two people, that's why. The scheming little bastard I saw so easily and the fine, intelligent boy under-neath that your grandfather, bless him, saw. But you're coming of age soon and you'll have to choose. A boy can be two, three, four potential people, but a man is only one. He murders the others.

There's a brute inside you, Duddel – a regular behemoth – and this being such a hard world it would be the easiest thing for you to let it overpower you. Don't, Duddel. Be a gentleman. A *mensh*.

Take care and God Bless,

Uncle Benjy

PS. I built the house on Mount Royal for my son and his sons. That was the original intention.

Duddy folded up the letter, replaced it in the envelope and, locked it in his suitcase.

'Hey,' Virgil said, 'where are you going?'

'Out.'

'It'll soon be time to pick up Yvette.'

'Tell her I might be late for dinner.'

The lake, as he suspected, looked splendid even in autumn. Some of the trees were going yellow, others burned a brilliant red. Duddy crouched by the shore. He searched for flat pebbles and made them bounce two-three times across the water before they sank. It's mine, he thought. This is my land and my water, and he looked around hoping for an interloper so that he could say, 'I'm sorry, there's no trespassing allowed here.' But all he could find were footprints, reasonably fresh, a man's and a woman's. The man had used a cane. Maybe two canes. The cane or crutch points dug deep near the water.

Duddy walked the length of the land he owned, tapping a tree here, picking up a piece of paper there. Lying on the grass he chewed on a weed and considered the topmost pine trees in the surrounding hills. The frogs began to croak. I could have salted the lake with trout, he thought. That would have been a fine attraction. He entered the cool damp woods and climbed to the top of the highest hill overlooking the lake and that land was his too. A natural ski-run, he thought. Around and around he could see all the land he owned and the rest, a third maybe, that was still in other hands. Beyond the woods he could make out the highway and Ste Agathe. Wheat, potatoes, and barley was being grown on some of the fields between and here and there wretched, skinny cows wandered, but already ranch-style houses were encroaching on the countryside, drawing nearer. I was right, he thought. I knew what I was doing. Five years from now this land will be worth a fortune.

There could have been a real snazzy hotel and a camp, the finest ski-tow money could buy, canoes, cottages, dancing on the lake, bonfires, a movie, a skating rink, fireworks on Israeli Independence Day, a synagogue, a Western-style saloon, and people saying. 'Good morning, sir,' adding in a whisper after he'd passed, 'That was Kravitz. He built the whole shebang. They used to say he was a dreamer and he'd never make it.'

There could have been his father, sitting on the porch and sucking sugar cubes maybe. 'My boy was broke,' he'd say. 'He hadn't made his name yet. He was just another kid at the time and he got this job as a waiter at Rubin's. But he wasn't going to be a waiter for long, you bet. All the while he's serving those *chazers* ideas are ticking over like bombs in his head. Tick-tock, tick-tock . . . He sets up a roulette game, can you imagine? There he is not even eighteen yet, a St Urbain Street punk, and he takes on all the B T O's at the hotel in a roulette game. On this side Fort Knox, so to speak, and on the other my kid, the house. And what does he say, "The sky's the limit, gentle-men", and he doesn't blink an eyelash. The money goes down one-two-three on the table, fives and tens and twenties, and the wheel begins to spin. Round and round she goes, where she stops nobody knows. It's up to fate. Kismet, as they say. Outside the stars don't care. They shine on and on. Midnight, the monkey-business hour. Bears prowl the woods, a wolf howls for its mate. Somewhere a wee babe is screaming for its mommy . . . The waiters and office girls are banging away for dear life on the beach: nature. PLUNK! The wheel stops. *Zero*. My kid rakes the table clean . . .'

There could have been his grandfather on the farm and every-body saying how Duddy was the easiest touch in town, allowing ten St Urbain Street boys into the camp free each season, helping out Rubin with his mortgage after the fire there, paying a head-shrinker fortunes to make a man out of Irwin Shubert, his enemy of old ('throwing good money after bad,' people said), building a special house for the epileptic who had been hurt working for him in those bygone days of his struggles, and giving so many benefit nights for worthy causes. They would have said that he was cultured too. 'A patron of Hersh in the early days. The great man's best friend.'

Duddy started back through the woods as the sun began to sink and he stopped twice to rest and reflect on the long walk home. Yvette was waiting for him on the porch steps.

'Are you all right?' she asked.

'I went for a walk.'

'You've been crying.'

'Don't be crazy. Where's our fighting editor?'

'Duddy! He's asleep. Listen, I've got some news for you.'

'Bad?'

'The notary phoned me at the office. The rest of the land has gone up for sale. There are two different owners and –'

'I'm not interested. Save your breath.'

'*What?*'

'Where could I raise any money now?'

'You'd need forty-five hundred dollars.'

'You might as well say a million. You mean for forty-five hundred I could have complete control?'

'Yes. But – well, other people are beginning to show an

interest. Everybody's beginning to buy land around here. The notary says there's a boom. Since the Korean War he says – '

'I'm not interested. No more.'

'If you really mean that I'm glad. You almost killed yourself running after that land, Duddy. And how would you have ever raised the money to develop it?'

'Sure.'

'We don't need to be rich.'

'Let's not rub it in, please.'

'We can do anything you want.'

'I own a house,' he said. 'A big one.' He told her about Uncle Benjy's letter. 'I think we should move in next week, before the winter. It's time I got started again.'

'What are you going to do?'

'I'm going to be a gentleman. Ha, ha, ha.'

'What?'

'How do I know what I'm going to do? We'll make out.'

'I've got faith in you. I'm not worried.'

'Good for you.'

'But I don't want you to start running again. I couldn't stand it.'

'Maybe Virgie will give me a job as a reporter?'

'Are you depressed?'

'Smiling Jack, that's me. Laugh-a-minute Kravitz from way back.'

'What's wrong?'

'Forty-five hundred bucks. How soon?'

'I thought you said – '

'Look, doll, with my name I'd be lucky if I could raise five. I'm just asking. You can't shoot a man for being curious.'

'Three weeks, Duddy, if you start running again I'll leave you. You'll ruin your health.'

'Running doesn't give you cancer.'

'What?'

'Skip it. I'm going for a walk.'

'Again?'

'Come with me. I'll buy you a smoked meat.'

It was the first time he had taken her near the lakeshore where the Outremont people, and tourists from the States, strolled arm-in-arm.

'The house will be a big help,' she said, taking his arm.
'There'll be no rent to pay. There's no point in killing yourself,
is there?'

'I'm not exactly the kind of shmo who opens a candy store,
you know. A paper route I'm not looking for.'

'There are lots of things you could do.'

'I could be a fireman.'

Yvette kissed him on the cheek. 'If you want to,' she said.

'I'm thinking of going to night school.'

'Oh, that would be wonderful. I can get work as a private
secretary and – '

' – and *The Crusader* brings in about eighty-two cents a
month. Listen, my little *katchka*, I'm not going to live off you
any more.'

'Duddy, you have to take it easy for a while. A little while,
anyway. Do you realize that you had a nervous breakdown?'

'Don't be ridiculous.'

'I'm just repeating what the doctor told me.'

'That's crazy. I didn't have a breakdown.'

'You had a nervous collapse. What do you want to study?'

'Things.'

'Like what?'

'I came so close, too. Jeez. Forty-five hundred fish.' They
entered the restaurant together. 'One minute, I want to get a
paper.' There had been a rush on the *Gazette* and there was only
one copy left. Duddy took a look at the headline and whistled.

DINGLEMAN LINKED WITH DOPE
SMUGGLING
Cote Alleges New York Tie-Up

He was out on bail, the bastard.

'Oh, Boy,' Duddy said. 'Jeez.'

'What is it?'

'Shettup. I'm reading.'

Cote had charged that Dingleman was connected with an
international smuggling organization with an Italian tie-up. He
was vague about proof, however. He wanted permission to
bring in some American witnesses and to use testimony that had
come up during Senator Kefauver's investigations in the United
States. Dingleman, questioned at his apartment, had denied

everything. The only comment he'd make on his frequent trips to New York was that they were 'of a highly personal nature'. He had, it seemed, been removed from the Montreal–New York train twice, but nothing had been found in his luggage. The rest of the story was a recapitulation of the gambling house and police bribery charges.

'Zowie!'

'Duddy, what is it?'

'I've got to make a phone call. I'll be right back.'

Luckily, Lennie was home. 'Listen,' Duddy said, 'is heroin white and does it smell like cinnamon?'

'Yes, but – '

'That's all, brother. I'll see you tomorrow morning. One minute. Could you make a lab test on some stuff for me and tell me for sure if it was heroin?'

'Duddy, you're not taking drugs?'

'Once a day and twice on Sunday. Don't – '

'Don't worry, Duddy. It's tough, but cures are possible. There are new techniques. I – '

'Don't be a jerk all your life. I'm no addict. Are you going to be in tomorrow morning?'

'Yes, but – '

'Good. Wait for me. And not a word about this to Daddy. Understand?'

'You're a dope-runner. Duddy, I'm warning – '

'The chief rabbi of the underworld, that's me. See you tomorrow. Good-bye, Lefty.'

He came running out of the phone booth, rubbing his hands together and grinning. 'I'll bet the last train has gone,' he said.

'What?'

'I've got to get to Montreal tonight. Kid Kravitz rides again. Boy!'

'Duddy, what's going on?'

'Aw, there's a bus at six in the morning. I'll take that. Listen, my little *chazer*-eater, tell the notary we're going to buy. Tell him not to advertise the land or even mention it out loud. I'll have the forty-five hundred in no time. Jeez, am I ever hungry.'

'Will you please tell me – '

'My luck's changed, that's all. Give me that paper again.'

Part Four

Chapter One

'O.K.' Duddy said, 'I'm here.'

Dingleman smiled. He wiped his neck with a handkerchief. 'Obviously you're here,' he said.

'You know why I'm here?'

'Certainly. You read I was in trouble and you owe me five hundred dollars.'

'Oh, a big joke. A *very* big joke.'

'You mean that's not why you're here?'

'No such luck. I'm here about New York.'

'Aha.'

'I need some money.'

'Yes?'

'A loan.'

'I see.' Dingleman burst out laughing. He slapped his desk. 'Aren't you afraid that a gangster with my reputation might take you for a ride?'

'Listen, Jerry, one thing let's get straight from the start. I'm tired of people making fun of me. That includes you. O.K.?'

'O.K.'

'I need forty-five hundred dollars.'

'Really?'

'Yeah.'

'Do you really think I'm going to give you forty-five hundred dollars? *Loan you*, that is?'

'I opened the suitcase in the toilet. I took some of the heroin out. I've still got it.'

'You're sweating. Are you frightened, Duddy?'

'This isn't blackmail. I'll pay you back. Honest, I will.'

'What if I told you I didn't have that much money?'

'The world is flat. Somebody once tried to tell me that too.'

'When the trial begins next Wednesday the lawyers will be costing me fifteen hundred dollars a day.'

'I feel for you. How much do your nightclubs bring in a week?'

'The nightclubs are finished. They cost me money these days. I'm selling out all over before television really gets going here.'

'Oh, yeah.'

'What I'm really interested in these days is real estate. Take my advice, Duddy. Buy land.'

'What do you mean by that? Why should I buy land?' Duddy shouted. 'Go ahead. Tell me.'

'What's wrong with you?'

'Look, let's not quarrel. I'll sign a note for the money. I'll pay you back at the rate of a hundred bucks a month.'

'I haven't got that much cash to spare.'

'Would you sign for me at the bank if they'd give it to me?'

'I'm not exactly what you call a good credit reference. Besides, any securities I own are tied up in bail money. Sorry, Duddy.' Dingleman looked at his watch. 'Come around again some time.'

'You must think I'm kidding. I could go to Cote. If I testified at the trial – '

But Dingleman began to laugh again.

'What's the big joke?' Duddy asked.

'You carried the suitcase across the border, sonny, not me. They took me off the train, remember? I was stripped. They searched me from top to bottom. I mean that literally.'

'I didn't know what was in the suitcase.'

'Duddy,' Dingleman said reproachfully, 'I don't pay three lawyers fifteen hundred dollars a day to let that kind of story stand up.'

'It's the truth, but.'

Dingleman didn't reply.

'It *is* the truth.'

'You must need that money very badly.'

'Oh, I'm the dirty guy eh? I'm the squealer. What do you call a guy who gets an innocent minor to smuggle dope across the border for him?'

'You got five hundred and fifty dollars for it.'

'I thought the five was a loan.'

'If I had given it to you just like that you would have suspected something. I never expected to get the money back.'

'Please lend me the money. I'll pay it back I promise.'

'What do you need it for?'

'Some land.'

'Where?'

'In Southern Siberia. What's your business? I'm sorry. I can't tell you.'

'Am I being asked to invest or – '

'You're definitely not being asked to invest.'

Dingleman looked at his watch again. 'I'm late,' he said.

'Aren't you worried I might go to Cote?'

'Go ahead.'

Duddy hesitated. 'I'm not scared. Give me the money or I go to Cote.'

'You're beginning to sweat again. Look at you.'

'You really think they wouldn't believe me?'

'Duddy, you sold some pinball machines up north. I saw one of them at Rubin's this summer. How'd you get them into Canada?'

'I imported them.'

'Not in somebody else's suitcase, I hope.'

'Jeez, I've got to get that money somewhere.'

'I wish I could help.'

Duddy walked to the door. 'I hope they put you away for life,' he said.

'Maybe they will. Good-bye now.'

'How'd you find out about the pinball machines?'

'Good-bye, Duddy.'

'Boy, when I was a kid I used to think you were some guy. My father used to – What a dirty son-of-a-bitch you are!'

'Mickey!'

'O.K. I'm going. I'm going.'

'One minute.'

'I thought you were in such a goddam hurry?'

'I'm interested in real estate. I wasn't kidding about that. If you're broke and have something you want to part with, or if you know of anything that might – '

'Hanging's too good for you,' Duddy said, slamming the door.

He knows, Duddy thought. He found out. Oh, Christ. Duddy began to bite his fingernails, he ordered another cup of coffee. Dingleman had said he'd seen the pinball machine at Rubin's.

Twice at least in the last six months Duddy had seen him with Linda. Oh, the dirty dogs. Those odd marks on the lakeshore. Canes my ass – crutches had made them. Choke to death on razor blades, Dingleman. Let them bury you on a Wednesday night with an onion in your stomach. Now I'm in for it, he thought. Jeez. Duddy hurried home and phoned Yvette.

'I've been trying to get you all day,' Yvette said. 'Have you got the money?'

'Not yet. Christ almighty.'

'Somebody else is after the land. A Mr Dingleman.'

Duddy sighed. 'What do you mean after it? He's got the money. Why doesn't he just buy it?'

'You know Dingleman?'

'It's Jerry Dingleman. The Boy Wonder.'

'Didn't you go to New York with him once?'

'Listen, this is long distance. Why doesn't he just buy?'

'Because our notary found out about the land going up for sale first. He put in a first offer and he's got an acceptance on paper. There's something else . . .'

'Wha'?'

'It's not important. Skip it.'

'Oh, come on. What else?'

'One of the farmers . . . well, he hates Jews. He'd prefer to sell to me.'

'God bless him. Listen you get a hold of that farmer and tell him Dingleman is the biggest, fattest, dirtiest goddam Jew who ever lived. If he gets hold of that land he's going to build a synagogue on it. You tell him that.'

'Are you coming back tonight?'

'No. Not tonight.'

'Dingleman's offering more money than we are. Our option's only good for twenty-one days.'

'I'll get the money. Don't worry.'

'There's something else. According to the agreement I signed we have to put up three hundred dollars option money tomorrow morning. Have you got it?'

'Oh, shit.'

'All right. I'll get it here.'

'Can you?'

'Yes.'

288

'Listen, tomorrow I'm going to see about the house. Maybe you and Virgie can move in by the weekend.'

Duddy went to see Mr Cohen at his office. He'd only just sat down when he realized it was a mistake. I should have waited until tonight, he thought, and seen him at home.

'Look,' Mr Cohen said. 'He's shaved. *Gottze dank*.'

'I'd like to take you up on your offer.'

'He hasn't even sat down yet. What offer?'

'I'd like to borrow some money.'

'I beg your pardon,' Mr Cohen said.

'You offered to lend me some.'

'Stop shouting. What do you want it for?'

'I've got my eye on some land.'

'Where?'

'No, sir.'

'You mean I should trust you and you won't even tell me – '

'You said you had a soft spot for me. You said – '

'A soft spot, Duddy, but not a hole in the head. You want to come to work for me?'

'No. I want forty-five hundred dollars.'

'*Azoi.*'

'I'll pay interest.'

'Duddy, if you're on to something good and it's too big for you to handle tell me about it. I might be interested. But to lend money at interest – Phooey.'

Boil in acid, Duddy thought. I hope all your teeth fall out. All except one. And the one that's left should give you a toothache for life.

'You're still a minor. Your signature is worth *kaduchus* to me.'

'You said you'd help me. That's why I'm here, Mr Cohen.'

'Don't cry, please. I told you that night that I don't offer loans every day of the week. I'm not the Marshall Plan. Unfortunately, I've had a very bad month. Believe me, Duddy, a terrible month.'

'A loan until you get on your feet again. Those were your exact words.'

'But forty-five hundred dollars? Some feet.'

'Lend me what you can.'

'Duddy, I've been speculating. Take a look out in the yard

and see how high the steel is piled. It's not moving, Duddy. The bank's on my neck too. Where's the land?'

'It's a good investment. I swear.'

'I'm sure it is. Tell me about it.'

'I'm not looking for a partner. I want a loan. Can you lend me three thousand?'

'Listen, to change the subject for a minute. Your friend Hugh Thomas Calder had got lots of other interests nearby besides the foundry. Who gets the scrap?'

'Funny you should bring that up,' Duddy said, lighting a cigarette. 'Hugh and I are having dinner again tonight.'

'He wants your advice on the market maybe?'

'I'll get you the rest of the scrap. But I want an advance against commission right now.'

'Why don't you come to work for me? Name the salary.'

'I want three thousand dollars.'

'What guarantee have I got that you can get me the contract? I'll give you five hundred.'

'You must have got up very late this morning. There – '

'I know. There are other scrap dealers in town – and they'd trust you about as far as they can throw you. Duddy, I'm going to take a gamble. I'll lend you a thousand dollars. You can give me a post-dated cheque for eleven hundred, just in case. But if you don't get me the rest of that scrap . . .'

Duddy picked up a couple of smoked meat sandwiches, hurried back to the house on St Urbain Street, and tried to locate Aunt Ida. Rosenblatt, the lawyer, thought she was at a hotel in Saratoga Springs. He phoned there, but she was gone. They said she and her son were at the Savoy Hotel in London. Duddy rang up London. Mrs Kravitz and her nephew had left four days ago. They were staying at the Ruhl Hotel in Nice. He phoned the Ruhl, and Mr and Mrs Kravitz were registered there, but they were out. Duddy put in another call for midnight, French time.

'Auntie Ida? Hullo. HULLO! It's Duddy.'

'Duddy, what are you doing in Nice? Come on right up here and we'll have a drink together. You *must* meet Gino. Gino, it's my nephew.'

'I'm not in Nice. I'm in Montreal.'

'Montreal? Then this is long distance.'

'Yeah. Listen, Auntie Ida – '

'Isn't that sweet! Gino. G I N O. It's my nephew phoning me from Montreal. Isn't that sweet? Duddy, can you hear me?'

'Yes,' he said, sighing. 'I can hear you.'

'What's the weather like there?'

'Warmish. Listen, Auntie Ida I need – '

'We've just come from the casino. I lost two hundred thousand francs, Duddy, isn't that just terrible? You must do me a favour. The minute you hang up I want you to call Mr Rosenblatt and tell him I simply must have my next cheque right away. I haven't a penny. What – Excuse me a minute, Duddy.' There was a pause. 'Gino says he can cable it care of the American Express.'

'Sure thing.'

'You sound so clear. Just like you were around the corner.'

'You don't say?'

'Are you sure you're not in the lobby and playing a trick on me?'

'No,' Duddy said, 'it's *long* distance.'

'Isn't that sweet! Gino, don't you think he's sweet? Duddy, you must – '

'I think I'd better hang up, Auntie Ida. Its – '

'Quick. Give me a lucky number for tomorrow night.'

'Ten. Good – '

'You'll call Rosenblatt?'

'Right away. Good-bye, Auntie Ida.'

'*Au revoir*. Call again sometime.'

Lennie had come in. He was sitting in the bedroom. 'It's nice to have you back, Duddy,' he said. 'Just like old times.'

'Yeah,' Duddy slumped back on the bed and groaned.

'Duddy?'

'Mm?'

'Riva and I are going to be engaged.'

'Isn't that sweet?'

'What?'

'It's very nice. I'm happy for you.'

'You're the first person I've told. I owe you a lot, you know.'

'Skip it.'

'We're going to go to Israel together.'

No reply.

'I wish you'd come. I think any Jew worth his salt ought to go. What is there for us here?'

'Balls all squared.'

'I've given a lot of thought to what happened to me, you know. To Sandra and Andy . . . I've come to realize that they're all anti-semites and out to use you. Every single one of them. They were never my friends. From the very first minute they were out to exploit my racial inferiority complex. They could have ruined me for life.'

'It's hard to be a gentleman – a Jew, I mean – it's hard to be. Period.'

'That's O.K. You have every right to tease me. Don't think I don't remember all those foolish things I said in Toronto. You're some brother, Duddy. Without you – '

'Listen, Lennie, how much did Uncle Benjy leave you?'

'It's all in trust. I don't get a penny until I graduate.'

'I see.'

'You need money?'

'Something terrible. And quick, too.'

'I've got eighty-five dollars in the bank. It's yours.'

'Come on,' Duddy said, 'I'll make us an omelette.'

'Like old times.'

Max arrived shortly after Duddy got to work in the kitchen. 'Have you seen the paper,' he said. 'Boy, the Wonder's lined up the sharpest battery of legal-eagles in the country. He's playing it smart too. He's got Shubert – that's the brains of the outfit, I figure – and two bigshot *goys* for display. Aw, they'll wipe the floor with Cote.'

Duddy stared at his father. He won't lend me any money, he thought, but if I got Lennie to ask him for a loan, pretending he needed it himself, then maybe, just maybe –

'You know what they say about Cote closing down all the whorehouses in town? He's a sadist. He hates dames.'

'I hope they put Dingleman away for life,' Duddy said. 'But they should burn his crutches first.'

'I oughta wash your mouth out with soap. What's the matter with you these days?' Max asked. 'That's what I'd like to know. You're not happy.'

'Jeez.'

'No. Don't turn your back on me like that. I can sense these things. Why, I haven't seen a smile cross your face ever since you moved back in here. Right, Lennie?'

Duddy forced himself to smile. It was hideous. 'There,' he said.

'Oi. Lennie you're a doctor. Almost, anyway. Diagnose. What's ailing the kid here?'

'He needs some money, Daddy. He – '

'Lennie, for Christ's sake – '

'No, Duddy. Daddy ought to know. Maybe he can help.'

That does it, Duddy thought. No chance of getting any money out of him any more.

'Duddy would like to borrow some money, Daddy.'

'Who wouldn't?' Max reached into the kitchen drawer for his backscratcher. 'Money,' he said, 'is the root of all evil. In olden times they used the barter system. I favour it.'

Duddy grinned in spite of himself. Standing behind his father he reached out to touch him. Gently, however, almost surreptitiously, just in case he moved away.

'For instance,' Max said, 'I would drive a guy from Windsor Station to . . . let's say the Town of Mount Royal and if he was, let's say, a baker he would give me six loaves of bread, or maybe three loaves and a tasty cake. You think that's so bad?'

'Will you lend him the money, Daddy?'

'How much?'

Duddy gaped. 'Are you kidding?'

'*Combien?*'

'Well, I've got to raise thirty-five hundred dollars,' he began, 'but – '

'Whew! Water, please. My heart.'

'Listen, Daddy, it's for something good. It's for land. If it works – '

'Your last brain-wave ended in bankruptcy.'

'This is land, Daddy. Valuable land. I already own plenty of it and in the eighteen months since I bought it it's value has doubled. Daddy, it's a lake. A whole lake. It's gonna be ours – it's gonna belong to all of us – and you'll be able to retire. We'll be rich.'

'What's under the lake? Oil.'

'Jeez.'

'Talk to him, Duddy. You mustn't get impatient.'

'Yeah,' Max said, 'and you could smile. It wouldn't hurt you.'

'All right. Let me put it this – '

'A smile, please. Just a little one.'

'THERE, O.K.?'

'So, did it hurt you? What did it cost you that smile?'

'Let me put it this way, Daddy. Dingleman is fighting me for the land. He's dying to have it.'

'You mean to say you're competing with the BW?'

'Right.'

'I can smell the burning fingers. I'm sitting right here waiting for my omelette and – '

'It's coming,' Lennie said.

' – and what do I smell? *Burning fingers*.'

'His you smell. Not mine. Help me, Daddy. Please help me.'

'You know,' Max said, 'I've seen plenty in my time. I have eyes and I see. Every day they come into Eddys' with sure winners, but – '

'This is not a horse, Daddy. It's land.'

' – but do I ever bet? Ixnay. That's how come I've got money in the bank.'

'How much?' Duddy asked, grabbing him by the arm.

'I've worked hard, you know. There's my old age to think about. If you think I'd risk my whole roll – '

'How much can you let me have?'

'He's never asked you for anything before,' Lennie said. 'Come on, Daddy. Be a pal.'

Duddy began to bite his fingernails.

'You're ganging up on me,' Max said.

'Jeez.'

'You've put me in a position where if I don't lend you any money I'm suddenly an s.o.b. Who put you through school? Do you know that when you had the mumps I stayed up with you three nights running? (At a great personal risk, brother, because I never had them, and you know about what the mumps can do to a grown man, I suppose?) I missed Lux Theatre and the last game of the Little World Series when you had the chicken pox. Some fathers, you know – '

'I give up,' Duddy said.

'He never told you the whole story, Daddy. He came to get

me in Toronto. If not for Duddy I would have been expelled from medical school.'

'Aw.'

'One minute,' Max said, 'I'm not paying Duddy a reward for helping you. He did that because you're his brother. Not for money. We're one family and we should stick together, just like the Rockefellers. In our own small way, I mean.'

'All right. You said it. Help him then.'

'He won't help me. Not in a million years. He's pulling my leg.'

'Would you help a boy who talked to his old man like that?'

'Wow!'

'If I was John D. Rockefeller would he talk to me like that?'

'He's nervous, Daddy. He's excited.'

'I was just on the verge of offering him –'

'I'm going out for a walk before I go nuts,' Duddy said.

'Wait,' Lennie said. He took a deep breath. 'Daddy, how much can you lend him?'

'A thousand dollars.'

Duddy stopped. 'Are you kidding?' he asked.

'I'm not kidding but, frankly speaking, I feel I've just kissed a grand good-bye.'

'You see, Duddy, I told you he'd help you.'

'I can see it,' Max said, 'right before my eyes. A bill with one thousand printed on it. It has wings this bill and it's flying away from me. Flap, flap, flap go the wings. Wham! There she goes through the ceiling. Good-bye grand.'

Duddy began to scratch his head.

'It'll be interesting to see what happens,' Max said, 'when I come to you for help in my declining years. Well, couldn't you give us a smile? It's cost me enough.'

Duddy sent Yvette a certified cheque and told her not to worry, he'd raise the rest of the money in time. Meanwhile he urged her to quit her job and come into town with Virgil. But twenty-two hundred dollars, he thought, where am I going to get it? The bank, of course, was out of the question after he'd already gone bankrupt once. He went to see Rosenblatt, picked up the keys and the deed to the house on Mount Royal, and hurried over to see his own lawyer.

'I'm sorry,' the lawyer said, 'but it's air-tight. You can't sell, you can't take out a mortgage, and you can't even rent.'

'Some gentleman. Some son-of-a-bitch. Listen, what about the stuff inside the house? The furniture, the books – He's got a fortune in liquor stashed away in the basement.'

'I don't advise it. You'd never get even a third of what it was worth.'

But when Yvette arrived with Virgil the following afternoon there was an enormous moving van parked outside and the men were busy inside.

'What on earth's going on here?' she asked.

'Aw, I'm getting rid of some of the old furniture.'

'Duddy, those are antiques. What are – They're not taking the books too? You haven't sold your uncle's library?'

'Quack-quack-quack. Can't you keep you face shut once in a blue moon?'

'Duddy, you can't do this. You've got to stop them. Your uncle left you this house as a trust.'

'My uncle's dead, I've got to go on living. When I've got the money we'll furnish the house according to our own tastes.'

'Oh, Duddy, this is terrible.'

'Terrible? It's robbery. Seven hundred and fifty bucks I got for the works.'

'You ought to be ashamed of yourself.'

'Listen, my little *katchka*, I'm not a British Lord and this isn't the old ancestral home. Lots of that furniture was stinky and uncomfortable anyway.'

'If your uncle knew . . .'

'Awright, he's spinning in his grave. If he'd set it up so that I could take out a mortgage on this place everything would be fine. I wouldn't have had to sell the furniture to a robber and I wouldn't be in such a spot either. Under normal circumstances I could raise at least ten thousand on a first mortgage on this house.'

'There's not a decent sentiment in your body.'

'I eat babies too, you know. Come around tomorrow morning at eight and you'll see. Listen, do you mind sleeping on a mattress on the floor? It's only for a couple of weeks.'

'Couldn't you sell the mattress?'

'Where's Virgie?'

'In the taxi. Is there a bed for him at least?'

'Oh, you're smart. You're so smart.'

Duddy couldn't sleep that night. Long after Yvette had scrubbed the floors and done her best to make a huge empty house seem hospitable, even as she slept exhausted on the mattress beside him, he scratched his head, bit his fingernails, and lit one cigarette after another. Twenty-two hundred dollars, he thought, it might as well be twenty-two thousand. Blood, he heard, sold for twenty-five dollars a quart. McGill paid something like ninety-eight cents for a man's body. Was there anything valuable he could steal? His stamp collection, that ought to be worth fifty dollars. Jeez, he thought, if one thousand people would lend me three dollars each or three thousand people one dollar each . . . This is crazy, he thought. It's not that much money, speaking objectively. I can raise it.

When Yvette rose at seven Duddy was in the kitchen, preparing an enormous omelette. He was singing. 'I'm going to call Hugh Thomas Calder,' he said.

'Don't count on anything.'

'He likes me. He takes a fatherly interest.'

'Just don't count on anything.'

'What's twenty-two hundred dollars to him? Beer money.'

'Are you going to eat all those eggs?'

'They're for the three of us. Hey, we could rent rooms here. There's nothing in the will that says I can't have friends staying with me.'

'What would your tenants do for furniture?'

'Sometimes I wonder what I'd do without you. Really, you know. You're wrong about Calder. I'm his pal. Maybe I ought to ask him for more than twenty-two hundred. A round figure, you know. Not too little, either. Those guys are never impressed if all you need is pin money. You've got to use psychology.'

Yvette went to wake Virgil.

'Well there, Mr Roseboro, how do you like your new abode?' Duddy asked.

'He's in a good mood,' Virgil said.

'Yes,' Yvette said. 'Take care.'

'I'll ask him for five thousand,' Duddy said. 'Excuse me.' And he went to phone.

'Does Duddy need more money?' Virgil asked.

'Don't you say a word,' Yvette said.

'But – '

'You heard me, Virgil.'

'That son-of-a-bitch,' Duddy said, re-entering the room, 'that king among anti-semites, I'll see him strung from a lamp post yet.'

'What happened?'

'Coffee, please,' Duddy shouted.

'You were in such a good mood,' Virgil said, grinning.

'You know, Virgil, sometimes you just give me one long pain in the — '

'Duddy!'

'COFFEE, PLEASE.'

'All right. Here you are. Now what did he say?'

'If I have to make it my life's work I'm going to see that Calder *dreck* busted. Anti-semitism's gone out of style. He doesn't know that yet but. I'm going to spread the word around about him. Hitler, that's what he is. Worse, maybe.'

'What did he say, Duddy?'

'He won't lend me the money. He had hoped we were friends. What in the hell's a friend for if you can't borrow money from him when you need it? He – he's hurt. Can you imagine? I've hurt the bastard's feelings. Oh, those white men. He ought to swallow a golf ball, that's what. The core of the ball should be stuffed with cancers and it should take years melting in his stomach,' he said, getting up.

'Aren't you going to drink your coffee?'

'Aw, stuff it. I'm going out for a walk.'

Duddy walked down the Park Avenue with his head lowered and his hands stuffed belligerently into his pockets. Guys rob banks every day, he thought, they rake in fortunes on the ponies, and me? Aw. Maybe, he thought, I should try Dingleman again? But he decided there was no point. A rich wife, he thought, that's what I need, but that kind of a deal takes time. You just can't find and pursue and bleed one in a week. All that work, he thought, so much struggle, heartache, nights without sleep, scheming, lying, sweats, fevers, and for what? *Bubkas*. I'm a failure. All I needed was to be born rich. All I needed was money in the crib and I would have grown up such a fine, lovable guy. A kidder. A regular prince among men. God damn it to hell, he thought, why was I born the son of a dope? Why couldn't my old man have been Hugh Thomas Calder or Rubin, even? What's twenty-two hundred bucks anyway? A piss in the ocean, that's what. But I haven't got it.

Duddy thought of forging Mr Cohen's signature on a cheque, depositing it to his own account, and writing another cheque against it, but dismissed the idea as unsound. There was a black market in babies, he'd read that in *Time*, but it was just his luck not even to have one of those. Maybe, he thought, if I got a passport, mailed it to Hersh, and asked him to sell it for me in Paris . . . He'd never do it. (There's not enough time, either.) The stock market, he thought, guys with no brains are shovelling it in like snow, but you've got to have a stake to start with. Suicide? Boy, would they ever be sorry to see me go. Virgil would – *Virgil!*

Wow, he thought suddenly, smacking the side of his face, why didn't I ever think of that before?

'Jesus Christ almighty!'

Yvette was waxing the dining-room floor when Duddy returned from his walk. He came with a bouquet of flowers for her, a book of poems for Virgil, and a bottle of whisky.

'You got the money,' she said.

'No.'

'You're sick?'

'Wrong again.'

Duddy waited restlessly, answering questions with curt nods, until Yvette went out to do the shopping. Then, turning his most expansive smile on Virgil, he asked, 'Join me in a drink, kid?'

'A small one.'

'You know something, Virgie, the two of us just don't sit around and chew the fat enough any more. We don't know each other as well as we could.'

Virgil ducked his head. He grinned.

'Once,' Duddy began, 'when we had the apartment on Tupper Street, I interrupted you while you were writing a letter to your father.'

'That's right. I remember.'

'Now you're obviously one of my most treasured friends, but – '

'Gee whiz, Duddy.'

' – but what do I know about your father. Nothing. Maybe – '

' I'll tell you all about him,' Virgil began enthusiastically. 'My father's name is John. He was born on January 18, 1901. He's five foot ten with greying hair and lovely blue eyes and – '

'*Maybe* . . . I mean for all I know he's . . .' Duddy hesitated. He jumped up and began to chew his nails again, ' . . . well, a man of means, as they say.'

Virgil looked grave.

'Virgie?'

He averted his eyes.

'I'm talking to you, Virgie.'

'Well, he's not exactly broke.'

'Here, old chap, let me refresh your drink.'

'No thanks. I think I've had enough.'

'Aw. Gwan.' Duddy poured him a stiff one. 'Cheers.'

Virgil hesitated.

'*Cheers, Virgie.*'

'Cheers.'

'You know, Virgie, we're buddies. Real buddies. Isn't that true?'

'Sure, Duddy.'

'And a friend in need, as they say, is a friend indeed. Right?'

Virgil, looking somewhat bewildered, a little oppressed, said, 'Yvette ought to be back soon, huh?'

'Sure. How's your poetry coming along?'

'All right, I guess. No, as a matter of fact, my muse hasn't exactly been – '

'Jeez, I wish I had your talent.'

'Do you mean that, Duddy?'

'Why, I'll bet E. E. Cummings would give his left ball for some of the stuff you've written. You make that Patchen look sick. Some day, boy, I'm going to be proud to have known you when.'

'Would you like me to read you some of my more recent efforts?' Virgil asked, and he began to wheel his chair towards the door.

'Later. Here, let me refresh your drink.'

'But I haven't even finished this one.'

'Aw. Gwan. Cheers.'

'Cheers.'

300

Duddy sat down, rose quickly, and began to pace. He cracked his knuckles. 'You know what I've been asking myself, Virgie? Where did you and Yvette get all the money to cover your hospital bills? How come Yvette was able to put her hands on three hundred bucks for the notary? Questions like that. That's what I've been asking myself.'

Virgil's head began to droop.

'How much have you got, Virgie,' Duddy asked, kneeling beside his wheelchair, 'and where did you get it?'

'I'm not supposed to say. I promised Yvette.'

'Aha.'

'She made me swear I wouldn't lend you one cent. She says I can't afford to gamble.'

'She's right too, you know,' Duddy said, rising. 'That girl's certainly got her head screwed on right.' The bitch, he thought.

Virgil smiled, relieved.

'But I'd never dream of asking you for a loan, Virgie. I'm only inquiring because I want to help you to invest your money wisely. Let's say you had as much as five thousand,' Duddy said tentatively, never taking his eyes off Virgil, 'or maybe ten . . . Ten, Virgie?'

'Well, I . . .' Virgil looked away. 'Yvette's taking a long time,' he said feebly.

'Where'd you get it?'

'My grandfather left me some. Well, in his will he left me . . . some, you know . . .'

'No kidding?'

'You mustn't tell Yvette I told you.'

'Of course I won't. But you know what, Virgie? That money's rotting in the bank like a lousy old apple left in the sun. Every day you leave it there it's worth less and less. It depreciates. You know what the real value of the dollar is today? Forty-five cents. Tomorrow it'll be forty-four and next year, wham, forty maybe . . . A guy's got to invest his money and invest it wisely. Where is it, Virgie?'

'What?' he asked, lifting his head heavily.

'Where do you keep the money? In a Montreal bank.'

'The Bank of Nova Scotia on Park Avenue,' he said, his voice beginning to wobble.

'You don't say?'

Virgil bit his lip. He nodded.,

'Are you O.K., Virgie?' Duddy asked, kneeling beside him again.

Virgil nodded again. 'A headache,' he said.

'I'm only asking you all these questions because I want to help. You know what, Virgie? Real estate, that's the thing. All the wise money's going into real estate today.'

It seemed to Duddy that Virgil's eyes were glassy, but he didn't feel so hot himself, his own hands were clammy. It's not like *I'm* enjoying this, he thought.

'I'll tell you something, Virgie,' Duddy said, pouring himself another drink, 'I close my eyes and before me I see a lovely spread of land before a lake, the land is all yours, and on it is a pretty white house and in the basement is a printing press . . . Health Handicappers, needy ones, come and go . . . I see you in the picture . . . Happy? *Happy.*'

'I can't,' Virgil screamed so sudden and loud that Duddy started.

'Wha'?'

Virgil gripped the arms on his wheelchair. His eyes were bloodshot. 'I promised Yvette. I can't.'

'Virgie, what are you yelling about? You can't what?'

'Yes,' Yvette said, entering the room. 'You can't what, Virgil?'

'Oh, for Christ's sake. Here comes the United States Cavalry. Right on the dot too.'

'What were you doing to him, Duddy?'

'Breaking his arms. Trying out the Chinese water torture. Jeez.'

'I can't,' Virgil muttered. His head fell, bobbed between his shoulders, and he began to sob brokenly.

Yvette set down her parcels with a bang and wheeled Virgil out of the dining-room. 'I'll speak to you later,' she said to Duddy.

Duddy poured himself a stiff drink. Speak your heart out, you lousy, *chazer*-eating Florence Nightingale, he thought. A lot I care. I'm going to get that land no matter what, see? I'm not giving up now, he thought, taking a big gulp of his drink. An hour passed before Yvette returned.

'He's sleeping,' Yvette said. 'What did you do to upset him?'

'I bopped him one. Wham! Right on the spine.'

'You're drunk.'

'A big deal.'

'Pour me one.'

'You've got hands. Pour yourself one. I'm going out,' he said. 'I require some ozone.'

Duddy didn't return for dinner. He stayed away for hours. He walked all the way downtown, played the pinball machines, drank some, chatted with whores in chromium-plated bars, stared into department store windows, weaving, his nose pressed against the refreshingly cold plate glass, drank some more, walked his feet sore, rested, was told to move on twice, and finally staggered into a taxi.

Yvette had waited up for him. 'Did you try to get any money out of Virgil this afternoon?' she asked.

'F— Virgil,' he said. 'You don't even ask how I am? Maybe—'

'How are you?' she asked.

'Drunk and sad.'

'Now then, did you try to get any money out of –'

'You've got a voice like a knife being sharpened,' he said. He began to giggle.

'*Answer me.*'

'Has he got any?'

Yvette hesitated.

'Jeez. Has he?'

'No,' she said.

'Listen,' he said, 'you're beginning to remind me of my family. That's a fact. I'm always in the wrong. *Why?*'

Yvette's face flushed.

'W,' he said, plucking one finger, 'H,' he said plucking another. 'Y. Cue-wesh-tion mark.'

'I'll help you undress,' she said.

'You can look,' Duddy said in a falsetto voice, 'but don't touch.' And in a moment he was snoring.

He was surly at breakfast and Virgil, embarrassed, did not say much either.

'What are your plans for today?' Yvette asked.

'I'm just going to hang around my house for a bit,' he said, 'if you and Virgil don't mind.'

'We're going out for a walk,' Yvette said quickly.

After they'd gone Duddy began to chain-smoke. It's their fault, he thought, they wouldn't help me, they're forcing me into it. Pushing me, he thought, and he went into Virgil's room. The cheque book wasn't even hidden. Jeez, he thought. It was on top of the dresser with the pass book. Duddy took a quick look at Virgil's bank balance, whistled, noted his account number and ripped out two cheques. He forged the signature by holding the cheque and a letter Virgil had signed up to the window and tracing slowly. This is a breeze, he thought. But the signed cheque frightened him. He concealed it in his back pocket. I'll wait an hour, he thought, well, three-quarters anyway, and if they show up before then I'll tear up the cheque. If not – Well, they shouldn't leave me alone for that long. Not in my desperate condition.

Duddy waited an hour and a half before he attempted to make the phone call. Even then he hung up three times (see, he thought) before he lit another cigarette off his butt and actually put the call through. Disguising his voice, he told the bank manager, 'This is Mr Roseboro speaking.' He gave the address. 'I'm sending Mr Kravitz down to have a cheque certified for me, please.'

Duddy hung up and waited. Just as he expected the bank manager called back to check. 'Yes,' Duddy said, 'Mr Kravitz just left. Thanks a lot, sir.'

Duddy's heart began to bang as soon as he entered the bank, but nobody questioned the signature on the cheque, and so he rushed down to his own bank with it and deposited it there. Zowie, he thought. Rushing into the house, he announced, 'I've got the money.'

'Really,' Yvette said.

'Duddy can do anything,' Virgil said.

'You said a mouthful, kid.'

But when the phone rang Duddy started. 'I'll take it,' he said swiftly. It wasn't the bank. 'All right,' Duddy said, 'we're all going out to dinner. Uncle Duddy pays.'

He got them out of the house as quickly as he could. Each time Yvette asked him where he had got the money Duddy winked and said, 'I found it under my pillow.'

'He can do anything he puts his mind to,' Virgil said. 'Duddy's going to be a tycoon.'

Early the next morning Yvette left for Ste Agathe to see the notary. Duddy met her at the station when she returned the same evening. He took her to a bar near by. 'Everything go O.K.?' he asked.

'The land's all yours now,' she said.

'At last,' he said. 'Jeez.'

'Are you happy?'

'Boy, would I ever like to see Dingleman's face now. The Boy Wonder? They'll soon be calling him the One-Day Wonder. You wait.' Duddy had some papers with him. He tried to produce them casually. 'Oh, you'd better sign these,' he said.

Yvette looked puzzled.

'It's about the land. You sign over all the deeds to my father. Just a formality, you know.'

She hesitated.

'What'sa matter? Your feelings hurt.'

'Give me a pen,' she said sharply.

'Listen, it's just a legal formality. My lawyer insisted. In case you were in an accident like. Aw, you know.'

'What if your father's in an accident?'

'Will you just sign, please?'

Yvette signed.

'Well,' Duddy said. 'Cheers.'

But she didn't lift her glass.

'Listen, if my father's in an accident the land automatically goes to me. But if you were – '

'Let's talk about something else.'

'Oh, boy. This is going to be a night. A real night.'

'I'd like you to take me home, please.'

All the lights were on downstairs.

'Virgil,' Yvette called.

There was no answer.

'He couldn't have gone to bed yet.'

'Maybe he went out dancing,' Duddy said.

Yvette walked ahead into the living-room. 'Oh,' she said, holding a hand to her cheek. 'Oh, no.'

Virgil lay twisted on the floor beside his overturned wheelchair. His face was thin and white and drying blood dribbled down his chin.

'He's had a fit. Duddy. Oh, Duddy.'

Above him the telephone receiver dangled loosely.

'Get me some hot water, Duddy. Quick!'

But Duddy had gone. Yvette reached the window just in time to see him pass outside.

Duddy ran, he ran, he ran.

Chapter Two

They took the taxi to go out to see the land. Duddy drove, his grandfather sat in front with him, and Max and Lennie sat in the back. 'Like customers,' Max said.

'Will we tip him, Daddy?'

'Into the lake. That's where we'll tip him.'

'Wait till you see that lake, *Zeyda*. Even where the water is twenty feet deep it's so clean and clear that you can see the bottom.'

'What about mermaids,' Max said. 'Have you got any of those?'

'You've got to see the sun set. You've just got to see the sun set over my land.'

'Did you buy the sun too?' Lennie asked.

'And *Zeyda*,' Duddy said, 'you just take your time and look around and pick a lot, any lot, and that's where I'll put up your private house.'

But Simcha seemed preoccupied. He merely nodded.

'Wait till you see the trees I've got there.'

'You're beginning to sound like a real dumb farmer,' Max said. 'What's so special about trees?'

'Aw, you'll love it, Daddy. It's so restful by the lake.'

'Oh, sure. I know all about the country. Ants and mosquitoes and skunks and – if you've got the appetite – bull-pies all over. You can have it, buster.'

'I'll tell you something,' Lennie said, 'I wouldn't want a lake here if they gave it to me on a silver platter. Why develop things for them? Now Israel, that's something else. There – '

'All right, Ben-Gurion. Keep the commercials to yourself.'

'Oh, it's easy to laugh,' Lennie said. 'I'll bet in Germany in 1930 they laughed too.'

'Lennie's got a point,' Max said.

'Jeez.'

'I'm only joking. He said that in Germany in 1930 they laughed too. I said he's got a point. *A point*. Get it? Lennie's got a point.'

Duddy groaned.

'Nobody in this family's got a sense of humour.'

'You've got enough for all of us,' Duddy said.

'Life should be approached with a smile. If you can't get laughs out – '

'That's enough,' Simcha said.

'We're almost there.' Duddy turned off on a dirt road. 'A couple or more miles and then we start walking.'

'Alaska here we come,' Max said.

They got out of the car and began to walk.

'Over there. Over the next hill. It's all mine. Everything.'

Duddy was always ahead of them, running, walking backwards, jumping, hurrying them, leaping to reach for a tree branch.

'That field,' he said, 'it's mine,' and he watched to see their expressions. Simcha, he noticed, remained grim.

'All you can see to the right, Lennie. Everything to the left. All mine.'

Lennie smiled encouragingly. But Max seemed let down. 'Just a bunch of crappy, godforsaken fields. What do you want them for?'

'Now close your eyes,' Duddy said. 'Close them until you reach the top of the hill . . . Keep them closed,' he said, taking Simcha's hand. 'Don't cheat . . . O.K. Look!'

Autumn leaves floated on the still surface of the lake.

'Injun territory,' Max said.

'Christ almighty!'

'A wilderness,' Max said.

'Sure,' Duddy said, jumping up and down, 'a goddam wilderness, and remember it, goddam it, take a good look, goddam everything to hell and heaven and kingdom come, because a whole town is going up here. A camp and a hotel and cottages and stores and a synagogue – yes, *Zeyda*, a real *shul* – and a movie and . . . well everything you can think of.'

'Dream,' Max sang, 'when you're feeling blue. Dream, let the smoke rings rise in the air – Hey, look over there!'

Mounting slowly and cumbersome, puffing and pausing to wipe his forehead, came a man on crutches and a young girl.

'It's the Boy Wonder,' Max said. 'Hey, here. Over here, Jerry.'

Duddy lit a cigarette and waited. 'Well,' he said as Dingleman approached, 'aren't you in jail yet?'

'Jesus,' Max said, smacking the side of his face.

'Hello, Linda,' Duddy said.

Max pulled Lennie over. 'This is my boy Lennie,' he told Dingleman. 'He's going to be a doctor. A specialist.'

'That's grand,' Dingleman said. 'Hullo, Duddy.' He extended his hand, but Duddy didn't take it. 'I came to congratulate you,' he said.

'Shake with him,' Max said.

Duddy shook hands with him.

'There. Isn't that how sports should behave? Jerry's a good loser,' Max said.

'This is a fine property your son's got here, Max.'

'Well, you know. He's a shrewd cookie. A chip off the old block.'

'Yeah,' Duddy said, 'and I'll tell you something funny about this land, Dingleman. No trespassing.'

'It's a joke,' Max said quickly. 'Duddy's a kidder. Natural born.'

'The sign goes up tomorrow. It reads, "Trespassers will be prosecuted."'

'Ah ha ha,' Max said, poking Duddy.

'You're a big boy now,' Linda said, 'aren't you?'

'I'm not a waiter any more, if that's what you mean?'

'It's going to cost you a fortune to develop this land,' Jerry said.

'So?'

'Who's the old man?' Jerry asked suddenly.

'He's not an old man, he's my grandfather. This is my property, sonny. Watch how you talk.'

'You're going to need lots of money, Duddy. A fortune.'

'A million,' Duddy began, 'maybe more. Because there's going to be a children's camp and a hotel and – What's the matter, *Zeyda*, where are you going?'

'Back to the car.'

'Have you picked your lot yet?'

'I don't feel well. I'm going to sit in the car.'

'But you haven't chosen your farm yet. *Zeyda*, wait.'

Dingleman stopped Duddy. 'Let him go,' he said.

Duddy watched the old man retire slowly down the slope. 'All his life he told me a man should have land. He said he wanted a farm. I don't . . .'

Dingleman laughed. 'Maybe he never expected you to get him one?'

'Wha'?'

'Have you ever read any Yiddish poetry?'

'*Zeyda*, come back. *ZEYDA!*'

But the old man continued towards the car.

'Certainly not,' Dingleman continued. 'But if you had you'd know about those old men. Sitting in their dark cramped ghetto corners they wrote the most mawkish, school-girlish stuff about green fields and sky. Terrible poetry, but touching when you consider the circumstances under which it was written. Your grandfather doesn't want any land. He wouldn't know what to do with it.'

'Will you shettup, please?'

'Duddy, don't talk like that. He's excited, Jerry. He – '

'He said a man without land was nobody.'

'He never thought you'd make it,' Dingleman said. 'Now you've frightened him. They want to die in the same suffocating way they lived, bent over a last or a cutting table or a freezing junk yard shack.'

'He can have any lot he chooses. Any one.'

'Duddy, listen to me.'

'He's listening, Jerry. *Listen*, Duddy.'

'I'm interested in this land. I'm interested in you too. I can raise the money for development. You can't.'

'Last time I saw you,' Duddy said, 'you couldn't even raise three thousand dollars. Remember, sonny?'

'We could be partners.'

Duddy watched his grandfather getting smaller and smaller. He disappeared behind a clump of trees.

'Alone, you'll never raise the money you need. With my help we could turn this into a model resort town in five years.'

Duddy began to laugh. 'You heard him, Daddy. You heard the man.'

'Imagine,' Max said, 'my boy and Dingleman. Partners.'

Duddy laughed some more. 'Listen, Dingleman,' he shouted, 'get off my land. Beat it.'

'Duddy,' Max began, 'what's got into you?'

'Take off, sonny.'

Max began to shake Duddy.

'You'll never do it alone,' Dingleman said.

Duddy broke free. 'I'm giving you five minutes to get the hell off my land. I'm the king of the castle here, sonny.'

'He's gone crazy,' Max said to Lennie.

'Duddy,' Lennie said. 'Why don't you listen to Mr Dingleman? He makes sense.'

Duddy picked up a stone. 'I'm giving you exactly five minutes to take Linda and get the hell out of here.'

Linda made as if to slap Duddy's face, but he caught her hand and held it. 'I remember you,' he said. 'You slap me and I'll kick your ass so hard you won't sit down for a week.'

Linda spat.

'It's good for my grass,' Duddy said.

Dingleman turned and began the long, difficult descent. Max pursued him. 'Listen, he's only a kid. You talk to me, Jerry.'

'You two-bit, dope-smuggling cripple!'

'Stop it,' Lennie said, alarmed.

But Duddy cupped his hands and hollered. 'On my land,' he shouted, 'no trespassers and no cripples. Except on Schnorrer's Day.'

'Duddy, please.'

Duddy jumped up and down, he laughed, he grabbed Lennie round the waist and forced him to dance round and round. 'Don't you understand,' he asked. 'Don't you realize that you're standing smack in the middle of Kravitz Town? This is a gold mine, don't you realize – He came all this way to beg me for an in. FASTER, YOU BASTARD. RUN, DINGLEMAN. LET'S SEE YOU RUN ON THOSE STICKS.'

'Take it easy, Duddy. Please try to calm down.'

Duddy whirled around and heaved the stone he still held into the lake.

'Boy,' Lennie said, 'are you ever the manic-depressive type.'

'Come on. Let's go see what's ailing the *Zeyda*.'

Max caught up with his boys half-way down the hill. 'You're my son, Duddy, but I'm going to be frank. You're in the wrong.'

'You don't so-say,' Duddy said.

'He's angry at you, Duddy, and when the Boy Wonder gets – '

'I know. He eats bread and it comes out toasted. I'm angrier but.'

Simcha sat silent and severe in the front of the car.

'Why didn't you pick a lot for yourself?' Duddy asked.

'I don't want a farm here.'

'Why?'

'The girl came to see me last week.'

'What girl?'

'Your girl.'

'I haven't got a girl.'

'Yvette came to see me.'

'You don't have to worry,' Max said. 'He's all washed up with her. A good thing too. Mixed – '

'Will you not interrupt, please?'

'She told me what you did,' Simcha said. 'And I don't want a farm here.'

'So you couldn't even wait to hear my side of the story? Is that right?'

'I can see what you have planned for me, Duddel. You'll be good to me. You'd give me everything I wanted. And that would settle your conscience when you went out to swindle others.'

'Will you all get into the car, please?' Duddy slammed the door. 'Nobody's ever interested in my side of the story. I'm all alone,' he said, pulling savagely at the gearshift.

'The boy's fits are getting worse and worse.'

'I didn't give him epilepsy.'

'What's going on?' Max asked.

'Would you have rather I married a *shiksa*, *Zeyda*?'

'Don't twist. Not with me.'

'You don't twist either. You don't want a farm. You never have. You're scared stiff of the country and you want to die in that stinky old shoe repair shop.'

Simcha took a deep breath.

'A man without land is nothing. That's what you always told me. Well, I'm somebody. A real somebody.'

'Why do we have to quarrel,' Max said. 'We're one family.'

'You couldn't even go to see Uncle Benjy before he died. Naw, not you. You're just too goddam proud to live. You – '

Simcha looked resolutely out of the window.

'I'm sorry,' Duddy said.

'You see, Paw. He's sorry. Kiss and make up,' Max said.

Eventually they reached the highway.

'I'm sorry, *Zeyda*. I . . . Please?'

But Simcha still stared out of the window. Duddy parked in front of Lou's Bagel & Lox Bar. And Simcha wouldn't get out of the car.

'We won't be long,' Duddy said. But inside he couldn't eat. 'Here, Lennie,' he said. 'Take him a coffee.'

'Forget it,' Max said. 'He gets like that. I know from long experience.'

'Shettup, please.'

'Time heals,' Max said.

'Will you shettup, please.'

Lennie returned with the coffee. 'Would you believe it,' he said. 'He's crying. I thought I'd never live to see the day . . .'

Duddy bolted out of the store. He did not pause to look into the car, but hurried past it and around the block. He began to run. The land is yours, he thought, and nothing they do or say or feel can take it away from you. You pay a price. Yvette wasn't at the house. Neither was Virgil. He found them in the park. Yvette saw him coming and motioned him back, behind a tree, before Virgil could see him. Then, after she'd whispered something to Virgil, she came to join him.

'Seeing you again,' she said, 'might be enough to bring on another fit.'

Duddy swallowed, he wiped his hand through his hair, he didn't speak. He looked exasperated.

'Now tell me quickly what you want,' she said. 'I've got nothing to say to you.'

'Maybe. Maybe that's so. But I've got plenty to say to you, sister. Why for two cents I'd wring your goddam neck. Why did you go to my grandfather? Of all the people in the world he's the only one – '

'That's exactly why I went.'

Duddy made a fist. He shook it.

'I told him about the cheque. I told him everything. I wanted to hurt you as badly as I could.'

'Gee, thanks. Thanks a lot.'

'Please go.'

'Look, I did it all for us. Do you think I enjoyed forging the cheque? Am I a thief?'

'I don't know what you are any more. I don't care, either.'

'I had to act quickly, Yvette. I had to think for all of us. What I did was . . . well, unorthodox. That's the word I'm looking for. But you know, like they say, he who hesitates – Don't you understand? It's mine now. At last the land is mine, Yvette. All of it.'

She tried to walk away. He stopped her.

'I'm going to pay him back. I swear it, Yvette.'

'We don't want your money. If we wanted it we could sue you. All we want from you is to be left alone. Can you understand that?'

'He'll get every last cent of his money back whether he likes it or not. And that's not all, either. I'm going to build him a pretty white house. Just like I said. So help me God I will.'

'We don't want to see you again, Duddy. Ever, I mean.'

'Oh, where do you get this "we" crap suddenly? We-we-we. Listen – '

'Are you finished?'

' – you listen, Yvette, you are looking at the man who is going to build a town where only bugs and bullshit was before. I'm going to create jobs. Jeez, I'm a public benefactor. But you've got to have faith in me, Yvette. You've got to help. Give me time.'

'You can have all the time in the world, Duddy. But I don't ever want to see you again.'

'I don't ever want to see you again,' he said, mimicking her voice. 'Quack-quack-quack. What do you think this is? Some dumb movie?'

'I'm serious, Duddy.'

He gave her an anguished look, started to say something, held back, swallowed, shook his fist, and said, his voice filled with wrath, 'I have to do everything alone. I can see that now. I can trust nobody.'

'We betrayed you, I suppose.'

'Yes. You did.'

He had spoken with such quiet and certainty that she began to doubt herself.

'You'll come crawling,' he said.

'I want you to know something. *I'd* sue you. I'd even get Irwin Shubert to take the case. But Virgil won't let me. He doesn't even want to hear about it any more.'

'You hate me,' Duddy said. 'Is that possible?'

'I think you're rotten. I wish you were dead.'

'You don't understand, Yvette. Why can't I make you understand? Listen, Yvette, I – '

But she turned away from him.

'You'll come crawling,' he shouted after her, 'crawling on your hands and knees,' and he walked off.

When Duddy finally returned to the store his father's back was to him. Max sat at a table piled high with sandwiches and surrounded by strangers. 'Even as a kid,' he said, sucking a sugar cube, 'way back there before he had begun to make his mark, my boy was a trouble-maker. He was born on the wrong side of the tracks with a rusty spoon in his mouth, so to speak, and the spark of rebellion in him. A motherless boy,' he said, pounding the table, 'but one who thrived on adversity, like Maxim Gorki or Eddy Cantor, if you're familiar with their histories. You could see from the day of his birth that he was slated for fame and fortune. A comer. Why I remember when he was still at FFHS they had a teacher there, an anti-semite of the anti-semites, a lush-head, and my boy was the one who led the fight against him and drove him out of the school. Just a skinny little fart he was at the time, a St Urbain Street boy, and he led a fearless campaign against this bastard MacPherson . . .'

The strangers looked up at Duddy and smiled.

'That's him,' Max said.

Duddy retreated. He raised his hands in protest.

'My brother,' Lennie said. 'Hey, what's wrong?'

'Nothing,' Duddy said. 'I'm fine.'

'Can't you ever smile,' Max said, turning to the strangers with a chuckle. 'Would it cost you something to give us a little smile?'

'I'm not driving back with you,' Duddy said gruffly. 'You take the *zeyda* home. I'm going by bus.'

'Why?'

'Never mind why. Christ Almighty. Just give me the money for my fare. I'm flat broke.'

'That's a laugh,' Max said, turning to the others again. 'Isn't that a laugh. He's broke.'

Duddy's cheeks burned red.

'Are you O.K.?' Lennie asked. 'You look sick, Duddy.'

'I'm fine. Just give me the money, please.'

'Aw, I know what it is. You can't hide anything from the old man. I'll bring in the *zeyda* and you'll kiss and make up.'

'In a minute,' Duddy said, 'I'm going to explode. I'm going to hit somebody so hard – '

'Easy,' Lennie said.

Max smiled at the strangers. 'It's been a big day for him. Red letter stuff. And you've never seen a nervier kid.'

Duddy started for his father, but the waiter got in his way. 'Mr Kravitz?' He smiled shyly at Duddy, holding out the bill. 'Are you the Mr Kravitz who just bought all that land round Lac St Pierre?'

'Yeah. Em, I haven't any cash on me. Daddy, can you . . .?'

'That's all right, sir. We'll mark it.'

And suddenly Duddy did smile. He laughed. He grabbed Max, hugged him, and spun him around. 'You see,' he said, his voice filled with marvel. 'You see.'

More about Penguins

Penguinews, which appears every month, contains details of all the new books issued by Penguins as they are published. From time to time it is supplemented by *Penguins in Print*, which is a complete list of all books published by Penguins which are in print. (There are well over three thousand of these.)

A specimen copy of *Penguinews* will be sent to you free on request, and you can become a subscriber for the price of the postage. For a year's issues (including the complete lists) please send 30p if you live in the United Kingdom, or 60p if you live elsewhere. Just write to Dept EP, Penguin Books Ltd, Harmondsworth, Middlesex, enclosing a cheque or postal order and your name will be added to the mailing list.

Some other books published by Penguins are described on the following pages.

Note: *Penguinews* and *Penguins in Print* are not available in the U.S.A. or Canada

John Braine

Room at the Top

John Braine's famous novel of the drivingly
ambitious, sexually ruthless Joe Lampton: hero of
our time

When Joe Lampton moved into Warley, he moved
into the plush life of a wool-rich town and the
waiting arms of two women. And he thought he
knew what he wanted . . .

Life at the Top

Readers of *Room at the Top* can now meet Joe
Lampton again after ten years amid the fleshpots.

'Mr Braine takes us into the same world as before,
listening to its dialogue with the same marvellous
ear . . . The book, like its predecessor, is alive from
the first moment to the last' – Laurence Lerner in
the *Listener*

NOT FOR SALE IN THE U.S.A.

Philip Roth

When She Was Good

Lucy Nelson, stuggling within the rigid framework of
American Mid-West moral and social codes, turns
to Catholicism to quell the hatred welling within
her. But, plagued by her drunken father and
frustrated by her weak directionless husband, she is
inexorably forced to destroy them. In this brilliant
three-part family saga, Philip Roth traces the
tensions that drive . . . and destroy . . . Lucy.

Praise for *Making Divorce Easier on Your Child*

"A must-read! This book is loaded with down-to-earth, practical advice pulled together by two leading experts in child clinical psychology. Parents who follow their fifty tips will immediately see that this is sound advice for helping children to navigate through the rough waters of divorce."

> —*Robert E. Emery, Professor, Director of Clinical Training, Director of the Center for Children, Families, and the Law, Department of Psychology, University of Virginia*

"Invaluable to parents who are divorced or contemplating divorce. The authors are leading experts on child development, and their book is based on the latest social scientific research. Yet, unlike many texts in this field, the authors' recommendations are straightforward, practical, and easy to understand. Divorcing parents can save their children a great deal of stress and emotional hardship by reading this book and taking its advice to heart."

> —*Paul R. Amato, Professor of Sociology, Pennsylvania State University*

"Much more than a how-to book, this book offers divorcing parents empirically supported, practical strategies for helping their children cope with divorce and, more importantly, empowers them to use the strategies it suggests."

> —*Gail Tripp, Ph.D., Director of the Clinical Psychology Training Program, University of Otago, New Zealand*

"Informative and sensible, offering realistic, clear-cut recommendations for successfully handling the many stresses and challenges that parents and children experience when divorce occurs. Not only provides research findings and important strategies but does so in a very compassionate, caring, empathic manner. I believe that this book will become a major resource in the area of divorce."

—*Robert Brooks, Ph.D., faculty, Harvard Medical School, and coauthor of* Raising Resilient Children

"A fantastic resource for divorced parents. It is clear, well written, and organized in a way that makes it easy to read (or re-read) the parts that are most relevant for a particular parent at a particular point in time. The authors are forthright concerning difficulties divorced parents and their children will face but very hopeful (and rightfully so) about the possibilities for parents to help their children adjust well during and after parental divorce."

—*Christy M. Buchanan, Associate Professor of Psychology, Wake Forest University, and author of* Adolescents After Divorce

"In this much-needed book, Drs. Long and Forehand clearly and concisely present a great deal of useful advice on what parents can do specifically to help children in terms of parenting and coparenting, including strategies to reduce the destructiveness of conflicts over everyday matters, how to protect children from over-involvement in conflicts, and numerous other specific concerns and issues articulated from the children's perspective. Moreover, the information is articulated in a way that will certainly help parents better understand and help their children."

—*E. Mark Cummings, Ph.D., Department of Psychology, University of Notre Dame*

"An enormously important set of guidelines for parents considering or experiencing a divorce. The range of topics is comprehensive, from understanding the laws that govern the termination of a marriage to methods for helping children cope with the separation of their parents. For each of these issues, the authors provide clear, specific steps that parents can take to deal more effectively with this extremely traumatic event. And each of the strategies for coping that they provide derives from sound scientific information as well as from many years of clinical experience. Readers of this book can have confidence that the information they receive is sound and will be truly helpful as they adjust to one of life's most difficult challenges."

> —*Rand D. Conger, Professor of Human Development and Family Studies, Department of Human and Community Development, University of California—Davis*

"Based on decades of research and clinical practice, Drs. Long and Forehand have produced an essential tool for not only divorcing parents but also mental health professionals and those in the legal system. This work should be required reading for the adults who endeavor to honor the principle of 'the best interests of the child.'"

> —*Michael W. Mellon, Ph.D., Codirector, Mayo Clinic—Dana Child Development and Learning Disorders Program*

"I highly recommend *Making Divorce Easier on Your Child* to both custodial and noncustodial parents. Nicholas Long and Rex Forehand have translated the research findings on children's post-divorce adjustment into an exceptionally clear set of guidelines for how to be a sensitive and effective parent during this transition in family structure. This book is an exceptional resource for parents."

> —*Sharlene A. Wolchik, Professor of Clinical Psychology, Arizona State University*

"A truly excellent guide for divorcing parents. It offers simple, clear, and invaluable advice on how to help their children adjust. The tone throughout is sympathetic and nonjudgmental, and the advice totally practical. It is a book that should be read by all parents going through the sadness of a divorce and indeed any professionals involved in counseling them or their children."

—*Bryan Lask, Professor of Child and Adolescent Psychiatry, St. George's Hospital Medical School, London*

"Provides detailed, sane advice, always grounded not just in careful consideration of research evidence but in humane recognition of the difficulties of real-life decision making by parents. The advice is not just about how to help the children but also a source of counsel for the parents themselves to assure their own welfare, a prerequisite of being able to help the children."

—*Masud Hoghughi, Professor of Clinical Psychology, University of Hull, United Kingdom*

"Provides practical, well-researched, theoretically consistent advice and guidance to parents to minimize any adverse consequences for children of family breakdowns. It provides state-of-the-art parenting advice, and it will be useful to any professional who works with families. I strongly recommend it."

—*Matt Sanders, Director of Parenting and Family Support Center, University of Queensland, Brisbane, Australia*

"Wonderful pearls of wisdom for divorcing parents, glowing with the extensive knowledge and clinical experience of two of the most prominent scientist professionals in the field."

—*Ann S. Masten, Ph.D., Director, Institute of Child Development, and Emma M. Birkmaier Professor in Educational Leadership, University of Minnesota*

Making
Divorce
Easier on
Your Child

Making
Divorce
Easier on
Your Child

50 Effective Ways
to Help Children Adjust

NICHOLAS LONG, Ph.D.,
and **REX FOREHAND, Ph.D.**

Contemporary Books

Chicago   New York   San Francisco   Lisbon   London   Madrid   Mexico City
Milan   New Delhi   San Juan   Seoul   Singapore   Sydney   Toronto

Library of Congress Cataloging-in-Publication Data

Long, Nicholas, 1956–
    Making divorce easier on your child : 50 effective ways to help
children adjust / Nicholas Long and Rex Forehand.
        p.   cm.
    Includes bibliographical references and index.
    ISBN 0-8092-9419-2
    1. Children of divorced parents—Psychology.   2. Divorced parents—
Attitudes.   3. Divorced parents—Family relationships.   4. Child rearing.
I. Forehand, Rex L. (Rex Lloyd), 1945–   II. Title.

HQ777.5.L66   2002
306.89—dc21   2001047322

Contemporary Books

A Division of The McGraw·Hill Companies

1 2 3 4 5 6 7 8 9 0   AGM/AGM   1 0 9 8 7 6 5 4 3 2

ISBN 0-8092-9419-2

This book was set in Scala
Printed and bound by Quebecor Martinsburg

Cover and interior design by Jennifer Locke

McGraw-Hill books are available at special quantity discounts to use as premiums and
sales promotions, or for use in corporate training programs. For more information, please
write to the Director of Special Sales, Professional Publishing, McGraw-Hill, Two Penn
Plaza, New York, NY 10121-2298. Or contact your local bookstore.

This book is printed on acid-free paper.

This book is dedicated to the many families who have

been willing to open their lives to the authors and other

behavioral scientists during the painful time of divorce.

These families are responsible for the knowledge base,

which we have translated into recommendations to

help divorcing and recently divorced parents raise

happy and healthy children.

Words to Remember

A hundred years from now it will not matter what

sort of house I lived in, what my bank account was, or

the kind of car I drove, but the world may be different

because I was important in the life of my child.

Author Unknown

Contents

Preface xvii

Introduction 1

Part 1

Planning the Divorce and Telling Your Child

  1 Understand the Divorce Laws and Process in Your
     Community 15
  2 Work Out the Immediate Issues 20
  3 Tell Your Child Together When the Decision to Divorce Is
     Made 23
  4 Anticipate Questions Your Child May Have 28
  5 Avoid Custody Disputes: Consider Mediation 32

Part 2

Looking After Your Own Well-Being During and Following Divorce

  6 Expect an Adjustment Period 37
  7 Examine Your Coping Style 41
  8 Develop a Support System for Yourself 44
  9 Manage the Stress in Your Life 48

Part 3

Issues Between You and Your Ex-Spouse During and Following Divorce

  10 Communicate Effectively with Your Ex-Spouse 55
  11 Do Not Argue with Your Ex-Spouse in Front of Your Child 59
  12 Do Not Use Your Child as a Messenger or Spy 64
  13 Do Not Use Your Child as an Ally 67

14   Do Not Place Restrictions on What Your Child Can Tell Your Ex-Spouse   70

15   Do Not Criticize Your Ex-Spouse in Your Child's Presence   72

16   Redefine Your Relationship with Your Ex-Spouse   75

Part 4

Visitation Issues

17   Encourage Involvement of the Noncustodial Parent   83

18   Ensure Frequent and Predictable Contact Between Your Child and the Noncustodial Parent   86

19   Make Visitation Transitions Smooth   91

20   Effectively Handle Birthdays, Holidays, and Special Occasions   95

Part 5

Divorced Parenting: General Guidelines

21   Change the Way You Think About Your Child   101

22   Expect Your Child to Play One Parent Against the Other   104

23   Maintain Regular Child Support Payments   107

24   Minimize Changes   110

25   Maintain Family Traditions and Rituals   115

26   Develop a Parenting Plan   118

27   Nurture Your Relationship with Your Child   123

28   Have Fun with Your Child   127

29   Communicate "I Love You" to Your Child   130

30   Encourage Your Child to Express Feelings   133

31   Be Consistent with Discipline   136

32   Monitor Your Child's Activities   140

33   Monitor School Performance   143

34   Build Your Child's Self-Esteem   147

35   Develop Greater Patience and Regain Your Lost Patience   150

36   Never Blame Your Child for the Divorce   153

37   Do Not Make Promises You Might Not Keep   155

38   Do Not Overcompensate for Your Divorce   157

39 Do Not Burden Your Child with Your Personal and Financial Concerns 159

40 Set a Good Example of How to Handle the Divorce 162

41 Deal with Your Child's Unrealistic Expectations Directly 164

42 Do Not Compare Your Child to Your Ex-Spouse in a Negative Way 167

43 Accept Your Child's Love for His Other Parent 169

Part 6

The Importance of Other Relationships

44 Honor Sibling Relationships 173

45 Encourage Your Child's Relationships with Extended Family Members 175

46 Help Your Child Cope if the Noncustodial Parent Becomes Uninvolved 180

47 Think About When and How to Introduce Individuals You Date 183

48 Effectively Handle New Family Combinations 186

Part 7

Seeking Professional Help

49 Seek Professional Help for Your Child if Needed 191

Part 8

Moving Toward the Future

50 Think Positive 199

Bibliography 201
Resources 209
Index 223

Preface

THE PURPOSE OF THIS BOOK is *not* to discuss whether parents who are experiencing problems in their marriage should divorce or stay married. For those of you who are contemplating divorce, we hope that whatever your final decision is, it will be made only after very careful consideration of all the issues concerned. Divorce should be pursued only after all the alternatives have been exhausted. For those of you who choose to divorce, or are already divorced, this book will provide you with information and practical ways to help your child both during and following the divorce.

Numerous research studies have found that children vary considerably in terms of how well they adjust to their parents' divorce. While some children experience significant problems, other children experience relatively few problems. What determines the degree to which your child will experience problems related to your divorce? We believe that many of the factors related to your child's adjustment have been identified and can be translated into practical recommendations for your use. The purpose of this book is to provide you with this information. More specifically, we present ways that you can minimize the negative effects of divorce on your child. The information and recommendations that we present are based not only on our own clinical and research experiences but also on the latest research findings and opinions of leading researchers in this area. Such research findings and opinions are published in the scientific literature and, for the most part, have been accessible only to professionals. In this book, we have attempted to translate this scientific literature into practical, well-grounded, and simply stated advice on how to best help your child.

This book is not intended to address the problems inherent in the relatively small percentage of divorces that are extremely bitter and/or involve a multitude of very complex problems. In such cases, we recommend that you seek assistance from an experienced professional who can assess your situation and provide individually tailored guidance. Fortunately, most divorcing or divorced parents do not fall into this category. This book targets the majority of divorcing or divorced parents who are confronting difficult, yet not hopeless, issues that affect their child.

Collectively, we have spent almost fifty years developing and evaluating programs for parents. A substantial part of our efforts has focused on parenting and children's adjustment during and following divorce. However, it is equally important to note that we each bring to this book the experience of being a parent. We know that parenting is not easy, even when there are two parents in the home who work together. As a parent who is divorcing or is already divorced, your job is even more difficult. We believe what we have to say in the following pages will make your job as a parent (yes, it is a job!) easier, more rewarding, and, most important, more influential in helping your child adjust to your divorce.

Before you start reading the book, we want to provide you with a brief overview of how the book is organized. The book starts with an Introduction that provides a synopsis of general issues related to divorce and children. Following the Introduction, we present fifty strategies for you to follow to help your child adjust to the divorce. Specific strategies that are in related areas are organized into eight parts (for example, Part I contains the strategies related to planning and telling the children). The Bibliography, which follows Part 8, contains references for the studies and professional writings on which we based many of our opinions. The work of the various researchers and experts we refer to throughout the book is referenced in the Bibliography for those of you who want to pursue more information about their work. At the end of the book you will find the resources section, which contains information about a variety of resources including books, organizations, and websites that you may find helpful.

This book could not have been written without the diligent work of many people. The William T. Grant Foundation provided not only financial support for our work with families undergoing divorce but also substantial emotional support and encouragement. Dr. Lonnie Sherrod, executive vice president, was always available and willing to respond to our needs.

Our agent, Amye Dyer, was a major source of encouragement and support. She patiently listened to our questions and sought out answers. Similarly, Judith McCarthy of Contemporary Books provided us with support, encouragement, and feedback. We also want to thank the other staff members at Contemporary Books for their valuable contributions, especially Michele Pezzuti.

Several additional people stand out as valuable contributors to this book. With patience and constant encouragement, Sandra Gary typed and retyped numerous versions of the manuscript. Her dedication and quality of work are exceptional—and greatly appreciated! Anne Shaffer and Mamie Johnson also read the text and made valuable suggestions. These individuals went substantially beyond the call of duty, and we greatly appreciate their efforts.

The first author (NL) appreciates the support and encouragement he has received for his work in the area of parenting from the Department of Pediatrics at the University of Arkansas for Medical Sciences and Arkansas Children's Hospital. The staff of the Center for Effective Parenting, and the parents who have participated in the Center's programs, have been a constant source of encouragement and inspiration.

The second author (RF) wishes to acknowledge the support of Dr. Richard Jessor and the Institute of Behavioral Science at the University of Colorado. An office, wonderful staff, and time to read and write were provided during a minisabbatical and allowed the completion of this book. Appreciation also is expressed to Dr. Joe Key, vice president for research, and Dr. Karen Holbrook, provost, at the University of Georgia for granting the minisabbatical.

The underlying theme throughout this book is that the support, love, and learning that comes from a family, whether the parents are married or divorced, should never be underestimated. This is certainly the case for both authors.

The first author (NL) wishes to thank his family for their endless love and support. My parents, John and Jean Long, provided me with many personal experiences of parents putting their children's needs ahead of their own. I will forever be grateful for their sacrifices. My own children, Alex and Justin, have taught me much about parenting and unconditional love. I hope that my influence on their lives will be as important as their influence has been on mine. Finally, I would like to thank my wife, Sharon, not only for her support and love but also for the many lessons she has taught me about life and relationships.

The second author (RF) has been fortunate to have experienced support and numerous invaluable learning experiences from his parents, Rex and Sara Forehand; wife, Lell; and children, Laura Forehand Wright and Greg Forehand. Thank you! I may be the only person who fell in love in the first grade, had the fortune to marry that person, and have experienced a continual growth in that love. Lell, thank you for "being the wind beneath my wings," which you truly are. But most important, thank you for your love, for your friendship, and for being!

This is our second effort as coauthors of a book designed to help parents. In our first effort we wrote *Parenting the Strong-Willed Child* (Contemporary Books) and experienced mutual inspiration, support, and encouragement. The writing of this book has been equally rewarding. Indeed, we are fortunate to have each other as not only colleagues but as friends, and to have had the opportunity to share this writing experience.

Authors' Notes: In referring to children, we decided to alternate the use of masculine and feminine pronouns for the different strategies discussed in the book. (Specifically, we use the feminine pronouns for the even-numbered strategies and masculine pronouns for the odd-numbered strategies.) However, all our strategies and recommendations apply equally to girls and boys. We use primarily feminine pronouns when referring to parents except when the great majority of parents in a particular situation are fathers. (For example, when referring to the noncustodial parent, we use masculine pronouns, as most noncustodial parents are fathers.) However, in all cases, our recommendations apply equally to fathers and mothers. Also, we refer to "your child" throughout this book but recognize that many of you have more than one child. Our recommendations apply to all of your children. Finally, new terms are regularly being introduced for different parts of the divorce process (for example, "parenting time" instead of "visitation" and "parenting responsibilities" instead of "custody"), for the individuals involved in divorce (for example, "nonresidential parent" instead of "noncustodial parent"), and, even, remarriage (for example, "bonus mom" instead of "stepmother"). For the sake of clarification, we elected to use the typical terms (for example, "custodial parent" for the parent with primary physical custody—whom the child lives with most of the time—and "noncustodial parent" for the other parent) but fully acknowledge that the new terms often remove some of the negative connotations associated with divorce—which is good.

The quotations of parents and children that are provided throughout the book reflect what various parents and children have told us over the years. The names, ages, and other information attributed to the quotes in the book are fictitious so as to protect the identity of the families we have worked with.

Making
Divorce
Easier on
Your Child

Introduction

Myths About Parental Divorce and Children

1. *Parents should always stay together for the sake of their children.*
2. *Parental divorce always has horrible, irreversible effects on children.*
3. *Children will adjust best to their parents' divorce at a certain age.*
4. *My divorce can be simple.*
5. *There is nothing that parents can do to promote the adjustment of their child during and after their divorce.*

Each of these is a myth. We will show you why and then present you with fifty ways in which you can help your child during and after your divorce. However, before doing this, let's quickly look at some of the demographics of divorce in the United States. If you are thinking about divorce or have already divorced, these figures will let you know that you are not alone.

Demographics

It is estimated that between 40 and 50 percent of all marriages in the United States will end in a divorce. About 60 percent of these divorces involve children. As a result, more than one million children experience their parents' divorce each year.

Children are most likely to be young when their parents divorce. This is because the risk for divorce is far greater early in marriage. Once parents divorce, children are most likely to reside with their mother in a single-parent home. However, this is usually a temporary situation, as most divorced women, as well as divorced men, remarry.

From the 1960s, and particularly from 1970 to 1980, the divorce rate in the United States accelerated rapidly. Since 1980, the rate has stabilized and shown a slight downward trend in the most recent years. Regardless of this trend, the United States still has a higher divorce rate than almost any other industrialized nation.

Divorce is a part of American life.

Should We Stay Together for the Sake of Our Child?

This is probably one of the questions most frequently asked by parents who are considering a divorce. Would our child be better off if we stayed married? Or, would our child be better off if we divorced and he did not have to experience our marital turmoil? There is no simple answer to this question.

We strongly believe that a child is best off in a happily married family where the parents get along, love each other, and love their child. Unfortunately, we also recognize that parents who argue and demean each other, particularly in front of their child, present a great risk to their child's adjustment. If divorce leads to a decrease in conflict between the parents, again particularly if that conflict occurs in front of the child, then divorce can be beneficial for some children. However, if parents divorce and continue to have high levels of conflict and involve their child in that conflict, then the child has to deal with both divorce and the ongoing conflict. This is the worst situation in which you can place your child.

Let's look for a moment at the relationships that can develop between you and your spouse when you divorce. Constance Ahrons of the University of Southern California and Roy H. Rodgers of the University of British Columbia have pointed out five possibilities.

Perfect Pals	Remain friends and share decision making and childrearing
Cooperative Colleagues	Do not remain friends but can cooperate for the sake of their children
Angry Associates	Have built-up anger that affects current relationship and diminishes the ability to coparent
Fiery Foes	Become so angry that coparenting does not occur
Dissolved Duos	Discontinue contact after the divorce

Whether you should stay married or divorce for the sake of your children depends on what happens after the divorce. And, as we have just pointed out, there are at least five possible relationships that can develop between you and your ex-spouse. Of course, you cannot fully predict what is going to happen between you and your spouse after the divorce. However, it is clear that your child's adjustment to the divorce will be more positive if you and your child's other parent can become "Perfect Pals" or "Cooperative Colleagues" rather than any of the other possibilities.

If We Divorce, How Will It Affect Our Child?

Before we address this question, let us acknowledge that divorce is stressful for children. It disrupts their lives in many ways just like it disrupts your life. What are some of the most difficult parts of parental divorce on children? Sharlene Wolchik and her colleagues at Arizona

State University surveyed eight- to fifteen-year-old children about the most stressful events of their parents' divorce. The following box presents a brief summary of the ten most stressful events. We will return to these often throughout this book, as there are many things you can do to prevent these events from occurring and, thus, reduce the stress on your child.

Children's Ten Most Stressful Events Associated with the Divorce of Their Parents

1. My dad or mom told me the divorce was because of me.
2. My parents hit each other or physically hurt each other.
3. My relatives said bad things to me about my parents.
4. My dad told me that he doesn't like me spending time with my mom.
5. My mother and my father argue in front of me.
6. My dad said bad things about my mother.
7. I had to give up pets or other things that I liked.
8. My mom acts unhappy.
9. My dad asks me questions about my mom's private life.
10. People in the neighborhood say bad things to me about my parents.

Let's now consider the effects of divorce on children—which is much more complicated than you may think. When we think about the effects of divorce on children, we need to consider both short-term effects and long-term effects. Furthermore, as Robert Emery of the University of Virginia has pointed out, we need to consider not only the effects on your child's adjustment, but the pain that your child may take away from experiencing his parents' divorce. Your child's adjustment and the pain he experiences can be quite different. For example, many children adapt or adjust to their parents' divorce and continue to function well throughout their lives; however, they may continue to carry the pain of the divorce with them for many years.

In terms of short-term effects, there is evidence from many researchers across the country that parental divorce is associated with adjustment difficulties for their children. These effects can include depressive symptoms, anxiety, anger, acting-out difficulties (belligerence, disobedience, and even delinquent acts), and falling school grades. Children may also exhibit a drop in self-esteem and self-confidence. However, not all children show such effects and, in fact, some children actually show fewer problems following parental divorce. This is particularly the case, as Alan Booth and Paul Amato of the Pennsylvania State University have shown, when children move from a home with a lot of conflict to a more harmonious one. There is great variability in how children respond to the divorce of their parents. What this says is that it is *how* you divorce and what you and your child's other parent do following the divorce, rather than the divorce per se (i.e., not living together anymore), that has the most impact on your child's adjustment. The recommendations in this book will provide guidance for you to help improve your child's adjustment to your divorce.

Let's put in perspective for a moment the magnitude of the effect of parents' divorce on children's adjustment. As we have stated, many children do show short-term adjustment problems. If we look at research studies (and there are a large number of them) that have examined how parental divorce affects children, the magnitude of the effect is modest. That is, across large numbers of children whose parents have divorced, the average disruption to a child's adjustment is relatively small, regardless of what area of adjustment you examine. As we have already stated, what is more apparent than the average size of the effect of parental divorce on children is the variability in children's reactions, with some showing more problems and some even showing fewer problems. Again, this emphasizes the importance of *how* parents handle the divorce.

Are the modest short-term effects of parental divorce on children likely to continue over time? There have been a number of research studies examining this question. When we look at these studies, the results show that children whose parents divorce have more difficulties for years, even into adulthood, after the divorce. As Mavis Hetherington of the University of Virginia has noted, children who experience parental divorce are less likely to complete college and more likely to be unemployed, have fewer financial resources, and have more difficulty in forming stable relationships (relative to children whose parents remain married). However, as with the short-term effects of divorce, these long-term effects are relatively modest. The magnitude of the difference in how children of divorce function in everyday life compared to their counterparts from married families is small. For example, there is a slightly greater proportion of children from intact families that do better in the areas noted previously (e.g., completing college) when compared to children from divorced families. And, again, what is more impressive is the variability among children in the long-term effects of their parents' divorce on their adjustment. Many children adjust relatively well, and others have significant problems.

There is little doubt that parental divorce is associated with difficulties in children's adjustment. However, the magnitude of the effect on the "average child of divorce" is not nearly as extreme as is often suggested in the media. Titles of articles about parental divorce in popular periodicals have included "Children After Divorce: Wounds That Don't Heal," "Children of the Aftershock," and "The Lasting Wounds of Divorce." These titles, while intended to attract attention and draw readers, do not present an accurate picture of most children's experience with the divorce of their parents.

At this point you may be thinking, "So, if the effects on my children are going to be small, why not get a divorce?" Before reaching a conclusion to divorce, there is another side of the picture to consider. Although most children adapt to their parents' divorce, many children experience painful feelings and unhappy memories about their parents' divorce. As Robert Emery of the University of Virginia has pointed out, there are costs to divorce, even for children who adjust well to it. Painful feelings may include grief, self-blame, hope for reconciliation, anger, worry about parents, and concerns about relationships with both parents. In one survey of young adults' painful feelings about their parents' divorce, Lisa Laumann-Billings and Robert Emery found that about half indicated that their parents' divorce still causes struggles for them, that they worry about both parents being present at the same time, and that they believe they had "a harder childhood than most people." What is important to note is that these are the painful experiences of well-functioning college students.

In a survey we completed with adolescents whose parents had divorced (see the box on page 8), we found that many of them did experience pain (for example, sadness and anger) initially; however, even with these initial painful feelings, after two years most of the adolescents had more pragmatic expectations, feelings, and thoughts about the divorce. Furthermore, most of these adolescents believed that both parents still loved them as much as before the divorce.

As we said at the beginning, the answer to the question about the effects of divorce on children is complicated. Let's see if we can summarize what we have said. On the average, children whose parents divorce function less well in both the short term and the long term than those whose parents are married; however, the magnitude of this effect is modest. Furthermore, among children whose parents divorce, there is considerable variability in their adjustment, indicating that *how* you as a parent handle the divorce is very important. Finally, for most children, regardless of how well they adjust to the divorce, there is a pain that accompanies the divorce and likely will stay with the child. Truly, the effects of parental divorce on children are complicated. However, if you decide to divorce, the important message in the rest of this book is that there are many things you can do to promote your child's adjustment during the difficult times both during and following divorce.

Before moving on, let's briefly consider two final issues. First is what has been called the "sleeper effect." The sleeper effect is when a child seems to be adjusting well to the divorce but may have long-hidden emotional problems from the divorce that may suddenly emerge many years later. This is a controversial idea and one for which there is very little support from well-conducted research studies. The important implication for you as a parent is that your focus should not be on worrying about whether or not problems will suddenly emerge in the future. Rather, your focus should be on promoting your child's adjust-

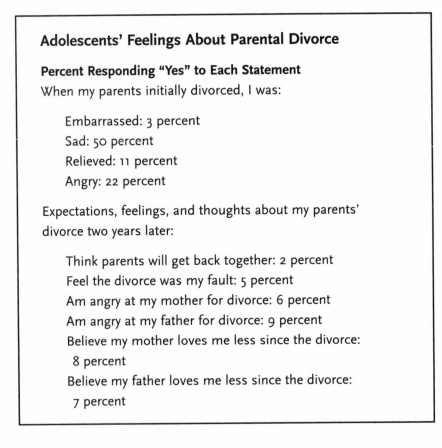

Adolescents' Feelings About Parental Divorce

Percent Responding "Yes" to Each Statement
When my parents initially divorced, I was:

   Embarrassed: 3 percent
   Sad: 50 percent
   Relieved: 11 percent
   Angry: 22 percent

Expectations, feelings, and thoughts about my parents' divorce two years later:

   Think parents will get back together: 2 percent
   Feel the divorce was my fault: 5 percent
   Am angry at my mother for divorce: 6 percent
   Am angry at my father for divorce: 9 percent
   Believe my mother loves me less since the divorce:
    8 percent
   Believe my father loves me less since the divorce:
    7 percent

ment now. The best way to ensure your child's future adjustment is by promoting her current adjustment, which this book will help you do.

Finally, we should point out that, when we consider the effects of parental divorce on children, you need to realize that some of the negative effects that have been attributed to divorce in both the scientific literature and the public media may actually have their roots in factors that occurred prior to the divorce. Although the scientific literature on this topic is sparse and the findings are not consistent, there is growing evidence—as exemplified by the work of Yongmin Sun of the Ohio State University at Mansfield—to support this notion, particularly when there are high levels of marital conflict and parenting problems prior to the divorce. Thus, it is not just what you as a parent do during and after the divorce that is important, but also what you did before the divorce.

It is also important to acknowledge that there are many things that are not related to the divorce that have an impact on a child's adjustment (e.g., genetic predisposition to problems and peer group pressure). In other words, the experience of divorce and your actions as a parent are important, but by no means are they the only things that determine your child's adjustment, both now and in the future.

Is There a Best Time for Us to Divorce Based on the Age of Our Child?

Many parents struggle with the feeling that there is an ideal time to divorce. Some think that it is while a child is young, that is, before she becomes too attached to both parents. Others think that they should wait to divorce until their child is old enough to "understand" the divorce. Even others think they should wait until their child has moved out of the home. There are a number of theories about the "best age" of a child for parents to divorce. However, there is little evidence to suggest that one age is better or worse than another age. Again, what is most important is how you handle the divorce, not the age of your child.

We should also mention that there are some people who believe that divorce is worse for boys than for girls. This belief is based on the fact that children primarily reside with their mother after divorce and, as a result, boys no longer have a male role model in the home. We agree that a male role model is important; however, there is little evidence to suggest that boys do worse following divorce than girls and, even where there is evidence, the magnitude of the difference for boys and girls is small. Again, it is how you handle the divorce, not whether your child is a male or female, that is most important.

Can My Divorce Be Simple?

When a child is involved, the answer to this question is a resounding "No." If a couple without children divorces, they can go their separate ways following the divorce, often without ever having to have contact with each other. However, when you have a child, it necessitates having an ongoing relationship with your ex-spouse. Redefining this relationship and having the responsibility for parenting your child through what is typically a very stressful time is never simple. Even though changes in laws governing divorce in recent years (for example, no-fault divorce) have made the legal process easier, even the legal issues are not simple when a child is involved.

Let's first consider some specific changes that occur with divorce. First, there is going to be one parent in the home to do the duties of two parents; in other words, work increases. Second, research studies indicate that for custodial mothers, total family income is often reduced by 50 percent within one year after the divorce; in other words, money decreases. Third, you are going to go through an adjustment period both personally and socially; in other words, uncertainty abounds. For example, are your mutual friends going to side with you or your ex-spouse? In either case, there is going to be a loss of social contacts that once revolved around your family. These social contacts involve not only friends but also relatives from both sides of the family. Fourth, there are going to be periods when you feel overwhelmed and lonely and wonder why you put not only your child but yourself through a divorce; in other words, you second-guess your decisions.

Next, let's consider some of the legal decisions you are going to have to make. First, what will be the legal custody arrangements for your child: mother sole custody, father sole custody, joint custody? Second, regardless of legal custody, what will be the physical custody arrangements? That is, how much time will your child spend with each parent, and how will that amount of time be arranged? There are an infinite number of ways that you and your ex-spouse can each arrange your time with your child, and you will have to come to an arrangement that is workable for both of you (and your child). Third, will there be alimony payments and, if so, how much? Fourth, will there be child support payments? Fifth, will you and your ex-spouse settle your differences through litigation or mediation?

These are just a sample of the legal decisions you will face, and, as is probably obvious, the answers are rarely simple. If you have just begun considering divorce, the important points are for you to realize that divorce is multifaceted and is a process that unfolds over an extended period of time.

Are There Things We Can Do to Promote the Adjustment of Our Child During and After Our Divorce?

The answer to this question is a resounding "Yes!" There are many things that you can do to promote the adjustment of your child both during the time you are divorcing as well as during the years after the divorce. In fact, that is the purpose of this book. To emphasize how you can help your child through this transition, look back at the first box where we listed children's reports of the ten most stressful events associated with the divorce of their parents. You will notice immediately that eight of the ten events directly involve things that you as a parent can address. You can make a difference in your child's adjustment to your divorce! The information in this book focuses on ways that you can facilitate the adjustment of your child.

Before we turn to the fifty strategies, let's touch on one final point. All children are unique and have different needs. This is probably not a surprising statement to you, particularly if you are the parent of more than one child. Some children are easygoing, some are intense, some are outgoing, some are withdrawn, some are impulsive, and the list goes on and on. Children come into the world with different behavioral styles or tendencies to act certain ways, which is referred to as a child's temperament.

As children are different from the beginning, you might suspect that they would react to the divorce of their parents differently. A child with an easygoing temperament typically will show less of a negative reaction to all phases of his parents' divorce than a child who is intense or is insecure. However, the situation is even more complicated as a child with a more difficult temperament often provokes poor parenting from his parents. For example, if you have a strong-willed child, she may continually try to argue with you or pester you to get her way. She just will not take "No" for an answer. Often, as a result of her persistence, you eventually lose control and scream at her. A child with a difficult temperament requires extremely consistent parenting, especially during times of stress such as when her parents are divorcing. Unfortunately, as we just pointed out, it is harder to effectively parent a child with a difficult temperament. What all of this means is that if you are a parent of a child with a difficult temperament, you are going to have to work extra hard with her during your divorce. Fortunately, the fifty strategies we present to improve your child's adjustment to your divorce apply to children of all temperaments.

Part 1

Planning the Divorce and Telling Your Child

"I was so overwhelmed with emotion that I didn't think much about the legal process. I was just concerned about making it through one more day. When we finally got to court, I soon realized that truth and fairness do not always prevail: it felt like a war."

Bonnie, thirty-six, mother of three young children

1

Understand the Divorce Laws and Process in Your Community

IN THE INTRODUCTION, we pointed out that divorce is never simple for parents. It is a process that involves numerous, and sometimes very difficult, decisions. Some of these decisions focus on legal issues. It is very important for you to understand the legal aspects of divorce and to realize that the laws pertaining to divorce can vary substantially from place to place. For example, in the United States, while many states have "no-fault" divorce laws, other states do not. If no-fault divorce does not exist where you live, or if your spouse does not want a divorce, you need to legally prove a reason (or grounds) for the divorce. This process involves placing blame on one spouse and often progresses to counter-complaints and a detailed and open dissection of the marriage. As you can imagine, such a process tends to open a lot of wounds and can drastically escalate the conflict between parents. This often leads to parents spiraling down a pathway of hostility and resentment that makes cooperative parenting much more difficult following the divorce decree.

Different states and areas also have different laws concerning the type of custody and whether a particular custody arrangement is an option, preference, or presumption. Thus, one place may have a presumption (which is "stronger" than a preference) for sole custody, whereas another place may have a presumption for joint custody. Taking this a step further, one place may require that joint custody be proved advantageous for a child before it can be ordered, whereas, with slightly different wording, another place may require joint custody unless it can be demonstrated to be detrimental to the child. These two laws are quite different and have implications for custody arrangements. Not only do laws vary across states, provinces, and countries but the laws applying to specific geographic areas are constantly being revised. Therefore, it is vital that you obtain up-to-date information for your community. Some of the websites listed in the resources section contain information on laws in each state in the United States. However, remember that the laws could have changed since the website information was last updated.

Let's continue to focus on custody arrangements for a moment, as this may be one of the first major issues you need to consider (also see Strategy #5, "Avoid Custody Disputes: Consider Mediation"). There are various types of legal custody arrangements, with the most common being sole custody by one parent (in more than 90 percent of the cases of sole custody, the mother gets custody), joint custody, and, on rare occasion, split custody. Split custody, where one parent has custody of one child and the other parent has custody of another child, is generally considered detrimental for a sibling relationship and is usually awarded only in unusual circumstances. Joint custody laws were implemented in many areas during the past several decades so that both parents could retain custody of a child following a divorce. Currently, most states in the United States have statutes that allow or encourage joint custody.

Is joint custody better than sole custody? Scientific evidence on this question is not very clear. There is some evidence to suggest that, with joint custody, fathers appear to stay more involved with their children and are more likely to continue child support payments. However, there are little data to support that children's adjustment is better in one type of custody arrangement than another. Eleanor Maccoby of Stanford University has perhaps best summed up the existing scientific evidence. In her opinion, joint custody is better if the parents can cooperate; however, if parents cannot cooperate, joint custody is worse than sole custody. It is not the type of custody that is most important but how parents interact with each other and with their children that is most important.

With so many legal issues that will need to be addressed, it is critical that you educate yourself about the divorce laws and legal process in your area as soon as possible after you have decided to separate and pursue a divorce. Typically, the best way to educate yourself about the legal aspects of divorce is to contact an attorney who specializes in divorce and family law. Most often the best way to select an attorney is through the recommendation of others. Talk to others who have gone through a divorce or are familiar with lawyers in your community. It is important to make sure that you try to identify attorneys who have a lot of experience in handling divorce cases. If you are having difficulty identifying an attorney who specializes in divorce and family law, you may want to contact the American Academy of Matrimonial Lawyers located in Chicago at (312) 263-6477 to see if they have any members who practice in your community. An additional resource for both identifying an attorney and locating information about your state's divorce laws is your local bar association.

Once you have names of some potential attorneys, you may want to briefly interview those at the top of your list before making your final decision. The purpose of these brief interviews should not be to "pump" the attorneys for legal information and advice but rather to determine which attorney you want to represent you in the divorce process. Think ahead about the type of attorney you will feel most comfortable with representing you and your desires. Some attorneys are very aggressive and adversarial. One parent described the attorneys involved in her case as "gladiators fighting to the death." Attorneys who are overly aggressive and adversarial may encourage revenge in the parents they represent. This can lead to even greater long-term conflict between you and your spouse. Remember that your attorney will serve as your advocate in the legal process, so it is important that you not only trust him or her but also feel comfortable with the approach that your attorney will use in representing you.

During your initial meeting with an attorney try to get a sense of his or her general feelings about joint custody, mediation, and other divorce matters. Make sure you ask the attorney to explain any legal terms that you don't understand. Throughout the divorce process you will probably come across some legal terms that you've not heard of before. There might also be other terms, such as "assets," that you think you understand, but within the legal system they are often much more complex than they are in other contexts. For example, assets might be determined based on replacement value, fair market value, or liquidation value. The bottom line is that it is very important to have an attorney who is willing and able to explain legal terms to you in a way that you can easily understand.

One issue that many people are hesitant to bring up when they meet with attorneys is their fees. Because the legal process, especially when divorces are contested, can become very expensive, you need to ask about fees and billing practices. Also check to see if a written agreement will be provided outlining the charges and when payments will be due.

Once you have selected your attorney, it is important to set up a meeting to discuss the laws in your state concerning matters such as child custody, child visitation, child support payments, grounds for divorce, property division with divorce, and alimony payments. In many states, booklets and sometimes even videos have been prepared for couples seeking a divorce that outline many of the legal issues regarding divorce. Many state governments and legal associations have websites containing information on divorce issues and laws in your state. Check for the availability of such materials and resources with your attorney, the local bar association, or the court that handles divorce cases in your community. To make informed decisions, you need to have a clear and detailed understanding of the process and resources available to you.

One final point: remember that attorneys are not therapists or peacemakers. Their job is to handle the business and legal aspects of the divorce, not the emotional baggage. Complaining to them about all the ways your spouse irritates or upsets you is not going to solve those problems. Your attorney's job is to offer legal advice and help you navigate the legal minefield.

Here is what we recommend:

- Educate yourself about the divorce laws and the legal process of divorce in your community.

- Consider possible custody arrangements, but remember that it is typically not the type of custody that is most important but how parents interact with each other and with their children that is most important in regard to your child's adjustment and well-being.

- Take the time and effort necessary to choose the right attorney to represent you.

"Right after we decided to get a divorce, I became

confused thinking about all the decisions that needed

to be made and all the things that needed to be done.

I had no idea what to focus on first."

Ronnie, twenty-nine, father of one

2

Work Out the Immediate Issues

A SEPARATION USUALLY goes more smoothly for the whole family when it is planned in advance rather than occurring in the heat of the moment. Having your child discover a parent gone when she wakes up one morning or returns from school one day can be very traumatic. While separation is always stressful for children, you can reduce this stress for your child with advance planning.

Once the decision to separate has been made, you need to address several important issues. Remember to talk to your attorney about these issues, because some of these initial decisions might have long-term implications. The major immediate decisions regard living arrange-ments, a temporary visitation schedule, temporary financial arrange-ments, and initial property divisions.

It is often in the best interest of all concerned to make sure that the parent who is moving out of the home has a suitable place to live. One of the first things many children want to know after they find out one parent is going to be moving out of the home is where that parent is going to live. Also one of the first things children want to do following the separation is to visit the place where the parent is going to live.

One of the most difficult issues that you will need to work out with your spouse is the time your child will spend with each of you initially. This can become a very complicated issue because of frequent competition between spouses over the amount of time each spends with the child. However, remember that the goal is to facilitate the adjustment of your child, not necessarily to satisfy either you or your ex-spouse. Try to work out a schedule for the first month for when your child will be with each of you (including dates and times), and then work on a month-by-month basis. If you and your spouse can work out a schedule, it will reduce the ambiguity and reduce the probability of conflict. As you develop a monthly schedule, be sure to consider how to handle birthdays, holidays, vacations, and other special occasions (see Strategy #20, "Effectively Handle Birthdays, Holidays, and Special Occasions") that occur during the month. Obviously, with older children and adolescents, your child's input should be solicited and given serious consideration. Although the courts may impose a standardized schedule (for example, every other weekend and one night per week), parents who allow for flexibility and fairness within an overall structure usually have children who experience fewer problems adjusting to the fact that their parents are not living together.

Financial issues that need your immediate attention include who will have access to bank accounts and charge accounts, who is going to pay what bills, and what temporary financial support payments will be made and by whom. You will also need to make some initial property division decisions. Who will get the car? If you have more than one car, who gets which car? What furnishings can the parent moving out take to furnish his or her new apartment or living space? This does not mean that all property decisions should be made at this time. Rather, the initial focus should be just on items that are needed immediately. More extensive and permanent property decisions can be made at a later time.

Beyond the financial and property issues, there are several more personal issues that need to be addressed at the time of separation. First, you will need to decide who to tell about the separation and what to tell them. After telling your child (see Strategy #3, "Tell Your Child

Together When the Decision to Divorce Is Made"), you will need to tell extended family members and several others that may include your child's teachers or childcare providers, friends and neighbors, people at your workplace, and creditors.

While the issues addressed previously are important, no decision is as important to children as their parents making specific commitments that they promise to follow. Such commitments require moving beyond the failed marriage. You should commit to encouraging a meaningful relationship between your child and her other parent. You and your child's other parent should each pledge to continue the parenting responsibilities you started. Finally, and most important, you should commit to avoid bringing your child into the middle of your battles with her other parent.

While there are many decisions that need immediate attention, there are many that do not. Try to avoid making major decisions during the early stages of the divorce process unless absolutely necessary. For example, this is not the time to make impulsive job and career decisions. Although you may start thinking about many major decisions that lie ahead, try to give yourself plenty of time to think through such issues before making final decisions. Waiting until you are more emotionally centered to make major long-term decisions can be one of your best immediate decisions.

Here is what we recommend:

- Make several immediate decisions regarding living arrangements, finances, and property.

- Decide together who to tell and what to tell about the divorce.

- Make an immediate commitment to your child that includes encouraging her relationship with her other parent and keeping her out of any conflict you might have with your ex-spouse.

- Put off making major long-term decisions until you are less emotional and can clearly think about both the positive and negative implications.

"I remember when my parents first told me they were

going to get a divorce as if it was yesterday. Even

though it was ten years ago, I remember it so clearly."

Jacob, sixteen

3
Tell Your Child Together When the Decision to Divorce Is Made

ONCE YOU HAVE WORKED out the immediate issues surrounding the divorce, tell your child together about the decision to divorce. This will be difficult. You and your spouse probably have different views about why the divorce is occurring, and each of you probably have very intense feelings about each other. However, whenever possible, it is important for both parents to be present when telling your child. Such a display of unity in regard to your roles as parents will help your child understand that although the relationship between his parents is changing dramatically, you will both continue in your parenting relationship with him.

Before talking to your child, it will be important for the two of you to discuss in advance what will be said—you need to have a game plan. It may be helpful to write down an outline of what you want to say. Remember that this is a discussion that will be remembered by your child for the rest of his life. You don't want to make it even more traumatic by having it become a forum for your negative feelings toward your spouse. For this reason, it is extremely important that you and your spouse make a firm commitment not to argue or put each other down when you are telling your child about the divorce.

Regardless of whether it is one or both of you telling your child, it is very important to plan a specific time to inform your child. This should be as early as possible after you have decided to divorce—you do not want your child hearing about the divorce from someone else. Remember that children are often more perceptive than most parents realize. Most children are aware of problems before parents sit down with them to tell them about the pending divorce. Of course, if you have been separated, your child will already be keenly aware of the possibility of divorce. The bottom line is not to wait too long before telling the child after the firm decision to divorce has been made.

You and your spouse should arrange a time that you can spend at least an hour with your child. You probably will not need an hour, but you want to make sure you have enough time to address all the issues and answer any questions your child may have. The time should be one that will not be interrupted. You should turn off the ringer on the phone and not allow any other distractions. This will be an important and difficult time for everyone involved. You need to give your child every opportunity to understand, to the extent possible, what is happening.

Children at different ages will have different levels of understanding of what divorce means. Obviously, the younger your child, the less understanding he will have. Terms we as adults use such as *love, marriage*, and *divorce* can be difficult for young children to understand. You might become very frustrated if your expectations for your child's level of understanding are too great. Therefore, it is important for you to have an awareness of what children at different stages of life usually understand about divorce. The following box presents a brief outline of how children typically vary in their initial understanding of divorce across different age groups.

What should you say to your child? First of all, there are no easy or perfect ways to tell your child you are getting a divorce. However, we have several suggestions that can help you with what to say. A very important point to remember is that *how* you say things may be just as

---

Children's Basic Understanding of Divorce

Infants	Have no understanding
Toddlers	Understand one parent no longer lives in the home but do not know why
Preschoolers	Understand parents are angry, upset, and live apart but do not understand why
Elementary Schoolchildren	Begin to understand what divorce means (for example, may understand that parents no longer love each other and will not live together)
Preteens and Adolescents	Understand what divorce means but do not necessarily accept it

---

important, if not more important, as *what* you say. Remember that non-verbal communication is much more powerful than verbal communication. Most children are very sensitive to their parents' emotional state. Children will often mirror the emotional reactions of their parents. If you appear devastated, it is likely your child will become devastated. If you seem to be managing the pending divorce well, your child will feel more secure and less anxious.

In terms of what to say, you will want to keep it simple and straightforward, especially for younger children. You want to be honest but nonjudgmental. This is not a time for blame. Honesty does not mean you should go into all the brutal details of what led up to the decision to divorce. The important point is to not lie to your child. Here is an example of a simple, honest, and straightforward explanation:

> *Your dad and I have been trying for a long time to work out our differences and problems in our marriage. We have reached a*

point where we realize we cannot be happy living together anymore and have decided to get a divorce. This is painful for all of us, but it will be OK. We both love you very much and will continue to love and care for you, but it will be from two separate homes.

This first discussion of the divorce should obviously not be the last. This will be an extremely emotional time for your child, and many of the details that you discuss will not be clearly remembered. You will need to repeat much of the information on more than one occasion. One of the best ways of assessing your child's retention and understanding of various issues is through the questions he asks. Be sure to encourage your child to ask questions by acknowledging his feelings and not overreacting to issues.

There are several other important points that need to be made to your child. Describe specifically what will remain the same and what will change from his perspective (e.g., where everyone will live and when he will spend time with the noncustodial parent). You also need to stress to your child that he, in no way, caused the divorce. Some children believe the stress that they created (for example, because of their behavior problems or school problems) for their parents contributed to the decision to divorce. This can be a tremendous burden for children, and the issue needs to be addressed and put to rest early on in the divorce process.

Here is what we recommend:

- Tell your child as soon as a definite decision is reached.
- Make sure all family members (including both parents) are present.
- Plan ahead about exactly when and what you are going to say.
- Be honest and straightforward.
- Give a simple reason for the divorce.
- Don't assess blame.

- Emphasize that your child did not cause the divorce.

- Emphasize that both parents will continue to love and care for him.

- Emphasize that your child is still part of a family.

- Describe things that will stay the same.

- Describe changes that will occur.

- If your child is older, outline steps that have been taken to save the marriage.

- Acknowledge your child's feelings.

- Encourage questions.

- Repeat the information on more than one occasion.

"My parents were so mad and upset I was afraid to

ask them any questions about the divorce. But there

were so many things I didn't understand."

Stacey, twelve

4

Anticipate Questions Your Child May Have

NOT ONLY SHOULD YOU follow the guidelines we previously discussed for telling your child about your divorce, but you and your spouse also should be prepared for questions that your child will ask. You may be surprised that most of the questions a child is likely to ask will pertain directly to herself. Parental divorce can be a scary time for children, and, as a result, a child typically is concerned with what is going to happen to her.

As we have already indicated, it is important for you and your spouse to encourage your child to ask questions. A major reason this is important is because children can have many misconceptions about the causes, consequences, and processes of divorce. A child may believe any or all of the following: one parent is totally to blame for the divorce, the child herself is to blame for the divorce, parents will get back together, or she will be abandoned. For example, you may be asked: "Will I have to go live with somebody I don't know?" This is a question that probably would never occur to you; however, it is the kind of question that a young child may think about and, if given the opportunity, ask. We have given some examples of questions that young children and adolescents may ask in the following boxes. Of course, we cannot tell you the specific questions your child will ask, and you will not be able to anticipate beforehand all the questions that she will ask. However, you need to be prepared as well as you can be.

Questions Children May Ask About Parental Divorce

"Who will take care of me?"

"Will I be left alone?"

"Where will I live?"

"Will I still be able to be with both of you?"

"What will happen if I get sick?"

"Will we live in the same house?"

"Who will feed me?"

"Will you still be my mommy and daddy?"

"Will I be with my brothers and sisters?"

"Will I get to keep my pet?"

"Where will Daddy live?"

"Who will take care of Daddy?"

Think about the potential questions, and also think about how you will answer. Your child will benefit if you and your spouse can have a "meeting of the minds" prior to telling your child about the divorce, in regard to how you are going to answer specific questions. One strategy that can be helpful is for each parent to separately generate a list of potential questions and answers. Ideally, the parents can then get together to review their lists and try to decide on mutually acceptable answers.

Your answers to your child's questions should provide her with factual information presented in as neutral a tone of voice as possible. Of course, you can state how you are feeling, but try to do so in a tone that will not upset your child. If you become emotional or upset, so will your child. You can and should also acknowledge her feelings. Regardless of how absurd a question may seem to you or how much it hurts you, try to answer it. Do not ridicule, humiliate, or reprimand your child. Your relationship with her and how she copes with this difficult time will be, at least partially, a function of how you handle these interactions with her.

Questions Adolescents May Ask About Divorce

"What do I tell my friends?"

"Will I have to move?"

"Will I have to go to Dad's apartment every weekend?"

"Will I have to change schools?"

"Why are you doing this to me?"

"Will I still get the same allowance?"

"Can I still have my friends spend the night sometimes?"

"Who will pick me up after basketball practice?"

"Why can't you just work it out?"

"Why don't you think about someone other than yourself?"

It is important for you and your spouse to not only encourage questions from your child when you initially tell her about the divorce, but to do so on at least several more occasions afterward. For example, you and your spouse may tell your child about the divorce and encourage questions. You can even say, "Sometimes when mothers and fathers divorce, children have questions, like 'Where will I live after the divorce?' Do you have any questions like this or any other questions?" In two or three days you should ask your child again if she has any questions. You can then repeat this again about two weeks later.

Talking about the divorce with your child and encouraging her to ask questions are not easy tasks. Furthermore, you likely will hear some very negative thoughts and feelings. However, you need to provide her the opportunity to acquire information and develop an understanding of what is happening. Let's hear about Barbara's experience, which highlights the idea that explaining divorce is an ongoing experience, not a one-time event. "I don't really remember much about when my parents told me they were getting a divorce; I was only five. I wanted to understand more, but my dad and mom would tell me that they told me before and I said I understood—but I didn't."

Here is what we recommend:

- Think carefully about potential questions your child may ask and how you would answer.

- Ask your child what questions she has about the divorce.

- Address questions in as neutral and factual a way as possible.

- Ask your child what questions she has on at least three occasions.

"I was so absorbed in winning the legal battle for

custody of my kids that I developed a 'win at all costs'

attitude. Many years later I realized what an

ugly process it was and what a heavy toll it took

on my kids."

Tom, forty-two, father of two boys

5
Avoid Custody Disputes:
Consider Mediation

THE "BEST INTEREST OF THE CHILD" standard is the principle currently used by courts for determining child custody. In essence, custody is awarded according to what is thought to be in the best future interest of the child. Although most state statutes have guidelines for determining a child's best interest, these are often too general and vague to give much direction to judges. As a result, if you and your spouse end up before a judge, you will be relying, at least in part, on that particular judge's interpretation of the law and his or her own discretion.

States vary substantially on the rules for awarding custody. Regardless of the rules of a particular state, parents often find that some of their most intense disagreements during the divorce proceedings are about custody. When these disagreements occur, each parent often lines up with his or her attorney, mental health professional, and friends to present reasons that "the custody decision should be in my favor." Of course, the other parent is lined up with his or her attorney, mental health professionals, and friends to present the exact opposite argument. A child also may be involved in a custody hearing by being asked his preference. Most divorce disputes are settled outside of court; however, the continual threat of a court hearing can make negotiations between ex-spouses very hostile, and this is exactly what is most harmful for your child. As a result, other methods of resolving custody disputes have been sought.

A promising alternative is divorce mediation. Both parents meet with one or more mediators, who are professionals (sometimes attorneys or psychologists) with specialized training in helping parents specify their disputes and negotiate compromises. The goal of divorce mediation is to reach a settlement that is agreeable to both parents. This cooperative method stands in contrast to the adversarial settlement of custody that occurs in the courtroom and tends to be viewed as a win-lose outcome. While mediation typically takes several sessions (the actual length depends on the complexity of the specific issues), it is often less expensive (both financially and emotionally) than litigation.

Some communities require an attempt at mediation before a court hearing, while other areas have voluntary mediation programs in which parents can choose to participate. In many communities judges will formally approve the mutual agreement to make it legally enforceable. If a mutual agreement cannot be reached in mediation, then the case is typically returned to the court for litigation. Dr. Robert Emery of the University of Virginia, an expert in divorce mediation, has pointed out that mediation has a number of benefits, including a significant reduction in custody hearings, better compliance with agreements reached (than with court orders), less conflict and more cooperation in coparenting, and more satisfaction by parents, particularly fathers, than with the adversarial process. (In regard to mother/father satisfaction, we want to point out that the research indicates that both fathers and mothers are typically very satisfied with mediation. However, fathers show a stronger preference for mediation over litigation than do mothers.) Finally, Dr. Emery also has pointed out that mediation itself has not been found to lead to improved mental health for children or parents. Nevertheless, as we will point out repeatedly in this book, a reduction in conflict between parents, which can occur with mediation, will most probably lead to better child adjustment.

So, our recommendation probably is obvious to you at this point. Give serious consideration to mediation for resolving disputes around child custody. While mediation is not a panacea, it offers a way for both parents to work together for the good of their child.

Here is what we recommend:

- Consider divorce mediation, which offers a potentially beneficial alternative to the adversarial legal process for resolving custody issues. Mediation resources can be found in the resources section.

Part 2

Looking After Your Own Well-Being During and Following Divorce

"I knew my child would have a hard time with the

divorce, but I wasn't prepared for the intense feelings

of loneliness, emptiness, and despair that I felt."

Pat, thirty-seven, mother of one

6

Expect an Adjustment Period

IT IS IMPORTANT TO REMEMBER that divorce is not a single event but rather a process that unfolds over months, years, or even decades. This unfolding process will be like a journey along a trail with many unexpected bends and forks. Although the specifics of your divorce will make your journey unique, you will share many actions and emotions with others who have experienced a divorce. Barbara Radford and her colleagues at Creighton University identified four phases of divorcing, each of which is accompanied by a set of actions and emotions. The phases, actions, and emotions are presented in the box on page 38. As can be seen in this box, negative emotions ranging from unhappiness to grief are typically experienced at each stage of the divorce process. You may very well be experiencing some of these emotions yourself. If you are, it can sometimes be helpful to realize that you are not alone in your feelings.

Many people inaccurately estimate how easily and quickly they will adjust to their divorce. The fact of the matter is that the first couple of years can be very difficult. You will be building a new life and a new

Phases of Divorcing

PHASE	BEHAVIOR	EMOTIONS
Emotional divorcing	Growing apart	Unhappiness
Making the decision	Moving to initiate action to divorce	Multiple emotions, such as anxiety, anger, and ambivalence— all intense and profound
Pulling apart	One spouse moving out; filing divorce papers	Pain
Moving beyond	Growing into a new life	Grief

Adapted from B. Radford, G. D. Travers, C. Miller, C. L'Archevesque, E. Furlong, and J. Norris (1997).

identity, and that takes time. You need to acknowledge that it will be a difficult adjustment period for you—probably more so than you currently anticipate. This adjustment period may be especially difficult for you if you did not initiate the divorce; however, this time is often difficult for both parties. Of most importance is the fact that how you handle your own adjustment will affect your child's adjustment.

What does the research literature say about changes in adjustment when divorcing? For many people there is a decline in self-esteem. There also are feelings of loneliness, distress, and second-guessing ("Did I do the right thing?" or "What could I have done differently to save the marriage?"). Among the most often reported feelings are depression, anger, and anxiety. Furthermore, many individuals who are divorcing indicate that they are "up one day and down the next." Especially difficult times might include holidays, birthdays, anniversaries, and other dates that held special meaning for you and your spouse or for your family. The intensity of emotions about an ex-spouse and the marriage will be like a roller-coaster ride, but one in which the highs and lows become less extreme with time. In addition to emotional reactions, there may be physical changes, such as weight loss and fatigue. It will be an important time to make sure you take care of both your physical and mental health. Unfortunately, some individuals turn to unhealthy ways to cope with their distress. For some this might involve excessive alcohol use, and for others it might mean plunging into another relationship too quickly. Be wary of such potential land mines.

Are women or men more likely to experience adjustment problems? This question has been proposed, examined, and debated by researchers. The evidence at this time suggests that the psychological and physical changes that occur for men and women, in general, are more similar than different.

Emotions experienced by a person divorcing appear to be related not only to the major stressors that are occurring in her life (for example, financial difficulties, moving, major argument with ex-spouse) but also the daily hassles or minor stressors (for example, your child is sick and can't go to school, your car runs out of gas, you have a disagreement with a friend). This suggests that it is not only major divorce-related events but also what occurs on a daily basis in your life during a divorce that can influence your adjustment. Therefore, it will be critical that you have, or develop, a strong support system to help you deal not only with the stress of the divorce itself but also with the daily hassles that occur in your life.

It is very important for you to have a realistic expectation of how difficult it will be to adjust to your divorce. There will be painful bumps along the way as you deal with many new experiences in rebuilding your life. At times it will probably be very difficult for you not only emotionally but also financially. Develop strategies for dealing with both emotional difficulties (for example, develop a strong support system) and potential financial problems (for example, develop a budget and stick to it) not only for your own sake but also for your child's.

Here is what we recommend:

- Expect and accept that there will be a period of adjustment.

- At the same time, work toward not only identifying and addressing adjustment problems but also enhancing your overall well-being. The remainder of this part, "Looking After Your Own Well-Being During and Following Divorce," will discuss some ways that you can do this. It is important that you seriously consider these approaches to facilitate your own adjustment, which will also improve your ability to help your child through this difficult process.

"Soon after my wife filed for divorce, I started to have

a drink at night to help me sleep. By the time the

divorce was final, I was drinking heavily . . .

every night. It was my way of avoiding having to

think about the realities of the divorce."

Joe, forty-one, father of two

7

Examine Your Coping Style

ONE WAY THAT YOU CAN promote your well-being during and following divorce is by examining, and perhaps changing, the way you cope with stress. When we are faced with a stressful situation such as divorce and the stressors that accompany it, each of us has a coping style that we come to rely upon. Some styles are healthy, and some are not. By recognizing the style of coping you may be automatically using, you will have made the first step toward changing that style, if it is one that does not work for you.

There are three basic types of coping styles:

1. A problem-focused style is one where you attempt to deal with a problem by changing or managing the situation in a way to reduce the stress.
2. An emotion-focused style is one where you do not attempt to change the problem but rather try to manage your emotional response to it.

3. An avoidant coping style is one where you attempt to cope with a stressor by denying its existence, refusing to deal with the situation, or perhaps resorting to alcohol, drugs, or other ways of numbing your reaction to the situation.

Let's take an example. Suppose that when your child is in the home of your ex-spouse, he rarely takes a bath, frequently goes to bed too late, or eats primarily unhealthy foods. If you use an avoidant style of coping, you might either imagine that these things are not happening (even though you know full well that they are) or avoid talking to your ex-spouse about your concerns. If you use a problem-focused coping style, you might plan a strategy for meeting with your ex-spouse and addressing these issues (possibly using the skills described in Strategy #10, "Communicate Effectively with Your Ex-Spouse"). If you use an emotion-focused coping style, you might acknowledge the problem but perhaps realize that your ex-spouse would not be willing to make changes based on your concerns. What you then try to do is find ways to cope with your worry about the situation. For example, this could involve talking to yourself about how these things are undesirable but, given the limited time your child spends with your ex-spouse, are probably not worth fighting over or worrying about. You might also focus more on the importance of your child spending time with his other parent even though your ex-spouse's parenting may not be exactly as you would like. In other words, you change the way you think about the situation by reducing its importance, or you try to think about the positive aspects of the situation rather than just the negative.

The scientific literature is convincing. An avoidant style of coping is not healthy. Such a style can lead to many problems, such as trouble sleeping at night, becoming a bitter person, or becoming extremely anxious about your child. Depending on the situation, a problem-focused or an emotion-focused coping strategy is better to use. If you are faced with a situation that you can actively change, then a problem-focused style of coping is best. On the other hand, if you are in a situation that is not under your control, focusing on your emotions and learning to cope with them is the best strategy.

As a person who is going through a divorce or is divorced, it is important for you to realize that there are some things over which you have control and some things over which you have no control. For example, you have minimum control over the behavior of your ex-spouse. On the other hand, you probably have substantial influence with your child, particularly if you are the custodial parent. Recognize what you can control, and use a problem-focused coping style to change it. Recognize what you cannot change, and use an emotion-focused coping style to help you cope emotionally with uncontrollable events.

Here are our recommendations:

- Examine your style of coping and identify which style you predominantly use.

- If you primarily use an avoidant coping style, identify a stressor in your life and attempt to use either a problem-focused coping strategy or an emotion-focused coping strategy, depending on whether the stressor is controllable or uncontrollable.

- Once you have tackled one stressor, implement either a problem-focused coping strategy or an emotion-focused coping strategy with a second stressor and then with a third stressor. By this time it should begin to be more natural for you to use active rather than avoidant coping strategies. However, for most people, it will continue to require thought and work to take yourself off "automatic pilot" when faced with a new stressor and to ask yourself how you should try to cope with it.

"I had so much I wanted to talk about but no one to

turn to. Our friends and family all sided with my wife

and I was on my own. As time went on, I became

more and more withdrawn and depressed."

Ted, twenty-seven, father of one

8

Develop a Support System for Yourself

UTILIZE THE SUPPORT OF family and friends to cope with your divorce. We all need companionship, understanding, sympathy, caring, trust, advice, and a good laugh to help us through life's difficult times. Divorce is a very stressful, intense, and emotionally draining process. Trying to handle it in isolation will just escalate your level of stress, which in turn will have a negative impact on your child.

As you move through the process of divorce, reach out to friends and relatives for support. Divorced parents who have the support of friends and relatives typically become less distressed and are better able to handle the many stressors associated with divorce. In addition to helping personal psychological adjustment, research with parents who are divorcing has found that satisfying relationships with friends and relatives lead to a greater sense of parenting competency and greater satisfaction in their relationships with their children. The support of friends is especially important during a divorce because there is often a tendency, as a marriage deteriorates, for couples to withdraw from their friends as well as from many of the social activities they participated in as a couple. While friends may rally to your side at the time of your separation and/or divorce, this support often fades over time. You will need to work to maintain it—call friends, schedule lunch dates, arrange activities to do with others. However, you need to realize that friends may be reluctant to "choose sides" when you divorce. Call upon friends for emotional support, not to gossip about or plot against your ex-spouse.

Although both practical (such as having someone help with babysitting) and emotional support are important, the latter appears to be of primary importance especially for women. Research by Nancy Miller and her colleagues at the University of Akron examined the relationship between the level of distress among divorced women and the type of social support they received from friends and relatives. They found that the most beneficial type of support was having someone listen to their personal problems. This was more helpful than practical or material support. Having a "sounding board" improves an individual's problem-solving skills and even improves feelings of well-being. A good listener is vital: look until you find one. The positive feelings that accompany "being heard" will go a long way in the healing process.

It is important that you have at least one person as a confidant, who will listen, remain neutral, give you honest feedback, and help you solve problems. Remember that friendships often change following divorce, and friends as well as relatives may take sides. It may become necessary for you to establish new friendships. Explore special-interest social groups (for example, groups that focus on specific hobbies), volunteer opportunities, and other activities where you might meet and interact with people who have similar interests. Also, you might want to look into the single-parent groups that are offered through many local churches, synagogues, and community centers. Such groups allow you the opportunity to meet others who have gone through divorce and may be facing similar problems.

Another possibility is to consider joining the international organization Parents Without Partners, which has more than fifty thousand members (55 percent women, 45 percent men) and approximately four hundred local chapters in the United States and Canada. To find out if there is a chapter in your community, contact their international head-quarters at (800) 637-7974, or visit their website (www.parentswithout-partners.org). If you become involved with such groups, it is important to remember that although social activities with groups of people can be helpful, they are not a substitute for the support of a close friend or relative. If you do not have any close friends, a goal should be to develop friendships that can offer you support on a one-on-one basis. If this is particularly difficult for you, consider contacting a counselor or clergy member.

It is important to remember that the need for support is not only for your own psychological well-being, but also for your child's well-being. The distress that parents often experience during and following a divorce almost always affects their parenting. This should not be surprising, as parenting is challenging even when there is marital support. Custodial parents face the challenges and demands of childrearing without such support and often with little, if any, relief from the daily routine of parenting. Research conducted by Ronald Simons and his colleagues at Iowa State University has found that parents' emotional distress is related to less effective parenting. Such distress may result in parents becoming less interested in their relationship with their children, spending less time having fun with them, becoming more irritable with them, monitoring their children less effectively, and not using discipline consistently. Therefore, it is critical that you take the time to nurture your relationships with friends and relatives so that you can receive the support it will take to prevent you from burning out and becoming a less effective parent. You owe it to yourself and to your child.

Here is what we recommend:

- Recognize the importance of social support.
- Make a commitment to nurture existing and establish new supportive relationships.

- Find supportive relationships to provide an opportunity to have someone objectively listen to you talk about the issues you face while also providing you with a sense of understanding and empathy. Choose your confidants carefully.

- Don't overburden your friends, and be prepared to return the support.

- Don't look for support where it isn't willingly available (for example, relatives of your ex-spouse).

- Seek the assistance of a counselor or clergy member if you are not receiving the emotional support you need.

"At times the stress got so bad that I couldn't

concentrate at work. I was so tense I would overreact

and yell at my coworkers. Eventually I lost my job

because of it. I felt like I'd lost everything."

Maria, thirty-three, mother of two

9

Manage the Stress in Your Life

IF YOU ARE IN THE PROCESS of divorcing or are divorced, you understand stress all too well. How you think about and manage this stress will be important for both you and your child. The more stressed you become, the less effective you will be in managing all areas of your life, including your parenting and your patience as a parent. As a result, if you do not effectively manage the stress in your life, not only will you be distressed, but your child may experience adjustment difficulties. Remember that children reflect their environment.

Fortunately, there are a number of general strategies that can help you manage the stress you experience around your divorce.

The first step is to identify what contributes to your stress. Make a list of all of the stressors, big and small, that affect you. Then go through the list and mark the stressors that you can change or eliminate. Develop a plan for changing one, and only one, of these stressors at a time. If you try to tackle multiple stressors simultaneously, you will not be successful with any of them. Also, keep in mind that not only the "big" things, like your finances, create stress but, for most people, the daily hassles of life can collectively cause even more stress. If this is the case for you, try to plan your day to minimize the small hassles. Organization is the key.

Take a break or change gears. You cannot spend twenty-four hours a day handling the stress of your divorce or working to do the job of two parents. You will burn out. A goal you should have is to spend at least several hours a week doing something you really enjoy. Your activity might be something you consider relaxing, such as reading, going to a movie, or spending time with a friend. Other kinds of breaks also can be helpful. For some people, just changing tasks and doing something different is helpful.

Learn how to relax. When most people become really stressed, they show signs of physical tension. Common symptoms are tense muscles, headaches, rapid and shallow breathing, and increased blood pressure. Do any of these sound familiar to you? Are you experiencing any of these symptoms? One way of managing stress is to learn how to relax in order to reduce these symptoms of physical tension. Many people believe they already know how to relax. However, effective relaxation is more than just sitting down in front of the television, taking a coffee break, or having a beer or glass of wine with friends. These activities may distract you from stress, but they generally do not reduce physical tension.

One effective technique for combating physical tension is to learn and practice specific relaxation exercises. Such exercises might include special breathing exercises or specific muscle-tension-relaxation exercises. There are many ways to learn such exercises. Mental health professionals often teach them individually. Your local hospital, community college, or other organizations may offer classes in relaxation or stress management. Or, you might be able to learn them on your own with one of many books on the subject (see the resources section for suggestions).

Learning problem-solving strategies can also help you more effectively manage the stress in your life. You are less likely to feel overwhelmed by the problems associated with your divorce if you learn and practice a strategy for solving the problems. One problem-solving strategy involves the following steps:

1. Try to relax and remain calm. You might want to use the relaxation techniques we just mentioned.
2. Clearly define the problem. Try to be as specific as possible.
3. Generate a list of possible solutions. Don't evaluate them at this stage. Just brainstorm ideas.
4. Evaluate the solutions on the list.
5. Choose what you think is the best solution.
6. Apply that solution, and then decide how effective it was.

Having a system to help you solve problems doesn't mean that you will be able to effectively solve all problems, but it can help give you a structured way to approach problems. Such a structure can be very helpful when you are overwhelmed by stress.

Make sure you get enough rest. Everyone is tired at times and, unfortunately, when you are a single parent you likely will be tired more of the time. Being tired can lead you to being less patient with your child, having difficulty seeing things objectively, and tending to blow things out of proportion and overreact to certain situations.

Eat a well-balanced diet. A poor diet can result not only in a lack of energy but also an inability for your body to fight off illness. Unfortunately, one of the things that often happens with the stress that accompanies a divorce is that the more stressed you become, the worse your eating habits become; the worse your eating habits, the less able your body is to help you deal with stress.

Make sure you get enough exercise. Just as nutrition is important to your general well-being, so is physical activity. The more physically fit you are, the greater your ability to handle the demands of your divorce and the stress associated with it. Unfortunately, when you are under stress, you are less likely to be physically active. The less physically active you are, the less physically fit you become. What this means is that the stress of the divorce will be greater on you. Regular exercise can actually help you manage stress—it gives you a chance to clear out your mind.

Try to keep a regular schedule. Not only should you have a regular schedule for sleeping, eating, and exercise, but also for other aspects of your life. By keeping a regular daily, weekly, and monthly schedule, you will work toward eliminating stress from your life and ensure that you accomplish activities that need to be completed. We realize that having a consistent schedule is often not typical, especially with children. However, you should strive for as much consistency as possible.

Have an outlet for releasing emotional steam. The stress of a divorce can lead to a buildup of emotions. It is important to release these emotions in healthy ways. As Barbara Radford and her colleagues at Creighton University noted, releasing your emotional stress will not necessarily solve any problems; however, it can provide a safety valve, which can prevent blowups from occurring unintentionally. Thus, you may need to do things like cry, scream, run, or be by yourself for a time. If you reach the point of needing to release emotional steam, recognize the need and find the way that is best for you to let go of these emotions—without harming yourself or anyone else.

Maintain a sense of humor even through the difficult times. When people are under stress, they tend to lose their sense of humor. They may fail to see any of the humor of what is going on in their life. This is unfortunate, because humor can be a very effective way to manage stress. It is also important for your child to learn that laughing can be healthy even during difficult times. Laughing about things, and about yourself, can really help you maintain a more realistic perspective about what is happening around you. Laughing also makes you feel good, and it can break the tension. So try not to take yourself and your situation too seriously, and look for the humor in the situation. You are going to need a big dose of humor, in addition to all the other strategies we have mentioned, to handle the stresses in your life associated with your divorce.

Here is what we recommend:

- Identify and reduce stressors.

- Take a break or change gears.

- Learn how to relax.

- Learn effective problem-solving strategies.

- Get enough rest.

- Eat a well-balanced diet.

- Exercise.

- Keep a regular schedule.

- Release emotional steam.

- Maintain a sense of humor.

Part 3

Issues Between You and Your Ex-Spouse During and Following Divorce

"Every time I brought up an issue she didn't want to talk about she would start riding me about all the things I had done wrong in the past."

Sam, twenty-seven, father of three

10

Communicate Effectively with Your Ex-Spouse

IN THE INTRODUCTION we told you about five possible relationships you can have with your ex-spouse: Perfect Pals, Cooperative Colleagues, Angry Associates, Fiery Foes, and Dissolved Duos. The type of relationship that the two of you have will be a factor in determining how your child adjusts to the divorce. Therefore, if Perfect Pals is not a possibility, it is important that you work toward being Cooperative Colleagues. Being Cooperative Colleagues means that although you are not friends (as is the case for Perfect Pals), you do agree to cooperate for the sake of your child.

How do you do this? First, you need to keep each other informed about your child. Her scheduled activities, school issues, medical issues, and any concerns you have about her behavior or discipline are just a few examples. You both are parenting your child and, to do this most effectively, both of you need to stay informed about all aspects of her life.

Second, how you keep your ex-spouse informed is equally important. You need to communicate clearly and effectively. Using effective communication skills can be difficult, especially if you have a lot of anger over the divorce and ill feelings toward your ex-spouse. However, let us stress again that it is important for the sake of your child that you communicate effectively and respectfully with your ex-spouse. If your communication patterns involve a lot of conflict, then there will be negative ramifications for your child.

Remember that it is not just what you say but how you say it that is important in communicating to another person. In one study, researcher Albert Mehrabian found that only 7 percent of what people communicate is accomplished through words, 38 percent is accomplished through vocal characteristics such as tone and volume, and 55 percent is accomplished through body language and facial expressions. When emotions are involved, as they are during and following divorce, remember that your ex-spouse is probably focusing more on your nonverbal language than on your words in "hearing" what you have to say.

Here are some suggestions that can facilitate effective communication with your ex-spouse. (These suggestions are from our book **Parenting the Strong-Willed Child** *and also adapted from materials developed by the Iowa Cooperative Extension Service.)*

- Pick a neutral location to discuss difficult issues. Choose to meet at a public place (e.g., coffee shop, park) rather than at your home or your ex-spouse's home. This will keep the discussion more balanced between the two of you.

- Be polite. Avoid disrespect and put-downs of your ex-spouse.

- Remain calm. When you become upset or emotional, you lose control of the situation and will accomplish nothing positive.

- Avoid generalizations, criticisms, accusations, threats, and sarcasm.

- Set goals prior to a discussion and stay on the topic. If you start dwelling on past problems, you will not resolve the issue that you wish to discuss.

- Work on one problem at a time. If you try to solve too many problems at one time, you run the risk of becoming overwhelmed and may end up not solving any of the problems.

- Be an effective listener. This is particularly difficult if you are thinking about the things that you are going to say to get "one up" on your ex-spouse. If you are not an effective listener, you cannot expect your ex-spouse to be one. Don't be preoccupied with your ex-spouse's listening skills. Focus on your own skills.

- Don't make assumptions. Ask your ex-spouse for her opinion or thoughts on an issue. Take them at face value.

- Avoid finger pointing and being judgmental. Attack the problem, not the person. Use "I" messages rather than "you" messages to do this. For example, your ex-spouse will likely become defensive and feel attacked if you say, "*You* are always letting her stay up as late as she wants. *You* are so irresponsible." Using an "I" message can often prevent the other person from becoming defensive. Basically, an "I" message involves you stating your feelings or how you are affected by a situation. For example, "*I* am worried that she is having a hard time at school because she may not be getting enough sleep. What can we both do to help make sure she gets enough sleep?"

- Request feedback from each other and take turns talking. You do not want to monopolize the conversation any more than you want your ex-spouse to monopolize the conversation.

- Focus on developing solutions. A solution to a problem is far more important than who is to blame. Use the problem-solving steps we discussed in Strategy #9, "Manage the Stress in Your Life," to help you generate a list of possible solutions.

- Request more time to consider issues or get more information. If you are uncertain about how to handle a particular issue, do not hesitate to ask for more information or time to think.

- Identify points of agreement. Once you have identified some things (or anything!) you can agree upon, both of you will feel like winners.

- Prepare and be willing to negotiate instead of remaining firm about getting "your way." That is what communicating and reaching compromises is all about. Your child will benefit and you will be glad you did.

- Communicate with your ex-spouse as you would like him to communicate with you. Remember the Golden Rule: do unto others as you would want them to do unto you (but don't expect it to always be reciprocated).

"They're always fighting. If they hate each other so much, why did they have me?"

Clay, eleven

11

Do Not Argue with Your Ex-Spouse in Front of Your Child

ALONG WITH CONTINUING to parent effectively, avoiding conflict with your ex-spouse in front of your child is of the most importance to your child's well-being. Cooperation between divorcing parents is always best for children; however, if cooperation is not possible, then absence of conflict is your goal. Unfortunately, in the great majority of cases, this also is often not realistic or easy—parents likely would not be divorcing if they did not disagree and have conflict. Thus, although conflict between parents may occur, there is substantial research to indicate that it should *not* occur in front of children. Regardless of the gender or age of your child, repeatedly exposing him to conflict between you and your ex-spouse is harmful.

Conflict between parents in front of children has been associated with a number of psychological problems for children, including aggression, anxiety, depression, poor self-esteem, physical complaints, and difficulties in school. While a child exposed to repeated conflict between parents probably will not have problems in all of these areas, one or more of these problem areas may well occur. Here is what one child has to say: "My parents would fight all the time. It got so bad that I started to get stomachaches and felt like throwing up. My mom thought I had some kind of illness and took me to a bunch of doctors. There was nothing wrong with me; it was just the fighting really got to me."

Just think about it. Conflict between parents is disagreement between two people a child loves. Children may feel a need to become an ally of one parent; however, they then worry about their relationship with the other parent. Furthermore, when parents argue or fight, they model for their children how *not* to solve problems. Not surprisingly, some children will learn to handle interactions with their peers in the same way—by being verbally or physically aggressive. Or, for some children who are fearful by nature, conflict between their parents may produce anxiety about what the conflict means for them or for you. "Will I not get to see my dad anymore?" "Are my parents fighting because of me?" "Will my parents hurt each other?" As is obvious from these examples, children can interpret conflict between parents in many ways. When you fight in front of your child, you do not know how he will interpret it, but one thing is certain: whatever the interpretation, it is not likely to foster his psychological adjustment or his relationship with either parent.

Here is some more food for thought. In contrast to children whose parents are married, children of divorcing parents often see their parents interact *only* around issues that frequently lead to conflict. Without some positive or cooperative times between parents to offset the times of conflict, children will become anxious when their parents interact. They will not only expect arguing and bickering but will learn to feel helpless to prevent or stop it. This can result in children showing high levels of problems whenever their parents are interacting.

It is important to note that the harmful effects of conflict for children whose parents are divorcing are not limited to times both parents and the children are physically together. Arguing during a telephone conversation when children are exposed to one end of the conversation can be just as stressful for them. Threatening, yelling, and slamming down the phone provide inappropriate examples of handling conflict and create anxiety for some children. You should assume that, if your child is in the house, he will overhear heated telephone conversations— even if you believe he is asleep.

Conflict between divorcing parents can occur over a number of topics. These include major matters such as money, property, custody, visitation, and how to parent. However, prepare yourself for conflict over minor matters, such as a child having dirty socks upon returning home from a visit with the noncustodial parent or a parent being five minutes late for a visit with a child, which can be just as intense and heated. At times you may well conclude that there are no simple matters in life between you and your ex-spouse.

Parental conflict in front of children can take different forms. It may be subtle, such as when parents make verbal "jabs" at each other, or, alternatively, such verbal conflict can be more overt and hostile, such as when threatening, screaming, and cursing occur. Furthermore, conflict may escalate into physical acts of parents pushing, shoving, or even hitting one another. Physical conflict is worse for children than verbal conflict; however, both are harmful for children's psychological adjustment.

Beyond the form (i.e., verbal or physical), there are other aspects of conflict that have been identified as particularly detrimental for children. As Robert Emery of the University of Virginia has noted, conflict that is frequent, remains unresolved, and involves the child in the dispute is especially damaging. When children are involved in the conflict, they may feel a need to stop it. Furthermore, they may feel forced to "take sides," which is a no-win situation for children. Having to referee a disagreement between parents in an attempt to reach a resolution or having to choose between parents are not roles for children!

Conflict in front of children around issues related to the children is particularly detrimental. These may involve child support payments, holiday visitation schedules, or any number of matters. Whatever the issue, the critical aspect is that it involves your child and can make him feel responsible. Guilt, the need to "make things better," and frustration from being helpless to do so are just some of the feelings your child may experience.

Here are our recommendations for how you should handle issues with your ex-spouse that are most likely to lead to conflict:

- Focus on what is best for your child, not on whether you can win an argument with your ex-spouse. With this as a guiding principle, you are on the right path. Following this principle leads to several specific strategies for dealing with your ex-spouse around issues that can lead to conflict.

- Do not argue or fight in front of your child. When you are in the presence of your child and your ex-spouse, avoid controversial issues. If your ex-spouse tries to start an argument, simply say, "Let's arrange a time to discuss that matter." If you can say this firmly but calmly, most of the time you can avoid conflict in front of the child. However, on some occasions this may not be sufficient. At those times, you need to say, "I will call you to arrange a time to discuss the matter," and then, if necessary, turn and walk away.

- When you do discuss the issue with your ex-spouse, without the child being present, follow these guidelines:

  - Make sure the child will not appear on the scene during the discussion.

  - Work diligently at remaining calm no matter how angry or verbally aggressive your ex-spouse becomes.

  - Always focus only on the issue of concern (i.e., avoid bringing up other issues or your ex-spouse's faults).

  - Use a problem-solving strategy. Clearly define the problem, brainstorm possible solutions, evaluate the possible solutions, decide which solution to use, and finally evaluate how well it worked. When you can successfully use such problem-solving skills with your ex-spouse about most issues, you then may want to begin addressing some issues in front of the child. Now, instead of arguing and fighting in front of the child, you are providing an example of how to appropriately resolve issues and, at the same time, creating a sense of security for him.

- Recognize when you need outside assistance to resolve an issue with your ex-spouse. Some different ways to resolve disagreements are listed in the following box. Obviously, you (and your ex-spouse) have more control with the first two approaches, which is what you want under most circumstances.

Resolving Disagreements with Your Ex-Spouse

Negotiation You and your ex-spouse discuss the issue and strive for a compromise that is acceptable to both of you.

Mediation A neutral third person, who has no decision-making authority, facilitates the discussion between you and your ex-spouse.

Arbitration A neutral third person listens to both your and your ex-spouse's views of the issue and makes a decision.

Litigation A judge makes the decision about the issue.

- If conflict between you and your ex-spouse does occur in front of your child, do not talk about it with your child until you have calmed down. Then in your conversation with your child about the conflict, do not put all the blame on your ex-spouse. It takes two to have a conflict! Explain that the two of you did not agree and that you are going to do everything you can to resolve the disagreement. Assure your child that the disagreement is not his fault.

"I remember lying to my mom when she asked whether

my dad's girlfriend spent time with us over

the weekend. I knew that if I told her the truth she

would have just gotten all mad."

Lora, ten

12

Do Not Use Your Child as a Messenger or Spy

ONE OF THE MOST DIFFICULT feelings for a child of divorced parents to cope with is feeling "caught in the middle" between her parents. Some parents put their child in the middle by asking her a lot of questions about the other parent. This might include questions about the other parent's personal life (e.g., if they are dating) or about details of the time she spends with the other parent that goes beyond normal interest (e.g., looking for things to be critical about). Parents can also place their child in the middle by sending messages to the other parent through their child (e.g., "Tell your father he's behind on child support" or "Tell your mother I give her enough money to be able to buy you those shoes").

Christy M. Buchanan and her colleagues at Stanford University have provided us with a substantial amount of information about the issue of children being caught in the middle. They found that almost two-thirds of adolescents from divorced homes said that they feel caught between their parents at least sometimes, and 10 percent indicated that they felt caught between parents very often. They also found that problems such as being used as a messenger or spy are rated by children as being among the most stressful events they associate with divorce. Some statements from children whose parents used them as messengers or spies, using the words of children who participated in the research of Dr. Buchanan and her colleagues, are contained in the following box.

Words from Children About Being "Messengers" or "Spies"

"When one parent tells me to tell the other one something, tell them this and tell them that. Tell her that I don't want you to do that any more or something. Things like that."

"Like when my parents disagree on paying for . . . something, usually I have to talk on the phone for them 'cause they don't want to talk to each other."

"[I feel caught] every time I go visit [my father]. I come home and I am bombarded with twenty questions."

"My father will tell my mom he is going to do something, and then she'll ask me if he's done it. I get caught in the middle."

Reprinted by permission of the publishers from Adolescents After Divorce *by Christy Buchanan, Cambridge, MA: Harvard University Press, Copyright © 1996 by the President and Fellows of Harvard College.*

What do we know about children who feel caught between their parents? First, this is more likely to happen to older children and adolescents than to younger children. In addition, girls are more likely to feel caught between parents than are boys. When parents have a relationship marked by high conflict and low parental cooperation, children are more likely to feel caught between their parents. Additionally, when adolescents have close relationships with their parents (yes, with both parents), they are less likely to feel caught between their parents. This occurs because parents who have close relationships with their children are more sensitive to their children's feelings and, as a result, less likely to behave in ways that put their children between them. Finally, and perhaps of most importance, children who feel caught between their parents have poorer psychological adjustment. These children may feel anxious or depressed or even become aggressive.

Here are our recommendations:

- Do not use your child to deliver messages to your ex-spouse.

- If your child brings a message to you from your ex-spouse, contact your ex-spouse and indicate that you would like messages to come directly to you, not through your child.

- Do not ask your child questions about your ex-spouse's personal life.

- Do not interrogate your child about the time she spends with her other parent.

- If you find out your ex-spouse is asking your child questions about your personal life, directly contact your ex-spouse and express your concern.

"When I was twelve, my mother told me all about the

affairs my father had. I told her I didn't want to know

all the details, but she told me anyway saying that I

needed to know what my father had done."

Cynthia, seventeen

13

Do Not Use Your Child as an Ally

WHEN DIVORCED PARENTS have disputes, both parents often call upon their child, either intentionally or unintentionally, to ally with them or take their side. Just like using children as messengers or spies, using your child as an ally in a dispute with your ex-spouse is very stressful for your child. Think about it for a moment . . . your child wants to love both of his parents. When you attempt to have him "take your side," you are creating a conflict for him by making him choose between two people whom he loves. Some divorced parents sometimes will even ask their child whom he loves the most. Even when parents don't demand such a direct choice, they may indirectly make demands on a child to choose one parent over the other parent. For example, a child might be asked with whom he wants to spend holidays, live, or spend time on a particular occasion. These types of choices are difficult for children, as they require a child to choose one parent over the other.

Many parents put pressure on their child to ally with them not by making them choose whom they want to be with or whom they love the most, but by trying to get their child to take their side on various divorce-related issues. For example, "I am going to go back to court to try to get your father to increase how much money he gives us each month. If we don't get the extra money, we won't be able to take a vacation this summer or buy you new clothes for school." Another example of such pressure is, "If your mother doesn't let me switch the night I see you next week, I won't be able to take you to the ball game." Sometimes this pressure can be unintentional and subtle, but it is hazardous to the child nevertheless. Some parents apply such pressure to try to have their child view them as the "good guy" and the other parent as the "bad guy." However, this usually backfires in the long run. In our experience, when a parent continually applies pressure on her child to take her side on various issues, the child usually ends up feeling more negative toward that parent over time.

The following box contains some statements from adolescents who felt that parents were trying to use them as an ally against the other parent. You can see that this can create a tremendous amount of stress for children and adolescents. Your child will have enough difficulty dealing with the divorce without being pressured to take sides.

Words from Children Caught Between Parents

"Well, sometimes my dad used to try to put me on the spot and ask me in front of my mom who I would rather live with."

"Sometimes they ask me who would I rather be with or who do I like the most."

"[When] they were going to split up . . . we had to choose who we were going to go with. . . . I didn't want to leave my mom or dad."

"My mom wants me, and my dad wants me at the same time that weekend, and he is making us choose."

"My mom and dad were fighting and I got upset and I ran from my mom to my dad and she said, 'Well, just take his side!' I just felt horrible."

Here are our recommendations.

- Try to recognize when you are putting even subtle or indirect pressure on your child to take sides.

- Make a commitment to yourself not to put any pressure on your child to choose sides. It is very stressful to a child to make him choose one parent over the other parent.

- Do not *ever* ask a child whether he loves you or your ex-spouse the most.

- As your child gets older, he will have more opinions about choices (for example, with whom he wants to spend special occasions). You may want to ask your child what he wants to do, but be clear about whether he, or you and your ex-spouse, have the authority to make the final decision. If he is given the authority, let him know that you will accept whatever decision he makes and continue to love him. However, you must be willing to actually accept and respect that decision.

"I didn't realize the problem until one day my daughter

got mad at me after I told her not to tell her father

about something. All of a sudden she blew up and

started screaming that I was always telling her not to

tell her father things. I had no idea how much

pressure she was under because of what I was doing."

Lynn, forty-one, mother of four

14

Do Not Place Restrictions on What Your Child Can Tell Your Ex-Spouse

SOME PARENTS WHO ARE divorced not only use their children as messengers or spies (see Strategy #12, "Do Not Use Your Child as a Messenger or Spy") and allies (see Strategy #13, "Do Not Use Your Child as an Ally") but also place restrictions on what their child can tell the other parent. This is a form of using your child as an ally in that you are attempting to have secrets shared between you and your child. As with being a messenger or a spy, this places an undue burden on your child.

For a child, having to keep secrets from someone whom she loves is difficult and stressful. This situation is aggravated further if the other spouse asks the child directly about the secret she is keeping. In this case, the child is faced with either telling the parent the secret or lying to that parent. In essence, a child is in a no-win situation.

The following box contains some statements from children who have restrictions placed on what they can tell the other parent. As is obvious in these examples, this is stressful for a child and another way children become caught in the middle of parental issues. Such loyalty binds can cause significant problems in a child's ability to adjust to her parents' divorce.

Words from Children Pressured Not to Tell Something to the Other Parent

"My dad told me he may take a job in another state. He then told me not to tell my mother. I am upset and I just don't know what to do."

"My mom really runs down my dad and then tells me not to tell him any of the things she says about him. It just makes me feel horrible."

"When my dad dates Cindy, sometimes she spends the night. If I am there, Dad tells me not to tell Mom because then I might not get to come see him anymore."

"Sometimes my mom asks me if there are things my dad says that I should not tell her. Well, there are things he told me not to tell her, and I don't know whether to lie or tell her."

Here are our recommendations:

- Think carefully before you tell your child something you do not want her to tell your ex-spouse.

- Don't ask your child to keep secrets.

- Make it clear to your child that she has your permission to talk to the other parent about any topics that she chooses to talk about.

- Talk to your ex-spouse about agreeing not to impose restrictions on what your child can tell each of you.

"I don't think my parents had a clue what their constant

ragging of each other was doing to me—until I became

really depressed and withdrawn."

Jennifer, sixteen

15
Do Not Criticize Your Ex-Spouse in Your Child's Presence

IN THE INTRODUCTION, we noted that one of the most stressful events for children associated with the divorce of their parents is when a parent says bad things about the other parent. Unfortunately, particularly if parents have high levels of conflict, it is not unusual for them to be critical of the other parent to their child. When you criticize your ex-spouse to your child, your child can do one of several things. First, he can defend your ex-spouse. This is more than likely going to end in an argument between you and your child. Second, he can say nothing but become angry at you for criticizing someone he loves. Third, and this is the least likely to happen, he may agree with you. What is evident here is that criticizing your ex-spouse is not very likely to improve your relationship with your child, which should be your focus following divorce. In fact, criticizing your ex-spouse in front of your child likely will have the exact reverse effect of the one you intended.

In recent years the term "parental alienation" has been increasingly used to describe the situation when one parent's actions and words encourage a child to reject the other parent. This would, of course, involve criticism of the other parent in the child's presence. The term "parental alienation syndrome," or "PAS," is often used to describe the problems of children in extreme situations involving a divisive campaign by one parent to alienate the child from the other parent. Although the term "PAS" has gained widespread use, it is not a clearly defined disorder. Professionals that use the term "PAS" tend to describe it as a loosely defined set of child behaviors, parent behaviors, and the parent-child relationship. This makes it a very subjective judgment as to when the term should be used in a specific situation. The lack of clarity has led to other professionals questioning whether a true syndrome actually exists. These professionals are not saying that children in such situations do not have problems but rather that there is not a unique syndrome of child symptoms that can be reliably diagnosed. Regardless of the validity of such a syndrome, it is clear that when a parent tries to alienate the child from the other parent, through criticism or other ways, the child suffers.

The box on page 74 contains some statements from children who have experienced one parent criticizing the other parent. As you read these examples, we hope that you will develop an even deeper understanding that criticizing the other parent creates a very difficult dilemma for children. As a parent, you can never justify criticism of the other parent that occurs in your child's presence. Words can hurt your child.

Here are our recommendations:

- Think carefully about how you talk about your ex-spouse to your child or when your child can overhear you.

- Never vent your hostile feelings toward your ex-spouse with your child, directly or indirectly.

- If you hear that your ex-spouse is criticizing you in front of your child, resist the temptation to "fight fire with fire." Rather, contact your ex-spouse in person, by phone, or by letter. Indicate that the goal both of you should have is helping your child during this difficult time. You can indicate that you know your ex-spouse has negative feelings toward you; however, voicing those negative feel-

Words from Children Hearing One Parent Criticize the Other Parent

"My mom says things about my dad, and I don't know what to say . . . sometimes my dad also will say things about mom, like she's taking all of his money."

"My dad just rags on my mom all the time. He just goes on and on and on until I feel like I am going to explode."

"Sometimes my mom just says really mean things about my dad. I want to defend him, but I know it will just lead to a fight. So I do nothing."

"My mom is so critical of my dad and my dad is so critical of my mom. I have to hear both sides, and I am just getting where I don't like either one of them."

"It is so hard. Every time I talk to my dad or see him, all he does is criticize my mom. It is like we don't ever have any fun together anymore."

ings to your child will only deteriorate the relationship between him and the child. Remember to use the "I" messages we discussed previously (see Strategy #10, "Communicate Effectively with Your Ex-Spouse"). For example, rather than saying "You are turning Jeffrey against me . . ." it is better to say something like "I am very concerned about how Jeffrey is responding to things he is hearing."

- If your efforts fail and your child continues to report the criticisms, talk to him about ways he might want to handle it with his other parent. For example, when the criticism starts he might want to say that it makes him feel uncomfortable or sad.

- Actively work on your relationship with your child rather than focusing on your negative feelings toward your ex-spouse.

"My ex-wife complained about everything I did

with our children. After every visit I knew she would

complain about what they ate, what they wore, and

what we did together."

Scott, twenty-six, father of two

16

Redefine Your Relationship with Your Ex-Spouse

ONE OF THE MOST IMPORTANT, yet difficult, issues that you will face as you go through the divorce process is how to redefine your relationship with your ex-spouse. As long as the two of you have a child with whom you are both involved, there will be an ongoing relationship between you. Obviously, that relationship is not going to be the same as when you were married. As a consequence, you are going to have to work at redefining the relationship that you have.

To most successfully coparent your child, the two of you need to separate your parenting roles from your past relationship with each other. That is, you need to work together to coparent your child without letting your negative feelings for each other influence how you parent. Obviously, this is a difficult task. However, there are many parents who have been able to do this successfully for the sake of their child.

Let's think about the boundaries that you are going to need to renegotiate with your ex-spouse. Robert Emery of the University of Virginia has pointed out that intimacy and power are the two major dimensions of relationships. Intimacy refers to emotional closeness to another person. Power refers to who has authority to make decisions. If divorced parents are going to be successful at coparenting, there must be significant changes in terms of their intimacy and power boundaries.

As you know, two people who are divorcing rarely have the same level of intimacy or emotional closeness. In most divorces, as Dr. Emery points out, there is a "leaver" and the person who is "left." That is, one person wants out of the relationship whereas the other person wants it to continue. As a result, the two people often have very different desires about where the boundaries around intimacy will be. For example, the "leaver" may want the marriage to end but want to preserve some aspects of the relationship. On the other hand, the partner who has been left may be angry and unwilling to "just be friends" or "get along for the sake of our child." Alternatively, the "leaver" may want to break off all aspects of the relationship whereas the person who is "left" may want to renew the relationship and actively pursue the "leaver." In both of these examples, what is evident is that two people who are dissolving a marriage will most likely have different needs for emotional closeness. And this often leads to conflict.

There also are often disputes over power boundaries between divorcing spouses. Power struggles can occur over any of a number of different issues, including finances, childrearing, amount of contact between ex-spouses, and amount of contact between each spouse and a child. The renegotiation of power relationships is typically less difficult than the renegotiation of intimacy boundaries, in part because there is usually not the same degree of emotional intensity and also because the legal system often decides power disputes.

In many ways the information we have just laid out for you may seem very academic. However, as you attempt to negotiate issues with your ex-spouse, you will need to think about each of your needs in terms of the intimacy of your relationship at this moment. Who was the "leaver" and who was "left"? What are the feelings that you are experiencing about your ex-spouse, and what do you think are your ex-spouse's feelings about you? Understanding these feelings will help you identify the current relationship you have with your ex-spouse and begin to redefine it. It will also help you understand the basis of some of the struggles between the two of you and, quite possibly, how to resolve them.

To redefine your relationship and renegotiate boundaries successfully, you must get past the need for vengeance. Your focus should be on building a different relationship rather than demolishing the old relationship. To help divorcing couples think about the need to define this different relationship, we often ask each parent to write down what they want for their child's future (i.e., what are their hopes and dreams for their child's life?). We then show them each other's answers. Usually their answers are very similar (e.g., success and happiness for their child in her personal life and job), or the answers at least complement each other (e.g., both want good things for their child). Next, we ask both parents what they think their postdivorce relationship needs to be like to help their child achieve the goals they delineated for her. Often the positive postdivorce relationship qualities both parents bring up are things such as cooperation, courtesy toward each other, and respect for personal privacy. Intimacy boundaries will have to change for such changes in a relationship to be successful. It might be extremely hard for you to shift from a marital relationship to a relationship that involves personal privacy. It is hard to let go of the emotional bonds with a former spouse, but you must work at doing it so your postdivorce relationship will be supportive, rather than destructive, for your child.

Many divorced parents have been successful in building a new and different relationship with their ex-spouse by viewing it as a type of "business" relationship. The goal of this business relationship is to focus on successfully rearing their child. In order for you to develop and maintain this new relationship, boundaries will need to be changed to reflect the rules that mark most relationships between businesspeople. New intimacy boundaries will support interpersonal interactions that are defined by politeness, courtesy, low personal disclosure, and personal privacy. New power boundaries will allow for explicit agreements (e.g., court-ordered financial support) and coparenting rights.

The power boundary that causes many divorced parents difficulty is related to coparenting. Whether right or wrong, in most married fam ilies one parent tends to assume the primary parenting role. It can be very difficult following divorce for that parent to accept the other parent doing things differently with their child. Obviously, the goal should be to strive for as much consistency as possible. But remember that no two parents (married or divorced) are going to handle all parenting situations in exactly the same manner. Following divorce, parents are going to have to accept differences in parenting (as long as no harm is being done to the children). This involves changing a major power boundary. If you have been the primary parent, you should discuss parenting issues with your ex-spouse and strive for agreement (see Strategy #31, "Be Consistent with Discipline"), but be careful not to insist he do it your way and stop yourself from falling into the role of supervising his parenting. You need to change that power boundary to be accepting of differences in parenting. Changing this power boundary to allow for less control by you is very difficult for most parents. If it is difficult for you, try to remember that there is not one perfect way to parent or care for children (even though you may think your way is best).

Children often handle different parenting styles in different homes better than most parents expect (and definitely better than being exposed to ongoing conflict between their parents over parenting issues). Many children accept and adapt to such differences in part because of their past exposure to many different caregivers such as teachers, childcare providers, and extended family members. All of these individuals approach caring for your child in a different way. From these experiences children learn that different caregivers in their lives interact with them differently and have different ways of managing their behavior. Even before the divorce your child was probably aware of the differences between her parents. After the divorce she can adjust more easily to these differences because each parent is in a different home (with different rules and expectations). Just like a child learns the rules and expectations of different teachers in different classrooms, your child will learn that her two parents have different rules and expectations. Although we encourage parents to strive for as much consistency as possible in regard to parenting across their homes, we realize there are always going to be inconsistencies to some degree. It is important to realize there is one type of consistency that you do have absolute control over, and that is the day-to-day consistency in your parenting of your child when she is with you. The more consistent you are, the more easily she will understand your rules and expectations when she is with you.

Here are our recommendations:

- Examine your emotions and feelings (positive and negative) for your ex-spouse.

- Strive for emotional distance from your ex-spouse.

- Separate your feelings for your ex-spouse as a marital partner from your feelings for him as a parent. Many individuals who are inadequate in one area may be adequate in another area.

- Decide on how power and intimacy boundaries between you and your ex-spouse need to change to create a relationship that is optimally supportive of your roles as coparents.

- Focus your energy on working together in a coparenting role to benefit your child.

- Develop a parenting plan (see Strategy #26, "Develop a Parenting Plan"). Such a plan helps define not only how the two of you will coparent your child but, to some extent, the relationship that you will have with each other. The more specific not only your parenting plan but your custody agreement, the less the feelings (again positive and negative) that you have for each other will interfere with how you coparent.

- Accept that you are going to have a loss of power over your child's life. This is the case whether you are the custodial or the noncustodial parent. What goes on in the home of the other parent is, for the most part, beyond your control.

- As you redefine your relationship with your ex-spouse, avoid further romantic involvement with him. A common scenario for many divorcing spouses is to have an occasional romantic interlude. This can happen for any of a number of reasons, but the end result is that it blurs the intimacy boundaries between the two of you. Unless you are both fully committed to reconciling, a romantic involvement can only hurt, not help.

Part 4

Visitation Issues

"I hated my ex-spouse so much that I did everything

I could to interfere with him being involved with our

children. Many years later I realized what a disservice

I had done to our children."

Gayle, forty-five, mother of three

17

Encourage Involvement of the Noncustodial Parent

UNFORTUNATELY, MANY noncustodial parents fail to stay very involved with their child after the divorce. This is especially the case when the father is the noncustodial parent, which of course happens most frequently. As a general rule, the longer the time since the divorce, the less involved the noncustodial parent is in his child's life. It is important that a noncustodial parent continue to be involved with his child not just in the time immediately following the divorce but throughout his child's life. If you are a custodial parent, you may have conflict and disagreements with your ex-spouse; however, this does not mean that your child should not be involved with his other parent. As we have said before, a divorce ends a marriage but not parenthood.

Why is it important that the noncustodial parent stay involved? As we will later elaborate (see Strategy #18, "Ensure Frequent and Predictable Contact Between Your Child and the Noncustodial Parent"), your child's adjustment will be enhanced by having the noncustodial parent involved in strengthening his relationship with your child.

There is another reason for encouraging a noncustodial parent to stay involved: noncustodial parents who are more involved are more likely to make child support payments. Child support payments are very important for your child—they can prevent events (for example, moving) that can set off a downward spiral in his adjustment (see Strategy #23, "Maintain Regular Child Support Payments").

Ex-spouses, particularly when they are fathers, may need encouragement to spend time with their child. They are often willing to do so but are uncertain exactly what role to take after the divorce. If you are the custodial parent, you need to make sure your ex-spouse understands that he still plays a very important role in your child's life.

If you are the custodial parent, how can you encourage your ex-spouse to stay involved with your child? Here are our recommendations:

- Maintain low levels of hostility and high levels of cooperation between the two of you to enhance the involvement of your ex-spouse with your child.

- We realize that it can be very difficult to change how you feel about your ex-spouse. If you are having a hard time trying to change your feelings, remember that it's not how you feel but how you act that has the greatest impact on your child. The important point is to prevent your negative feelings from controlling what you say and do in your child's presence.

- Do not criticize your ex-spouse in your child's presence (see Strategy #15, "Do Not Criticize Your Ex-Spouse in Your Child's Presence"). This can hurt your child's perception and relationship not only with his other parent but also with you.

- Encourage your child to initiate activities with your ex-spouse. These might involve going to a movie or special event together or any other activity that is beyond the usual and customary visitation time.

- Encourage phone calls, letters, and E-mails between your child and his other parent, especially if the other parent lives far away.

The Internet offers an additional opportunity for children to interact with their parents who live far away. Parents and children can now play games with each other over the Internet. While many parents and children do not have Internet access, such access will continue to become less expensive and more widespread in the coming years. Many public facilities such as libraries also offer free Internet access.

- Encourage your child to take items, such as his artwork and photographs, to show or give to his other parent.

- Keep a folder with information to share with the other parent. Items to keep in the folder might include report cards, schoolwork, school calendars, activity schedules, photographs, and videos. You can give these items (or copies) to your ex-spouse. Keeping him regularly informed about your child's life can make him feel more connected and thus more likely to continue involvement.

- Talk to your ex-spouse about the good things, not just the problems, about your child and coparenting.

- Make visitation transitions smooth (see Strategy #19, "Make Visitation Transitions Smooth"). If you can do your part to make these transitions pleasant, your ex-spouse will not shun visits to avoid conflict or problems with you.

- Incorporate your ex-spouse into your child's special events, such as birthdays, sports activities, and holidays. By doing this, you will help your ex-spouse feel that he still plays an important role in his child's life.

- Help your child select cards and gifts for his other parent's birthday and special occasions (Mother's Day, Father's Day, Christmas, etc.).

- Communicate to your ex-spouse that you appreciate his parenting role.

"I remember not wanting to let my mom know how much it hurt me each time my dad had to cancel a weekend visit with him. If she knew, she would just have gotten even madder at my dad. I would just go to my room and cry myself to sleep."

Abby, seventeen

18

Ensure Frequent and Predictable Contact Between Your Child and the Noncustodial Parent

IF A PARENT IS TO maintain involvement and a meaningful relationship with his child following divorce, the parent and child must have sufficient contact with each other. Unfortunately, as a number of national surveys suggest, many noncustodial parents have only minimal contact with their child. For example, Susan D. Stewart of Bowling Green State University found in a survey that only one-third of noncustodial fathers saw their child at least once a week, and only 37 percent had contact by phone or letter at least once a week. Furthermore, more than one-fifth of fathers did not see their child and had no phone or letter contact during the past year.

Is frequent contact with the noncustodial parent good for a child? When a child's psychological adjustment is considered, a review of the research by Paul Amato and Joan Gilbreth of Pennsylvania State University indicates that the answer is a weak "yes." When considered in light of several other research findings, it is clear that contact with the nonresidential parent becomes quite important for a child.

First, as Frank Furstenberg and Christine Nord of the University of Pennsylvania found, most children view their noncustodial parent as significant in their lives. This is a critical piece of information and one that divorced parents should not ignore. Second, the review by Paul Amato and Joan Gilbreth indicates that in divorced families, children are generally better adjusted when they have a positive relationship with the noncustodial parent. And, as Mary F. Whiteside of the Ann Arbor Center for the Family found in her research, the more frequent the visitation between a noncustodial father and his child, the better the relationship. Third, if you are the custodial parent, let's face it, you need support. Child visitation with your ex-spouse can allow you some free time—time to organize yourself, complete some tasks, and perhaps even relax. Fourth, as we previously pointed out (see Strategy #17, "Encourage Involvement of the Noncustodial Parent"), more frequent contact with the noncustodial parent is related to more consistent child support payments, which itself is very important.

Taken collectively, the evidence suggests that frequent contact with the noncustodial parent is beneficial for children. Of course, there are exceptions. There are some conditions under which frequent contact may be less than beneficial for children. Before you look at the following four conditions, it is important to remember that they do not mean visitation should not occur; rather, these circumstances may need to be addressed so that visitation can be more pleasant and beneficial for a child.

1. Frequent contact between a noncustodial parent and a child typically means more interchanges between you and your ex-spouse. Thus, if you and your ex-spouse are engaging in high levels of heated conflict in front of your child around visitation or when the two of you meet to exchange your child, this can be detrimental.

2. Inconsistent contact, such as visits not occurring as scheduled, can have a negative effect on children. A child needs consistent routines. She also may interpret broken visits as indicating a parent does not love or care for her.

3. When a particularly high conflict relationship exists between a noncustodial parent and a child, being forced to spend relatively long periods of time together may be detrimental. As we pointed out earlier, contact is important, as it allows a positive relationship to build between a child and a noncustodial parent; however, if a relationship is not positive, extended time together may have the opposite effect.

4. If a noncustodial parent is irresponsible, incompetent, or perhaps mentally disturbed, the amount of time spent with that parent likely should be limited. However, if you are the custodial parent, remember that you may have hostile feelings that influence your perceptions of your ex-spouse. It is very likely that he is not as bad as you think. Also, just because an ex-spouse may not have been a good spouse does not mean that he is not an adequate parent. Remember that you chose to marry and have a child with your ex-spouse; thus, he cannot be all bad, right?

The right frequency of contact between a child and a noncustodial parent is dependent on a number of things, two of which are the gender and age of the child. A noncustodial parent and a child of the same gender may have developed a bond around gender-specific activities. For example, a divorced father who has been actively involved in coaching his son in youth football may spend more time with the son because of this activity. Of course, parent-child bonds around activities do not have to be gender-specific. Mothers may coach their sons and fathers may coach their daughters.

The age of your child is likely to be an even bigger issue when contact with the noncustodial parent is considered. As children grow, peers become increasingly important, particularly in the teenage years. During these years, adolescents spend less time with parents and more time with friends. Removing a teenager, or in some cases a younger child, from her peers every other weekend may be difficult for everyone and beneficial for no one. Flexibility and creativity will be required with teenagers when contact with the noncustodial parent is considered.

How can divorced parents arrange the right amount of contact between a child and the noncustodial parent? First, the legal arrangements of your divorce likely will specify the noncustodial parent's time with the child. In ideal situations, this arrangement will be (or was) negotiated and acceptable to you, your ex-spouse, and your child. If needed, use a mediator to help find an arrangement agreeable to all (see Strategy #5, "Avoid Custody Disputes: Consider Mediation"). Second, for a very young child, more frequent short visits may be better initially than prolonged visits. For older children, let them have some input into the visitation schedule. The guiding principle should be the following: "What is in the best interest of your child?" Third—and this can be difficult—work cooperatively with your ex-spouse and your child. Take her needs, as well as yours, into account as visitation is arranged. Develop a predictable, but flexible, schedule. Allow flexibility to accommodate your child's activities. Don't drag her, kicking and screaming, away from important activities in order to visit.

Here are some additional important points surrounding visitation with the noncustodial parent:

- If you are the custodial parent, don't withhold contact between your ex-spouse and your child as a way to punish your ex-spouse. You are hurting your child the most.

- If you are the noncustodial parent, focus on the quality of contact, as much as the quantity. Quality time does not mean being a "Disneyland" parent but rather working (yes, it is work!) on building a positive relationship with your child (see Strategy #27, "Nurture Your Relationship with Your Child"). This means doing activities together, being positive with your child, and having clear rules that you consistently enforce. With an older child or teenager, you may want to involve her friends in some of these activities. Of course, all of this becomes substantially more difficult when you have multiple children who are different ages and genders or have different interests.

- If you are the noncustodial parent and your relationship with your child is primarily negative at the moment, go slowly. Spend brief periods of time with your child and make those times very positive. Gradually, through your efforts, the relationship will turn around.

- If you are the noncustodial parent and your relationship with your child is positive, longer visits may be beneficial. They will allow you to establish regular routines where your child is more a part of your life rather than being just a visitor in your home.

- If you are a noncustodial parent, especially one who lives some distance away, there are forms of contact other than being physically together. As we pointed out previously (see Strategy #17, "Encourage Involvement of the Noncustodial Parent"), you can telephone, write letters, and, in this age of computers, E-mail your child.

"My parents would always get into it whenever my dad

came to pick me up. They would always argue

about something or be mean to each other."

Erika, fourteen

19
Make Visitation
Transitions Smooth

As we have emphasized, it is important for your child to have frequent and predictable contact with his noncustodial parent. What this means is that there likely will be an interaction between you and your ex-spouse when your child moves from one home to the other. This transition time, which has been labeled as a "switchover," can be difficult for both of you and, particularly, for your child.

Janet R. Johnston and her colleagues at Children's Hospital of San Francisco found that most children experienced distress during this time of switching from one parent to the other. Among the ways that the distress was manifested were the following: withdrawal, apprehensiveness, physical complaints (e.g., stomachaches, headaches, nausea), aggression, and acting like a younger child. Obviously, when a child shows such symptoms around switchovers, it indicates that this is a difficult time for him.

Why do children have difficulty when making the transition from one parent to the other? The foremost answer is that, when parents are actively engaged in conflict with each other, children display more problems. Think about it for a moment: you and your ex-spouse may interact with each other only during times of switching your child from one home to the other. As a result, he sees the two of you together only at these times. If you spend this time fighting over issues like visitation and money, your child soon comes to expect the time when he switches from one parent to the other to be loaded with conflict. As a consequence, it is not surprising that he might display symptoms of distress.

Another reason making the transition from one parent to the other may be difficult for your child is the change that occurs as he moves from one home to the other. Even if parents strive for consistency between their homes, there will be differences. It sometimes takes children a while to adjust to different parenting styles, rules, and surroundings. Many children have a particularly difficult time when they return from a weekend visit. Such postweekend difficulties are sometimes referred to as "reentry problems." Switching at this time is often made more difficult by the child having to return to the reality of regular life (e.g., school night) from a relatively unstructured time over the weekend.

Children also may have difficulty with switchovers due to uncertainties. If your child, particularly if he is young, is unsure of when he will be with each parent, how long he will be with that parent, and exactly when and where he will be picked up when time with a parent ends, he may experience anxiety and distress. Be sure to tell your child, very clearly, all the details of the visitation schedule.

As Mary Elizabeth Curtner-Smith of the University of Alabama has pointed out, switchover sites should be determined, first, by the needs of your child and, second, by the preferences of you as parents. If you and your ex-spouse frequently engage in open, hostile conflict, you are probably better off having the switchover take place in a public setting where the two of you are less likely to lose your tempers. If you find it almost impossible to interact without engaging in conflict, then you should consider having the switchover occur where there is little or no contact between the two of you. For example, one of you can drop your child off at a grandparent's house or at an after-school activity, and the other spouse can pick him up there.

Here are our recommendations for making visitation transitions smooth:

- Develop a month-by-month visitation schedule, taking into account holidays, vacations, and special occasions (see Strategy #20, "Effectively Handle Birthdays, Holidays, and Special Occasions"). Each parent should have a copy of this schedule to minimize misunderstandings over when visits will occur.

- Confirm with your ex-spouse about when and where visitation "switchovers" will occur.

- Communicate clearly with your child when and how the switchover will occur (e.g., "Your dad is going to come to the house to pick you up at 6:00 P.M. on Friday"). Also, communicate clearly with your child how long he will be with the other parent (e.g., "I will come pick you up at your dad's apartment at 5:00 P.M. on Sunday").

- Have your child ready in advance of the switchover time. Have all his clothes and other items he is taking with him packed and ready to go.

- If your child is going to need to bring anything special with him for the visit, let the other parent know in advance.

- Speak to your ex-spouse in advance of any changes in your schedule regarding visitation.

- Realize that visitation schedules may change as a function of your child's activities. Do not try to resolve these changes in front of your child during a switchover.

- Don't make your child responsible for making, canceling, or changing visitation plans. Those are your and your ex-spouse's responsibilities.

- Do not be late or fail to show up for a switchover. If this happens frequently, there is a good chance that your child will think you do not care about him.

- Deal with issues that need to be resolved with your ex-spouse at times other than the transition of your child from one home to the other.

- Remember, don't use your child to convey messages to your ex-spouse during the transition.

"My parents both came to all my birthday parties.

It was probably difficult for them, but it really meant

a lot to me."

Ryan, seventeen

20

Effectively Handle Birthdays, Holidays, and Special Occasions

As we have previously indicated, when you work with your ex-spouse to schedule the time that each of you spends with your child, you need to consider birthdays, holidays, and other special occasions. How will these occasions be spent? Unfortunately, there is no magic formula that will work for all occasions. Many factors will need to be taken into consideration including what occasions have had the most meaning to your family, distance between parents' homes, and fairness. When deciding on the schedule, try to put yourself in your ex-spouse's shoes and think what would be fair from his perspective (be honest with yourself!).

There are more of these holidays and special occasions than most parents initially think. The box on the next page lists some holidays that you may need to consider. Obviously, depending on your cultural heritage and religious affiliation, some of these may not be holidays or events that you would celebrate. Nevertheless, the list does give you an idea of some days you may need to consider. There certainly may be others.

Some Holidays and Special Occasions

- New Year's Eve
- New Year's Day
- Martin Luther King Jr. Day
- Kwanzaa
- Chinese New Year
- Valentine's Day
- Presidents' Day
- St. Patrick's Day
- Good Friday
- Easter
- Cinco de Mayo
- Mother's Day
- Father's Day
- Memorial Day
- Flag Day
- Independence Day
- Labor Day
- Rosh Hashanah
- Passover
- Hanukkah
- Columbus Day
- Halloween
- Thanksgiving
- Christmas Eve
- Christmas Day
- Mother's Birthday
- Father's Birthday
- Child's Birthday
- Sibling's Birthday
- Grandparent's Birthday
- School Holidays

You need to take into account these holidays in your month-by-month planning. Here are some of the options that you have. Your child might spend part of a holiday with you and part with your ex-spouse. Or, you might rotate so that your child spends a holiday with you one year and with your ex-spouse the next year. Or, she might spend one holiday with you and the next holiday with your ex-spouse. Or, believe it or not, there might be some holidays and special occasions, like your child's birthday, that you want to celebrate together. If you are able to cooperate with your ex-spouse, spending certain occasions (e.g., child's birthday) together with your child can send a strong and positive coparenting message to your child. Obviously, there are going to be many other options, and it is up to the two of you to work together to decide which of these is best for your child and for the two of you as parents.

The most difficult decisions will be those related to the occasions that have the most meaning to you and your child.

Children's input, particularly for older children and adolescents, needs to be given serious consideration. However, it is important that we point out that children (like many of us as adults) often have unrealistic views and expectations of holidays. For example, they may want the three of you to spend time together on a holiday. Depending on the relationship between you and your ex-spouse, this may or may not be feasible.

Here are our recommendations:

- Decide for each holiday how the two of you want to handle time with your child: splitting time, rotating holidays, or rotating a holiday across years.

- Be flexible and put your child's best interest first.

- Plan times for phone calls to and from the other parent when your child is spending holidays with you.

- Decide on holiday schedules well in advance, especially if travel plans need to be made.

- Talk to your ex-spouse about gift plans for your child so you don't buy the same things.

- Realize that it might be hard for you to spend some holidays (e.g., birthday, Christmas) without your child. If your child is not going to be with you and you anticipate difficulties, make sure you plan activities to occupy your time.

Part 5

Divorced Parenting: General Guidelines

"I was convinced that my child was doomed to a life of

psychological problems because of my divorce."

Debby, thirty-one, mother of one

21

Change the Way You Think About Your Child

WHEN YOU ARE WITH your child, you probably experience a wide range of thoughts and emotions about his behavior. Some are good; some are not so good. Most parents think that these thoughts and feelings are caused directly by their child's behavior. As an example, suppose your child has a temper tantrum in a store, and you then become upset. You might conclude that the temper tantrum caused you to become upset. However, your child's temper tantrum does not directly cause you to become upset; instead, it is the way you view the temper tantrum that determines whether or not you become upset. For example, you might view your young preschooler as "bad" or "mean" for having a tantrum, which may lead you to become angry and start yelling at him. Or, you might start thinking that he is having a tantrum because he is upset about the divorce, and as a result you start feeling guilty and do nothing to address his tantrum because you hold yourself responsible. A third, and often more realistic, view may be that the tantrum resulted from his being exhausted. In this case, you probably do not become very upset but rather deal directly with the tantrum and decide that it is time to go home so that he can rest.

Certain common ways of thinking about a child's behavior often occur when parents are going through a difficult time with a divorce. Here are some examples:

"We really messed up our child by divorcing."

"My child never behaved this way before the divorce."

"It is terrible since the divorce—my child always behaves so horribly."

"My child is behaving that way to get back at me for divorcing."

"It is always necessary for me to get angry to correct my child's behavior, especially since the divorce."

"I am a bad parent because I divorced."

When parents start thinking in these ways, they become upset. It is not so much their child's behavior that is causing them to become upset, it is their own belief system. A belief system is a habitual way a person thinks about or interprets what is going on, in this case his or her child's behavior. One example of a belief system is negative absolute thinking, which occurs when you start thinking negatively in absolute ways about something (which typically involves using absolute words such as *should, must, never,* or *always*). When under the stress of a divorce, many parents are particularly likely to think this way. Let's face it: all children are going to misbehave sometimes, and it may have nothing to do with your divorce. Therefore, it is not terrible or awful when your child misbehaves, unless you convince yourself that it is terrible or awful. This does not mean that you should be content with or condone your child's misbehavior. However, you do need to have a realistic perspective regarding his behavior, and you need to avoid negative absolute thinking. Instead, try to replace your negative thinking with more realistic thoughts.

Many parents who are prone to negative absolute thoughts have found it helpful to consciously start reciting to themselves more realistic and helpful thoughts when their child misbehaves. Here are some sample statements:

"I am not a bad parent because I divorced."

"My child's negative behavior is not necessarily related to my divorce."

"My child will misbehave sometimes even when he knows the rules."

"It is undesirable and irritating when my child misbehaves, but it is not terrible."

This realistic self-talk helps avoid the trap of thinking negatively out of habit. Forcing yourself to think more realistically will not be easy at first. However, with practice, it will become more natural and help you have a more positive view of your child.

"She would always tell me that her dad would let her

do this and do that. It made me so angry."

Sylvia, thirty-two, mother of one

22

Expect Your Child to Play One Parent Against the Other

ALL CHILDREN ARE going to test limits. In fact, most of us test limits every day. Do you always follow the speed limit when you drive? If you are like most people, you probably drive over the speed limit at times. In fact, the average speed of cars on most highways is a few miles per hour over the posted speed limit. People drive over the speed limit because they think that they can get away with it—and in most cases they do! However, if a system existed to ticket drivers every time they went over the speed limit, people would not speed. The bottom line is that people are going to test limits if they think they can get away with it.

Following a divorce, children often test limits more frequently because they are more successful at it. Why are they more successful? Well, one reason is that with poorer communication between parents, children are often more successful playing parents against each other. Many parents find themselves competing for their child's affection, and they don't want to be seen as the "mean" parent, so they acquiesce. You know your child is playing you and your ex-spouse against each other when you hear statements such as these:

"But Dad lets me stay up until 11:00 P.M."
"Mom lets me watch R-rated movies."
"Mom said I didn't need to study this weekend."
"But Dad lets me do it."

It is important to realize that playing one parent against the other doesn't have to always work for your child for her to keep doing it. Why would a child continue to do this if it often doesn't work? From a child's perspective, she just needs to think that there is a chance that it might work this time. In many ways it's a game of odds. Let's look at casino gambling to help clarify this point. People continue to put money into slot machines knowing that the machine is not going to pay off every time (or even most of the time) they insert their money. However, in their minds they think that just maybe the next time they will hit the jackpot. If the slot machines were reprogrammed to never pay off, people would stop inserting their money (and casinos would go out of business). But the people who run casinos are very smart; they program their slot machines to pay off just enough to keep people playing. So let's get back to what all this means in regard to your child playing you against your ex-spouse. The bottom line is that if it works just occasionally, it might be enough to keep her doing it.

Here is what we recommend:

- When your child tells you that her other parent lets her do something that you don't allow, state matter-of-factly that when she is with you, she has to follow your rules.

- Remember that children are sometimes prone to absolute thinking. "My dad *always* lets me stay up past my bedtime" may mean it happened a few times. You need to realize this. Don't argue with your child about it or become upset with your ex-spouse. Rather, as we have just said, enforce your own rules.

- Discuss with your ex-spouse incidents where you feel your child was playing the two of you against each other. Do not come across in an accusing manner; instead, ask for clarification. You may discover that "Mom lets me watch R-rated movies" really means that your child once saw three minutes of an R-rated movie.

"He was always coming up with some excuse about

why he couldn't send the money."

Jackie, thirty-five, mother of four

23
Maintain Regular Child Support Payments

AN IMPORTANT ROLE that a noncustodial parent, usually the father, can play in his child's life is to make regular child support payments. When payments are made, a child's standard of living is more likely maintained and, as Paul Amato of Pennsylvania State University has pointed out, a child's health, educational attainment, and general well-being also are more likely maintained. Just think about this for a moment: following divorce the custodial parent and child typically face a significant decline in their standard of living. Child support payments can help offset some of this decline for your child. If lack of finances results in moving, decreasing extracurricular activities, changing schools, and losing friends, it can cause a downward spiral of negative influences on your child.

Unfortunately, as I-Fen Lin of Princeton University has noted, only about half of the custodial mothers have an active child support order and only one-fourth of mothers actually receive the full amount of support they are mandated to receive. What are some reasons why fathers don't make child support payments? Both a father's ability to pay and the extent to which he perceives the amount to be paid as fair have been identified as significant factors. Unfortunately, about half of noncustodial fathers do not view their child support orders as fair.

You have to realize that money has tremendous emotional overtones, and financial issues can bring out the worst in people. If money was a big issue during your marriage, you can bet that it will probably be an even bigger issue in your divorce. Nonpayment of child support is not confined to noncustodial fathers. Fathers with custody are even less likely than custodial mothers to receive eligible child support from their ex-spouse. If you are a noncustodial parent, you must separate your negative feelings about your ex-spouse from the needs of your child. You must convince yourself that child support payments are important to your child and make a personal commitment to yourself to make the payments as arranged.

How large should a child support payment be? This is not an easy question to answer, and the actual payment depends to a great extent on the state in which you live. Some states, such as Massachusetts and Wisconsin, require substantially higher payments than other states. The District of Columbia and some states, such as Mississippi and South Carolina, are at the lower end of the scale. If possible, you and your ex-spouse need to work together to reach an amount that you both, more or less, perceive as fair. If you can't, find a mediator to help you reach an agreement. If the two of you alone or with the help of a mediator cannot reach an agreed upon amount, a judge will do it for you. This is generally not best for either you or your ex-spouse, as you both are giving up all control. You will also be paying more legal fees and helping pay your attorney's house payments or rent rather than your own.

States also vary in their effectiveness to enforce child support payments. In general, legislation reforms in the past several years have focused both on nonresidential parents paying more child support and on providing the government with new methods of ensuring that the payment is made. Remember that it is illegal not to pay court-ordered child support. The resources section contains information on resources to help you collect child support when you are not receiving payments on a regular basis.

As noted, regular child support payments are important in enhancing your child's life and adjustment. Here are our recommendations:

- View the child support payments as primarily benefiting your child, not your ex-spouse.

- Try to work out child support payments that are—to the extent possible—agreeable to both you and your ex-spouse.

- Seek the help of a mediator if you and your ex-spouse cannot agree.

- If you are the noncustodial parent, make the commitment to prioritize the payment of the agreed upon child support payments in a timely and regular fashion.

- If you are the custodial parent, do not plan for the future anticipating that the child support payments will always be stable. What happens if your ex-spouse loses his job or becomes ill? You will need to be flexible if such problems arise. Have a plan for what you can do to lower expenses or increase income if for some reason your ex-spouse cannot, or does not, make child support payments.

- If you are the noncustodial parent, do not withhold payments as punishment for your ex-spouse. You are really punishing only your child.

- If you are the custodial parent, do not withhold contact with your child from his other parent for nonpayment of child support. You are punishing your child even further. Remember the old saying, "Two wrongs don't make a right."

"The worst part of my parents' divorce was having to

move to a different town where I didn't know anyone."

Caroline, fifteen

24

Minimize Changes

CHILDREN TYPICALLY function best when there is routine and stability in their lives. Unfortunately, parental divorce often leads to instability and major change in children's lives. Such changes are associated with a sense of uncertainty, and, for some children, uncertainty can lead to feelings of fear, anxiety, and, in some cases, depression.

Let's think a little further about change in the life of children. Many key decisions that significantly affect children, especially young children, are made by adults. Examples of such decisions would include the decision for parents to divorce, where the family will live, and whom the parent dates or remarries following the divorce. With little control over such major decisions, children rely on day-to-day routines and predictability for a sense of stability and security in their lives. When parents divorce, children naturally experience feelings of uncertainty and instability that are worsened if there also is a lot of change in their day-to-day routines. Therefore, it is important for parents to be keenly aware of such changes.

Changes in daily routines that follow divorce are instantly obvious to a child and may have fairly immediate consequences. Some children may respond by withdrawing, and others may respond by acting out. In both cases the child is probably communicating that the sense of security she felt through the predictability of her daily life has been compromised.

Let's look at some of the changes that may occur with parental divorce. First, consider routines within your home. For many parents who divorce, routine family activities (for example, mealtime, bedtime, homework time) become less consistent. One child gave us this example, "My whole family used to always have dinner together right after Dad came home from work. Now, Mom works night shifts and we all kind of fix our own dinner and eat whenever we want to." In many families there are a multitude of changes that, when combined, can lead children to have even more difficulties adjusting to divorce.

Let's look at another type of change that often occurs following divorce. Because of the stress related to divorce, many parents no longer have the time or energy to supervise their child completing her homework as closely as they did prior to the divorce. A set time for homework (for example, before dinner) may be discarded because of other responsibilities falling on the parent. With more variability in when homework is done, the parent also might be less likely to effectively monitor how well a child is doing her schoolwork and to provide assistance when needed. Such changes in routine obviously will influence a child's achievement in school.

Sometimes we don't recognize the significance to our children of certain changes. In the Introduction we presented children's ratings of the ten most stressful events associated with the divorce of their parents. One of these stressful events was having to give up a pet. Because many children rely on pets for friendship and companionship, it is understandable why having to give up a pet is stressful. Unfortunately, divorce may mean moving to a place that doesn't allow pets, or it may cause financial pressures that can lead to a child no longer being able to keep the pet. The loss of a pet can be very difficult for any child, but when the child is also coping with the divorce of her parents, it can be particularly painful. As Jennifer, a young adult, told us, "My parents divorced when I was four years old. All I can really remember is that I was upset because I could not understand why my dad, instead of mom and me, kept our dog."

Let's next consider change in routines that may occur outside the home when parents divorce. For some children, attending preschool, church, or other such activities may become more erratic because of the stress and demands on the family. When attendance is irregular, it can lead to a child becoming more resistant and emotional around getting ready to go to these activities. Because parents are already stressed, they may give in to this resistance, and over time attendance will become less and less frequent.

Some changes affect older children and teenagers through their peer relationships. For example, after divorce there is less money available for a child's activities. As a result, the teenager may be cut off from her regular peer activities because she no longer has the money to go to a movie or events with her friends. This change, especially for a teenager, can be frustrating and, again, may lead to either withdrawing from the family or acting out.

A change that occurs all too often is that the custodial parent and child have to move. This is understandable, as their income may be cut by half or more when a divorce occurs. As a result, a move becomes a necessity. Unfortunately, a child already may feel like she has lost a parent and now must experience the loss of the familiar surroundings of her home. Let's consider for a few moments what a move following a divorce means to a child. It frequently means loss of friends and familiar adults in the neighborhood. Furthermore, moving may take a child farther away from relatives, such as grandparents. Finally, and of significant importance, a move may require that a child change schools, which means leaving her classmates and teachers. In the words of Kristi, "Most of all I hated having to leave my house and my school. It just wasn't fair. Why did I have to leave? I wasn't the one getting the divorce."

Finally, let's consider one other change associated with divorce: a child's loss of time with each of her parents. For a noncustodial parent, time with his child is going to be limited to visitation days. This can be difficult for a child; however, the problem is compounded when the custodial parent also has to decrease her time with a child. Frequently, this parent has to work more hours to make an adequate income for the family as well as handle added responsibilities at home—not an easy task for a parent. Unfortunately, a busier schedule for a parent also means less time with her child.

Let's now consider some solutions. Minimize change as much as possible. This is obviously an admirable solution but one that is very difficult. Nevertheless, we encourage you to make as few changes as possible, at least for one year following the separation. By minimizing change during the first year, you will make it much easier for your child to realize that she is in a stable family where her physical and emotional needs will be met.

To minimize changes within your home, you are going to have to make concerted efforts. We recognize that these efforts will be difficult, especially considering the additional demands and stresses put upon you as a single parent. However, by minimizing changes in household routines, not only will your child's life remain more consistent and pre-dictable, but so will your life. Remember that this is as important for you as it is for your child.

In addition to maintaining routines within the home, try to be consistent in maintaining routines outside of the home. Your child should not be allowed to skip important activities because you are too "stressed out," do not have the energy to fight the battle of going to the activity, or feel guilty about the divorce. Activities that your child was involved in prior to the divorce (e.g., scouts, sports, music, dance) should be continued following the divorce, whenever possible. These will provide your child with ongoing contact with other children and adults that she is used to being around, as well as send the message to your child that her life is continuing in a predictable and stable manner.

In terms of maintaining activities outside of the house, you obvi-ously need to carefully examine your resources. We would propose that a priority for you is to continue to provide as many opportunities for your child to interact with her friends as she had before the divorce. This will help prevent her from feeling that she is "suffering" (and chil-dren, particularly teenagers, will think they are suffering!) as a result of the divorce. Furthermore, after the divorce, friends may act as a stabi-lizing influence for a child.

In terms of moving, it is important not to move in the first year after divorce if at all possible. Research by Christy Buchanan and her colleagues at Stanford University has provided support for the premise that changing residences after parental separation is associated with adjustment difficulties for children. Moving can be stressful for all children but it is often much more difficult for children when they are already coping with their parents' divorce.

Also of importance is maintaining, as much as possible, the amount of time you spend with your child. Simply being there and being available to your child is critical, whether you are the custodial or noncustodial parent. Obviously, if you are the noncustodial parent you can't be with your child as much as you might like, but you can make yourself available to your child by phone or other means. We know that maintaining your time with, or availability to, your child following your divorce can be very difficult, but it can make an enormous difference in the life of your child.

If a major change does have to occur, it is important that you prepare your child for that change. Sit down with her and explain why the change is necessary (e.g., why you are having to move). This should be done in a matter-of-fact and nonblaming manner (i.e., don't say "because your father won't give us enough money" but rather something like "we need to live within our budget"). Also, tell her when this change will occur. Have this discussion with your child several weeks before the change is to occur so that she will have the opportunity to adjust to it. You also should repeat the "why" and "when" discussion a second time to make sure your child understands and to provide her with the opportunity to ask questions and express her feelings. It may be unpleasant, but it is important.

Here are our recommendations:

- Minimize change as much as possible.

- Maintain household routines and time you spend with your child. These are things over which you do have some control.

- When changes have to occur, prepare your child for them.

"Both of my parents had always taken me out to eat

on the last day of school. After the divorce, they still

did it every year. It made me feel like they really

supported me together."

Jake, seventeen

25

Maintain Family Traditions and Rituals

WHEN PARENTS DIVORCE, family life, as it has been known, forever changes. As we have already discussed, it is important for your child's adjustment that you minimize these changes as much as possible. One area of change that is often overlooked is the family's traditions and rituals.

We as parents often don't realize the important role these traditions and rituals play in our child's sense of security and identity. Family traditions, especially those that are passed down from your own childhood, can become very meaningful to your child and help give him a sense of his family roots. Having a Halloween party, helping cook on Thanksgiving, or singing carols on Christmas Eve are important activities to many children. They are the things your child will remember when he has children of his own. Therefore, you don't want your divorce to end all of these family traditions. Unfortunately, following divorce most parents are unable to equally participate in established family traditions around holidays because they are not together with their child. This can be hard on children and on the parents. However, the important message to get across to your child is that both of you as parents will work to maintain as many of your traditions as you can, with as few modifications as possible. Whenever possible, try to develop win-win situations for all involved. For example, on Halloween your child could trick-or-treat with Mom in her neighborhood for an hour and then go with Dad to his neighborhood for an hour. Splitting holiday time traditions can also work well for many families (Christmas Eve celebrations with one parent and Christmas Day with the other parent).

There is also an opportunity following divorce to establish new traditions, which can supplement the old traditions. These new traditions can become just as meaningful over the years as the old ones were. The new traditions do not have to be associated with major holidays. The traditions can be unusual, idiosyncratic, and important to only your family. For instance, a family was playing tennis for the first time one year on the day before Easter. A rabbit ran by the tennis court, and the youngest child thought it was the Easter Bunny. Following tennis, they went to Waffle House to eat dinner. Nothing else was said, and they didn't play tennis again that year. The next year at Easter time the young children remembered, to their parent's amazement, seeing the "real" Easter Bunny, playing tennis, and going to Waffle House on the day before Easter and wanted to do the same thing. Well, they played their annual game of tennis and went to Waffle House that year and for the next ten years, although they never saw the rabbit again. That became a very important tradition for those children and helped identify the uniqueness of their family. The point of this example is that family traditions can be almost anything that helps children see their family as special and unique.

While family traditions are important, so are the minor rituals that occur on a much more frequent basis. Rituals, such as all family members telling at dinner each night what they did that day, bedtime routines with stories, or Saturday trips to the park, can be very important to a child. While both parents will not participate together in most of these activities following divorce, each parent should try to maintain the activities when they are with their children. They really do provide a sense of stability and security that is critically needed following divorce.

Here are our recommendations:

- Identify your family's traditions and rituals.

- Next, and of primary importance, maintain these traditions and rituals as much as possible following your divorce.

- Consider developing new rituals to supplement the old ones.

"When we said we would share in all decisions that would impact our child, I wasn't thinking about all the little decisions that would need input from both of us. I wish we had created a list and gone over it together at the time we were going through the divorce."

Kelly, thirty, mother of two

26

Develop a Parenting Plan

THE WAY TO PARENT most effectively is to have a plan! It is much better to be proactive than reactive, especially following a divorce. Some states now require that parents submit specific plans for how they are going to parent their child after the divorce. As Robert Emery of the University of Virginia has pointed out, the purpose of a parenting plan is to encourage creative, individualized, and clear arrangements, as well as to facilitate cooperative parenting. Having a plan can make it easier for you and your ex-spouse to work together as parents and reduce the amount of conflict between you.

The place where you live may not legally require a parenting plan. However, as we have just noted, a parenting plan can be beneficial for you, your ex-spouse, and, particularly, your child. Therefore, we would encourage you to give consideration to developing such a plan whether it is legally required or not. The example on pages 120 to 121 represents a typical parenting plan. At a minimum, you need to consider the topics that are usually addressed in a parenting plan because these will be ones that you eventually will have to address with your ex-spouse.

Joan McWilliams, an attorney and mediator in Colorado, points out that a parenting plan contains at least three sections:

1. Decision Making—How will you make decisions for your child?
2. Visitation—How will your child spend time with each parent?
3. Dispute Resolution—What happens if you and your ex-spouse do not agree?

Let's look at each of these three components of a parenting plan.

There are decisions that you will need to make in each of the following areas. First are health decisions, which involve issues such as who will be responsible for paying medical insurance, who will make medical appointments, who will take your child to the appointment, who will care for your child when she is sick, and who will pay the medical expenses not covered by your health plan. Second are decisions regarding education. These involve issues such as how you will decide what school your child will attend, how each of you will participate in school activities, how school announcements and report cards will be shared, who will have access to your child's school records, and who will be identified on school records as the parent to be notified in case of an emergency. Third are religious decisions. These include who will decide about the choice of religion for your child, how each parent will participate or not participate in religious training, and how religious holidays will be celebrated. Finally are decisions that can promote the general welfare of your child. These can include almost anything, but some examples are how you and your ex-spouse communicate with each other, rules regarding how each of you entertain dates in the presence of your child, what happens if one of the two of you decides to move to a distant location, and who will be the guardian of your child in the event of both of your deaths. As is obvious, there are a number of decisions that you face, and the clearer you can be about how each of these will be addressed, the better it will be for your child.

Excerpts from a Sample Parenting Plan

The purpose of this plan is to help us, Pat Wood and Todd Wood, better meet our responsibilities as parents and to help our child, Christina Wood, adjust to our divorce. We both support Christina's need to love each of us regardless of our marital status or where we live. We both realize that it is in Christina's best interest for us to cooperate as partners in parenting and to each provide her with the love and caring she needs from both of us. We agree to cooperate with each other in developing mutually acceptable plans for handling Christina's education, health, and other aspects of her care and development.

Decision Making

Education: Christina will continue to attend Eastside Elementary School. Pat will provide Todd with a copy of all semester report cards and inform him of any significant school event (e.g., open houses, plays, parent-teacher conferences). Any decision to change schools will be mutually decided. Pat will be listed on school records as the first person to contact in case of emergency, and Todd will be listed second. Any significant school-related problems (e.g., academic or behavioral problems) that come to the attention of either parent will be shared with the other parent.

Health Care: Christina will continue to be covered by Todd's health and dental insurance plans. Todd will communicate any changes to these plans to Pat. Todd will be responsible for 80 percent of noncovered health- and dental-care costs and Pat the remaining 20 percent. Pat will be responsible for making routine health-care and dental appointments. Day-to-day health-care decisions (e.g., whether she needs to go to the doctor) will be the responsibility of the parent Christina is with at the time. Any significant health-care issues will be communicated to the other parent. Major health- and dental-care decisions (e.g., nonemergency surgery, orthodontic work) will be shared.

Religion: We both agree to continue raising Christina in the Methodist church. We each agree to attend church with Christina on a regular basis when she is in our care.

Discipline: We agree to discuss issues related to Christina's behavior and discipline on a regular basis so that we can strive for mutually agreeable approaches. However, where differences exist, we will each honor the other's parenting style and authority, recognizing that there is not one right way to parent and that rarely will two parents consistently handle behavior problems or issues in exactly the same way.

Contact with Extended Family: We both agree to support Christina's continued contact with both Todd's and Pat's extended family members.

- _____
- _____
- _____

Handling Disputes

Each year in June (or at any time if serious problems develop), we will review this plan and, if revisions are necessary, we will attempt to negotiate mutually agreeable changes. We both commit to trying our best to resolve issues pertaining to the plan and to disagreements regarding parenting issues. If we are unable to resolve disagreements, we both agree to work with a mutually selected mediator or objective third party to help us develop solutions with which we can both agree. We will split the cost of the mediator or other professional (Todd and Pat will each pay 50 percent).

_____ _____   _____ _____
Signature   Date   Signature   Date

The second component of a parenting agreement has to do with the time your child will spend with each of you. We have already identified a number of issues and recommendations around visitation (see Part 4, "Visitation Issues"). Obviously, in trying to develop a visitation schedule, you have to work around what is best for your child and what is best and most feasible for each of you as parents. This requires a great deal of thought, patience, and cooperation.

The final component of a parenting plan is how to handle disagreements. Obviously, you are not going to agree all of the time. Sometimes when you disagree, you may be able to reach a compromise. At other times, one parent may have the authority to make the final decision. In other cases, you may have to seek outside help, such as mediation, to resolve a conflict (see Strategy #5, "Avoid Custody Disputes: Consider Mediation"). The more you can specify in advance how you will resolve disagreements, the less conflict you will have.

Parenting plans can cover a lot of issues that are decided in court or in mediation. So you will need to work in collaboration with your attorney/mediator. However, if you are able to resolve many of these issues outside of the courtroom, it will put you on the right track to helping your child adjust to the divorce.

Here are our recommendations:

- Develop a parenting plan with your ex-spouse as soon as possible. Focus on decision making, visitation issues, and dispute resolution. A professional mediator can often help the two of you develop a plan if you are having a hard time on your own.

- Emphasize with your ex-spouse that the goal of a parenting plan is to clarify parenting issues, avoid conflict, and help your child. The earlier in the divorce process this can be accomplished, the less conflict there will be and the better your child will adjust.

- Set a time with your ex-spouse to reevaluate the parenting plan. Your plan will need to be modified at times, but by working together in the best interests of your child, the two of you will be able to make modifications acceptable to all parties.

"I really liked the times I spent with my parents talking

to them about when they were little kids."

Jose, sixteen

27
Nurture Your Relationship with Your Child

CHILDREN ARE AFRAID that when their parents divorce, their relationship with one or both parents will suffer. Unfortunately, this fear is often well founded. While it is easy to imagine that the relationship between the noncustodial parent and his child will deteriorate, it is also a problem for a custodial parent. Paul Amato of Pennsylvania State University and his colleagues have carefully examined a large number of studies in this area and have concluded that children in divorced, single-parent families have less positive relationships with their custodial parents than do children in intact families. Simply stated, the parent-child relationship is at risk for deterioration after divorce for both custodial and noncustodial parents.

Research by Carolyn Webster-Stratton at the University of Washington offers some insight into what can happen if the parent-child relationship deteriorates following divorce. She studied the mother-child interactions of single mothers, married mothers in families where there was a supportive marital relationship, and married mothers in families where there was marital distress. When compared to mothers in the two married groups, the single mothers issued more critical statements, questions, and commands when interacting with their children, and, in turn, their children displayed more behavior problems. While this study focused on mothers, other research studies suggest that it is the father-child relationship that typically deteriorates the most following divorce.

It is critical for you as a divorcing parent to understand the importance of the parent-child relationship following a divorce: a positive parent-child relationship is among the best predictors of children's post-divorce adjustment. Research by Robert Hess at Stanford University and Kathleen Camara at Tufts University indicates that the negative effects of divorce on children are greatly reduced when there are positive relationships with both parents. In their study, children who maintained positive relationships with both parents had lower scores on measures of stress and aggression and higher ratings on schoolwork style (preparedness, concentration, attentiveness, task completion, and toleration of delay) and social interactions with peers (peer acceptance, friendship patterns, and sociability). Hess and Camara also found that children can do relatively well even if a positive relationship with only one parent can be maintained. It is the children who have a poor relationship with both parents who do not fare well at all following divorce. The importance of the parent-child relationship in promoting a child's adjustment during parental divorce has been replicated in a number of scientific studies, including work from our own research.

If your child is to adjust well to your divorce, nurturing the parent-child relationship is paramount. A positive parent-child relationship involves affection, warmth, effective communication, appropriate boundaries and discipline, mutual respect and caring, child-oriented time spent together, and a general enjoyment of each other's company. It is vital to recognize the importance of developing a more positive relationship between you and your child.

Here are our recommendations on how this can be accomplished:

- Be an "askable" parent. A child needs to feel comfortable asking parents any type of question without fear of ridicule or rejection.

An "askable" parent does not withdraw love or support if what is heard is disappointing or less than appropriate. By listening with your mouth closed, you are inviting your child to communicate with you. We want our children to ask questions and express feelings; therefore, we must be willing to hear what they have to say. This means developing the valuable skill of talking less and listening more.

- Beyond being an "askable" parent, utilize other effective communication skills. The same general skills for effective communication with your ex-spouse (see Strategy #10, "Communicate Effectively with Your Ex-Spouse") will improve your communication and relationship with your child—or with anyone! Communication skills, which will help you solve problems between you and your child, include these: be polite, set goals for a discussion, work on one problem at a time, state your opinion or feelings, request feedback and take turns talking, and focus on developing solutions. Of course, the language you use will depend on the age of your child; however, the message is the same: be polite, focused, honest, open, and receptive.

- Spend special time with your child. With limited time and frazzled emotions, a parent going through a divorce might aim for at least twenty minutes a day of special time with your child (when the child is with you). This special time is simply sharing your child's experience "in the moment" without judgments, criticisms, or questions. It might involve talking with your child about issues of interest to him when there are few distractions (e.g., right before he goes to bed), playing a game with him, or having a hobby you work on together. Let your child choose, within reason, what he wants to do during his special time. Such special time is a wonderful gift to a child. It should be consistent throughout good times, bad times, chaotic times, and even mediocre times. It is the foundation for a positive parent-child relationship. (Remember that it is never too late in a child's life to start with special time. This works as well for teenagers as it does for preschoolers.)

- Have fun with your child (see Strategy #28, "Have Fun with Your Child"). Find activities that you both enjoy and can have fun doing together. Make sure that they are things that involve the two of you interacting and not just being in each other's presence. Provide your child with plenty of affection, encouragement, and praise during these times. It is through the fun times you spend together that you both develop a greater sense of caring, under-standing, appreciation, and cooperation.

- Express your love for your child (see Strategy #29, "Communicate 'I Love You' to Your Child"). Many parents love their child in their hearts but do not do a good job of communicating that love to their child. Don't be hesitant to tell your child that you love him. However, actions speak louder than words. Hug your child. Try to be creative in expressing your love in a manner that will be mean-ingful to your child. For some children this might involve creating a photo album or scrapbook for them; for others it might be more meaningful to hang their artwork in your home or for you to wear something they made for you. For some children of divorce, the greatest expression of love is a parent's understanding and true acceptance of the child's love of their other parent.

"My favorite times growing up were when my dad

and I went fishing together."

Sidney, sixteen

28

Have Fun with Your Child

YOU CAN STRENGTHEN your relationship with your child during and after the divorce by making sure you have fun together. The best way to do this is to find activities that you can both enjoy. If you are doing something that you don't enjoy as much as your child does, the activity will become more of a chore than a means to further strengthen the relationship between you and your child. Always keep in mind that while having fun is enjoyable, the primary benefit of doing fun things together is that it allows your relationship with your child to be strengthened.

The activities that you do with your child should be interactive. You need to be observing and responding to each other. It's that type of interpersonal interaction that deepens and strengthens relationships. Some examples of interactive activities, particularly for preadolescent children, can be found in the box on page 128. Having fun together often is more difficult with adolescents; however, there are many things you can do even with an adolescent. And, both of you can actually enjoy the activities. For example, hiking, bike riding, shopping (as long as you are buying something for your adolescent, of course), and playing board or video games together are some potential activities. As Alex told us, "One of my most favorite memories growing up was helping my dad restore a '57 Chevy on the weekends I spent with him."

Examples of Interactive Activities

Collecting things	Hiking
Camping	Cooking
Collecting sports cards	Fishing
Making crafts	Gardening
Doing puzzles	Participating in sports
Going to sports events	Hunting
Biking	Building models
Playing board games	Exercising
Sewing	Playing music
Jogging	Needlepoint/sewing
Creating art	Skating
Doing community service	Participating in church activities

Doing fun things together helps you to understand your child better, including her strengths and weaknesses. It also provides both of you with the opportunity to develop a greater sense of caring and respect for each other. This can lead to your becoming a more "askable" parent. In other words, your child will feel more comfortable asking you any type of question, even about the divorce, without fear of ridicule or rejection.

As expressed in one of our favorite verses, which can be found at the entrance to the Louisiana Children's Museum in New Orleans, you can teach your child most effectively through play:

> *I tried to teach*
> *my child with books.*
>
> *He gave me only*
> *puzzled looks.*

I tried to teach
  my child with words.

They passed him by
  often unheard.

Despairingly
  I turned aside.

"How shall I teach
  this child?" I cried.

Into my hand
  he put the key.

"Come," he said,
  "play with me."

Author Unknown

Here is what we recommend:

- Decide on interactive activities that you and your child both enjoy.

- Regardless of the stress you are experiencing in your life, make the time to do these fun things with your child. We guarantee you will feel better by doing these activities. And, you will deepen and strengthen your relationship with your child.

"My mom used to always put little notes in my lunch

bag telling me how much she loved me. It made me

feel real special and lucky to have my mom."

Christina, thirteen

29
Communicate "I Love You" to Your Child

MOST OF US THINK we communicate our love for our children to them more effectively than we actually do. This can be especially true during the stressful times of divorce. However, this is exactly the time that you need to let your child know you love him: he may mistakenly think that because you no longer love your spouse, you also no longer love him. Although you may feel an enormous amount of love in your heart for your child, how well do you let him know the depth of your love? How often do you tell him that you love him through both your words and actions?

Of course your words must be consistent with your actions. Just telling your child that you love him is not enough. Just like adults, children will look at your actions to determine whether your words of love are sincere. As Jackie told us, "My dad would tell me how much he loved me and all that stuff. But then he would forget about promises he made to me. A lot of times he would just not show up to pick me up. He would always come up with some lame excuse, and I remember thinking: if you really loved me, you wouldn't be doing this to me."

Being there for your child's sports events, music recitals, dance performances, school plays, and other activities is extremely important. If an event is important to your child, you should be there if at all possible. It can mean a lot to children if both parents can attend such events and be cordial toward each other. This, of course, requires good communication between parents (and we know that may be difficult) in terms of making sure both of you are aware of all significant events on your child's schedule. It is also important for parents to be involved in their child's school activities. This communicates not only your care and love for your child but also the importance of school and learning. Volunteer to help with field trips, class parties, dances, and other school activities even if it means taking some time off from work. This is just as important for dads as it is for moms.

The following list includes some additional suggestions from our book *Parenting the Strong-Willed Child* of how you can communicate your love to your child. Of course, these need to be tailored to your particular child, which will be partially dependent on his age and personality. What is a clear message of "I love you" to a young child may be a real turnoff to an adolescent. Also, remember that communicating your love through both your words and actions is important.

- Say "I love you." Simply saying this is important and needs to occur on a regular basis.

- Leave little signs with hearts or "I ♥ U" on them around the house in places your child will find them (for example, by his bed and in his coat pocket).

- Give your child a lot of physical affection. Hugs can really make a child feel loved.

- Let your child overhear you talking to someone else about your love for him. Sometimes this can be more powerful than telling your child directly.

- Start and maintain a family photo album or scrapbook for your child. This lets him know that you think he is important and loved. Put selected photos, artwork, and other information about your child in the album and let him keep it in his room.

- Have photographs of your child displayed around your home.

- Write letters to your child about his positive qualities.

- Display your child's successful school projects, artwork, and athletic awards. Be creative! One family had their children's artwork framed in museum-type frames and hung them throughout their house alongside their professional artwork.

Spend some time generating a list of ways to say, "I love you" that will be especially meaningful to your child.

"I am just so thankful that my mom and I had the

kind of relationship where I could really open up

to her and tell her exactly how I was feeling."

Jordan, seventeen

30
Encourage Your Child to Express Feelings

As ADULTS, ONE OF the things that some of us do when we are faced with stress, such as the stress that accompanies divorce, is to "bury our feelings inside." In essence, we avoid thinking about our problems and feelings. This is what we were talking about earlier when we discussed the avoidant style of coping (see Strategy #7, "Examine Your Coping Style"). If you remember, the research has found an avoidant style of coping to be generally unhealthy. Just as it is important to avoid bottling up your own emotions, it is also important to help your child avoid bottling up her emotions. This may be particularly difficult for you if you are prone to avoidant coping yourself.

Annie's words highlight the importance of trying to help your child express her feelings: "I used to hold it all inside of me. I'd be walking around just full of all these feelings, thinking I was going to explode. It made me mad at everyone and after a while my friends didn't want to hang out with me. I finally found someone who would listen and I could trust. I found that when you talk about how you feel about things, things don't bother you as much."

Fortunately, some children, like some adults, do not have difficulty expressing their feelings. However, if your child tends to bottle up her emotions, it is important to realize that you can't force her to talk about her feelings. What you can do, however, is "set the stage" for her to feel comfortable enough talking to you to express how she feels. This means providing frequent opportunities for the two of you to talk about a variety of issues privately and without interruptions. It also means that you develop your relationship to the point where you are "askable" and she feels safe in being honest with you without fear that you'll discount her feelings (see Strategy #27, "Nurture Your Relationship with Your Child"). With the stage set, you can provide prompts (for example, "How do you feel about . . .") to give her the opportunity to reveal her feelings. If she doesn't want to share her feelings, back off and don't try to force the issue. Wait and try again another day.

There are many books about divorce that have been written for children of various ages. There are books that you can read to young children and books that older children and adolescents can read themselves (see the resources section for a listing of some of these). You should consider using some of these books to help your child realize that many of her feelings are normal. After reading the books, discuss them with your child. This can create a great opportunity for you and your child to talk about her thoughts, concerns, and feelings.

When your child does express her feelings, do not overreact or discount them. Use the opportunity to help her learn how to best cope. You can help her explore the different options that emotion-focused and problem-focused coping strategies provide (see Strategy #7, "Examine Your Coping Style"). Remember that the problem-focused approach can be the best approach if your child has control over the situation that is causing the problem. Unfortunately, when it comes to divorce-related problems, children often have little control over the situation. Therefore, an emotion-focused approach, where your child learns how to best deal with her emotions, is often what you need to focus on with your child. This might involve looking at the issue from a different perspective, learning to control anger, or just accepting the reality of the situation. Sometimes just talking about feelings can be helpful, as we saw in Annie's words previously.

Here is what we recommend:

- Acknowledge that talking about feelings is helpful.

- Create the opportunities and relationship necessary for your child to open up to you about her feelings.

- Encourage, but don't try to force, your child to express her feelings about divorce issues.

- Utilize books written for children about divorce (see the resources section) to provide opportunities for your child to talk about her feelings.

"I knew I could always get my dad to give in if I told him

that mom let me do it—even though she usually didn't."

Rachel, sixteen

31

Be Consistent with Discipline

BEFORE DISCUSSING consistency of discipline, let's take a few moments to understand what we mean by discipline. Most parents equate discipline with punishment. However, discipline is more than just punishment. To discipline means "to teach." So when we talk about disciplining children, we are talking not only about using punishment to teach them what *not* to do but also about using positive feedback and guidance and providing examples to teach them what *to* do. If we are going to be effective in disciplining our children, we need to make sure that we don't focus just on the punishment side of discipline.

It is understandable that being consistent in discipline is difficult even under the best of circumstances. Following divorce, it often becomes infinitely more difficult. But it is very important for your child that you make the effort to strive for as much consistency as possible. The more consistency there is, the easier it will be to teach your child how to behave appropriately.

There are really two types of consistency of discipline. While most of us initially think about consistency between parents, the first type of consistency we are going to discuss is consistency within ourselves in how we discipline our child. For example, you may be harsh with your child when you are under a lot of stress and in a bad mood, and you may be overly lax when you are in a good mood. When you are inconsistent like that and perhaps punishing your child for something he does one day and not punishing him for doing the same thing on another day, your child is more likely to misbehave and test limits. Your child needs to know that when he breaks a rule or misbehaves there will be consistent consequences. As we recommend in our parenting book *Parenting the Strong-Willed Child*, time-out, when used correctly and in combination with positive approaches for appropriate behavior, is an effective strategy for handling the misbehavior of young children. For older children, taking away privileges and grounding can be effective. Regardless of your child's age, by having clearly stated rules about what behaviors are and are not allowed and consistent consequences (both positive and negative), you will be more effective in teaching your child to behave well.

Let's consider for a moment some factors that may lead to your becoming inconsistent in your disciplinary parenting strategies. One good example is drinking alcohol. Some parents become more lenient whenever they drink in that they let their children do things they normally would not allow them to do. On the other hand, other parents become less tolerant and more harsh in discipline when they drink. In either case, discipline becomes inconsistent, and the child may become confused about what is or is not allowed.

Let's look at another example. For most parents, when they are stressed, their discipline becomes more inconsistent. This particularly happens for parents who do not have good coping skills (see Strategies #7, "Examine Your Coping Style," and #9, "Manage the Stress in Your Life"). When you are under stress and cope poorly, the consistency of your discipline may change, as you may become less tolerant or, on the other hand, ignore behaviors you typically discipline. Again, neither is beneficial for your child.

Let's consider one final example. If you are the custodial parent, a particularly difficult time to be consistent is immediately after your child has spent time with your ex-spouse. Your child likely will have been living under a different set of rules during his time with your ex-spouse. You may feel that it will be too hard on him to reinstitute the rules and disciplinary practices you have been using in your house. However, it is critical that you remain firm in upholding your rules, even when your child tests you to see if you will loosen up. (And, as we indicated in Strategy #22, "Expect Your Child to Play One Parent Against the Other," he will test you!) Be prepared to respond to, "But dad lets me. . . ." We recommend that you clearly state something like, "Well, when you are with your dad that might be OK with him, but when you are with me the rule is. . . ." When you are consistent in upholding your rules, your child learns that testing limits won't work, and he learns to abide by your rules.

The second type of discipline consistency is *across* parents. That is, you and your ex-spouse will vary in how you discipline your child. Some parents are obviously more consistent in how they discipline their child than other parents are. Research by Christy Buchanan and her colleagues at Stanford University found that, when divorced parents are inconsistent with each other in terms of how they manage their child's behavior, it takes an emotional toll on their child. Thus, in terms of discipline, a goal is for parents to be consistent not only within themselves but also with each other. Obviously, this is a difficult task because no two parents are ever going to be totally consistent, especially following divorce. However, it is important for parents to talk to each other about discipline and try to agree on using a similar approach. Unfortunately, some parents cannot agree on a common approach to discipline. If this is the case with you and your ex-spouse, then you need to focus on these two things:

1. Most children will handle differences in parenting styles better than you expect (see Strategy #16, "Redefine Your Relationship with Your Ex-Spouse").
2. You can still be consistent in the way you deal with your child across time, as we discussed previously.

Here is what we recommend:

- Carefully monitor the stress level you are experiencing. Unless you are aware of your distress, you are not going to be able to cope adequately. And, if you do not cope well, you are not going to be consistent in your discipline. (See Strategies #7, "Examine Your Coping Style," and #9, "Manage the Stress in Your Life.")

• Develop clear guidelines for your child about what behaviors are and are not allowed, and make the consequences clear. It may help to write down behaviors that are and are not allowed, post them somewhere in your home, and review them daily with your child. With clear guidelines and defined consequences, both you and your child will know what is going to happen.

• Remember that being consistent in discipline involves more than punishment. You also need to work on building a positive relationship with your child (see Strategy #27, "Nurture Your Relationship with Your Child"). Research by Sharlene Wolchik and her colleagues at Arizona State University suggests that children are best protected from the stresses of parental divorce when they have both a positive relationship with a parent and consistent discipline.

• As difficult as it may be, work toward consistent discipline with your ex-spouse. If you can be consistent in terms of discipline, it will lead to your child not needing to test limits and question rules that may be enforced in one house but not in another. However, this is probably the biggest complaint of custodial mothers: the "Disneyland Father" who has few or no rules on his weekends with the children. Of course, in some cases, the non-custodial father has the same complaint about the custodial mother. If possible, you need to communicate and work with your ex-spouse to reach a compromise on consistency across the two households. But, if your spouse is not willing to work with you, you need to accept the level of consistency (or inconsistency) that exists. Give it a good effort and then move on. Focus your energy on your own consistency from day to day.

• Be firm in your rules and disciplinary practices as soon as your child returns from time spent with his other parent.

"I didn't realize that on the nights my daughter

said she was staying at her girlfriend's house, she was

really spending the night with a boy. Now she's

pregnant at sixteen."

Diana, thirty-eight, mother of four

32

Monitor Your Child's Activities

BOTH DURING AND AFTER a divorce, older children and adolescents often rely on friends for support. This is important, as friendships can help a child deal with the potential negative impact of parental divorce. However, as a parent, it is important that you monitor the activities of your older child or adolescent when she is outside the home with friends. Although friends can be a source of support, without appropriate monitoring your child may start hanging out with others who will have a bad influence on her. The wrong friends could lead to your child's becoming involved in problematic activities like smoking, drinking, early sexual involvement, and delinquent acts.

What do we mean by monitoring the activities of your child? Let's look at some examples. Do you know who your child is "hanging out" with? Do you require your child to let you know where she is when she is away from home? Does your child have a regular curfew time, both during the week and on weekends? Do you know the parents of your child's friends? If you can answer "yes" to these questions, then you seem to be doing an excellent job of monitoring your child's activities outside of the home.

Unfortunately, with divorce, parents often experience stress of their own and, as a result, are less effective at monitoring their adolescent's activities. For example, in one of the classic studies on children of divorce, Mavis Hetherington and her colleagues at the University of Virginia found that, six years following divorce, adolescents from divorced families were monitored less closely by their custodial mothers than were adolescents who lived in two-parent homes. Try to make sure you are the exception to this statistic.

So, what can you do to effectively monitor your child's activities? Here are our recommendations:

- Keep your child involved in structured activities that are supervised by adults. Youth sports, dance lessons, extracurricular school activities, and church groups are examples of such activities.

- Establish reasonable curfews for your adolescent on both weeknights and weekends. To establish such curfews, you need to take into account the age of your child, her performance in school, and who her friends are. Later curfews should be allowed only if they are earned by demonstrating responsible behavior.

- Know your child's friends. Encourage your child to invite them to your home so you can have the opportunity to get to know them.

- Know the parents of your child's friends. Call them up, talk to them, and meet them.

- If your child is going to a friend's house, find out if the parents will be home.

- Combine monitoring your child's activities with building a close relationship with her (see Strategy #27, "Nurture Your Relationship with Your Child"). Our own research with our colleagues indicates that it is the *combination* of these two skills that is best in promoting the adjustment of children. Furthermore, as research by Margaret Kerr and Hakan Statten from Sweden suggests, without a close relationship and good communication, adolescents who are closely monitored may feel overcontrolled by parents, which can have a negative effect on their mood. Your child is less likely to feel that you are being unfair and too strict by setting curfews and monitoring her activities if you also work on your relationship and communication with her. However, regardless of your child's feelings about being monitored, our view is that this is your parental obligation. In the long run, your child will benefit from your monitoring.

"Tommy had been telling me that everything was going fine for him at school. It wasn't until I got his report card that I realized he was having some major problems in school."

Martha, thirty-four, mother of one

33

Monitor School Performance

YOUR CHILD'S PERFORMANCE in school can be a good indication of how he is coping with your divorce. When a child is not coping well, grades often deteriorate and behavior problems increase in school. Thus, as a parent who is divorcing or divorced, you need to closely monitor your child's school performance. As Robert Emery of the University of Virginia has summarized, children in divorced families do not do as well as those from two-parent families on grades, standardized test scores, school behavior, and school completion. While there are many possible explanations for these findings, the important point is to try to prevent your child's school performance from becoming problematic. This is critical because if a child's school performance does deteriorate and his behavior problems in school increase, it can place him on a pathway that leads to less investment in school, which, in turn, leads to even lower grades and more behavior problems in school. This downward spiral can lead to a child losing his motivation to complete his education.

Here are some recommendations that can keep your child on the right pathway in school:

- Work on strengthening your relationship with your child. Several studies, including our own research studies, have indicated that, if a child has a good relationship with at least one parent following divorce, his grades are higher. In our work with divorced families, one of our studies found that, on the average, adolescents who had a poor relationship with both parents had a low C grade point average. In contrast, when adolescents had a good relationship with both parents, their grade point average was a high B on average.

- Closely monitor your child's school performance. This means three things: (1) check on whether he has homework and whether it is completed, (2) review tests and other assignments of your child, and (3) establish and maintain a close working relationship with your child's teacher or teachers so that they will contact you if difficulties arise. Your involvement in your child's school life is essential.

- Tell your child's teacher or teachers that you are going through a divorce. Teachers are probably going to figure it out anyway. And, by telling them, you can work together closely to make sure the divorce does not interfere with your child's progress at school.

- Try to have a regular time for doing homework. Typically, this should be before your child watches TV or plays video games. By setting a regular time for doing homework, you will not only help ensure that homework is completed but your child also may benefit from the sense of stability and security that are often associated with routines.

- Try to coordinate how to manage homework, review assignments, and other school-related activities with your ex-spouse, especially if your child spends time with him during the week.

- If your child starts having problems in school, consider using a daily report card. For children who are in the second grade and above, a daily report card can make clear to your child what is expected, open communication between you and a teacher, and provide motivation for your child to do well in school.

  With the daily report card, you and your child's teacher first identify and clearly define the problem or problems (for example, not completing homework assignments, not completing in-class work, or talking in class). You then identify incentives that your child can earn for doing well in the targeted areas. Incentives might be extra TV time, staying up a little later, or playing a board game after dinner. Your child can help identify possible incentives that are reasonable and that he will not receive if he does not earn the privilege. Sit down and explain to your child that he will take a card to school (see the example on page 146) each day and he will give it to the teacher to complete and sign. The daily report card should focus on the problem identified by the teacher. It is your child's responsibility to have the teacher check off and sign whether he completed the task. It also is your child's responsibility to bring the daily report card home and, when he has reached the goal for earning the incentive, it is your responsibility to provide that incentive to him. (For more information about using daily report cards, see the book by Mary Lou Kelley that is listed in the resources section. There are also free parent handouts on daily report cards and on other school-related issues at the Center for Effective Parenting's website, www.parenting-ed.org.)

- If your child falls behind in his academic performance, ask his teacher to recommend a tutor or other ways to help your child.

An Example of a Daily Report Card for Homework Completion

Child's Name: _____

Date: _____

_____

Was homework assignment
turned in?   Yes   No   N/A

Was it completed
appropriately?   Yes   No   Not yet checked

Give grade if known. _____

_____

Give brief description
of new homework.
(Circle None if there is no homework.)   None

_____

_____

_____

_____

Teacher's Signature:

_____

"I'll always remember the look on Paulette's face

the first time she was able to complete her science fair

project without any help. She was so proud of

herself—and I was too."

Janet, thirty-seven, mother of one

34

Build Your Child's Self-Esteem

MANY PARENTS WORRY about whether their divorce will affect their child's self-esteem or how a child feels about herself. This is a valid concern, as a child's self-esteem is related to a number of positive outcomes in her life, including success in school, positive interpersonal relationships, and the ability to resist peer pressure. Children with positive self-esteem tend to be more successful in almost all areas of life than do children with low or poor self-esteem.

As a parent, you can have a major impact on how your child's self-esteem develops during her early years. Children look to their parents and other adults in their lives for evidence that they are lovable, likable, smart, and capable. It is during the early years that a child's sense of self starts to develop and provides the foundation upon which her self-esteem will build over her lifetime.

Before looking at how to increase your child's self-esteem, it is important to understand the relationship between self-esteem and ability. We usually feel good about ourselves in areas in which we have a high level of skill. For instance, if your child has strong academic skills, she probably feels good about her abilities in that area. What if your child does not have strong academic skills? In this situation you do not want to focus primarily on building self-esteem. Instead, the focus should be on improving her academic skills. This same principle applies to other areas in her life (e.g., interpersonal skills, music, sports).

How do you go about building your child's self-esteem? Here are our recommendations:

- Encourage your child's interests and abilities. Focus on developing the skills and interests in which she shows particular promise. This will help her feel she is better than, or at least as good as, other children her age in at least one activity.

- Offer frequent praise and encouragement.

- Recognize your child's efforts and accomplishments. Don't wait until she has done something outstanding to recognize her efforts.

- Encourage your child to make decisions. By making decisions, children develop a sense of self-control and accomplishment. As children learn to make "good" decisions, over time they develop a sense of both ability and self-worth.

- Let your child take some risks. Don't overprotect your child by helping her to avoid all activities and situations that carry the risk of failure. It is important that your child learns to cope with failure. Everybody fails at some time or another. However, by taking some risks, your child will also learn that she can sometimes do things that she did not think she could do. Taking risks and succeeding builds positive self-esteem. The key is for you to try to make sure most (but certainly not all) of the risks will end on a positive note.

- Give your child responsibilities. A child needs to grow up believing that she can make an important and meaningful contribution to her family. One way of achieving this is to give her household responsibilities from an early age.

- Don't demand perfection. Instead, encourage your child's best effort. Remember that she needs to know you accept her, flaws and all.

- Avoid absolutes in describing your child. Avoid saying your child "always" does something wrong or "never" does something right. Instead of using absolutes, describe your child's behavior within a particular situation. Rather than saying, "You are always so messy," you could say, "You have really messed up your room this afternoon." This avoids labeling your child in an absolute manner.

- Limit negative feedback. No one, whether a child or an adult, likes to be criticized. However, many parents make more negative statements than positive statements to their child. This is especially true for parents undergoing stresses related to divorce. Try to be mostly positive in the feedback you give your child. For every instance of negative feedback you give her, try to give positive feedback to her at least three or four times.

"For months following my divorce, I was so emotionally

upset that almost anything my child did wrong sent

me into a screaming fit."

Tammy, twenty-five, mother of one

35
Develop Greater Patience and Regain Your Lost Patience

ONE OF THE GREATEST challenges of parenting, especially during stressful times, is maintaining your patience when your child does something that upsets you. As you well know, divorce is associated with a lot of stress. As a result, many children whose parents are divorced are frequent targets for such feelings of frustration. If you frequently lose your patience with your child, it can lead to a deterioration of your relationship with him, which can make it even more difficult for him to adjust to the divorce. Given the problems losing your patience can create, you need to work on maintaining your patience if this is a problem area for you.

As we discussed earlier in the book (see Strategy #21, "Change the Way You Think About Your Child"), your thoughts often control your emotional reactions about your child. When your child does something that is upsetting to you, it is how you interpret and think about his actions that will determine how upset you become and how likely it will be that you lose your patience. For example, your child has just returned from the weekend with his dad, and he is whining a lot. Your emotional reaction (which affects whether or not you lose your patience) will depend to a large extent on to what you attribute his whining. If you think the whining is because your ex-spouse gave in to his whining and now he thinks he can get away with it with you, then you are more likely to become upset than if you attribute the whining to his being tired because it is close to bedtime. Your thoughts control your emotional reactions. Try to not assume the worst. Your child is not always behaving poorly because of your ex-spouse or because he's trying to upset you. Consider less negative explanations for your child's behavior and you are less likely to lose your patience. However, almost all parents will lose their patience at times. As we noted previously, this is especially true for parents who are experiencing the stress of divorce.

If you think that you should never lose your patience, that you should always be patient, and that it is *terrible* if you lose your patience, you may very well become upset or depressed whenever you can't help losing your patience. And becoming upset or depressed is not going to help you become more patient. Instead, when you lose your patience, you should acknowledge that it is undesirable and unfortunate, but also human. Expecting yourself to always be patient, particularly during the stress of a divorce, is unreasonable. Do not make excuses for losing your patience, but acknowledge and understand that it is going to happen occasionally.

What can you do to minimize the negative effects of losing your patience with your child when it does happen? In our book *Parenting the Strong-Willed Child*, we recommend using the four R's of damage control:

1. Recognize that you are losing or have lost your patience.
2. Remove yourself or step back from the situation.
3. Review the situation.
4. Respond to the situation.

The first step is to recognize as soon as possible that you are losing or have lost your patience. Because we all react somewhat differently, try to identify your personal signals that you are losing or have lost your patience. For one of the authors (we will not tell you which one), it is when he grits his teeth and speaks in a low tone. The key is to identify, as early as possible, that you are losing (or have lost) your patience. With early identification, you can regain self-control more easily.

The next step is to remove yourself from the situation as soon as you recognize that you are losing or have lost your patience. If you cannot leave your child (e.g., you are alone with your child in a public place), try to step back—literally. Take a couple of steps away from your child, look at something other than your child, and try to regain your composure. Take some deep breaths and try to calm yourself as much as possible. Recite to yourself realistic thoughts about your child's behavior (see Strategy #21, "Change the Way You Think About Your Child"). This type of positive self-talk can be effective in managing anger and regaining self-control. It surely beats exploding!

Once you have regained your self-control, pause and quickly review the situation. Think about what happened, how your thoughts may have led you to start losing your patience, and how you could potentially respond to the situation. Then decide on what you think is the most effective way to handle the present situation.

The final step is to confront the situation and respond in the way that you have decided is most appropriate. Maintain your self-control. If you sense yourself losing control again, start back at the beginning and go through the four R's: recognize, remove, review, and respond.

Here is what we recommend:

- Don't take your frustrations out on your child.

- Try to increase your patience by controlling how you interpret your child's behavior. Reread Strategy #21, "Change the Way You Think About Your Child."

- When you lose your patience, practice the four R's: recognize, remove, review, and respond.

- When you lose your patience, never—and we repeat *never*—threaten to send your child to live with his other parent.

"My greatest regret in life is when I told my seventeen-

year-old, in a fit of anger, that if he hadn't been so

bad, maybe his father and I would still be together.

After that fight he left home. And I rarely see him

anymore."

Linda, forty-two, mother of three

36
Never Blame Your Child for the Divorce

As you might remember from the survey of children we discussed in the Introduction, the most stressful event for a child associated with the divorce of her parents is one of the parents telling her the divorce was her fault. It is imperative that you never say this to your child. A child has enough to deal with when her parents are divorcing without being directly blamed for the divorce. In addition, a divorce is *never* a child's fault: we, as adults, make these decisions; children do not.

You may be one of the majority of parents who immediately say, "I would never tell my child she is responsible for our divorce!" We would certainly hope that is the case, but we also need to point out that you may indirectly and unintentionally lead a child to feel that the divorce is her fault. For example, you might make a comment like the following to your child: "It was just too hard with all of us living together." What you may mean by this is that you and your ex-spouse could not get along; however, a child may interpret this to mean that it was because she lived in the house and, therefore, the divorce is her fault.

Another way that you may inadvertently lead a child to believe that she is the cause of the divorce is through predivorce fighting that occurred over issues pertaining to your child. For example, you may have bought your child an expensive coat, and your spouse may have thought that you spent too much money. As a result, the two of you got into an argument. Your child may believe that if it weren't for her and her coat, the fight would never have taken place. If episodes like this occurred repeatedly and prior to the divorce, your child may feel responsible for the divorce.

Finally, another way that you may inadvertently lead your child to think she is responsible for the divorce is by failing to make it clear that the divorce is not her fault to begin with. When children don't understand things, they sometimes have a tendency to expect the worst. As Laura told us, "I blamed myself for the divorce because my parents had always fought a lot about me and my behavior. They never told me I wasn't the reason for the divorce. I figured that they didn't tell me that because I was the reason." Your child may feel that your divorce is her fault. It is your job as a parent to dispel this false belief clearly and repeatedly.

Here are our recommendations:

- Never blame your child for the divorce, directly or indirectly.

- Carefully think about how you discuss family matters when your child can hear what is being said. She may misinterpret what is said and blame herself for the divorce.

- Emphasize to your child when you initially tell her about the divorce that it is not her fault. Repeat this often, and be receptive to your child's talking to you about her feelings regarding the causes of your divorce.

"I remember my parents promising that I would still be able to go to the same school so I could graduate with my friends. Three months later we had to move and I had to go to a different school for my senior year."

Zach, nineteen

37
Do Not Make Promises You Might Not Keep

MOST PARENTS DESPERATELY want to make the divorce as easy on their child as possible. Unfortunately, in their efforts to help make the divorce easier, parents often make promises that they will not be able to keep. These promises might be that the family will not have to move following the divorce, that the noncustodial parent will visit every week, or that the child will still be able to go to an expensive summer camp. Unfortunately, divorce changes many things, and what you promise may not be possible. As a result, it is important to be very careful about what you promise your child.

James told us the following story: "When I divorced my wife, I felt a tremendous amount of guilt. You know—concern about what I had done to my kids. I wanted to make it up to them so I promised I would take them on a cruise every summer. I wasn't sure how I was going to pay for it but I figured I could find a way somehow. A year after my divorce, I was laid off from my job and couldn't find another job that paid as well. When I told them we couldn't go on the cruise as I had promised, I could see the look of 'but you promised' in their eyes and on their faces."

If you repeatedly make and break promises, your child may believe that you do not care about him enough to follow through with your promises. Just because you no longer have enough income to stay in your current home or you have to move for a job usually will not be satisfactory reasons to your child for breaking a promise. As you break promises, he may start questioning the value of his relationship with you and, perhaps, his own self-worth.

Keeping promises is also important for another reason: you want your child to view you as honest and true to your word. If you, as a parent, tell the truth and keep your word, your child will not only trust you but will also value those qualities and, we hope, develop the same qualities himself. In the long run, such qualities of character will help him cope with the stresses of life, including your divorce.

Here is what we recommend:

- The surest way to keep your promises is to think very carefully about what you are promising. Before you speak, ask yourself, "Am I sure I can follow through on this?" If you are not sure you can, do not make a promise.

"I knew that if I laid a guilt trip on my dad, I could

ask him for anything and he would get it for me"

Alex, fourteen

38
Do Not Overcompensate
for Your Divorce

MANY PARENTS WHO divorce experience anxiety and guilt about how
their child will feel and react. Some worry that their child will not love
them as much as she used to. Others worry that their child is being
deprived of time with the other parent. Furthermore, when a parent
sees her child as sad, she may have even more guilt and anxiety. Also,
older children and teenagers may directly tell parents how much their
life has changed for the worse with the divorce. Such experiences do
not make it easy for you to feel good about yourself as a parent. As a
result, many parents attempt to overcompensate for what they feel they
have done to their child.

There are many ways that parents can overcompensate, and we will
give you just a few examples here. First, parents may continually apologize to their child for divorcing. Second, parents may lavish gifts on
their child, such as new bicycles, video games, and clothes. Third, parents may attempt to constantly entertain their child or provide her with
excessive money for going to movies, skating, or doing activities with
other children. Finally, parents may let their child do whatever she
wants to do with few rules and no discipline. All of these are attempts
to overcompensate for the divorce or to buy your child's love—they will

not work! You cannot buy your child's love. Your child needs to maintain as normal a life as possible following the divorce, not one in which you overcompensate and try to make life easier and better for her.

The potential consequences of overcompensating for divorce are evident in Patti's story. "My daughter was six years old when we divorced. At first I didn't want to punish her when she misbehaved because she had been punished so much by the divorce. I didn't want her to hate me. I used to just let her behavior slide and tell myself it was no big deal. But her behavior eventually got so bad that she was suspended from school three times. Now I am seeing a therapist so I can learn how to help her control her behavior."

Here are our recommendations, which are adapted in part from the University of Iowa Cooperative Extension Service's recommendations and from our own experiences in working with divorcing parents:

- Do not continually apologize for the divorce. Divorce is a decision made between two adults. Yes, it likely will disrupt your child's life—at least temporarily. However, your job as a parent is to do the best you can for your child under the circumstances. You can do this by following the fifty strategies presented in this book, not by repeatedly apologizing for the divorce.

- Don't let your child blackmail you by demanding or expecting that you make up for the divorce by buying something for her. If you are the noncustodial parent, do not let your child refuse to visit unless you buy her something or do something she requests.

- Be realistic about gifts and money that you give your child. You may have financial restraints, and, besides, excessive gifts are not the way to build a positive relationship with your child.

- Don't feel that you have to spend every minute occupying your child's time. Children need to learn how to entertain themselves.

- Do not feel that you have to be your child's best buddy or chum. Yes, you need to focus on your relationship with your child, but remember that you are a parent.

"My mom would always blame my dad for not giving

us enough money. My dad would always tell me that

mom wasted a lot of the money he gave her."

Juan, seventeen

39
Do Not Burden Your Child with Your Personal and Financial Concerns

DURING AND FOLLOWING divorce, many parents have few people, if any, with whom they can discuss their own concerns. These concerns might include their feelings for their ex-spouse, financial hardships, feelings of isolation, and negative feelings about themselves. This is unfortunate, as having a support system is critical for handling the stress of divorce (see Strategy #8, "Develop a Support System for Yourself"). When a strong support system does not exist, some parents turn to their children, especially older adolescents, for support. As Mavis Hetherington of the University of Virginia has pointed out, children are sometimes called on by a parent to provide emotional support or even act as an advisor or confidant for a parent. In addition, some children may take over certain household tasks for the parent, like planning and preparing meals and making decisions about younger siblings.

Placing your personal responsibilities, concerns, and problems on your child is not good for either him or you. A child has enough concerns and issues of his own when his parents divorce without having to take on the concerns and problems of his parent. As far as household and family responsibilities are concerned, children should have routine chores and responsibilities that are appropriate for their ages and abilities. It becomes a problem when a child has to take on parental responsibilities, such as providing primary care for his younger siblings.

For most families, financial problems are a natural but very unpleasant part of divorce. Two cannot live as cheaply apart as together. Having fewer available finances has far-reaching ramifications. As John Grych of Marquette University and Frank Fincham of the University at Buffalo have pointed out, a decline in family income can lead to poorer housing in poorer neighborhoods, poorer schooling, and poorer quality of day care. Divorce often leads to financial problems that can be very stressful to parents.

Some divorced parents let their financial concerns dominate their life—their thoughts, conversations, and behavior. If this happens to you, your child can easily become burdened with your financial problems. Of course, financial difficulties will affect your child. However, for your child's sake, you must try to protect him from being exposed to all of your financial concerns and worries. Your child needs to feel confident that you are able to handle your concerns and problems, including financial issues, in an effective manner.

Here are our recommendations:

- Carefully assess the topics of your conversations with your child. You might do this by writing them down in a journal. If you find that the conversations are focusing on *your* personal issues, you need to make a change.

- Do not burden your child with your personal concerns. If you need a sympathetic ear, advice, or support, rely on an adult, not your child. If you do not have a good support system, work to build one (see Strategy #8, "Develop a Support System for Yourself").

- Carefully assess the responsibilities that you have given your child. Have these increased since the divorce? If so, ask yourself whether your child is doing tasks that are appropriate and are not a parent's responsibility.

- Negotiate financial matters directly with the other parent. Do not involve your child. Your child should not be asking the other parent for money for clothes, recreational spending, or anything else. Finances are adult matters that should be handled between you and your ex-spouse.

- Explain financial changes to your child in a very matter-of-fact manner. For younger children, a brief explanation, such as "We are not going to be able to do some of the things that we used to do because we do not have as much money since Mommy and Daddy are no longer living together," is sufficient. You can follow up by answering any questions that a child has. For older children, a more detailed explanation is warranted, and you can expect more "give and take" with older children and particularly with adolescents.

- Do not blame your ex-spouse for financial problems. It may be the case that your ex-spouse is primarily responsible; however, your child does not need to hear this and be placed in the middle of your financial conflicts.

- Do not continually bring up financial problems. Again, divorce is an adult matter. After you have explained it once or twice to your child, do not continue to burden him with it.

- If you are experiencing significant problems and are not able to get the support and help you need from your friends and relatives, consider seeking professional assistance.

"I remember my mother always breaking down and

crying. I didn't know what to do."

Lynn, sixteen

40

Set a Good Example of How to Handle the Divorce

As the old saying goes, your children will learn more from your actions than from your words. Your actions in regard to how you handle the divorce will send very important messages to your child. They will indicate how worried she needs to be about the divorce. They will teach her how to manage stress. They will also teach your child how to interact with other people who might make her angry. The lessons learned will depend on you.

As we mentioned earlier, children, especially younger children, look to their parents for signals of how anxious or worried they need to be about the divorce. If they see their parents as in control and managing things relatively matter-of-factly, they tend to feel more secure and worry less. On the other hand, if they see their parents as being very upset and having significant difficulties emotionally, then they are going to feel less secure and worry more about the divorce and their future.

Your child also will learn from you how to deal with stress and with individuals who make her mad and upset. You and your ex-spouse will serve as role models for such learning. Will your child learn to scream, slam down the phone, make threats, and criticize others in her life? Or will she learn to control her anger and deal with others and with stressful situations in a more matter-of-fact and effective manner? The choice is yours.

Let's hear what Helen told us. "One night my ex and I got into a major screaming battle over the phone. I thought our four-year-old was asleep, but after I got off the phone I found out that Mary had heard the whole thing. The next week her preschool teacher called to tell me about what happened at school. She and another little girl had decided to play 'mommy' and 'daddy' with a doll as their baby. They were talking to each other over a play phone when Mary started yelling. When the teacher told me what she had said, I realized that it was just like what I had said to my ex over the phone a few days earlier."

Here are our recommendations:

- You are your child's most important teacher. Make sure your actions teach her how to handle the divorce and other stressful situations effectively.

- Do not expect your child to handle stress any better than you handle it.

- If you are having a difficult time adjusting to the divorce, review Part 2 of the book.

"One year I received a Valentine's Day card from

my ex-spouse! As I looked at it, I soon realized

that our daughter had forged the card. It was

her attempt to get us back together."

Marilyn, thirty-one, mother of two

41
Deal with Your Child's Unrealistic Expectations Directly

WHEN PARENTS DIVORCE, children often have a number of unrealistic expectations about what is going to happen. This is to be expected because they are in a situation where you, as the parent, are making all the decisions about what will happen. Many of their expectations are unrealistic because they are based on their desires and not on the realities of the situation.

What are some of the unrealistic expectations that children may have? By far the most common is that many children believe that their parents are going to get back together. This is an expectation or desire that can last for years, even after one of the parents remarries. Such reunification fantasies can be strengthened if a child sees his parents being affectionate toward one another. This is why it is so important to clearly redefine your relationship with your ex-spouse (see Strategy #16, "Redefine Your Relationship with Your Ex-Spouse").

How should you handle it when your child asks if the two of you will get back together? You need to clearly and unequivocally state that it will not happen. Here's an example of a mother addressing this issue with her young son. "Will Dad ever come back to live with us?" the boy asks. His mother replies, "No, he will never come back to live with us. But he still loves you so much. And always remember that he will never stop being your dad."

This interchange between a young child and his mother highlights the question that many children think about and some, like this boy, ask. His mother directly dealt with the issue of whether his father would come back to live with them. Of great importance, she also emphasized that, although he would not come back to live with them, he would always love the child and always be his father.

Let's look at another type of unrealistic expectation that some children have: that their parents will be together on holidays. If holidays have been an important occasion for your family, a child may think that on these special days everyone can get together and enjoy each other as they did once before. This is an unrealistic expectation for many families and should be addressed simply and directly. Explain to your child that it would be wonderful if all of you could spend the holidays together as you used to as a family; however, it is no longer possible to do this. Reassure your child that both of you love him and want to spend time with him individually, and one of you will be with him on holidays. (See Strategy #20, "Effectively Handle Birthdays, Holidays, and Special Occasions," for more information.)

Let's consider one final unrealistic expectation your child might have: that you should never date. Remember that your child continues to love your ex-spouse even when you do not. As a result, he may have difficulty understanding how you can date someone else. You need to explain to your child that his feelings for your ex-spouse are exactly as they should be; however, you no longer love the other parent in a romantic way, and after a divorce it is normal for people to start dating. (See Strategy #47, "Think About When and How to Introduce Individuals You Date.")

Here are our recommendations:

- Deal directly with any unrealistic expectations that your child has.

- Add to your explanations to your child that both you and your ex-spouse love him, and both of you will always be his parents.

- Try to help your child understand that there are things that he can and cannot change. He can control things that have to do directly with him. For example, he can choose some of the activities he will do with you, and he can decide what to wear. However, there are other things that he cannot change. Those are matters about which adults make decisions.

"My mom would always tell me that I had a temper

just like my dad. I hated it when she said that."

Erica, sixteen

42

Do Not Compare Your Child to Your Ex-Spouse in a Negative Way

YOUR CHILD IS LIKE *each* of her parents, because of the genes that you passed to her and the experiences she has had with each of you. Through such influences, you pass on not just physical characteristics but also such things as mannerisms, talents, interpersonal skills, and personality characteristics. Some of these qualities you pass on to your child will be positive, and others will be negative.

Unfortunately, due to hostility or other negative emotions associated with the divorce, you might tend to view your ex-spouse as a person who has far more negative characteristics than positive characteristics. As a result, you tend to focus on and think about those negative qualities more often than about your ex-spouse's positive qualities. So, it is not surprising that you may notice negative characteristics and behaviors in your child similar to those of your ex-spouse more easily and frequently than you notice similar positive characteristics. If you find yourself comparing your child to your ex-spouse in negative ways, make sure you keep it to yourself and don't make statements like these:

"You ignore what I'm saying just like your dad did."

"You get crazy just like your mom!"

"You don't ever help me out around here. First it was your dad who just sat around and did nothing, and now it's you!"

"You're as mean as your mom."

Comments such as these do no one any good. They make your child feel bad about herself, and it is likely to make her defend your ex-spouse. This can only lead to an argument between the two of you.

It is also important to point out that comparing your child to your ex-spouse in a negative way can have a damaging effect on your child even when you don't say anything to her directly. For example, you may be complaining over the phone about your child's behavior and how it is similar to your ex-spouse's behavior. Your child may overhear this. Furthermore, the friend with whom you are talking on the phone may say something to her child, which is then repeated back to your child.

Here are our recommendations:

- Do not make negative comparisons of your child to your ex-spouse, either directly or indirectly.

- If your child behaves in ways that you do not approve of, directly address these behaviors with your child without making any comparisons to your ex-spouse.

- Try to notice and point out the positive characteristics your child has acquired from your ex-spouse. There are some.

"I still remember the cold stare I got from my mom

when she heard me tell my dad that I loved him

over the phone."

Allison, fourteen

43
Accept Your Child's Love for His Other Parent

As we have pointed out several times, just because the love between you and your ex-spouse ends, your child's love for both of you does not. In fact, his love for each of you and your love for him are critical in helping him adjust to the divorce. It is important that your child be allowed to love both of you and spend time with both of you. Furthermore, you need to remember that, just because your child loves your ex-spouse, this does not mean he loves you any less. As we noted previously, children feel caught in the middle when parents cannot accept that their child loves both of them and wants to spend time with both of them.

Amy's comments highlight the importance of this issue. "One of the greatest gifts my parents gave me after their divorce was their support and encouragement for my relationships with each of them. My dad would always remind me about my mom's birthday and Mother's Day. He would even take me to the store to buy her presents. My mom did the same. She even encouraged me to make things for my dad that he liked—paintings and needlepoint. In the fifteen years since their divorce, I've had the chance to talk to a lot of people my age whose parents divorced. After hearing their stories about their parents, I realize how blessed I am to have parents who truly love me."

Here are our recommendations:

- Accept and encourage your child's love for your ex-spouse. It is natural and beneficial for your child to want to talk about and do things for his other parent; allow this to occur.

- Separate your feelings for your ex-spouse from your child's feelings for your ex-spouse. This is difficult, but it is an important part of your role as a parent.

- Encourage your child to talk on the phone to, write letters to, or E-mail his other parent. These give him avenues, beyond visitation time, to communicate with and express his love for the other parent.

Part 6

The Importance of Other Relationships

"If it hadn't been for my sister, I don't know

what I would have done. She really helped

me through our parents' divorce."

Liz, fourteen

44

Honor Sibling Relationships

As we have repeatedly emphasized, *both* parents play critical roles in helping children adjust to divorce. Others, including friends and relatives, are also important. If your child has one or more siblings, they can play an important role during and after your divorce. After all, siblings often spend more time with each other than they do with their parents.

Siblings are a constant during parental divorce. As Lori Kaplan and her colleagues at Miami University have pointed out, siblings can provide a safe and predictable world in a family breaking apart. Some parents have told us about how siblings came to rely on and comfort each other during the divorce. An older sibling may assume a protective role and, with this new responsibility, feel like she is "making a difference." A younger sibling may look to an older brother or sister for reassurance, stability, and an understanding of what is happening in the divorce process. Clearly, there are several types of support that siblings can provide each other, including emotional support, advice, information, and companionship. All of these can lead to siblings developing closer relationships, which is associated with better adjustment of both children.

However, your children will not automatically grow closer during and after your divorce. In fact, some research by Mavis Hetherington and her colleagues at the University of Virginia suggests that siblings often are more negative toward each other when their parents divorce. Furthermore, adolescents often begin distancing themselves from their younger siblings when their parents divorce. Thus, although siblings can be a source of support for each other, you may have to play a role in helping this to happen.

What can you do to encourage your children to help each other during the divorce? Here are some suggestions:

- Work on strengthening your relationship with your child; this is one of the most important things that you can do. As Hetherington and her colleagues have shown, the quality of the relationship between siblings in divorced families is closely linked to the quality of the relationship that parents have with each of the children. You need to be positive with your children and demonstrate consistent discipline. Furthermore, it is important to not show preferential treatment of one sibling over the other. Preferential treatment will lead to siblings having hostile or jealous feelings toward each other and will interfere with the development of a positive relationship between them.

- Recognize that a sibling can play a role that you cannot play. You are one of the individuals going through a divorce. Your children will often look to others, including a sibling, who they think will not have a one-sided view.

- Don't be jealous of the relationship between your children. If they can provide support to each other, it will facilitate the adjustment of all.

- Don't split up your children. We urge you to generally avoid split custody where some children are in the custody of (and live with) one parent and other children are in the custody of (and live with) the other parent.

"I spent a lot of time with my grandparents when

my parents were going through the divorce. It was

such a relief to get away from all the stuff that was

going on between my parents."

Scott, fourteen

45
Encourage Your Child's Relationships with Extended Family Members

CHILDREN ARE NOT members of just their immediate family—grandparents, uncles, aunts, and cousins are often important extended family members for them. This includes not only those extended family members on your side of the family but those of your ex-spouse as well. Just because you and your spouse are divorcing or have divorced does not mean your child is "divorcing" his relatives. In fact, during the time of divorce, these relatives can play an important role in promoting your child's adjustment.

Most of what we know about what happens between children and their extended family members when parents divorce comes from examining the relationships of children and their grandparents during divorce. Of course, this is not surprising, as there is often a special bond between grandparents and grandchildren. In fact, from many children's perspective, it is their grandparents that often provide them with the most support and security during the divorce.

When a divorce occurs, both the amount of contact and the amount of active involvement a grandparent has with a child (for example, a child spending the night with his grandparents) depend on whether the grandparent is the parent of the custodial parent or of the noncustodial parent. Because mothers are most often the custodial parent, her parents (the maternal grandparents) are more likely than the parents of the father to have contact and active involvement with their grandchildren.

What should be the role of the parents of the custodial parents? W. Glen Clingempeel of the Francis Marion University and his colleagues have pointed out that these grandparents often are like "firefighters." That is, when there is a problem in the family, such as too much stress for the mother to handle, these grandparents, just like volunteer firefighters, should come in and provide assistance. Once things are running smoothly again, they should withdraw, again just like volunteer firefighters. Of course, this does not mean that these grandparents should have contact and involvement with their grandchildren only when there is a problem; however, it does mean that the grandparents should take on a different role when there is stress in the family versus when there is no stress. In times of stress, these grandparents should be available to help solve problems and provide relief. When the stress is reduced, these are the times the grandparents should focus on maintaining and strengthening their relationship with their grandchildren.

Thomas Hanson and his colleagues at the University of California have found that with divorce a custodial mother's contact with her parents increases. As we have just noted, this is not surprising, as many custodial mothers frequently call upon their parents for assistance. Hanson and his colleagues also found that, unfortunately, with increasing contact between a mother and her parents, the quality of their relationship deteriorates. This suggests that if you are a custodial parent and rely on your parents for assistance, you need to communicate clearly about your role as the parent of your child and their role as the grandparents. Also, remember that this can be a time of stress for your parents as well as for you. You need to communicate clearly and nurture your relationship with your parents similar to the way you would strengthen your relationship with your children.

What about the other set of grandparents, typically the paternal grandparents? They often play a very different role. Unfortunately, for many of these grandparents, it is not unusual for their contact and involvement with their grandchildren to diminish after the divorce. And, as a result, both the grandchildren and grandparents report feeling less closeness and less satisfaction with their relationship. As Gary Creasey of Illinois State University has found, grandparents can sustain their relationship with their grandchildren by working (and in many cases we do mean "working") to maintain contact, even if it is by telephone. It may be harder for paternal grandparents to maintain and strengthen the relationships with their grandchildren, but it is worth it because the relationships with *both* sets of grandparents are important in terms of providing children in divorced families with stabilizing influences in their lives.

What we know about grandparents very likely applies to other extended family members. Uncles, aunts, and cousins of your child often have played and can continue to play important roles in your child's life. These roles can include providing a stabilizing influence for your child, being role models, being playmates, and even being historians about your family origins. These are all important roles for any child, but particularly for a child whose parents are divorcing.

Finally, we want to mention the issue of "grandparents' rights." In recent years there has been a lot of media attention focused on such rights. These rights include the basic right for grandparents to be allowed to continue their relationship with their grandchildren following the divorce of the parents. Unfortunately, the hostility that engulfs some divorces sometimes involves the grandparents, and some parents try to eliminate, or severely limit, their child's contact with grandparents. Such cases have prompted some grandparents to advocate for legislative action to guarantee their right to have ongoing contact with their grandchildren.

We want to make it absolutely clear that when grandparents get involved in the hostilities surrounding a divorce, the children always suffer. Grandparents need to provide a refuge from the hostilities, not another battleground. It is very important that you and your ex-spouse talk to your parents and request that they not make matters worse by further exposing your child to the negatives surrounding the divorce. You might want to share this book with them so they can better understand things that they can do to help minimize the negative effects of the divorce on their grandchild.

Here are our suggestions regarding extended family members:

- Maintain continual contact and involvement of extended family members on *both* sides of the family.

- Remember that your extended family members and those of your ex-spouse may play different roles with your children, often depending on who is the custodial parent of the children.

- If you are the custodial parent, you need to call on your parents when necessary for support, if possible; however, you also need to make clear your role as the parent of your child and their role as the grandparents. Grandparents related to the custodial parent often have more contact and more involvement with grandchildren than grandparents of the noncustodial parent. These grandparents often play important roles in times of stress and crisis. Grandparents related to the noncustodial parent are equally important but often play a different role. These extended family members may be less active in a child's life; however, it is important that your child's relationship with these grandparents and other extended family members on that side of the family be maintained. Whether you are the custodial or noncustodial parent, you need to work to sustain the relationship between your child and *both* sets of grandparents, as well as other extended family members, on both your and your ex-spouse's side of the family.

- If you live a long distance from relatives, you will have to make extra efforts to maintain your child's (and your) contact with relatives. Remember that phone calls, letters, and E-mails are important ways to keep communication channels open between your child and his relatives.

- Tell your relatives that they should remove their personal feelings about your divorce and for your ex-spouse from their interactions with your child. Your child needs nurturing relationships with them, not exposure to more hostility and negativity.

"How could my father just walk out of my life like that? I thought he loved me."

Kyle, fourteen

46
Help Your Child Cope if the Noncustodial Parent Becomes Uninvolved

UNFORTUNATELY, THERE are many research studies that indicate non-custodial parents often do not remain involved with their children. There are a number of reasons this can happen including mental health or substance abuse problems, guilt, conflict with the custodial parent, financial problems, or focusing energy on new relationships. As we have previously discussed, frequent and predictable contact with the noncustodial parent is important (see Strategy #18, "Ensure Frequent and Predictable Contact Between Your Child and the Noncustodial Parent"), and there are things you can do to promote your ex-spouse's involvement with your child if you are the custodial parent (see Strategy #17, "Encourage Involvement of the Noncustodial Parent"). However, despite your best efforts, some noncustodial parents will still become uninvolved.

Fortunately, the research suggests that a strong positive relationship with one parent can help buffer your child from the negative impact of having a poor or nonexistent relationship with the other parent. While having a strong relationship with your child will not totally compensate for the absence of your ex-spouse, it can go a long way toward helping your child adjust to having a noninvolved parent.

Jane's story provides an example of this issue. "After my parents divorced, my father moved to another town about forty minutes away. After a couple of years he remarried and we hardly saw him at all. He didn't always call on our birthdays. He didn't come to see me or my sister play basketball or soccer. He didn't come to see us graduate from high school. We invited him, but he never came. Because Mom had to be both our mom and our dad, my sister and I would always buy her a card and present on Mother's Day and on Father's Day. It was our way of thanking her for being such a great parent."

If you are the custodial parent, what can you do to help your child cope with an uninvolved parent? Here are our recommendations:

- Encourage your child to express her feelings appropriately (see Strategy #30, "Encourage Your Child to Express Feelings"). Keeping her sadness or anger pent up will not help.

- Do not criticize the other parent for his lack of involvement; rather, encourage his involvement. Let him know that his contact with your child will always be welcome.

- Do not be critical of your ex-spouse's noninvolvement in the presence of your child. Acknowledge your child's feelings, and let her come to her own conclusions about her other parent without your direct or indirect influence.

- If your ex-spouse is not involved with your child due to substance abuse or mental health problems, seek assistance from a professional or from organizations such as Al-Anon [(800) 356-9996] to help your child understand what is going on with her parent.

- Realize that you cannot play the role of both parents. Regardless of how hard you try to do everything two parents normally do, you can't. Be the best parent you can be, but realize that you cannot, by yourself, make up for your ex-spouse's lack of involvement.

- Involve other individuals who can serve as "parent" figures. These might include a grandparent, an uncle, or someone from outside the family such as a coach or a teacher.

- Work on strengthening your relationship with your child and enhancing your parenting skills to help her cope with having a noninvolved parent.

"My mother went out on a date, with someone she

didn't even know, to 'celebrate' her divorce. She didn't

realize how much that hurt me. It was a sad

time for me, not a time to celebrate."

Jason, fourteen

47

Think About When and How to Introduce Individuals You Date

MANY PARENTS WHO divorce, especially those who have been "left," are ready to "swear off" of future romantic relationships. They may feel that they have been too deeply hurt to ever get involved with anyone again. If these are feelings that you are experiencing now, it is important for you to realize that they typically do not last. The majority of women and men who divorce do remarry. Furthermore, among those who do not remarry, romantic involvement with someone almost always happens at some point after divorce.

When you start to think about dating, you need to think about how it will affect you and your child. As Robert Emery of the University of Virginia has pointed out, dating would seem to be a normal part of being divorced; however, it is not a simple process. You probably have "emotional baggage" from your marriage as well as practical considerations surrounding your child.

Given that dating is a normal part of being divorced, you should feel comfortable with the idea of it. However, as you begin to consider dating, carefully evaluate your reasons for doing so. Is it because your ex-spouse is dating someone? Is it a way to punish your ex-spouse? There can be many reasons for dating and most, but obviously not all, of them are good ones. For example, companionship, support, and fun are appropriate reasons for dating.

After examining your reasons, you next need to consider how difficult it will be for your child when you first begin dating. More than likely, it will not be easy for him. As Christie told us: "I hated it when my mom started dating. I got so mad when I saw my mom kissing one of her dates. I remember thinking that she was going to start loving him and she wouldn't love me as much. I was definitely jealous!"

There are a number of reasons that your dating may be upsetting for your child, including feelings of personal rejection, feelings of not wanting to share you with anyone else, and thoughts that you are replacing your ex-spouse with someone else. These are not simple matters for a child. In fact, they are not simple matters for your child even if he is grown and living independently.

Here are our recommendations:

- Don't start dating immediately after the divorce. Give your child a chance to adjust to the divorce before moving on to this next step.

- Before you start dating, consider whether your child is ready for you to date. We are not saying that your child should prevent you from dating; however, if a child is still experiencing distress from your divorce, introducing another change in your life may be very difficult for him.

- When you have the opportunity to date, carefully examine the reasons why you would choose to go out with this person.

- If you decide to date someone, do not try to hide it from your child. This will cause more distress and fear about the future for your child.

- Tell your child in advance that you are going to have an evening out with someone. Reassure your child about your love for him, what time you will be home, and who will be looking after him. If your child asks you if this is a date, you can tell him the following: "You could call it a date. I like to think about it as going out with a new friend."

- Generally, it is not a good idea to have your child meet your dates on the first date. This is especially true if you think you will be dating a lot of different people. You don't want to confuse your child by introducing him to a lot of strangers whom he may never see again. However, if you are being picked up at your house for your date, you will need to briefly introduce your child to your date. Do this in a matter-of-fact manner: "Jimmy, this is Mr. Jones. He and I are going to dinner together and then I will be back home." On the other hand, if you are dating someone repeatedly, it is appropriate for your child to spend more time with your date.

- If your child is awake when you arrive home, tell him about something you did on the date. This will give him permission to ask you questions about the date. If your child is asleep when you get home, wait until the next day and then tell him something you did on the date.

- Remember to always reassure your child of your love for him.

- Don't let dating significantly interfere with the amount of time that you and your child spend together.

- Never ask your child to keep the fact that you are dating a secret from your ex-spouse.

"When my dad first told me he was going to marry

his girlfriend, I was worried that they would move

to Illinois, where she was from, and I wouldn't

get to see him anymore."

Sheila, twelve

48
Effectively Handle New Family Combinations

As ROBERT EMERY of the University of Virginia has reported, about 75 percent of divorced men and 66 percent of divorced women do eventually remarry. Furthermore, many of those who don't remarry do spend time living with a partner. These figures point to an important aspect of divorce in the United States: most children are going to live in new family combinations after the divorce of their parents.

If you, your ex-spouse, or both of you choose to remarry, the possible family combinations are almost infinite. Let's think about it for a minute. If you divorce and you marry someone else who has divorced and has children, your child may live with the two of you the majority of the time. However, at some point in time, your new spouse's children may also live with you and your child. There may be other times when your child spends time with your ex-spouse and potentially his or her new spouse. Furthermore, that new spouse may have children who are in your ex-spouse's new family part of the time. It can become very complicated.

There has been a lot written about children and remarriage of their parents following divorce; in reality, there are few studies to provide us with conclusions about whether remarriage is good or bad for children. The existing studies seem to suggest that preadolescent boys often do better in remarried families than in divorced single-parent families. Some have speculated that this is because a boy, who typically resides with his mother following a divorce, now has a male role model in the home. On the other hand, the existing studies suggest that preadolescent girls appear to do somewhat worse in a remarried family than in divorced single-parent families. Some have speculated that this is because, following divorce, a girl may develop a closer relationship with her mother and, with remarriage, the closeness of this relationship may diminish as the mother refocuses some of her time and energy into the new marriage.

When adolescent-age children are considered, there do not appear to be as many differences between boys and girls and their adjustment to remarriage; however, adolescence has been viewed by many as the most difficult age to have parents remarry. This is, in part, because adolescence is a time when children usually begin to withdraw from the family and, with the introduction of another adult into the family, adolescents may distance themselves from the family even more.

Again, we must point out that at this time the scientific literature supporting the statements we have just made is limited. Perhaps the most important point is for you to realize that, with remarriage, you need to plan carefully and focus on your relationship with your child. There is nothing more crucial than a strong relationship and good parenting in a time of transition. Furthermore, what is probably most significant for your child's adjustment is how you handle the remarriage and your parenting during this time—not whether you remarry.

Here are our recommendations:

- If you have been dating someone for a period of time and the relationship is becoming serious enough to consider marriage, keep your child informed about your strong feelings for this person. This does not mean that you should immediately discuss with your child that you may get married, but it does mean that you should communicate to your child your feelings for this person so a marriage announcement won't come as a complete shock to her.

- If the two of you do decide to marry, designate a two-week period when you will work together to plan the practical details, including what you will tell your child, what you will do about financial and living arrangements (for example, will you and your child move, or will your new spouse move into your house?), what role your new spouse will take in parenting, and, if applicable, when and how children from your new spouse's previous marriage will spend time in your home. Preparation and planning will help you deal with these and other issues. Seek outside help in developing a plan. This may be a friend who has been through a similar situation, an attorney, or a counselor. The more information you can gather and consider, the more problems you will prevent.

- In terms of parenting your child after remarriage, your new spouse should not attempt to take over the family and change the rules and the way you have been handling things with your child. For example, if you have certain rules set up for a teenager in terms of a curfew and chores, these should not change when you remarry. The role of your new spouse should be to support, not change, the rules that you have in effect. You should still be the primary person who presents the rules to your child and who imposes discipline if the rules are violated. If your new spouse attempts to undertake the primary parenting role too soon, it is going to lead to your child saying, "You aren't my parent. You can't tell me what to do!" As time passes, your spouse gradually can begin to assume more direct responsibilities for parenting. However, remember that imposing rules and applying discipline will not work unless a nurturing, positive relationship exists between your child and your new spouse.

- Remember that your new spouse does not replace your ex-spouse as a parent for your child. With remarriage, it is important that your child continue to maintain a strong relationship with her other parent.

Part 7
Seeking Professional Help

"My child participated in a twelve-week program at school for children whose parents had divorced. I was amazed at how much it helped her."

Carolyn, thirty-three, mother of one

49
Seek Professional Help for Your Child if Needed

As WE POINTED OUT in the Introduction, children often experience pain from the divorce of their parents and may have difficulties in adjustment. As we also have pointed out throughout this book, there are things that you can do to help the pain heal and to promote your child's adjustment. Nevertheless, for some children, more is going to be needed. If your child is experiencing significant or ongoing difficulties, we suggest that you turn to a professional. In this section we are going to give you information on when to seek professional help, the types of help that are available, and from whom to seek the help.

The box on page 192 contains a list of some problems that should alert you to the possible need for professional help. In the list, we use the word *persistent*—we mean that these problems have continued for three or more months. However, if you have one of these problems with your child that is severe enough, it may well warrant seeking professional help even if it hasn't been going on for three months. Alternatively, you may see several of the problems listed but none of them are extreme. This also may warrant seeking professional help. Finally, we should note that your psychological resources in terms of dealing with your child's problems also should be considered. That is, it is not just the behavior of your child that should be taken into account, but it is also your ability to cope with that behavior. If you find that you are having difficulties coping with your child, even though his behavior is not extreme, you should consider seeking professional help. Our main point is that there are a number of factors that determine whether or not you should seek professional help. In the end, typically you alone or in conjunction with your ex-spouse (depending on how the legal custody agreement is written) will make the decision for your child.

Persistent Problems Suggesting the Need for You to Seek Professional Help for Your Child

- Constant conflict with you or your ex-spouse
- Persistent defiance and/or oppositional behavior
- Repeated angry outbursts
- Significant sadness and/or withdrawal
- Significant peer problems
- Significant school problems: grades or behavior
- Significant relationship problems with other adults (for example, teachers, coaches, relatives)

If you decide to seek help, from whom should you seek this assistance? You want to seek help from a mental health professional (psychologist, psychiatrist, or social worker) who specializes in working with children, adolescents, and families. You also want to make sure the person has expertise in working with children of divorce. After conducting an evaluation to examine the nature of the problems, the professional should discuss with you different treatment or intervention options. Assuming the evaluation determines that the problems your child is experiencing are related to the divorce (many problems children have may not be), there are several different types of interventions that may be used. You want to try to ensure that the intervention approach selected is one that has been demonstrated to be effective. Next we will discuss the different types of interventions that have been found to be effective when the problems are related to divorce. We hope that this brief overview will help you become more knowledgeable in discussing treatment options with the mental health professional you have selected.

What are the intervention options? Basically, as John H. Grych of Marquette University and Frank Fincham of the University at Buffalo have explained, there are three types of interventions that have been studied. First, there are child-focused interventions for children from divorced families. The structured format usually lasts between eight and fourteen sessions. These are usually group interventions where there are typically five to ten children participating, all of whom have had difficulty adjusting to their parents' divorce. These groups often are conducted in mental health centers or schools. There are three goals of most of these group interventions. The first goal is to help children clarify divorce-related events so that they can understand why their parents divorced and begin to adjust to it. A second goal is to help children learn new ways to cope with dealing with their feelings about the divorce and all of the issues that surround it, such as visitation problems. Finally, most of these interventions attempt to increase a child's level of social support from others. Probably the program that has been most extensively evaluated is the Children of Divorce Intervention Project by JoAnne Pedro-Carroll and her colleagues at the University of Rochester, which is being used in many schools around the country.

Your second choice is a parent-focused intervention. These interventions focus on teaching you, as a parent, ways to help your child during and after divorce. The goals of these programs are similar to much of the information we have given you in this book. The primary focus is typically on parenting principles, but other issues related to divorce often are included (for example, information about the effects of conflict with your ex-spouse on your child). Two programs that have been evaluated are one by Kelly Shifflett and E. Mark Cummings at the

University of Notre Dame and one by Marian S. Forgatch at the Oregon
Social Learning Center in Eugene, Oregon.

Your third choice is a program that combines interventions for parents and children. In these sessions, typically children meet in a group
and parents meet in a separate group. Goals for the children and for the
parents are similar to those already presented. One program that has
been evaluated is by Arnold Stolberg and his colleagues at Virginia
Commonwealth University.

We hope that this information is helpful to you in seeking professional assistance and in deciding what intervention approach to pursue.
However, it is important to realize that professional help is not a
replacement for your efforts to help your child. The parenting
approaches and strategies we have presented in this book will still be
more important than ever.

Here are our recommendations:

- If you feel that that you need assistance because of your child's
  problems or your inability to cope with your child, you might want
  to use a relative, friend, or clergy member as a sounding board.
  Tell the person about your concerns. Ask for advice on whether
  you should get professional help.

- Before seeking assistance, be sure you have the legal right to
  make this decision. Look at your legal custody agreement. Consult
  your attorney if you are not certain.

- Involve your ex-spouse in the decision-making process about seeking help and in the therapy itself when appropriate. Also, prior to
  beginning therapy, decide who is going to pay for the costs of
  therapy that are not covered by your medical insurance (which can
  be most, if not all, of the cost).

- Consider attending a local meeting of Parents Without Partners
  (see the resources section for contact information). These parents
  who have been through divorce can provide you with support,

information about how they handled similar situations with their children, and advice for seeking professional help.

• When you begin selecting a mental health professional, ask the person about her experience with children of divorce and about her experience with programs that research has found to be effective. Organizations such as the Association for the Advancement of Behavior Therapy [New York, NY; (212) 647-1890], the American Psychological Association [Washington, DC; (202) 336-5700], and the American Academy of Child and Adolescent Psychiatry [Washington, DC; (202) 966-7300] can provide you with some suggestions on choosing mental health professionals. Furthermore, your child's physician should be able to make local recommendations and referrals for you.

Part 8

Moving Toward the Future

"When I stopped focusing on the hate and resentment

and started to see the positive aspects of my ex-spouse's

parenting—my whole perspective on the future changed."

Carla, forty-one, mother of three

50

Think Positive

YOUR DIVORCE MARKS the end of one phase of your life but the beginning of a new phase. This new phase can be characterized by blame, guilt, self-pity, and pessimism, or it can be characterized by hope and optimism. The choice is yours! Much of your future happiness will depend on your attitude and your perceptions. Do you see your future like a glass half empty or half full? It is critical to have a positive mental attitude as you start this new phase of your life. Although times may be tough right now, you need to be able to envision the light at the end of the tunnel. (Don't worry, it is not a train!)

Divorce brings with it many opportunities. You have the opportunity to make new friends, to have new experiences, to explore old dreams, and to find happiness. However, if you focus on the past, you will not be able to move forward in your life. You must let go of the past, rather than let it control your future.

If you tend to be a pessimist, you need to learn how to become more of an optimist. Yes, it can be done! Martin Seligman of the University of Pennsylvania has spent much of his career studying optimism and pessimism. It is clear from his research and that of other researchers that people can learn to be more optimistic. One of the keys in becoming more optimistic lies in changing how you think about things. As we discussed previously (see Strategies #21 "Change the Way You Think About Your Child," and #35, "Develop Greater Patience and Regain Your Lost Patience"), the actions of others do not control your emotions. It's the way you think about and interpret their actions that determines how you feel. The beliefs that we have determine how we think about and interpret what happens. What if one of your beliefs is that your life and your child's life are forever ruined by the divorce? Well, the next time your child misbehaves, you may start thinking that she is destined for a life of problems and you might very well feel depressed. You must challenge such negative beliefs and replace them with more positive beliefs. If your belief is that you both will make it through the bad times and the future will be good, then you will start becoming more optimistic in your thinking. If you are interested in learning how to become more of an optimist, we recommend you read Martin Seligman's book *Learned Optimism: How to Change Your Mind and Your Life*. Remember that changing the way you think can change your life!

Bibliography

Ahrons, C. R., and R. H. Rodgers. 1987. *Divorced families: Meeting the challenge of divorce and remarriage*. New York: W. W. Norton & Company.

Alpert-Gillis, L., J. L. Pedro-Carroll, and E. L. Cowen. 1989. The children of divorce intervention program: Development, implementation, and evaluation of a program for young urban children. *Journal of Consulting and Clinical Psychology*, 57: 583–589.

Amato, P. R. 1993. Children's adjustment to divorce: Theories, hypotheses, and empirical support. *Journal of Marriage and the Family*, 55: 23–38.

Amato, P. R., and A. Booth. 1996. A prospective study of divorce and parent-child relationships. *Journal of Marriage and the Family*, 58: 356–365.

Amato, P. R., and J. G. Gilbreath. 1999. Nonresident fathers and children's well-being: A meta-analysis. *Journal of Marriage and the Family*, 61: 557–573.

Amato, P. R., and B. Keith. 1991. Parental divorce and the well-being of children: A meta-analysis. *Psychological Bulletin*, 110: 26–46.

Amato, P. R., and F. Rivera. 1999. Paternal involvement in children's behavior problems. *Journal of Marriage and the Family*, 61: 375–384.

Armistead, L., A. McCombs, R. Forehand, M. Wierson, N. Long, and R. Fauber. 1990. Coping with divorce: A study of young adolescents. *Journal of Clinical Child Psychology*, 19: 79–84.

Booth, A., and P. R. Amato. 2001. Parental predivorce relations and offspring postdivorce well-being. *Journal of Marriage and Family*, 63: 197–212.

Buchanan, C. M., E. E. Maccoby, and S. M. Dornbusch. 1991. Caught between parents: Adolescents' experience in divorced homes. *Child Development*, 62: 1008–1029.

Buchanan, C. M., E. E. Maccoby, and S. M. Dornbusch. 1996. *Adolescents after divorce*. Cambridge, MA: Harvard University Press.

Carson, L. 1999. *The essential grandparent's guide to divorce: Making a difference in the family*. Deerfield Beach, FL: Health Communications, Inc.

Cherlin, A. J., F. F. Furstenberg, P. L. Chase-Lansdale, K. E. Kiernan, P. K. Robins, D. R. Morrison, and J. O. Teitler. 1991. Longitudinal studies of effects of divorce on children in Great Britain and the United States. *Science*, 252: 1386–1389.

Clingempeel, W. G., J. J. Colyar, E. Brand, and E. M. Hetherington. 1992. Children's relationships with maternal grandparents: A longitudinal study of family structure and pubertal status effects. *Child Development*, 63: 1404–1422.

Creasey, G. L. 1993. The association between divorce and late adolescent grandchildren's relations with grandparents. *Journal of Youth and Adolescence*, 22: 513–529.

Emery, R. E. 1999. *Marriage, divorce, and children's adjustment* (2nd ed.). Thousand Oaks, CA: Sage.

Emery, R. E. 1999. *Renegotiating family relationships: Divorce, child custody, and mediation.* New York: Guilford.

Emery, R. E., and R. Forehand. 1994. Parental divorce and children's well-being: A focus on resiliency. In R. J. Haggerty, N. Garmezy, M. Rutter, and L. R. Sherrod (Eds.) *Stress coping and development: Risk and resilience in children* (pp. 64–99). Cambridge, England: Cambridge University Press.

Fauber, R., R. Forehand, A. M. Thomas, and M. Wierson. 1990. A mediational model of the impact of marital conflict on adolescent adjustment in intact and divorced families: The role of disruptive parenting. *Child Development,* 61: 1112–1123.

Ford, M., A. Ford, S. Ford, and J. B. Ford. 1997. *My parents are divorced, too.* Washington, DC: Magination Press.

Forehand, R. 1992. Parental divorce and adolescent maladjustment: Scientific inquiry versus public opinion. *Behaviour Research and Therapy,* 30: 319–327.

Forehand, R., L. Armistead, and C. David. 1997. Is adolescent adjustment following parental divorce a function of predivorce adjustment? *Journal of Abnormal Child Psychology,* 25: 127–164.

Forehand, R., and N. Long. 2002. *Parenting the strong-willed child* (2nd ed.). Chicago: Contemporary Books.

Forehand, R., A. McCombs, N. Long, G. Brody, and R. Fauber. 1988. Early adolescent adjustment to recent parental divorce: The role of interparental conflict and adolescent sex as mediating variables. *Journal of Consulting and Clinical Psychology,* 56: 624–627.

Forehand, R., K. Middleton, and N. Long. 1987. Adolescent functioning as a consequence of recent parental divorce and the parent-adolescent relationship. *Journal of Applied Developmental Psychology*, 3: 305–315.

Forehand, R., B. Neighbors, D. Devine, and L. Armistead. 1994. Interparental conflict and parental divorce: The individual, relative, and interactive effects on adolescents across four years. *Family Relations*, 43: 387–393.

Forehand, R., A. M. Thomas, M. Wierson, G. Brody, and R. Fauber. 1990. Role of maternal functioning and parenting skills in adolescent functioning following parental divorce. *Journal of Abnormal Psychology*, 99: 278–283.

Forgatch, M. S., and D. S. DeGarmon. 1999. Parenting through change: An effective prevention program for single mothers. *Journal of Consulting and Clinical Psychology*, 67: 711–724.

Furstenberg, F. F., S. P. Morgan, and P. D. Allison. 1987. Paternal participation and children's well-being after marital dissolution. *American Sociological Review*, 52: 695–701.

Furstenberg, F. F., and C. W. Nord. 1985. Parenting apart: Patterns of childrearing after marital disruption. *Journal of Marriage and the Family*, 47: 893–904.

Garfinkel, I., C. Miller, S. S. McLanahan, and T. L. Hanson. 1998. Deadbeat dads or inept states? A comparison of child support enforcement systems. *Evaluation Review*, 22: 717–750.

Girard, L. W. 1987. *At daddy's on Saturdays*. Morton Grove, IL: Albert Whitman & Company.

Grych, J. H., and F. D. Fincham. 1997. Children's adaption to divorce: From description to explanation. In S. A. Wolchick and I. N. Sandler (Eds.). *Handbook of children's coping, linking theory and intervention* (pp. 159–193). New York: Plenum.

Hanson, T. L., S. S. McLanahan, and E. Thomson. 1998. Windows on divorce: Before and after. *Social Science Research*, 27: 329–349.

Healy Jr., J. M., J. E. Malley, and A. J. Stewart. 1990. Children and their fathers after parental separation. *American Journal of Orthopsychiatry*, 60: 531–543.

Hess, R. D., and K. A. Camara. 1979. Post-divorce relationships as mediating factors in the consequences of divorce for children. *Journal of Social Issues*, 35: 79–96.

Hetherington, E. M., M. Bridges, and G. M. Insabella. 1998. What matters? What does not? Five perspectives on the association between marital transitions and children's adjustment. *American Psychologist*, 53: 167–184.

Hetherington, E. M., M. Cox, and R. Cox. 1982. Effects of divorce on parents and children. In M. Lamb (Ed.), *Nontraditional families* (pp. 233–288). Hillsdale, NJ: Lawrence Erlbaum.

Hetherington, E. M., M. Cox, and R. Cox. 1985. Long-term effects of divorce and remarriage on the adjustment of children. *Journal of the American Academy of Child Psychiatry*, 23: 518–530.

Hetherington, E. M., and M. Stanley-Hagan. 1999. The adjustment of children with divorced parents: A risk and resiliency perspective. *Journal of Child Psychology and Psychiatry*, 40: 129–140.

Iowa State University Extension. 1996. Divorce matters: A children's view. Available at www.extension.iastate.edu/Pages/pubs/fa.htm.

Iowa State University Extension. 1996. Divorce matters: Talking with your child's other parent. Available at www.extension.iastate.edu/Pages/pubs/fa.htm.

Iowa State University Extension. 1996. Divorce matters: Visitation do's and don'ts. Available at www.extension.iastate.edu/Pages/pubs/fa.htm.

Johnston, J. R., M. Kline, and J. Tschann. 1989. Ongoing postdivorce conflict in families contesting custody: Effects on children of joint custody and frequent access. *American Journal of Orthopsychiatry*, 59: 576–592.

Kaplan, L., L. Ade-Ridder, and C. B. Hennon. 1991. Issues of split custody: Siblings separated by divorce. *Journal of Divorce & Remarriage*, 16: 253–274.

Kelley, M. L. 1990. *School-home notes: Promoting children's classroom success*. New York: Guilford Press.

Kelly, J., and R. E. Emery. 1989. Review of J. S. Wallerstein and S. Blakeslee, Second chances: Men, women, and children a decade after divorce. *Family and Conciliation Courts Review*, 27: 81–83.

Kempton, R., L. Armistead, M. Wierson, and R. Forehand. 1991. Presence of a sibling as a potential buffer following parental divorce: An examination of young adolescents. *Journal of Clinical Child Psychology*, 20: 434–438.

Kerr, M., and H. Stattin. 2000. What parents know, how they know it, and several forms of adolescent adjustment: Further support for a reinterpretation of monitoring. *Developmental Psychology*, 36: 366–380.

Laumann-Billings, L., and R. E. Emery. 2000. Distress among young adults from divorced homes. *Journal of Family Psychology*, 14: 671–687.

Lin, I. F. 2000. Perceived fairness and compliance with child support obligations. *Journal of Marriage and the Family*, 62: 388–398.

Long, N., and R. Forehand. 1987. The effects of parental divorce and parental conflict on children: An overview. *Developmental and Behavioral Pediatrics*, 8: 292–296.

McWilliams, J. H. 1998. *Creating parenting plans that work*. Denver: Bradford Publishing Company.

Miller, N. B., V. L. Smerglia, D. S. Gaudet, and G. C. Kitson. 1998. Stressful life events, social support, and the distress of widowed and divorced women: A counteractive model. *Journal of Family Issues*, 19: 181–203.

Pedro-Carroll, J. L., and E. I. Cowen. 1985. The children of divorce intervention program: An investigation of the efficacy of a school-based prevention program. *Journal of Consulting and Clinical Psychology*, 53: 603–611.

Pedro-Carroll, J. L., S. E. Sutton, and P. A. Wyman. 1999. A two-year follow-up evaluation of a preventative intervention for young children of divorce. *School Psychology Review*, 28: 467–476.

Peterson, J. L., and N. Zill. 1986. Marital disruption, parent-child relationships, and behavior problems in children. *Journal of Marriage and the Family*, 48: 295–307.

Radford, B., G. D. Travers, C. Miller, C. L'Archevesque, E. Furlong, and J. Norris. 1997. Divorcing and building a new life. *Archives of Psychiatric Nursing*, 11: 282–289.

Seligman, M. E. 1998. *Learned optimism: How to change your mind and your life*. New York: Pocket Books.

Shifflett, K., and E. M. Cummings. 1999. A program for educating parents about the effects of divorce and conflict on children: An initial evaluation. *Family Relations*, 48: 79–89.

Simons, R. L., K. Lin, L. C. Gordon, R. D. Conger, and F. O. Lorenz. 1999. Explaining the higher incidence of adjustment problems among children of divorce compared with those in two-parent families. *Journal of Marriage and the Family*, 61: 1020–1033.

Stewart, S. D. 1999. Nonresident mothers' and fathers' social contact with children. *Journal of Marriage and the Family*, 61: 894–907.

Stolberg, A. L., C. W. Camplair, and M. A. Zacharias. 1991. *Children of divorce: Leader's guide*. Circle Pines, MN: American Guidance Service.

Stolberg, A. L., and K. M. Garrison. 1985. Evaluating a primary prevention program for children of divorce: The divorce adjustment project. *American Journal of Community Psychology*, 13: 111–124.

Stolberg, A. L., and J. Mahler. 1994. Enhancing treatment gains in a school-based intervention for children of divorce through skill training, parental involvement, and transfer procedures. *Journal of Consulting and Clinical Psychology*, 62: 147–156.

Summers, P., R. Forehand, L. Armistead, and L. Tannenbaum. 1998. Parental divorce during early adolescence in Caucasian families: The role of family process variables in predicting the long-term consequences for early adult psychosocial adjustment. *Journal of Consulting and Clinical Psychology*, 66: 327–336.

Sun, Y. 2001. Family environment and adolescents' well-being before and after parents' marital disruption: A longitudinal analysis. *Journal of Marriage and the Family*, 63: 697–713.

Webster-Stratton, C. 1989. The relationship of marital support, conflict, and divorce to parent perceptions, behaviors, and child conduct problems. *Journal of Marriage and the Family*, 51: 417–430.

Whiteside, M. F., and B. J. Becker. 2000. Parental factors and the young child's post-divorce adjustment: A meta-analysis with implications for parenting arrangements. *Journal of Family Psychology*, 14: 5–26.

Wolchik, S. A., I. N. Sandler, and B. Fogas. 1989. Events of parental divorce: Stressfulness ratings by children, parents, and clinicians. *American Journal of Community Psychology*, 14: 59–74.

Wolchik, S. A., K. L. Wilcox, J. Y. Tein, and I. N. Sandler. 2000. Maternal acceptance and consistency of discipline as buffers of divorce stressors on children's psychological adjustment problems. *Journal of Abnormal Child Psychology*, 28: 87–102.

Resources

Books

General Parenting

Bennett, Steven, and Ruth Bennett. 1991. *365 TV-free activities you can do with your child*. Boston: Adams Media Group.

Brooks, Robert, and Sam Goldstein. 2001. *Raising resilient children*. Chicago: Contemporary Books.

Buntman, Peter H., and Eleanor M. Sairs. 1990. *How to live with your teenager II*. Saline, MI: McNaughton & Gunn.

Farber, Adele, and Elaine Mazlish. 1999. *How to talk so kids will listen and listen so kids will talk*. New York: Avon Books.

Forehand, Rex, and Nicholas Long. 2002. *Parenting the strong-willed child* (2nd ed.). Chicago: Contemporary Books.

Lansky, Vicki. 1991. *101 ways to make your child feel special*. Chicago: Contemporary Books.

Vannoy, Steven. 1994. *The 10 greatest gifts I give to my children*. New York: Fireside.

Webster-Stratton, Carolyn. 1992. *The incredible years.* Toronto: Umbrella Press.

Wycoff, Jerry, and Barbara Unell. 1991. *How to discipline your six- to twelve-year-old . . . without losing your mind.* New York: Doubleday.

Books for Young Children About Divorce

Brown, Lawrence, and Marc Brown. 1988. *Dinosaurs divorce: A guide for changing families.* New York: Little Brown and Company.

Girard, Linda W. 1987. *At daddy's on Saturdays.* Morton Grove, IL: Albert Whitman and Company.

Johnston, Janet, K. Brunig, C. Garritz, and M. Baris. 1997. *Through the eyes of children: Healing stories for children of divorce.* New York: Free Press.

Lansky, Vicki. 1998. *It's not your fault, KoKo Bear.* Minnetonka, MN: Book Peddlers.

Nightingale, Lois, and Blanca Apodaca. 1997. *My parents still love me even though they're getting a divorce.* Yorba Linda, CA: Nightingale Rose Publications.

Rogers, Fred. 1996. *Let's talk about it: Divorce.* New York: Putnam's Sons.

Thomas, Pat. 1998. *My family's changing.* Hauppauge, NY: Barron's Educational Series, Inc.

Books for Older Children and Adolescents About Divorce

Ford, Maxine, A. Ford, S. Ford, and J. B. Ford. 1997. *My parents are divorced, too.* Washington, DC: Magination Press.

Johnson, Linda C. 1992. *Everything you need to know about your parents' divorce.* New York: Rosen.

Joselow, Beth, and Thea Joselow. 1996. *When divorce hits home: Keeping yourself together when your family comes apart.* New York: Avon Books.

Krementz, Jill. 1998. *How it feels when parents divorce.* New York: Knopf.

Books for Divorcing Parents to Facilitate Their Own Adjustment

Benson, Herbert, and Miriam Klipper. 2000. *The relaxation response.* New York: Avon Books.

Davis, Martha, Matthew McKay, and Elizabeth Eshelman. 2000. *The relaxation and stress reduction workbook.* Oakland: New Harbinger.

Ellison, Shelia. 2000. *The courage to be a single mother: Becoming whole again after divorce.* San Francisco: Harper.

Fisher, Bruce, and Robert Alberti. 1995. *Rebuilding: When your relationship ends.* Atascadero. CA: Impact Publishers.

Prengel, Serge. 1999. *Still a dad: The divorced father's journey.* New York: Mission Creative Energy.

Seligman, Martin E. 1998. *Learned optimism: How to change your mind and your life.* New York: Pocket Books.

Trafford, Abigail. 1993. *Crazy time: Surviving divorce and building a new life.* New York: Harperperennial.

Books on Divorced Parenting

Ahrons, Constance R. 1995. *The good divorce: Keeping your family together when your marriage comes apart.* New York: HarperCollins.

Benedek, Elisa, and Catherine Brown. 2001. *How to help your child overcome your divorce: A support guide for families* (2nd ed.). New York: Newmarket Press.

Blau, Melinda. 1995. *Families apart: Ten keys to successful co-parenting.* New York: Perigee.

Knox, David, and Kermit Leggett. 2000. *Divorced dad's survival book: How to stay connected with your kids.* New York: Perseus Books.

Lansky, Vicki. 1996. *Vicki Lansky's divorce book for parents: Helping your children cope with divorce and its aftermath.* Minnetonka, MN: Book Peddlers.

McWilliams, Joan H. 1998. *Creating parenting plans that work.* Denver, CO: Bradford Publishing Company.

Ricci, Isolina. 1997. *Mom's house, dad's house: A complete guide for parents who are separated, divorced, or remarried.* New York: Fireside.

Rothchild, Gillian. 1999. *Dear mom and dad: What kids of divorce really want to say to their parents.* New York: Pocket Books.

Books on Parental Conflict

Darnall, Douglas. 1998. *Divorce casualties: Protecting your children from parental alienation.* Dallas: Taylor Publishing Company.

Kline, Kris, and Stephen Pew. 2000. *For the sake of the children: How to share your children with your ex-spouse in spite of your anger.* iuni verse.com.

Books on Legal and Financial Issues

American Bar Association. 1996. *The American Bar Association guide to family law: The complete and easy guide to the laws of marriage, parenthood, separation, and divorce.* New York: Times Books.

Friedman, James. 1999. *The divorce handbook.* New York: Random House.

Margulies, Sam. 1992. *Getting divorced without ruining your life: A reasoned practical guide to the legal, emotional, and financial ins and outs of negotiating a divorce settlement.* New York: Fireside.

Woodhouse, Violet, and D. Fetherling. 2000. *Divorce and money: How to make the best financial decisions during divorce.* Soquel, CA: Nolo Press.

Books on School Issues

Kelley, Mary Lou. 1990. *School-home notes: Promoting children's classroom success.* New York: Guilford Press.

Books for Grandparents

Carson, Lillian. 1999. *The essential grandparents' guide to divorce.* Deerfield Beach, FL: Health Communications, Inc.

Cohen, Joan. 1994. *Helping your grandchildren through their parents divorce.* New York; Walker & Company.

Books on Stepparenting

Visher, Emily B., and John S. Visher. 1991. *How to win as a stepfamily* (2nd ed.). Bristol, PA: Brunner/Mazel.

Ziegahn, Suzen. 2001. *7 steps to bonding with your stepchild.* New York: St. Martin's Griffen.

Academic Books Written for Professionals

Buchanan, Christy M., Eleanor Maccoby, and Sanford Dornbusch. 1996. *Adolescents after divorce.* Cambridge, MA: Harvard University Press.

Emery, Robert E. 1999. *Marriage, divorce, and children's adjustment.* (2nd ed.). Thousand Oaks, CA: Sage.

Emery, Robert E. 1999. *Renegotiating family relationships: Divorce, child custody, and mediation.* New York: Guilford.

Garrity, Carla B., and Mitchell Baris. 1994. *Caught in the middle: Protecting the children of high-conflict divorce.* New York: Lexington Books.

Hetherington, Mavis (Ed.). 1999. *Coping with divorce, single parenting, and remarriage: A risk and resiliency perspective.* Mahwah, NJ: Lawrence Erlbaum Associates.

Saposnek, Donald T. 1998. *Mediating child custody disputes.* San Francisco: Josey-Bass.

Organizations

Single Parents

Parents Without Partners International Office
1650 South Dixie Highway, Suite 510
Boca Raton, FL 33432
(800) 637-7974
(561) 391-8833
www.parentswithoutpartners.org

The Parents Without Partners (PWP) organization has approximately four hundred chapters and more than fifty thousand members in the United States and Canada. It provides advocacy services for single parents at the national level. Local chapters provide social, family, and educational activities for single parents. An online newsletter is available.

Single Parent Resource Center
31 East Twenty-Eighth Street, Second Floor
New York, NY 10016
(212) 951-7030

Single Parent Resource Center provides information packets, which are mailed by individual request only. The packets include resources for single parents regarding education, support, and legal issues in the state that the individual requests.

Mothers

National Organization of Single Mothers
P.O. Box 68
Midland, NC 28107
(704) 888-5437
www.singlemothers.org

The National Organization of Single Mothers provides advice on parenting and on meeting the challenges of daily life as a single mother. It publishes a bimonthly newsletter with tips on parenting, money management, handling former family members, custody, and visitation. It also has an interactive website.

Fathers

National Congress for Fathers and Children (NCFC)
9454 Wilshire Boulevard, Suite 907
Beverly Hills, CA 90212
(310) 247-6051
www.ncfc.net

The NCFC provides assistance to local and state efforts to support parents who desire to remain actively involved in the lives of their children. The main focus is on helping single fathers stay actively involved in their children's lives. It publishes a newsletter and a member manual.

National Fatherhood Initiative
101 Lake Forest Boulevard, Suite 360
Gaithersberg, MD 20877
(301) 948-0599
www.fatherhood.org

The National Fatherhood Initiative provides national advocacy for, and promotes public awareness of, fatherhood issues. The organization encourages fathers to be actively involved in the lives of their children. It publishes a quarterly newsletter and a fatherhood resource catalog.

Grandparents

Grandparents' United for Children's Rights, Inc.
137 Larkin Street
Madison, WI 53705
(608) 238-8751
www.grandparentsunited.org

This organization provides information to grandparents on raising grandchildren. It also provides information on protecting visitation rights. It publishes a national directory of support groups and services for grandparents. There are also local chapters in various parts of the country.

Mediation
Association of Conflict Resolution
1527 New Hampshire Avenue NW
Washington, DC 20036
(202) 667-9700
www.mediate.com

This organization is for professionals in the field of mediation. However, it does provide referrals to mediators and has a directory of organizations involved in mediation.

Child Support
Office of Child Support Enforcement (OCSE)
U.S. Department of Health and Human Services
370 L'Enfant Promenade SW
Washington, DC 20447
www.acf.dhhs.gov/programs/cse

This federal government agency encourages the economic and social well-being of families, children, individuals, and communities through child support enforcement efforts. It provides information on child support enforcement issues. Contact OCSE by mail or through their website.

Legal
American Academy of Matrimonial Lawyers
150 North Michigan Avenue, Suite 2040
Chicago, IL 60601
(312) 263-7682
www.aaml.org

This association of lawyers encourages the study of, and improved practice in, matrimonial law (which includes divorce). It publishes a directory of its fellows (leading lawyers in matrimonial law) and several online articles.

American Bar Association (ABA) Service Center
541 North Fairbanks Court
Chicago, IL 60611
(312) 988-5222
www.abanet.org

The ABA is the major professional association for lawyers. ABA provides legal and professional resources, as well as general public resources regarding legal issues. It provides lawyer referral services and information on divorce.

Association of Family and Conciliation Courts
6515 Grand Teton Plaza, Suite 210
Madison, WI 53719
(608) 664-3750
www.afccnet.org

This international and interdisciplinary association for professionals is dedicated to the constructive resolution of family disputes. It publishes model standards for the practice of mediation and is a source of books and materials for professionals.

Stepfamilies
Stepfamily Association of America
650 J Street, Suite 205
Lincoln, NE 68508
(800) 735-0329
www.stepfam.org

This nonprofit organization is dedicated to successful stepfamily living through education, advocacy, and support. It provides educational information and resources on stepfamily issues, including its quarterly magazine *Stepfamilies*.

The Stepfamily Network
555 Bryant Street, Number 361
Palo Alto, CA 94301
(800) 487-1073
www.stepfamily.net

This nonprofit organization is dedicated to helping stepfamilies achieve harmony and respect through education and support. The website includes a listing of recommended books and an online forum.

Additional Websites

General Parenting
Center for Effective Parenting
www.parenting-ed.org

This website offers information on a variety of parenting topics. Go to the "Parent Handouts" section for practical suggestions on how to handle many different issues.

Connecting with Kids
www.connectingwithkids.com

This website provides extensive information on various children's problems and practical ways to address those problems.

Kid Source
www.kidsource.com

This website contains a wide variety of information on children and parenting. Areas covered include health, education, recreation, and parenting.

National Parent Information Network
www.npin.org

This website allows access to numerous publications written by professionals on a variety of topics. It also provides reviews of books for parents. Parents can access a bimonthly electronic newsletter called *Parent News*. Perhaps the most unique feature of this site is the ability for parents to submit parenting questions, which are later responded to by NPIN staff.

Parents Place
www.parentsplace.com

This website contains general parenting information, including question-and-answer columns from experts in a variety of fields. There is also a chat room for parents to interact with other parents.

ParentSoup
www.parentsoup.com

This major website offers parenting information on a variety of topics. It includes parenting tips, discussion groups, chat groups, and the opportunity to access "expert" advice on numerous topics.

Practical Parenting
www.practicalparent.org.uk

This website provides services for parents and practitioners wanting advice and support on children's behavior and family relationships. It publishes *The Practical Parenting Newsletter*, which is free and provides practical parenting tips.

Divorce Information
Divorce Online
www.divorce-online.com/index.html

This website provides legal, financial, and psychological information about divorce for both the general public and professionals.

Divorce Source
www.divorcesource.com

This commercial site provides information and materials related to divorce. It has a direct link to each state, as well as Canada, for divorce information relating to that state.

Divorce Support
www.divorcesupport.com

This website provides information and materials about divorce topics such as child custody, visitation, and state laws.

DivorceNet
www.divorcenet.com

This website provides extensive information regarding divorce, especially legal issues.

Legal Issues

American Bar Association, Section on Family Law
www.abanet.org/family/home.html

This ABA website provides numerous documents on legal issues related to divorce, custody, and other issues. It also contains information about finding an attorney and expectations for attorneys.

Divorce HelpLine
www.divorcehelp.com

This website provides information on legal and parenting issues related to divorce. It also provides information about working through the legal issues of divorce with your spouse.

Divorce Law
www.law.cornell.edu/topics/divorce.html

This website provides extensive legal information compiled by the Legal Information Institute at Cornell University. It provides information on divorce laws by individual states.

Federal Office on Child Support Enforcement
www.acf.dhhs.gov/ACFPrograms/CSE

This website provides information related to enforcement of child support.

Mediate.com
www.mediate.com

This website provides extensive information on various aspects of mediation, including mediation related to divorce. Numerous articles are available to read. This site also contains a directory of mediators.

Children's Issues
Children's Rights Council (CRC)
www.gocrc.org

This website contains advice for parents, a newsletter, and information about books, conferences, and state chapters.

Index

Activities
    interactive, 126, 127–29
    monitoring child's, 140–42
Adjustment period for divorced peo-
    ple, 37–40
Adjustment problems, children's
    long-term, 4, 6, 7
    professional help for, 191–95
    short-term, 4, 5, 7
Adolescents. *See also* Children
    curfews for, 140, 141, 142, 188
    feelings of, 7, 8
    as messengers, 64–66
    peer relationships of, 88, 112
    questions from, 30
    remarriage and, 187
    school performance of, 144
    visitation issues with, 88
Age of child
    impact of divorce and, 9, 24, 25
    visitation and, 88–89

Ahrons, Constance, 3
Al-Anon, 181
Allies, using children as, 67–69
Amato, Paul, 5, 86, 87, 107, 123
American Academy of Child and
    Adolescent Psychiatry, 195
American Academy of Matrimonial
    Lawyers, 17
American Psychological Association,
    195
Angry associates, 3, 55
Apologizing for divorce, 157–58
Arbitration, defined, 63
Arguments with ex-spouse
    avoiding, 59–63
    communication tips, 55–58
    criticism, 72–74
    redefined relationships and, 3,
        75–80
Artwork, children's, 85, 126, 132
Askable parents, 124–25

Association for the Advancement of
  Behavior Therapy, 195
Attorneys, 17–20
Avoidant coping style, 42, 43

Birthdays, 85, 95–97
Books about divorce, 134
Booth, Alan, 5
Buchanan, Dr. Christy M., 64, 65,
  114, 138

Camara, Kathleen, 124
Changes in routine, 110–14
Child support payments, 17, 84,
  107–9
Children. *See also* Communication
  with child
  age of, 9, 24, 25
  as allies, 67–69
  commitments to, 22
  communicating love to, 126,
    130–32
  discipline for, 136–39, 157–58
  effects of divorce on, 3–9
  fun activities with, 126, 127–29
  limit testing by, 104–6
  as messengers or spies, 64–66
  noncustodial parent's contact
    with, 86–90
  nurturing relationship with,
    123–26
  parental conflict and, 59–63
  professional help for, 191–95
  questions from, 28–31, 124–25
  school performance of, 143–46
  self-esteem in, 5, 59, 147–49
  sharing secrets with, 70–71
  stressful events for, 4, 11
  temperament of, 11–12
  unrealistic expectations of,
    164–66

Clingempeel, W. Glen, 176
Commitments to your child, 22
Communication with child
  blaming child, 153–54
  building self-esteem, 147–49
  burdening child with financial
    concerns, 159–61
  comparing child to ex-spouse,
    167–68
  conveying love, 126, 130–32
  expressing feelings, 133–35
  making promises, 155–56
Communication with ex-spouse
  arguments, 59–63
  criticism, 72–74, 84
  guidelines for, 55–58
  keeping secrets from ex, 70–71
  parenting plans, 118–22
Consistent discipline, 136–39
Cooperative colleagues, 3, 55
Coping styles, 41–43
Creasey, Gary, 177
Criticisms of ex-spouse, 72–74, 84
Cummings, E. Mark, 193
Curfews, 140, 141, 142, 188
Curtner-Smith, Mary Elizabeth,
  92
Custody arrangements. *See also*
  Noncustodial parent; Visitation
  issues
  mediation for, 32–34
  types of, 16–17, 19

Dating, 183–85, 187
Demographics, 2
Disagreements with ex-spouse
  avoiding arguments, 59–63
  communication tips, 55–58
  criticism, 72–74
  redefined relationships and, 3,
    75–80

Discipline
consistent, 136–39
curfews, 140, 141, 142, 188
parent's guilt and, 157–58
school performance and,
143–46
Disneyland Father, 139
Dissolved duos, 3, 55
Divorce
age of child(ren) and, 9, 24, 25
blaming child for, 153–54
effects of divorce on children,
3–9
myths, 1
overcompensating for, 157–58
phases of, 37–38
rate, 2
telling child about, 23–27
Divorce attorneys, 17–20
Divorce laws, 15–19
Divorce rate in United States, 2
Divorced parent, well-being of
adjustment period, 37–40
coping styles, 41–43
stress management, 48–52
support systems, 44–47
Divorced parenting. *See also*
Communication with child
changes in routine, 110–14
child support payments, 17, 84,
107–9
discipline, 136–39, 157–58
family traditions, 115–17
monitoring activities, 140–42
monitoring school performance,
143–46
nurturing parent-child relationship, 123–26
patience and self-control for,
150–52
plan for, 79, 118–22

playing parents against each
other, 104–6
viewing misbehavior realistically,
101–3

Education
decisions regarding, 119, 120
school performance, 143–46
Emery, Robert, 4, 6, 33, 61, 75, 76,
118, 143, 183, 186
Emotional distress of parents, 46
Emotion-focused coping style, 41,
42, 43
Emotions of divorcing person,
37–40
Ex-spouse. *See also* Noncustodial
parent
accepting child's love for, 169–70
arguments with, 59–63
comparing child to, 167–68
constructive communication with,
55–58
criticizing, 72–74
plan for coparenting with, 118–
22
redefining relationship with, 3,
75–80
Extended family members, 175–79

Family combinations, new, 186–88
Family members, extended, 175–79
Family traditions, 115–17
Feelings, expressing, 133–35
Fiery foes, 3, 55
Fighting parents
arguments in front of children,
59–63
communication tips for, 55–58
criticisms, 72–74
redefined relationship of, 3, 75–80
role models instead of, 162–63

Financial concerns
　burdening child with, 159–61
　child support payments, 17, 84,
　　107–9
　custodial mother's income, 10
　during separation, 20, 21
Fincham, Frank, 160, 193
Forgatch, Marian S., 194
Friendships, child's, 140–42
Friendships, parent's, 44–47
Fun activities, 126, 127–29
Furstenberg, Frank, 87

Gifts, excessive, 157, 158
Gilbreth, Joan, 86, 87
Golden Rule, 58
Grandparents, 175–79
Grych, John H., 160, 193
Guilt, 157–58

Hanson, Thomas, 176
Health care issues, 119, 120–21
Hess, Robert, 124
Hetherington, Mavis, 6, 141, 159,
　174
Holidays
　family traditions, 115–17
　noncustodial parent and, 85
　unrealistic expectations during,
　　165
　visitation schedules and, 95–97
Homework, 144, 145, 146
Hugs, 131
Humor, maintaining sense of, 51, 52

"I" messages, 57, 74
Immediate issues, 20–22
Income, custodial mother's, 10
Inconsistencies in parenting, 78–79

Interactive activities, 126, 127–29
Intimacy boundaries, 75–76, 77,
　79–80

Johnston, Janet R., 91
Joint custody, 16–17

Kaplan, Lori, 173
Kelley, Mary Lou, 145
Kerr, Margaret, 141

Laughing, 51
Laumann-Billings, Lisa, 6
Lawyers, 17–20
Legal decisions
　custody arrangements, 16–17,
　　19
　mediation and custody disputes,
　　32–34
　overview of, 10
Limit testing, 104–6
Litigation, 33, 63
Living arrangements
　custody arrangements, 16–17, 19,
　　32–34
　as immediate issue, 20
　remarriage and, 188
Love
　child's love for ex-spouse,
　　169–70
　communicating, 126, 130–32

Maccoby, Eleanor, 17
Male role models, 9
McWilliams, Joan, 119
Mediation
　custody arrangements and, 32–34
　defined, 63
Mehrabian, Albert, 56

Mental health professionals, 192–93,
    195
Messengers, using children as,
    64–66
Miller, Nancy, 45
Money
    child support payments, 17, 84,
        107–9
    custodial mother's income, 10
    excessive gifts, 157, 158
    talking to child about,
        159–61
Monitoring child's activities,
    140–42
Monitoring school performance,
    143–46
Myths, divorce, 1

Negative feedback, 149
Negotiation, defined, 63
No-fault divorces, 15
Noncustodial parent. *See also*
    Ex-spouse
    frequent contact with, 86–90
    involvement of, 83–85
    uninvolved, 180–82
Nord, Christine, 87

Parent, divorced
    adjustment period for, 37–40
    coping style of, 41–43
    stress management for, 48–52
    support systems for, 44–47
Parent, noncustodial
    frequent contact with, 86–90
    involvement of, 83–85
    uninvolved, 180–82
Parental alienation syndrome (PAS),
    72–73

Parenting, divorced. *See also*
    Communication with child
    changes in routine, 110–14
    child support payments, 17, 84,
        107–9
    discipline, 136–39, 157–58
    family traditions, 115–17
    monitoring activities, 140–42
    monitoring school performance,
        143–46
    nurturing parent-child relation-
        ship, 123–26
    patience and self-control for,
        150–52
    plan for, 79, 118–22
    playing parents against each
        other, 104–6
    role modeling, 162–63
    viewing misbehavior realistically,
        101–3
Parenting the Strong-Willed Child, 151,
    222
Parents Without Partners, 45–46,
    194
Paternal grandparents, 177
Patience, 150–52
Pedro-Carroll, JoAnne, 193
Perfect pals, 3, 55
Pets, 29, 111
Phases of divorcing, 37–38
Photo albums, 131–32
Positive thinking, 199–200
Power struggles, 76
Problem-focused coping style, 41,
    42, 43, 134
Problems, children's adjustment
    long-term, 4, 6, 7
    professional help for, 191–95
    short-term, 4, 5, 7

Problem-solving strategies, 49–50,
57, 62–63
Professional help, 191–95
Promises, 155–56
Property divisions, 20, 21

Questions from children
askable parents and, 124–25
preparing for, 28–31

R's for self-control, four, 151–52
Radford, Barbara, 37, 51
Religious decisions, 119, 122
Remarriage, 186–88
Report card, daily, 145, 146
Risks, 148
Rituals, family, 115–17
Rodgers, Roy H., 3

School performance
decisions regarding education,
119, 120
monitoring, 143–46
Secrets, keeping, 70–71
Self-control, four R's of, 151–52
Self-esteem
child's, 5, 59, 147–49
parent's, 38
Self-talk, realistic, 102–3
Seligman, Martin, 199, 200
Separation, 20–22
Shifflett, Kelly, 193
Sibling relationships, 173–74
Simons, Ronald, 46
Simple divorces, 1, 9–11
Sleeper effect, 7
Social contacts, loss of, 10
Sole custody, 16–17
Spies, using children as, 64–66
Split custody, 16, 174

Spouse. *See* Ex-spouse
Statten, Hakan, 141
Staying together for child's sake, 1,
2–3
Stewart, Susan D., 86
Stolberg, Arnold, 194
Stress management for parents
exercise, diet, and rest, 50
humor and, 51
importance of, 48
problem-solving strategies, 49–50,
57, 62–63
recommendations on, 51–52
relaxation, 49
Stressful events for children, 4, 11
Sun, Yongmin, 8
Support systems for parents,
44–47
Switchovers (visitation transitions),
91–94

Talking to ex-spouse
arguments, 59–63
criticism, 72–74
guidelines for, 55–58
keeping secrets from ex, 70–71
parenting plans, 118–22
Teenagers. *See also* Children
curfews for, 140, 141, 142, 188
feelings of, 7, 8
as messengers, 64–66
peer relationships of, 88, 112
questions from, 30
remarriage and, 187
visitation issues with, 88
Telephone conversations, 60–61
Telling child about divorce decision
guidelines for, 23–27
questions from children, 28–31
Temperament, child's, 11–12

Visitation issues
  holidays and birthdays, 95–97
  noncustodial parent's involve-
    ment, 83–85
  predictable contact, 86–90
  separation and, 20, 21
  smooth visitation transitions,
    91–94

Webster-Stratton, Carolyn, 123
Well-being of divorced parent
  adjustment to divorce, 37–40
  coping styles, 41–43
  stress management, 48–52
  support systems, 44–47
Whiteside, Mary F., 87
Wolchik, Sharlene, 3, 139

About the Authors

Nicholas Long, Ph.D., is a Professor of Pediatrics and Director of Pediatric Psychology at the University of Arkansas for Medical Sciences and Arkansas Children's Hospital. He is also Director of the Center for Effective Parenting. Dr. Long has been appointed to the editorial boards of many pediatric and psychology journals and has extensively published in the areas of divorce and practical approaches to parenting. His research has been published in leading professional journals and books and presented at numerous national and international professional meetings. He is coauthor of *Parenting the Strong-Willed Child* (with Rex Forehand), which has received international acclaim for providing parents with a proven program for changing child behavior. Dr. Long has developed strategies to help parents manage common behavior problems of young children and for parents who are going through stressful times, such as divorce. These strategies have included the development of various parenting classes and written materials for parents and pediatricians. In addition to his clinical and research activities, Dr. Long plays an active role in training pediatricians and psychologists in the science and art of helping parents cope with stress in the family.

Dr. Long is a noted public speaker whose parenting presentations are in high demand. He conducts ongoing divorce groups for parents and is a frequently requested speaker on parenting at the regional, national, and international levels. Dr. Long is a recipient of the Rivendell Foundation Award for Outstanding Contributions to Improving the Research and Delivery of Mental Health Services to Children and Adolescents and of numerous teaching awards. He is married and the father of two teenage sons.

Rex Forehand, Ph.D., is Regents Professor of Clinical Psychology and Director of the Institute for Behavioral Research at the University of Georgia. Dr. Forehand, a child clinical psychologist, has devoted more than thirty years to studying behavior problems of children and developing strategies for parents to use to change those problems. Furthermore, his research has addressed the role of divorce and its influence on parenting and child behavior. His work on divorce has been published in many journals, presented at national professional meetings, and presented to parents and mental health professionals in workshops both nationally and internationally. His research and applied clinical programs have been published in more than three hundred professional journal articles and book chapters. His book *Helping the Noncompliant Child* (coauthored with Robert J. McMahon) has received national acclaim for its delineation of a proven clinical intervention program for therapists to use with parents of children with behavior problems. Dr. Forehand's clinical and research efforts have resulted in his recognition as one of the most frequently cited authors in psychology, his identification as one of the leading child mental health professionals in the United States, his frequent citations in the public media, and his appointment to many editorial boards of professional journals. He has received the American Psychological Association's Award for Outstanding Contributions to Child Clinical Psychology, the Rivendell Foundation Award for Outstanding Contributions to Improving the Research and Delivery of Mental Health Services to Children and Adolescents, the William A. Owens Jr. Award for Creative Research in Social and Behavioral Sciences, and the Creative Research Medal. Dr. Forehand is married and the father of two grown children.